ILLUMINOSITY

Transcender Trilogy Book 3

Vicky Savage

ISBN-10: 0985901942
ISBN-13: 978-0-9859019-4-3

DEDICATION

To all the remarkable women who have touched my life and
inspired me to be a more loving, strong, and resilient person,
especially Josephine, Shelly, and Jessica—mother, sister, daughter.
I hope we have perpetual contracts with each other.

ONE

A deal's a deal, right? Except when one party secretly plans for the other party to be dead by the end of the deal, then I'm thinking all bets are off.

I had a straight up deal with the Inter-Universal Guidance Agency, the self-appointed destiny police—they return me to my parallel life in Domerica for thirty days, after which I get to decide whether I want to stay here, go home to Connecticut, or join up with a community of Transcenders like myself. What I didn't know at the time was that IUGA had already determined the highest and greatest good of the multiverse would best be served by ridding it of one pain-in-the-ass Transcender—namely me. They don't know it yet, but that ain't gonna happen.

My mentor, Ralston, sniffs around the panorama of dusty old windows in the tower room of Warrington Palace—the only place we can be sure of having a private conversation. The silvery afternoon light slants through the grimy panes causing the mostly empty space to seem incongruously cheerful and cozy.

"How long have you known about this room?" he asks in his soft British accent.

"Not long," I say. "I discovered it the night of Mother's funeral … I mean Farewell Celebration. I couldn't sleep after Ryder shared the news about Erica being pregnant, so I came exploring up here."

"Ah yes, the timing of all of that was regrettable. Misfortunes seem to come in threes, don't they? The queen's passing, Erica's pregnancy, and now this conspiracy to assassinate you and the royal family."

I rest my forehead against the warm windowpane, admiring the stunning view. Domerica may be just a tiny, backward dome world, but its sloping fertile hills and valleys lush with fruit orchards and richly hued wildflowers are breathtakingly beautiful. My heart grieves at the thought of never seeing my adopted homeland again, but that's nothing compared to the utter devastation I feel at the idea of never seeing Ryder again. Ralston tells me I have no choice—either I leave or we all die. My heart hasn't fully accepted that yet.

"Rals, I've been thinking about it. We know IUGA wants me out of the way because they see me as a threat to their existence. And we know Dome Noir originally planned this bloody coup so they could take over Domerica and get control of the dome materials. What if we just give them what they want?"

"What do you mean?" He drops his brow and peers at me over the frames of his glasses.

What if we contact King Philippe or Prince Gilbert, whoever's calling the shots, and tell them they can have the dome materials if they just leave us in peace?"

"That's a bit like arming the security system after the burglars have broken in, Jaden." He smiles indulgently. "The Noirs are already inside Domerica. Why would they settle for stealing only the silver when they believe they can have the cash and jewels too? Not to mention that IUGA will still consider you a danger."

"I guess you're right." My shoulders slump in defeat. "But I've decided something, Rals, and don't be upset with me. I'm going to marry Ryder anyway."

"That's preposterous!" he splutters. "As I've already explained, the attack is set to take place on your wedding day. You can't possibly—"

"I don't mean on the scheduled day. I mean tomorrow when he gets back, after we tell him about this whole scheme. I'm going to ask him to marry me right away since the royal wedding's never going to happen."

Ralston stands next to me and gazes out the window. I can almost hear his computer brain sifting through the one hundred and twenty thousand possible responses to this seemingly harebrained idea. "You would marry him knowing that you two cannot ultimately be together?"

"Yes," I whisper, my fingers caressing the wolf-head necklace at my breast. Ryder's necklace. The one I promised to wear always—to keep him safe from harm.

"Is that really necessary, my dear?" he swivels to look at me. "I know you two have not had much time alone, but now that things have settled down a bit, that should be easier to arrange."

"I'm not doing it for the sex if that's what you're thinking. Well … truthfully, that's partly why I'm doing it. I want my first time to be with Ryder. I'm not sure I'll ever want anyone else—not with this kind of passion. But the thing that bothers me is I don't know what will happen after I'm gone. He turned to Erica once before, and now she's expecting his baby. Odds are they'll end up together." Tears press at the back of my eyes. "I just love him, Rals. I want to be his *first* wife at least, if only for a few days. Is that hideously selfish of me?"

A trace of sadness muddies his light blue eyes, and he shifts his gaze out the window again. "No, it is not, my dear. You deserve whatever small happiness you may glean from this unfortunate situation. But …" He turns back to me. "It is imperative that any ceremony take place in absolute secrecy. IUGA must not get a whiff of it. Perhaps Ryder can arrange for you to be married in Unicoi. To my knowledge, IUGA has no presence there at this time."

"Okay. Good idea. Thanks, Rals." We both know I'm thanking him more for not going ballistic on me rather than for his suggestion.

"Jaden, I trust you realize this decision will make it even more difficult for you to leave him when the time comes. *But leave him you must.*"

"I know, I know …" An involuntary sob escapes my throat. "I'll do what I have to do."

Ralston squeezes my shoulder and wanders over to the small door leading out to the rickety walkway surrounding the tower. He rattles the rusty knob.

"Hey, I wouldn't go out there if I were you." I swipe away my tears so I can see what he's up to. "That walkway's practically rotted through. Not even an automaton could survive a fall like that."

He cracks open the little door and peers out. "Yes, I'm certain you're right. It appears quite treacherous." He pokes a boot outside and gingerly tests the crumbling wood while holding tightly to the frame. "Actually, this is rather wonderful. I believe it may be just what we need."

"If you say so, Rals. Exactly what do we need it for?"

"For staging your death, my dear." He closes the door and dusts off his hands. Then he eases himself down into the faded chintz chair in the center of the room.

"We're going to stage my *death*?" My voice goes all squeaky.

I seat myself on the matching ottoman facing him. The only other piece of furniture in the room is a black Bombay chest which holds a collection of personal treasures tucked away long ago by the princess.

"I'm afraid we must, old girl, if you wish for our plan to work. Your loved ones' safety depends upon it. I hadn't worked out all the details before, but I believe this room will serve quite nicely for what I have in mind. Now that you're queen, the advent of your death has far greater significance."

I pull my legs up and rest my forehead against my knees. "I was hoping I could just sort of disappear like I did last year. So maybe I could come back someday."

"Absolutely not!" The force of his voice makes my head jerk up. "Queen Jaden's body must be recovered," he says. "There can be no question this time that you are, in fact, dead. It's the only way Lady Lorelei may rightfully assume the throne and rule Domerica. The country will be on the brink of war with Dome Noir, its very survival threatened."

"Okay, okay. Don't yell. Just how is the queen's body supposed to be recovered? I can't play dead that convincingly."

He removes his glasses and massages the bridge of his nose. "I have a solution for that. We'll use Princess Jaden's body. As you know, IUGA has it stored in cryostasis. The fact that she died from a fall on the day of your first shift to Domerica makes this staged plunge from the tower a rather perfect conclusion to your brief tenure here. There's a sort of symmetry to it."

"That's a really twisted way of looking at it, if you ask me. Still, I guess it could work. But how are we going to get the body out without alerting IUGA to what we're doing?"

He replaces his glasses. "I'll simply inform them that you wish to have your body discovered in Connecticut, as a way to make a clean break with your family there. That's consistent with IUGA's belief that you've elected to remain in Domerica. I'll requisition the princess's body and make some behind the scenes arrangements to have it diverted here instead of Madison."

"*Eww.*" I scrunch up my nose at the visual. "This whole thing is getting kind of convoluted, Rals."

"The plan necessarily involves some complexities. But it's nothing we can't handle. It's crucial that there be witnesses to your death. We'll arrange for you to be in hiding up here in the tower. The palace will be heavily secured during the planned attack, but IUGA will be able to identify your exact location. The Noirs will likely then dispatch a small party of black knights to your hiding place. But we'll be ready for them."

"Wait a minute. How will IUGA know where I am if I'm hiding? Nobody really knows about this room."

"They have your imprint, my dear. All objects—living, nonliving, animate, inanimate—have a certain energy field or illuminosity unique to that object. It's more distinct than a fingerprint and cannot be faked."

"How did they get my imprint?"

He sighs mildly. "If you must know, I recorded it at the time of your first shift in order to protect and keep track of you. Instruments exist which can locate and track these energetic imprints. Your TPD bracelet contains a similar device. That's how it pinpoints the location of all other Transcenders."

I throw up my arms. "Well, that's just great. So you're saying I can *never* hide from IUGA?"

"Not on this earth, old girl—which is why the assassination party and your own guards must witness your actual fall. You simply take your spill and make an immediate shift to Arumel."

"You're kidding, right? You want me to swan dive off that walkway? Can't I use a stunt double or something?"

"You'll have your bracelet. You'll be fine. We'll alert Narowyn and the other Transcenders to our plan and seek their assistance. The princess's body will be staged down below in your clothing to be discovered by those on the ground. And, thus, your death will be confirmed. It's quite simple really."

It sounds the opposite of simple to me, and I'm the one likely to get pancaked on the ground if this whole thing fails. "Geeze Rals, how can you be sure you'll have all the timing calculated correctly?"

"I've been working on this ever since I was informed of the Noirs' plan. My abilities to sort and assimilate information into a cohesive strategy are rather extraordinary, if I may say so myself. I've worked out most of the specifics, but certain variables must still be finalized.

"That's where you come in, my dear. I have the computer power, but you have all the contacts. You should visit with the Transcenders tonight. Then, I suggest you ask your father to meet us at Prince Andrew's estate tomorrow after Ryder's return. I believe we can safely discuss our plan with them at Meadowood."

Cool beads of sweat collect at my hairline. "That's a hell of a lot to accomplish in a week. Do we really stand a chance pulling it off?"

"We'll do our best to ensure the highest odds of success, but one can never be one hundred percent certain. I do have something here that will give us a significant edge."

Ralston reaches inside his jacket and draws out a compact black case. He opens it out flat on his knees. It resembles a small computer with two screens. He presses a button and a three-dimensional holographic figure composed of hundreds of tiny colored dots rises from one screen. It looks like a miniature mountain range.

"What's that?"

"A little something I pilfered from headquarters. It's a mini QP. A quantum predictor, used to generate sophisticated prediction models. State of the art, really. This scatter graph depicts our chances of success against the upcoming attack. Each dot corresponds to a specific variable that could impact our plan positively or negatively. Blue represents the highest probability of success," He points to the mostly blue end of the model. "Red is the highest probability of failure. Yellow, orange, and green are everything in between."

"Seriously, Rals? You stole a prediction model thingy?"

He nods soberly.

"So we can use it to find out everything we ever want to know about our futures?"

"That's not what this is about, Jaden. This is about making certain we have futures. Now, look here."

He presses another key, and a figure composed of only blue dots rises from the opposite screen. "I've structured a plan based upon all variables falling within the blue spectrum. It's our best shot. We'll plug in this new tower room location as your hiding spot and run a reassessment. A few adjustments may be required. But, all in all, we should have a decent chance of saving the royal family and ourselves."

"*Decent!* That's it? That's the best you can do? I'm not feeling real warm and fuzzy here, Rals." In reality, I'm scared witless and reasonably convinced his whole plan is doomed.

"Maybe we need to rethink this," I say. "If I can't stay with Ryder, and I can't go back to my family in Connecticut because IUGA will hunt me down and kill me, is this even worth it?"

I rub the knotted muscles in the back of my neck. "I mean if I'm going to be forced to move to a foreign earth with a bunch of weird strangers because they're the only ones who can protect me, maybe I'm better off letting destiny unfold the way IUGA wants it to. I don't know … maybe I *am* better off dead." Tears topple down my cheeks once more, and my throat seizes up.

Ralston sighs heavily. "Jaden, please spare me the teenage histrionics at this crucial juncture. You are perfectly capable of facing this obstacle and overcoming it brilliantly. Do not underestimate me or yourself. Remember, other lives are also at stake here—mine included. Now is not the time to fall apart."

His words sink sharp teeth into my pride, and my tears instantly dry up. "Fine. I'll just schedule falling apart for a later date—if I'm still alive. But I sure as hell hope we can work together to improve our chances of survival to something slightly better than decent."

His lips press together in the barest of smiles, then it's all back to business. "Let's begin with what you will need to tell the Transcenders this evening. We shall require their assistance in a number of areas."

"Okay, but wait a second. What's going to happen to you when this is over? What will IUGA do when they find out that you stole their machine and are helping me to escape?"

He runs a hand across his wispy sandy-colored hair. "I suppose they'll dismantle me and use me for parts, if I'm lucky. Betrayal is not taken lightly at the agency."

I reach over and put my hand on his arm. "That's a no-go, Rals. We need to find a way to get you out of here before IUGA can touch you. I know the Transcenders will help us. I'll ask them tonight. You can choose where you want to end up, but I hope you'll think about coming to Arumel with me."

His eyes soften and he pats my hand. "I'd be honored to accompany you to Arumel, my dear, if the Transcenders are in agreement."

"They'll agree, or you and I will find someplace else to land. If we can really make this work, Rals, I'll owe you much more than my life."

"Just keep your wits about you, my dear. This is not going to be easy, but I'm confident we can beat IUGA at its own game."

Ralston and I plug the new information into the QP and finish going over all the details of his plan. He swears it's air-tight, and everything on his computer model is flashing blue, but I'm still not completely convinced. A lot of planets and stars will need to align perfectly over the next several days for this to work.

TWO

Shortly before dinner, Ralston and I climb quietly down from the tower room and put the wheels of our plan in motion. I quickly dispatch a messenger to my brother's estate to let him know we'll be visiting Meadowood tomorrow and would like the use of one of his guest houses for the night. I send a second messenger to my father's home at the Enclave with a letter requesting that he meet Ryder and me at Drew's tomorrow evening. Finally, I dash off a note to General LeGare, head of the Royal Guard, asking to see him for a few minutes in the morning.

Ralston goes off to arrange for a small dinner to be served in my office, as a cover for my planned visit to the Transcenders tonight.

Narowyn Du Lac, head of the Transcenders, is a nice lady, but I can't predict how she'll react to me showing up unannounced asking for some huge favors. The last time we met, I stubbornly assured her that I'd never change my mind and decide to join the Transcender community. Yet, in a matter of days, I've made a complete turnaround. Now I'm going to her, hat in hand, asking not only that she put her people in harm's way for me, but also that she make room for Ralston and me at the Chateau du Soleil in Arumel City. I hope to god she still wants me, especially after she hears I'm predicted to be her replacement someday.

At six o'clock, my maid, Maria, breezes into my room for our usual evening ritual of making me look regal for dinner at the palace. To her and everyone else at Warrington Palace it must appear as if nothing's changed, but while she brushes out my hair, my brain obsessively goes over everything Ralston and I discussed. I can't afford to forget even one small detail.

Ryder's due to return early tomorrow afternoon, and now that the initial steps of our plan are underway, the realization hits me— tomorrow may be my wedding night. All at once, a frenzy of pixies begins using my stomach as a bounce house.

Maria lifts a gem-encrusted tiara from the jewelry chest. "No crown tonight," I tell her. "Ralston and I are having dinner alone in my office."

She cocks an admonishing eyebrow like I'm supposed to wear it anyway, but I stare her down until she replaces it in the chest. A dab of make-up here and there and Maria deems me fit for dinner. Ralston and I have arranged to meet up in my third floor office at seven o'clock, where we'll pretend to have weighty matters to discuss privately.

Within a few seconds of leaving my room, I'm joined by my dark and strapping personal bodyguard, Patrick. "Good evening, Your Majesty," he says with a slight bow.

Patrick's been practically glued to my hip since the brutal attack on my traveling party last week left several of my guards dead. I was the obvious target, and until Ralston discovered this plot to assassinate me, we didn't know who was responsible. I feel bad keeping Patrick in the dark, but the risk of a leak is too great for me to share the information with anyone in the palace.

"Hi, Patrick," I say. "I'm just on my way to meet with Professor Ralston. We have several important things to go over before our foreign wedding guests arrive, and we don't have much time to get all the details in order and …" I realize I'm over-explaining myself, so I shut-up.

"Yes, ma'am."

When we reach the office, my conference table has already been set with sparkling crystal, shiny white china, and glittering silver. Dinner waits for us beneath gold domed platters, and a uniformed butler stands ready to serve. I never experienced this kind of luxury growing up in Connecticut, but now it's become my normal chowtime routine. Ralston stands and bows as I enter.

"Good evening, Professor Ralston." I promptly dismiss the butler and turn to Patrick. "Please make sure we're not disturbed for any reason."

"As you wish, ma'am." He follows the butler out and closes the door.

I can't resist a peek under the golden food warmers on the table. Roast pheasant and vegetables, strawberry and spinach salad, and chocolate cake for dessert. Looks delicious but my insides are still doing the rumba, so I decide to pass on having samples. Traveling across dimensions leaves me a little queasy anyway.

"Would you care for a bite before your journey?" Ralston asks.

"No thanks. But save some of that chocolate cake for when I get back."

I push up my sleeve exposing my gold TPD bracelet, and twist it so that the Transcender coat of arms medallion with the three shooting stars is positioned on top. When I flip open the medallion, a holographic map of the city of Arumel rises up. The coordinates for the Transcenders' headquarters are already programmed into the trans-dimensional positioning device inside, and I use my index finger to lock-in a spot near the entrance.

"Will you be okay here, Rals?"

"Yes, I have this fine meal to eat, and your shelves are amply stocked with pithy reading material if I get bored. Don't worry. I'll handle whatever arises here."

"Wish me luck." I double click the latch on the side of the medallion and *Zzzt!*

Instantly, I'm flying through silken space. My body glows brilliantly leaving a wake of tiny golden stars streaming behind me. The whole thing lasts only seconds, but it's a rush like nothing else imaginable.

Arumel is bathed in muted purple twilight when I alight on the sidewalk outside the Chateau du Soleil. I hurry through the gate and up the steps to the cerulean double door. As I reach for the brass lion head knocker, the door swings open. My heart pirouettes in my chest when I stare up into the striking pale green eyes of Asher Steele. I open my mouth to ask how he knew I was here, but he takes my arm and whisks me inside before I have a chance to speak.

"Jade." He pulls me into a quick embrace and then holds me out at arm's length studying my face. "It's great to see you, but why are you here? Is everything all right?"

"Hi Ash," I say, realizing how foolishly happy I am to see him. He looks amazing as usual, dressed in a loose linen shirt and jeans, and he smells wonderful—kind of spicy and masculine.

"Actually, things aren't okay. That's why I came. I need to speak with you and Narowyn."

His eyebrows quirk up. "That doesn't sound good. I think Narowyn is in her office. Let's check."

I follow him down a side hallway. The Chateau is nearly castle-sized. Most of the Transcenders have apartments on the upper floors. In addition to the main kitchen, dining rooms, and other public spaces, a number of offices are located on the first floor. The décor is sort of shabby French-chic, with impressionist paintings, Persian rugs, softly plinking fountains, and comfortably worn furniture throughout. I've always found it charming and inviting, but tonight I scrutinize it with new eyes, knowing it will soon be my permanent place of residence. If the circumstance weren't so stressful, I might actually enjoy the idea of living here.

When we reach Narowyn's office, Asher opens the door and pokes his head inside. "We have a visitor," he says.

Narowyn lifts her head from her work and smiles. The little crinkle lines around her eyes convey warmth and welcome. She rises fluidly and comes around her desk to embrace me. "Jaden, so good to see you. Please sit down." She motions to a small sitting area in the cozy lamp-lit room.

"Thanks." I seat myself in a silk-upholstered chair, and Narowyn and Asher take seats opposite mine. The scent of citrus potpourri wafts from a bowl on the table next to me.

"Despite my pleasure at your visit, I sense this is not a social call." Narowyn clasps her hands on her lap. "Is there something we can do for you?"

"Well, yes." I take a deep breath. Ralston and I rehearsed everything I need to say, but now that I'm here, it's hard to know where to begin. "I just found out that Dome Noir has plans to kill me and as many other members of the royal family as possible next week on my wedding day." My delivery is not as eloquent as I'd wished, but it's succinct.

"That's extraordinary. Are you quite certain of this?" Narowyn asks.

"Yes. Ralston described the whole plot to me today." I quickly fill her in on the basics of the scheme as it was reported to him at IUGA headquarters.

"Then IUGA is aware of this plan and is prepared to ensure that it will not happen?" she says.

"Not exactly. IUGA's aware of it, all right, but they're doing everything they can to make sure that it *does* happen. They want me out of the picture, and the sooner the better."

She and Asher exchange surprised glances. "What possible reason could IUGA have for wishing to see you assassinated?" she asks.

It's embarrassing to have to say the words, but I need to lay it out for them the way Ralston told it to me. "The prediction models indicate within a ninety-six percent probability that eventually, I will succeed you as Chief Executive of the Transcender Society, and I will spearhead a campaign that seriously weakens and eventually leads to the downfall of the agency. Long story short: the Inter-Universal Guidance Agency goes kaput, and I'm to blame."

Asher's previously gaping mouth forms itself into a huge grin. "Oh my god! That's fantastic!"

Narowyn slumps back in her chair, seemingly stunned. "The Auguaries told us of this, and we hoped this day would come," she says.

"The who?" I ask.

"The Auguaries, a distinguished organization of clairvoyants, telepaths, and empaths dedicated to maintaining balance and peace on the planet. We share our exploration reports with them on a bi-annual basis, and they reciprocate with information helpful to us.

"At a conference a few years ago, they made some rather startling revelations. We were told of a new Transcender who would join our ranks and whose presence would launch a new movement, greatly expanding our influence on this earth. Advocates of enlightenment and free will—the volitionists—are predicted to rise in power, and advocates of guided destiny will fall. Among other things, it was foretold that this person will expose corruption and graft inside the IUGA, which ultimately leads to its collapse."

"And you think I'm that person?" *Because I'd really rather let someone else take care of that.*

"Apparently IUGA does, and their prediction models seem to bear it out. But do you know how long they've been aware of this prediction involving you?"

"From the beginning, according to Ralston. That's why they kept me away from the Transcenders last year and hustled me back to Connecticut in such a hurry."

"While this is wonderful news for the Transcenders, I'm afraid it has placed you in a dreadful situation," Narowyn says. "We must put an end to this planned attack at once."

"We can't stop it. That's the problem," I say. "Ralston plugged in every scenario he could think of, and the prediction models all show that the battle takes place in one form or another no matter what we do. If we try to attack them in their caves, they use explosives to decimate our army. Most of them escape and proceed to attack the palace anyway. If we try to bar the two princes from entering the dome, word is sent to those inside to attack immediately. Some scenarios even lead to an all-out war between Domerica and Dome Noir—like if we try to sink their ships, or confiscate their firearms."

Narowyn frowns. "But I'll go immediately to the Inter-Galactic Confederation Court, tell them of IUGA's involvement in this criminal plot, and demand an emergency injunction."

"Yep, we ran that model too. If the Noirs find out we're on to their plan, their orders are to attack at once. So, by the time you're able to get an emergency hearing, the battle has already taken place … and I'm dead."

Asher mutters a curse under his breath and Narowyn's normally glowing skin blanches. "Good god, we shall not allow that to happen," she says. "You must not go back. You must stay here where we can protect you."

"Yeah, I could do that. But if I do, nearly everyone I love in Domerica will end up dying at the hands of the Noirs. The battle will take place whether I'm there or not. We also ran that scenario. Dome Noir is hell-bent on taking over Domerica, and IUGA is hell-bent on destroying me. There's only one way I can survive and possibly save my family too."

"What is it? Please tell us," she says.

"Ralston's put together a strategy that has a pretty good probability of working if we can get all the elements in place before the princes arrive." Lowering my eyes to my hands, I twist my engagement ring back and forth. "I'm going to need your help in making my escape. I'm also going to need a place to live when this is all over."

"Of course," Narowyn says. "You'll always have a home with the Transcenders. I've told you that. We'll do whatever we can to assist you in executing your plan."

I raise my eyes to hers. "You should know this will probably involve some danger. Your people may find themselves in the thick of the fighting."

"I see." She pauses and laces her slender fingers through the long strand of onyx beads around her neck. "With your permission, before you go into the details of Ralston's plan, I'd like to include Captain Watterson of the Transcender Police Force in this discussion. His people are well trained and could prove quite useful in this matter."

I gape at her. "The Transcenders have a police force? You never told me that."

"A certain class of crimes exists which requires inter-galactic cooperation to solve. Because of our ability to travel among different worlds, Transcenders are uniquely qualified to address such matters expeditiously and without the need of special equipment. The Inter-Galactic Confederation has granted us broad jurisdiction in such cases."

She holds up her index finger, like *just a moment*. "Call Captain Watterson, please," she says, seemingly to no one.

"Calling Captain Watterson," a disembodied woman's voice replies.

I glance at Asher. "Voice activated assistant," he says softly.

"Good evening Chief." A male voice answers the call.

"Captain would you join me in my office please? And bring your Lieutenant."

"Yes, ma'am."

Focusing on me again, she says, "We mentioned the Garugians to you last time you were here. They're illegal dimension jumpers.

Mercenaries, if you will. Hired by others to commit crimes on different earths and then disappear back into their own realm before their employers' identities can be discovered. Our officers spend much of their time pursuing Garugians, but occasionally a situation such as yours arises."

"How come I didn't meet any Transcender Police officers when I came for lunch?"

Asher pipes up. "They don't live in the main Chateau. They have their own barracks and training facilities on the edge of the property. So they're not always here for meals. And, to be honest Jade, some of them can be a little *different*. They stay to themselves mostly."

Narowyn's lips curve into a small smile. "Since you had made your decision not to join our community, we did not wish to overburden you with information you'd likely never need. Now that circumstances have changed, you have many things yet to learn."

I draw in a breath and hold it. I can only imagine what other surprises may be in store for me as a full-fledged Transcender.

THREE

Within minutes, the office door opens, and two men in black uniforms stride inside. Narowyn stands to greet them. The older of the two reaches across the desk to shake her hand. His skin is dark and smooth as a polished chestnut, his black hair cropped short.

"Nice to see you, Chief," he says. "We were about to depart for a laserball game. What can we do for you?"

The younger man lingers near the doorway scanning the room with fierce, yellow-brown eyes set in an oddly angelic face. His thick, golden hair hangs to his hulking shoulders. A menacing gun rides low on his hip reaching nearly to his knee. He'd make the perfect model for a Black Ops Viking action figure. I swallow loud enough for everyone to hear. His wolf eyes fix on me for an instant before moving on again.

"Captain, I'm afraid you're going to miss your game. We have a matter that requires your immediate attention. Urick, please come in." She nods at Viking Man and he obeys. "Gentlemen, please sit."

Narowyn seats herself behind her desk. Her normal gracious demeanor is now replaced by an air of steely power. It's obvious who's in charge here. We adjust our chairs so that we all face her way.

"Captain Watterson, Lieutenant—this is Jaden Beckett." She gestures toward me.

The captain reaches over and shakes my hand. "Miss Beckett, we've heard a lot about you. I believe we were out on assignment when you visited last. Nice to finally meet you."

"Thanks. Call me Jaden."

"Jaden has come to us with a serious problem," Narowyn says. "Her life and those of the royal family in Domerica are being threatened. Our friends at IUGA appear to be assisting those who would do her harm."

A hard smile creeps across Captain Watterson's face. "Surprise, surprise," he says. "And why has the illustrious agency chosen to vent its wrath on our Miss Beckett?"

Narowyn steeples her fingers. "It seems the Auguaries' information was correct. IUGA's own prediction models indicate that, in the not too distant future, the Transcenders will succeed in discrediting the agency sufficiently to cause its complete demise. Jaden appears to be the lynchpin in that momentous event. I believe she is the one of whom the Auguaries spoke."

Captain Watterson slaps the arm of his chair loudly and jumps to his feet. "Well I'll be goddamned! That's the best news I've heard in a decade." He beams at me. "Congratulations, Miss Beckett. It's high time someone put an end to those meddling, manipulative, self-serving bastards."

I shrink a little at his outburst. Congratulations don't seem to exactly fit the situation, since my whole life is crumbling like a stale vanilla wafer. Not to mention my considerable discomfort at being slotted in some kind of savior role. I don't need that kind of pressure right now.

"Captain, I appreciate your enthusiasm," Narowyn says. "But Jaden finds herself in a grave and life-threatening situation. She has requested our assistance. I wanted you to be present while we go over the details."

"Of course," the Captain says, reseating himself.

Narowyn focuses on me. "Jaden, please take us through the

specifics of your plan, and tell us what you would like from us."

I lean forward and prop my elbows on my knees. "According to our information, Dome Noir has decided to attempt to conquer Domerica because conditions inside that country are dire at the moment. Food shortages, overcrowding, rampant crime, and now a revolutionary army threaten the existing monarchy. The bottom line is, they need a new dome to survive, and Domerica is in possession of the only existing plans and materials for a new dome."

"But aren't your domes virtually impenetrable?" Watterson asks. "How can they gain entrance if you're aware of their intentions?"

"In point of fact, a bunch of them, hundreds maybe, are already inside. Some of them came to Domerica last year with Prince Damien of Dome Noir. After pretending to leave the country, they stole the powerful energy source reserved for the new dome. Damien threatened to use this energy source to completely destroy Domerica if his demands weren't met. Eventually he was captured and the power cell recovered, but most of his men are still hidden in the countryside. They've supposedly helped to smuggle in other soldiers and have recruited some local criminals and ex-prisoners as well."

"Could they realistically have amassed an army strong enough to capture the palace?" Watterson asks.

"That's what we're told. They expect reinforcements when the wedding party from Dome Noir arrives. Prince Gilbert plans to lead the attack himself on my wedding day."

"Oh ho," Watterson whacks the arm of his chair again. "Cunning. So they're relying heavily on the element of surprise for their success."

"Yes, that and the fact that the Royal Guard isn't exactly well trained or well outfitted for an attack like this. We plan to ask for assistance from my fiancé's people, the Unicoi, and from my father's army at the Enclave. I'll brief General LeGare, head of the Royal Guard at Warrington Palace, but his men won't be informed until the very last moment. Ralston—the IUGA agent who's helping me— says there are too many informants at the palace, and word will certainly leak out if the Guard is told in advance."

"Surely your combined forces will be large enough to quell the Dome Noir army," Narowyn says.

"We'll definitely outnumber them," I say. "The problem is they'll have firearms and explosives. The only firearms in the dome belong to my father's army. Possession of guns or explosives in Domerica is strictly illegal, so we can't match them in terms of firepower. We're hoping the reverse element of surprise will play in our favor. Plus, we plan to surround them and trap them inside the palace grounds."

Captain Watterson rubs his chin thoughtfully. "You have a strategy in place for accomplishing that?"

"Yes, we have a solid plan, but we have to coordinate things quickly."

"I wish we could offer you firearms, but the laws prevent us from doing that." He shakes his head. "I assume part of your strategy includes moving you and the other members of the royal family to a safe, remote location well before the attack."

"We're hoping we can arrange for the royal family to hide out under guard in Old Unicoi," I say. "It's a mostly deserted city located outside the dome, deep inside a mountain. I doubt my father will agree to go, and Ryder and I will need to be visibly present at Warrington Palace or it'll be obvious to everyone that something's up."

The Captain nods in understanding, Viking Man just stares, but Narowyn appears troubled. "What is the plan for your escape?" she asks.

"We plan to stage my death," I say. "When the battle breaks out, my guards will hustle me to safety inside the palace tower room. When the Noir's discover my hiding place, I'll make a dash for the broken-down old walkway. The wood's so rotten it won't hold me, and it's a fifty foot fall."

"Good lord." Narowyn frowns and twists her necklace nervously.

"Obviously, I'll never hit the ground. After the floor gives way, I'll immediately shift here. The real Princess Jaden's body will be found on the ground beneath the tower room. IUGA still has it stored somewhere, and Ralston's arranging to have it transported to Domerica."

"I don't like it, Jaden," Narowyn says. "This is the weakest part of your plan. The rest seems fairly straight forward. But you're leaving too much to chance here. It requires split-second timing, and many things could go wrong. Your life is too important to risk."

"May I make a suggestion?" Watterson asks. "If IUGA can infiltrate this group of renegades, why can't we? We could have Urick here approach them about joining their band. Who would turn this guy away?" He slaps Urick on the shoulder, and for the first time a spark of interest shines in his lupine eyes.

"He'll already know Jaden's location, and he can ensure that when they send men to find her, none of them harms her before she makes her shift to Arumel. If all else fails, he can at least warn her to get out early."

Narowyn swivels her chair from side to side while considering this. "I suppose it would be beneficial to have someone on the inside. Someone to manipulate the things we can and to report back to us should anything significant change. Yes, I'm more comfortable with that scenario."

"But won't IUGA know he's a Transcender?" I ask. "I mean won't his illumo-whatever give him away?"

"They won't be looking for him, so his imprint won't set off any alarms," Watterson says.

"He should be fine," Narowyn agrees. "But if Urick is unable to infiltrate the group, we need to revisit this entire plan, Jaden."

"Okay, sure, whatever you say. I'm just happy you've consented to help. I have one other request, though. My friend, Ralston—he may be just an automaton to you," I glance at Asher who thinks automatons are little more than machines, "but he's saving a lot of lives by helping me. IUGA will destroy him or use him for spare parts or something once they find out what he's done. I want to bring him to Arumel with me. Is there a way to do that?"

Narowyn looks to Captain Watterson. He straightens his shoulders and runs a hand across his chin. "Yeah sure, since he's non-human, it can be done. We probably won't need any extra equipment. Maybe we can do it as a team shift. Strap him to one of the larger guys. We'll take care of it."

"And he can stay here?" I look to Narowyn.

"Certainly, if that's what you wish. We have quarters for him."

"Thank you," I say, letting out a relieved sigh.

"All right then, I think we have a clear idea of what must be accomplished." Narowyn pushes away from her desk. "Jaden, we'll need regular updates from you once you've spoken with your fiancé and your father and the details begin to be filled-in. Timing will be crucial. Asher will be your liaison."

She turns to Watterson, "Captain, you will be in charge of efforts to have Urick gain access to the Dome Noir group, and you'll put together a team to be on the ground in Domerica on the day of the attack. I'll need daily reports from you."

"Yes, Chief." Watterson gets to his feet, and Urick follows suit.

"Thank you both. I look forward to hearing of your progress." Narowyn comes around her desk and shakes hands with each of them. "Good luck, Lieutenant," she says to Viking Man.

He grunts in return. The Captain tips his head to Asher and me as the two men leave.

"Asher," Narowyn says, "please arrange to have a polycom assigned to Jaden. That way you two can communicate back and forth, and she can let you know in advance when she's coming for an update."

"What's a polycom?" I ask.

"An inter-galactic communication device, developed by our own Dr. McDonald."

"Okay, that'll be good." I check my watch. "But I really need to get back to the palace soon, before somebody comes looking for me."

"No problem," Asher says. "This'll only take a few minutes." He heads for the door.

Once Asher's gone, Narowyn and I take chairs in the sitting area again. Her eyes seek out mine. "Jaden, this is a very courageous thing you're doing. I'm certain you are heartbroken to leave your Ryder and your chosen home. As you know, I've experienced a similar separation, though not against my will or accompanied by violence. I cannot tell you that it won't be painful for a very long time. But I can tell you that you will survive and come to know happiness again. We will do everything in our power to make your transition to Arumel as pleasant as possible, and rest assured you'll be safe with us."

"Thank you." The heaviness of it all sinks deep into my bones. "I saw you in the crowd at Queen Eleanor's Farewell Celebration," I say. "It was kind of you to come."

"I was concerned for your wellbeing, and wished to convey my support, but without interfering."

I nod. "You knew all along I'd be coming back to live in Arumel, didn't you? I saw it in your eyes the last time I was here."

She rests her elbows on the arms of her chair, lacing her fingers together. "I didn't *know* it, of course. But after meeting with you, I suspected you might be the one of whom the Auguaries spoke. You have a very intense and colorful energy field."

"You can see it?"

She shrugs. "It's a minor talent. After many years of dwelling with Transcenders, I've become more sensitive to it. In any event, Jaden, the moment you're safely established here in Arumel, we'll file papers with the IGC Court setting forth the deceptive and illegal behavior of IUGA in this matter. We'll make certain the court understands that the agency poses a threat to you, and we'll ask for all appropriate protections."

"Okay. It would be nice not to have to be looking over my shoulder at all times."

"Good. Now, may we discuss your family in Connecticut for a moment?"

"What's there to talk about? Ralston says I can't go back or I'll be in danger." My voice quavers, and I lower my head, hiding my watery eyes.

"While it may be true that you can no longer safely reside there, I believe we can arrange a short-term visit for you."

My head pops up. "What do you mean?'

"You're due to graduate high school in a few weeks, aren't you?"

"Yes."

"It may be possible for you to return home and be with your family until you graduate. I wouldn't expect IUGA to attempt anything after we file our court papers, but we would need to be certain you are adequately protected. In the meantime, we'll work on a cover story for you. One that will allow you to visit home occasionally."

"Like Asher does? You think that's possible?" My pulse picks up.

"Yes. I believe we can come up with something that will work quite nicely."

"Oh my god. That would be fantastic." My spirits are instantly lightened. "I'm not sure I can handle losing everything all at once."

She reaches over and pats my knee. "I know, dear. We shall endeavor to find ways to take some of the sting out of this. Let me see what I can do."

"You don't know how much I appreciate that."

We get to our feet, and Narowyn hugs me tightly. I lean into her soaking up her maternal warmth and floral scent. I don't remember ever needing a hug so much. She's given me a tiny sliver of hope. Home sounds like heaven right now ... even if only for a short time.

We walk together to her door. "Peace be with you, little sister," she says. "Be safe and check in every day or two at a minimum, please." She kisses both my cheeks.

"I will, and thanks ... for everything."

Asher waits in the hallway, a small black device in his hand. He holds it out so I can see its face. It looks like a fat stubby iPhone. "This works a lot like your cell phones at home." He touches the display and it lights up with a menu. "I've programmed our numbers in here." He touches the *Dir* button and a list of names appears. In addition to his, I see Narowyn, Captain Watterson, and Urick.

"Press a name and choose a function. The voice only works if you're on an earth that has communications satellites." He goes back to the menu and points to a silhouette of a talking head. "In Domerica, you'll only be able to script me." He touches the *abc* button and a keypad appears.

"Okay, that looks easy enough," I say.

"It's got photo and video too, if you need them. Oh, and if you're in Arumel City, you can press this red button on the side and the device works like an instacom."

"A what?"

"I believe on your earth it's called a talkie-walkie. Anyway, it gives you immediate contact in case of an emergency or something."

I smile, but don't correct him. "Gotcha."

He places the polycom in my palm and closes his own warm hand around mine. "We won't let anything happen to you, Jade, I promise." He's close enough that I feel the heat radiating from his body.

"I'm so sorry for what you're going through," he says, "but I'd be lying if I said I was sorry that you're not getting married."

I tug my hand away and take a step back. "I'm still getting married, Ash."

"How do you plan to do that?" An edge of irritation slices through his words. "You just finished telling us your wedding ends in the apocalypse and you barely escape by the seat of your pants."

"I'm marrying Ryder tomorrow. When he gets back from Old Unicoi."

"Seriously? That's the most crazy ass thing I've ever heard. You'll be married, what … three or four days? And then you're just going to bail on the guy? Real nice."

"It's not like I have a choice about leaving." My annoyance level quickly surpasses his. "I love him, Ash. I want this for *me*. Can't you understand that?"

He shakes his head sadly. "No, I can't. But let me know how it works out for you. We need to meet after you've spoken with your father … if you can tear yourself away from your honeymoon, that is." He wheels around and stalks off down the hall. I stare at his retreating back, shaking my head. *The last thing I need right now is attitude from Asher.* He may be a few years older than I am, but sometimes he acts like such a baby.

I flip open my TPD bracelet, touch the virtual key for my office back in Domerica, and *Zzzt,* I'm gone.

FOUR

Ralston sits with a book in his lap and a cup of tea next to his chair. He raises his head as I land softly back inside my office. "There you are, my dear," he says. "How did it go?"

"It was okay." I pour myself a cup of tea and take a huge slice of chocolate cake. "I met with several people. They're going to help us. They weren't completely shocked by the news. They'd already heard some weird prophesies about a Transcender taking down IUGA. It's all part of some social movement on their earth—volitionists, or something like that."

He sets aside his book. "That's remarkable. What kind of prophesies?"

I take the chair next to his. "Narowyn said some group called the Auguaries made them. I don't really understand it, but supposedly the people in the universe who advocate directing and controlling destiny for the greater good are going to be defeated by the free will movement. I guess that means the scumbags at IUGA will be out of work soon."

Ralston sips at his tea. "I'm afraid it's all become very politicized these days. Because of IUGA's proficiency in predicting future events over the last centuries, the agency has assumed a role as a kind of director of human affairs. Many people believe it has overstepped its bounds and abused its authority."

"So, it acts kind of like *Big Brother*?" I say with a mouthful of luscious cake.

"Yes, in the sense that it attempts to control destiny in a way it believes is best for the common good. But whenever an entity takes it upon itself to foist its values and vision upon the general populace, the endeavor is doomed to fail. The human spirit will not be denied. Free will and righteousness will inevitably prevail."

"If you say so, Rals, but honestly, I'm just trying to stay alive until Sunday."

"Your priorities are sound, my dear. Saving lives must be our number one goal."

I wash down the cake with a swallow of tea. "Speaking of that, Narowyn has agreed to transport you to Arumel. You can live at Chateau du Soleil. She says they have a place for you."

"Excellent. I am eternally indebted to you, Jaden. Most people wouldn't bother with …"

"Don't even say it, Rals. You're saving my life and Ryder's and Father's and Drew's. I can never repay you. You could've just let me sign those papers. You could've just let us die."

"You know I could never do that." His eyes shine with a determined glow.

"Hey Rals, did you know the Transcenders have a police force?"

"I had heard of it. Yes."

"They're going to try to get one of their officers, a big mean looking dude, to join up with the Noirs. The Captain says if they can get him on the inside, he can lead the black knights to the tower room and make sure no one takes any potshots at me before I do my cannonball off the rail."

"That's brilliant. It will be most helpful to have a cool head and strong ally on the scene."

"Yeah, that's what Narowyn thinks." I yawn loudly. "Let's talk more in the morning. I need some rest. Tomorrow's going to be a big day." My heartbeat goes all kind of jagged when I think of seeing Ryder and asking him to marry me.

* * *

Ralston and I go over our plans once again in the morning before I meet with General LeGare. I trust Charles. He was unwaveringly loyal to—and not-so-secretly in love with—my mother before she died. He'd never betray my confidence, but he might inadvertently let something slip to the wrong person, or non-person, so I keep my visit with him short and light.

He's flattered when I ask him to join us for a family dinner at Meadowood, and readily accepts. It's good to see him smile. Since Mother's death, he seems to have lost his usual swagger. I hope he can muster up some of his old chutzpah for this operation.

Up in my room, I pull out a bag and begin packing for my trip. Maria knocks on my door as I tuck the box containing Ryder's ring in with the rest of my things. She carries my Skorplings in her arms.

"Hey guys." Ethel reaches out for me, and Fred hops onto my back and grasps a handful of my hair.

Ethel wears her favorite miniature pink dress. She touches a gray furry hand to my cheek. "Jay, go for walk?" she says in her tiny melodic voice.

"Sorry Sweetie, I can't go today. I have some things to do."

Fred bounces up and down on my back. "Walk, walk, walk," he chants.

"Fred, quit." I pull him off my back and set him on the floor. He makes a beeline for my bed and burrows under the mounds of pillows.

"Are you traveling somewhere, Your Majesty?" Maria asks eyeing my bag.

"Yes, just a short trip to see Drew and Adelais. I'll be back tomorrow evening."

"May I do something to help you?"

"If you have time to take these guys for a walk, I'd appreciate it."

"Of course."

"Ethel, I'll see you tomorrow," I say. She plunks a tiny wet kiss on my nose.

Maria fishes Fred out from beneath my pillows and takes Ethel in her other arm. "You two be good," I call as she carries them out my door. I make a mental note to leave written instructions for what happens to the Skorplings after I'm gone. They're so sweet and loving. I want to make certain they're well taken care of.

Shortly before noon, I glimpse Ryder passing through the palace gates, and I race down the front steps to greet him. He leaps from his horse and sweeps me up in his arms, kissing me sweetly. He smells of fresh air, road dust, and newly mown hay. His smile is wide and boyish, his deep blue eyes glitter.

"I missed you," he says, holding me close.

"Same here."

I soak in his unrestrained joy, but my heart aches with the knowledge that within minutes I'll have to lay out the heavy facts of our precarious predicament, and we'll be forced to face the seriousness of our shaky future. I wish with every fiber of my being that I could make this euphoric moment last—spend an hour or two pretending our fairytale is really coming true. But we have no time for that. We're expected at Meadowood in a few hours, and we have a battle to plan.

"Come inside, love," I say. "Ralston and I need to speak with you."

Sensing something's up, his expression changes quickly to one of concern. Taking my face into his hands, his eyes bore into mine.

"What is it, Jade? What is wrong?"

I scan the courtyard busy with workers and palace staff, paranoid that someone will overhear us. "Let's discuss it inside."

Ralston greets us at the door. "Ah, Chief Blackthorn, so happy you have returned safely." The men shake hands. "Perhaps Her Majesty's office would be the most appropriate place to have our discussion," he says. We walk in tense silence up the stairway to my office.

The moment Ralston closes the door, Ryder turns to me. "Why the secrecy, love? Do not keep me in suspense a moment longer."

"Please sit for a minute, we have something to tell you," I say.

He perches on the edge of an armchair, and I take the seat facing his. Ralston stands stiffly beside my chair.

"We received word yesterday from very reliable sources that Dome Noir is planning an attack on Warrington Palace on our wedding day. They already have a large fighting force inside Domerica, and when Prince Gilbert arrives a few days from now he's bringing reinforcements and additional firearms."

He snorts a small laugh. "How can Dome Noir have a sizeable army already inside Domerica? Who are these *reliable sources?*"

I have an answer ready for this question. "They're the same sources who told me the whereabouts of the Skorplings after they'd been kidnapped. So I trust them completely. The squad of black knights who tried to assassinate me a few weeks ago was a small faction of this army. Apparently Damien's remaining men have been quietly amassing a militia over the past months. My sources have also provided us with very specific information as to where they are holed up."

Ryder rakes a hand through his hair, his handsome face now marred with fury, his legs bouncing nervously. "Have you confirmed any of this? Where are they hiding?"

I cut my eyes to Ralston. "They're spread out in a series of interconnected caves in the Northern Hills," he says. "We have a map." He pulls a folded map from his jacket pocket and gives it to Ryder.

"We haven't confirmed it yet," I say. "We hoped you could help with that—maybe have some of your trackers locate the caves and gather as much information as possible without tipping them off that we're onto them. We're told if they learn that we've uncovered their plot, the Noir army has been instructed to attack the palace and hold it until Prince Gilbert arrives."

Ryder unfolds the map and studies it a moment. "I see," he says softly. His legs become still. The adrenaline spike seems to wane a bit. "If this is true, we must act with haste. I will have my best men investigate at once."

I place my hand lightly on his knee. "I've asked Father to meet us at Meadowood tonight. He and Drew need to know about this, and … well, Ralston and I have sketched out a plan that we think will work if we can bring your warriors and the Enclave army together to help us. The Noirs are counting on confronting only the Royal Guard."

He leans forward in his chair refolding the map. "Certainly, if we coordinate efforts we have a greater chance of success. But when do you intend to have General LeGare ready your soldiers?"

"Let's discuss the timing tonight. He'll be at the meeting too. Will you come?"

"Of course. But I must go to Unicoi first and dispatch my trackers to locate this hideout." He bursts out of his chair and stuffs the map into his pocket. *Good Lord, the man can't sit still.*

"Don't run off yet," I say, standing. "I have something else important to speak with you about."

I glance at Ralston. He takes his cue and coughs lightly into his hand. "If you two will excuse me, I'll fetch my things and meet you downstairs."

Taking Ryder's hands in mine, I feel him vibrating with tension.

"Ryder, look at me."

"What is it, love?" His eyes blaze with purpose.

My mouth goes dry as a fleeting wisp of doubt wafts through my mind. *Am I being fair, knowing what I know?*

Then he visibly calms and smiles gently. "I'm so sorry for all of this." He tucks a strand of hair behind my ear. "It is not what we had planned for our wedding day, but I shall make it up to you once this is behind us."

"That's kind of what I wanted to talk with you about." My pulse thrums loudly in my ears. "I've thought about it, and with all this chaos about to happen in the middle of our wedding, I wondered ... will you ... marry me ... now? Tonight?"

His smile wavers. "Jaden, this does not seem to be the most favorable time for—"

"Please." It comes out a mournful plea.

He lightly brushes my cheek with his knuckles. "Are you frightened, love?"

"Yes. I'm very frightened for the future." More than he'll ever know. "I want to be with you tonight as your wife."

He lifts my hand to his lips and tenderly kisses the inside of my palm. "You have nothing to fear. We will easily crush this band of intruders. But I will do whatever you wish. Are you certain you would not prefer to wait until we can have the elegant royal wedding your mother originally planned?"

"I don't want to wait another second. I want to marry you now."

He bows formally. "Then I would be honored to marry you tonight, my lady."

My heart practically flies out of my throat. "Thank you," I whisper.

"Have you worked out a plan for that also?" he tilts his head, smiling again.

"Um, no. I was hoping you might know someone in Unicoi Village who could perform the ceremony privately. Someone you trust."

He nods slowly. "Yes. Abraham Phoenix, the spiritual leader of our tribe will help us. I'm certain of it. I've mentioned him to you before. I will send a message asking him to meet us at my house—"

"No! I mean *yes* to Abraham Phoenix. I know he means a lot to you, but *no* to doing it at your house. I don't want your sister in on this. She hates me. I know she'd find a way to ruin everything."

He frowns. "Perhaps you are right. It may be best if Catherine's not involved. The situation is complicated enough. When we meet with the trackers at my office, I'll send word to Abraham that we will be stopping by his home for a visit."

"Perfect. It's settled then. Are you ready to go?" I take his hand and start for the door.

He pulls me back and folds me into a strong embrace. "This is a wonderful idea, by the way." His full lips graze across my ear. "I'm glad you thought of it," he whispers, sending a hot chill from my scalp to my toes.

FIVE

Unicoi Village is a bustle of goings and doings as we approach. The Unicoi are an industrious and colorful tribe. Signs of the Cherokee influence are visible throughout the town in the form of totems and circular structures. Construction is on-going in most parts of the new village. It's been thirteen months since the Unicoi population was relocated to Domerica, but many families are still without homes— some living in tents, others staying with friends or relatives.

All activity on Main Street comes to a standstill as our entourage, led by Patrick, enters the city and the villagers pause to gawk. We didn't need to bring this large an escort for such a short a trip, but since the recent attack on my travel party, extraordinary precautions are taken whenever I leave the palace grounds.

Most of the villagers bow or wave as we pass. Some call out to me or Ryder. Others barely glance at us and go on about their business. Ryder directs us to Sequoya Hall, the official tribal building. Work on the perfectly round structure has not yet been completed, but the eastern wing is finished and that is where our party comes to a stop.

We dismount, and Ryder leads Ralston and me through double doors to a hallway lined with offices. He takes us through a door marked *Tribal Affairs*. A slight woman in a gray dress is seated at a polished mahogany desk. She rises immediately.

"Chief Blackthorn, we weren't expecting you this afternoon," she says.

"I know, Grace. My plans were to be at Warrington Palace, but I must speak with Adahy and Liam as quickly as possible. Would you ask them to join us please? And let Abraham Phoenix know that we plan to call on him within the hour."

"Yes, sir. Right away."

When Adahy and Liam arrive, Ryder and I spend some time summarizing the unstable situation for them. Ryder spreads out Ralston's map on the desk. As the men study it, he emphasizes the importance of locating the caves before nightfall.

"You must gather as much information as possible while maintaining absolute secrecy," he says. "If you are discovered it could be disastrous for Domerica."

Adahy picks up the map and refolds it. "We will not fail you."

"I will be at Meadowood," Ryder tells them. "Please come to me there in the morning with whatever information you have gathered."

Adahy and Ryder grasp each other's forearms, the Unicoi version of a handshake. "Peace be with you brothers," Ryder says.

"And with you," they reply.

Once the trackers have left, Ryder turns to me. "We can easily walk to Abraham's home from here. Patrick can join us on foot and one or two others if you wish."

"I think Ralston and Patrick will make the perfect wedding party," I say. "Are two witnesses enough?"

"Yes. Are you ready?" His eyes glint cobalt as he holds out his arm for me.

I am so ready.

* * *

A large shade tree dominates the small front yard of Abraham Phoenix's home. The new cottage is freshly painted a pale yellow with a sloping slate roof and jumbles of bright orange and scarlet flowers spilling from white window boxes.

The front door opens as we step onto the stone pathway, and a small, stooped woman with white hair and a girlish smile beckons to us. Ryder goes to her quickly and bends to embrace her. She places a gnarled hand on his cheek.

"Ryder, it is wonderful to see you. It has been too many days since you last called on us. Abraham is so pleased you have come for a visit."

"Thank you for welcoming us, Inola," Ryder says. "This is my betrothed, Jaden."

"How lovely to meet you, my dear." She takes my hand in both of hers. "Peace be with you." Her kind eyes sparkle with grandmotherly warmth.

"And with you," I say. She betrays no sign that she knows or cares that I'm Queen of Domerica, and I'm grateful for that.

"These are our friends Professor Ralston and Patrick Stillwater," Ryder says. "We have a favor to ask of Abraham. May we come in?"

"Yes, yes, please." She gestures us inside. "He's just in the parlor."

As we enter the tiny and sparsely furnished parlor, an elderly man with a single gray braid reaches for his cane and balances carefully as he rises from a worn leather chair. "Ryder, my son." He stretches out his hand. His voice sounds like the crunching of autumn leaves underfoot.

Ryder claps his forearm in greeting. "Peace, Abraham."

"And to you. Please come in and sit, all of you."

We each take a chair, leaving no empty seat for Inola, but she perches comfortably on the broad arm of Abraham's chair.

Ryder introduces each of us to the aging minister.

"Congratulations on your engagement," Abraham says to me. His youthful blue eyes belie his profoundly lined face. "I have known your betrothed since birth. You could not have chosen a better man."

"Thank you. I agree," I say.

"I hope you plan to stay and have tea with us. Inola has just put some almond cakes into the oven." He gazes affectionately at his wife, patting her knee.

"We do not wish to impose," Ryder says, "but we've come to ask an important favor of you."

Abraham leans forward attentively. "Of course, my son. What can I do for you?"

"Jaden and I wish to be married tonight. No one other than those in this room must know. The reasons are complex and political, involving the security of Domerica and of the queen herself. I hope you will consent to perform the ceremony for us, but if you are not comfortable with that, we will understand."

Abraham rests his cool, clear eyes on me for a moment and then refocuses on Ryder. "This is no favor you ask, my boy. It is a privilege. I shall be honored to perform the marriage ceremony for you. Allow me a few moments to change into something more appropriate and find my ceremonial book. I've not done one of these for years."

Ryder reaches for my hand, and we exchange relieved looks. "Thank you, sir. Take whatever time you need," Ryder says. "We are comfortable here."

Abraham grasps his cane and rises once again. Inola helps him from the room. In a few moments she returns and beckons to me from the doorway. "Come, my dear. We must make you presentable also."

I'm not sure what she means. Granted, I'm not wearing a dress, but I think I look just fine in my riding pants and jacket. Ryder's imploring look tells me it would be rude to refuse her, so I follow her into the hallway.

She leads me to a small bedroom in the rear of the house. It's furnished femininely in a powder pink shade with a single ruffled bed and a compact dressing table and stool.

"Allow me to take your coat, my dear." She helps me out of my jacket and appraises my ivory silk blouse with a shrewd eye. "Lovely. That will do," she says. "I'll return momentarily. You'll find a brush in the top drawer." She points to the dressing table.

Okay, I can take a hint. I sit on the small tufted stool and check my reflection in the mirror. My hair does look a bit wind-blown after the ride from Warrington Palace. I pull out the brush and go to work.

Inola returns in a few minutes with her arms full. "Stay right there," she says as she piles several items on the bed. She lifts a lace shawl from the top of the heap and carefully arranges it around my shoulders.

I lightly finger the delicate fabric. "This lace is so fine, Inola. You really don't need to do this."

"Nonsense, my dear. You're a queen, not a stable hand, and this is your wedding day. You can't get married looking like that."

Ah, so she does know who I am, and isn't shy about insulting me.

She plucks a blue velvet pouch from the pile on the bed and unties the strings. Inside is a stunning gold and diamond tiara.

"Inola, that's too precious," I tell her.

"Oh, I haven't worn this in years, and I can't think of a better use for it." Her bent fingers are surprisingly nimble as she anchors the tiara securely in my hair.

I admit I do look more like a queen and less like a stable girl with the crown in place. "Thank you. It's lovely," I say.

She slides a small case off the bed and places it on the table. "I'm not much for makeup, but I believe a touch of rouge for your cheeks and a hint of stain on your lips will do wonders." She's been right so far so I don't argue with her. I'd probably lose anyway.

When she finishes fussing over me, she turns me toward the mirror, and we both smile at the results. Seeing myself all made up to look like a bride crystallizes the fact that in a few minutes I'll be married to Ryder Blackthorn. Inola catches the flicker of panic in my eyes as my heart stumbles over itself and topples into my stomach.

She lightly touches my shoulder. "My dear, it is normal to be nervous on your wedding night. I am so sorry your beloved mother is not here to counsel you, but if I may speak in her stead, there is one bit of advice I will give you."

For a second, I'm worried she's going to reveal the secret of the birds and the bees, but she cups my chin in her nubby fingers and says, "Do not allow the sun to set upon your anger. It is always wise to patch things up before saying goodnight."

"Thanks, Inola. I'll remember that. And thanks for dressing me so beautifully."

"I enjoyed it, my dear. Now let me make certain all is in place for the ceremony. I'll return for you shortly."

Alone in the tiny room, I pace while taking deep calming breaths. This is what I wanted, but a sharp sliver of conscience jabs at me for being so selfish. How can I go through with this when I know I must leave? I face the mirror, willing myself to run to Ryder and call the whole thing off.

But then the door opens, and Inola waits at the threshold with a bouquet of orange and red flowers for me. "Your true love awaits, my dear."

Ah yes, he *is* my one true love. Pledging myself to him body and soul cannot possibly be wrong. I embrace the bouquet with trembling hands and go to take my wedding vows.

Abraham stands at the far end of the parlor wearing a navy blue, silk shirt and two long neckpieces—one made of large animal teeth and the other of eagle feathers. His gray hair has been loosened from its braid and hangs in waves around his shoulders. He holds a small white book in his right hand.

Patrick and Ralston stand to his left. Inola stations herself on his right. Ryder is positioned directly in front of Abraham, and he holds out his hand for me as I take my place by his side.

Abraham begins the ceremony with a short Cherokee blessing. *"Man cannot measure the earth and sky. They are gifts from above. So it is with love …"*

The inspiring words seep into my heart, and my entire universe shrinks down to this instant in time. I feel more alive than ever before. Every cell in my body is newly awake and alert, savoring the most important few minutes of my life. I'm acutely aware of everything around me—the slow ballet of dust motes in the shaft of light behind Abraham, the soft cadence of his scratchy voice, the sweet smell of freshly baked almond cakes, the harsh chatter of magpies in the old shade tree, the heat of Ryder's strong hand in mine.

After a few words about the sanctity of the institution of marriage, Abraham asks if we have rings. Ralston, our combination best man/maid of honor, reaches inside his jacket pocket and withdraws the diamond and emerald engagement ring Ryder designed for me. He places it in Ryder's palm. Then he extracts a black velvet box from his other pocket and hands me the thick gold band with interlocking circles that Lorelei crafted from my drawings.

Ryder smiles broadly at the appearance of a ring he knew nothing about. My heart thrills at his genuine delight. Once we have slipped the rings onto each other's fingers and recited our mutual promises, Abraham wraps a white satin ribbon and a brown leather thong around our joined hands and pronounces us husband and wife. Relief and joy flood through me as I kiss my new husband, more certain than ever that this is right.

SIX

Ryder and I make the journey to Meadowood together on his horse, suffused with happiness and wonder at the enormous step we've just taken and the mutual commitment we've made. Neither of us mentions the dark threat hanging over our heads. We laugh and talk about the ceremony and Inola's delicious almond cakes and what my family will say when we tell them, both of us anticipating the moment when we will finally be alone.

The winding lane leading to Meadowood is a stunning, shaded path that follows a narrow, mossy stream. The estate once belonged to Princess Jaden, but this is the first time I've ever seen it. The main house is a lofty white ante-bellum style mansion, with soaring pilasters and black shutters bracketing the windows. The grounds feature rolling lawns, giant shade trees, and what looks like an English hedge maze off to one side. A number of outbuildings— stables, guest houses, and servants' quarters—are visible behind the main house.

We steer our horses under the porte couchere and dismount. Patrick and the other guards take the horses around to the stables, while Ryder, Ralston, and I make our way up the sweeping front stairway. Two bowing butlers open the front doors for us, and Drew welcomes us inside.

"Your Majesty," he says, kissing my cheek. "Late as usual. Is this

44

attributable to your desire to make a grand entrance, or was it designed to heighten the suspense surrounding this secret meeting you so hastily called?"

"We had a stop to make. I'll tell you all about it," I say. "Is Father here?"

"Yes, as well as General LeGare. Adelais is entertaining them in the drawing room. I've asked her *not* to play piano, though. She's really quite terrible, so we'd better hurry before she runs out of small talk."

Drew shakes hands with Ryder and Ralston, and we follow a butler down the cherry-wood paneled hallway.

"Your Majesty," Adelais says with a curtsey as I enter the room. I've asked her several times to call me Jaden, but she hasn't gotten the hang of it yet. General LeGare bows, and Father comes to embrace me.

"You look lovely, sweetheart," he says, taking in my rosy cheeks and painted lips.

"Thank you, Father. We have something to tell you." I can't control my ecstatic grin as I reach out for Ryder. "Drew, do you mind if we close the door?"

"Not at all." He nods to the butler who pulls the door shut as he exits.

"Please sit down, everyone," I say. "I apologize for being late. We had some business in Unicoi, and while we were there ... well, we were married by a minister in Ryder's church."

"Huh?" Drew says, scratching his head.

Father gets to his feet and takes my hands in his. "Married? That is wonderful news, Jaden. But aren't we all invited to a grand royal wedding next Saturday? Has that been cancelled?"

"No. The wedding is still on schedule, but we have our reasons." I glance nervously at Ryder.

"Well, whatever the reason, this calls for champagne," Drew says heading for the door.

"Hold off on that for now," I tell him. "We have more news, and it's not so pleasant, I'm afraid. The reason we eloped today is because we've become aware of a plot to attack Warrington Palace on our wedding day."

"A plot?" General LeGare springs from his chair. "What kind of plot? Who is behind it?"

Questions fly at us from Drew and Father also.

"Please, just sit. We'll explain everything," I say.

I lay it all out for them—everything we know of the plot to massacre the royal family, Prince Gilbert's plan to bring more firearms into the country, the isolated location of the Noirs' army, and the difficulties of trying to attack them in their caves.

The responses from those present range from shock to outrage.

"Ralston has put together a plan," I say. "We believe it is our best chance of not only defeating our attackers once and for all, but also placing Domerica in the most favorable position possible to avoid an all out war with Dome Noir."

"Ralston?" General LeGare says. "He's a professor not a military man. Theory is one thing, but—"

"Just hear him out," Ryder says quietly. "He's a learned man and is well acquainted with military strategy."

Ralston rises confidently from his chair ignoring the slight from LeGare. "Thank you. As General LeGare has pointed out I am not a military man, but I am rather well versed in the art of war. The backbone of my plan is borrowed from a maneuver employed by Hannibal at the Battle of Cannae. It's called the double-envelopment, or pincher movement."

I catch Drew rolling his eyes, but I'm pretty sure he'll come around once he hears the whole thing.

"Quite simply, we lure the Noirs onto the palace grounds by allowing them to believe we are completely unaware of their plan. Their goal is to attack at the heart of the Royal Guard. Our plan is to have soldiers from the Enclave hidden on the right flank of the palace grounds and Unicoi warriors hidden on the left. With your permission, of course," he says looking from Father to Ryder.

"The entire contingent of Noirs will be allowed to enter the grounds," he continues, "and the gates will be secured behind them, thus blocking the only avenue of retreat. Our hidden forces will then surround them and strike. Due to our superior numbers, the Noirs will have no choice but to surrender or die."

"Why don't we just pick them off as they enter through the gates?" Drew asks. "Seems safer than allowing them all inside the palace grounds."

I answer for Ralston. "Because most of them will scatter and regroup at their hideout once they're aware of the trap. We can't risk a big chunk of their army escaping."

"Why not? It's classic divide and conquer," Drew says. "Eventually, we'll get them all."

I shake my head. "You don't understand. I'm going to have Prince Gilbert and Prince Jean Louis arrested prior to the attack and secretly transported to Wall's Edge Prison. I don't want anyone staging a prison break for them. Remember, the Noirs have explosives. Also, this whole incident could trigger a major war with Dome Noir. If that happens, we can't chance having people on the inside helping the Noir army gain access to the dome."

Father rubs his whiskered chin. "You're going to arrest the princes?"

"Yes. I don't want them killed in the battle. They're our biggest bargaining chip with King Philippe. Plus, we've been informed that he's frail and barely makes a move these days without Gilbert. We're counting on the fact that he's not strong enough to lead an attack on Domerica without his sons. His monarchy's on the verge of collapse as it is. His only hope of saving it is to make a deal with us. If he's not smart enough to see that, I believe Gilbert is. We can use him to persuade his father."

"I will prepare the Royal Guard immediately, Your Majesty," LeGare says. "We will train from now until your wedding day. We'll strengthen the palace with extra fortifications. They will not penetrate our defenses."

"That poses a bit of a problem, Charles," I say. "The key to this entire plan is secrecy. Our sources have informed us that spies have infiltrated the palace over the last few weeks posing as household staff and new Royal Guard recruits. With all the new people hired in preparation for the wedding, it'll be impossible to know who the spies are. The Noir's have a standing order to attack without delay if their plot is uncovered."

"But how am I to defend the palace?" LeGare asks.

"You need to identify those men who have been with the Guard for more than a couple of years. Those are the only ones we can trust. On the morning of the wedding, you'll inform them of the impending attack and provide them with assignments. By that time, it will be too late for anyone to alert the Noirs."

A knock at the door halts the conversation. Adelais goes to speak with a maid and returns to the group.

"I apologize for interrupting, Your Majesty, but dinner has been ready for nearly an hour now," she says. "Do you wish to continue this discussion in the dining room?"

I glance at Ralston and he shakes his head. "It is not wise to discuss this where we may be overheard. Even a servant innocently passing along the information may pose a threat."

"Dinner will have to wait," Drew says.

Adelais wrings her hands. "Perhaps I should have the servants lay out a buffet before the meal is ruined. We can fill our plates and bring them back here. Does that suit you, Your Majesty?"

My stomach feels a little hollow, and I'm sure I'm not the only one. "Yes, that's fine. We should eat. Thank you, Adelais."

After we're all seated again with plates of food in our laps, General LeGare asks, "Have you given any thought to moving members of the royal family to a safe haven prior to this battle?"

"Yes. In fact we thought the best idea would be to move everyone the night before the wedding to Old Unicoi. It's in the opposite direction from where the Noirs are holed up." I turn to my new husband. "Ryder, I'd be willing to offer Alexander amnesty in exchange for his help. He could be with his wife and child again."

"That's a wonderful plan," Ryder says. "Alexander will be overjoyed. I'm certain he would have helped us without your generous offer. But this will ensure his complete cooperation. He may be in a position to supply us with a cache of firearms also."

"Old Unicoi is a good choice," Father says. "What about your Uncle Harold and Osrielle? Are they in danger also?" he asks.

"Yes. The Noirs believe Osrielle is still the next in line to the throne. The family's probably safe if they stay in Hempstead, but we should inform them of the plot and give them the opportunity to go to Old Unicoi. Father could you take care of that? Harold and I haven't spoken since our last contentious meeting."

"Of course," Father says. "I'll pay them a visit tomorrow."

"Isn't the air poisonous in Old Unicoi?" the pregnant Adelais asks. Her hand goes protectively to her midsection.

"Alexander and the others live in a safe zone," Ryder says. "No uranium has been found to be present, and the air is constantly monitored for radon gas."

"We'll make certain it's completely safe, for everyone," I say. "Ryder and I will need to stay put at Warrington Palace to continue the charade that we know nothing of their plan."

"Jade!" Father and Ryder say in unison.

I hold up a hand. "Don't even try to talk me out of it. I've made up my mind. When the fighting begins, I'll be safely inside the palace under heavy guard. So, there's nothing to worry about."

"Well, I'm not going either," Drew says. "I'll not turn tail and run while a band of thugs attempt to murder me and my family. I welcome the fight."

"Drew, you are a grown man, and I respect whatever final decision you make," Father says gently. "There is nothing cowardly in choosing to go to Old Unicoi to care for and protect your pregnant wife. But, Jaden," he says more forcefully, "I'm afraid I must strongly object to your decision to remain at Warrington. You are the queen. For the sake of your people you must take all necessary precautions to ensure your own safety."

"I hear what you're saying, Father, but in my opinion, my people will be better served if I continue the pretense that the wedding is taking place as planned. Also, nothing in this world could keep me from seeing those two royal vipers from Dome Noir shackled and carted off to Wall's Edge."

Father turns pleadingly to Ryder. "She is your wife now, man. Will you not order her to Old Unicoi?"

Without hesitation Ryder says, "Surely you have mistaken me for someone else. My wife makes up her own mind about what is best for her. Besides, I would never ask my wife to do something I am unwilling to do myself."

SEVEN

It's nearly ten o'clock when Ryder and I finally break away from the meeting and walk hand-in-hand across the expanse of lawn to the guest house.

Drew and Adelais have furnished it lavishly and made certain it was adequately prepared for the queen. Enormous arrangements of freshly cut flowers are positioned in every available corner, a bowl of fresh pommeras—my favorite—and a golden tray of chocolate truffles are laid out on the coffee table, the faux fire-place has been turned on, and the crystalline logs dance merrily with red and gold light. The setting couldn't be more romantic, and I twine my arms around Ryder's waist.

"Are you tired, love?" he asks.

"No. You?"

He shakes his head and draws me closer, bending low to brush my lips with his own.

"I'm ready to see the rest of the house," I say. "Let's put out the lights to discourage any visitors."

Ryder turns off the silk-shaded lamps and follows me down a small hallway. We pass beautiful bedrooms on both our left and right, but I head straight for the French doors at the end of the hall. They open onto an enormous master suite with thick, colorfully patterned rugs, sumptuous artwork, and a gigantic four-poster bed. Our bags have been strategically arranged on luggage stands on either side of the bed.

"This is amazing," I say, goggling the luxurious furnishings.

"You act as if you've never seen it before."

Oops. I forgot Princess Jaden used to own the place. "Well, Drew and Adelais have done a great job redecorating."

"It is very beautiful," he says, resting his hands on my shoulders. "Do you wish to shower before we retire?"

My stomach does a little flip-flop. I'm ready to get the honeymoon started, but a shower is probably a good idea after the day I've had. "Yes. Do you mind? I'll be quick."

"Take your time, love. I'll shower in the other room." He scoops up his bag and disappears down the hall.

I drag my bag into the ballroom-sized bathroom and peel off my dusty clothes, tossing them into the corner. I climb under the warm shower spray, allowing it to ease the tension collected between my shoulders. After lathering up with vanilla-scented bath gel, I rinse off and towel myself dry. Poking through my bag, I come across an uber-sexy nightgown I took from the princess's hope chest.

I slide it on and straighten the lace on my shoulders. Staring at myself in the mirror, I can't decide if the filmy gown makes me look seductive or ridiculous. I'd die if Ryder laughed when he saw me. *That settles it* ... I yank off the gown and stuff it back in my bag, choosing instead to wear the silky white underdress I brought along.

Back in the bedroom, I switch off the brilliant chandelier in favor of the soft lighting of the bedside lamps. I tug down one side of the gloriously plush gold comforter and am pleasantly surprised to find ivory silk sheets beneath. *Nice touch.*

Ryder saunters shirtless through the French doors wearing only a pair of low slung cotton drawstring pants. Holy Mother of Mercy, he's so freaking beautiful fireworks explode inside my chest.

"Is this all right?" he says gesturing to his extraordinary bare torso.

I nod, tongue-tied, and continue to gape at him like a starving man at a banquet. For the briefest of seconds Erica's stunning face flashes through my mind, but I quickly shove it out. I'm the one he married today, not her. And I know beyond a doubt that whatever happens after I'm gone, I'll always be *the one* for him.

He tosses his towel on a chair. "Would you care for a glass of champagne?"

I shake my head mutely.

He moves in close, lifting his hand to tenderly cradle my cheek. I quiver at his touch. "Are you frightened?" he asks.

"No." It comes out a hoarse whisper.

"I will be gentle. I promise." His eyes hold concern.

"I know."

"We do not have to do this tonight, love. I can just hold you …"

"Shh," I whisper. My fingers find the straps of my underdress, and I slip them from my shoulders. The flimsy hank of fabric wafts to the floor like a feather. Ryder's breath hitches in his throat. His look of concern quickly vanishes, replaced by something deeply primal.

We glide together as naturally as puzzle pieces sliding in place. His sturdy arms surround me, and my bare skin tingles at his touch. He kisses the tender spot just below my ear, and I grip his muscled back with both hands. His lips trace along the length of my jaw line, and then his hungry mouth smothers my own. A low moan of longing comes from somewhere—whether him or me I don't know because all thought has ceased, and the only thing that matters is Ryder's electric touch and the remarkable way our bodies move together.

I shift my hand to the drawstring on his pants and he obliges by slipping out of them. Lifting me to the bed, he stretches full length next to me and takes me in his arms once more. We hold each other close, heartbeat to heartbeat. He covers my skin with hot kisses, causing me to writhe with pleasurable excitement. My body sinks and swells beneath his touch, and I ache for more of him. I won't stop until I have every last bit of him.

Love everlasting may be only a fleeting dream for us, but this is real. This man of flesh and bone, honor and passion, is worth whatever price I must pay. Tomorrow be damned, Ryder Blackthorn is mine tonight.

We cling to each other throughout the night, lost in the wonder of being together completely, knowing each other in ways we'd only dreamed of up until now, reaching for each other over and over again. I float in a twilight of alternate longing and fulfillment, shunning sleep, unwilling to miss even a single moment of this precious night.

When silvery-pink streaks of morning light stream into our room, I lie completely still, fearing to stir in case Ryder should say it's time to rise and face the day. But he only tightens his arms around me and kisses my hair.

"Morning, love," he whispers.

I nestle deeply into his warmth. "Shh. Just hold me," I say.

He nuzzles my ear and softly kisses my neck. My whole body shivers with delight, and I wrap myself around him.

A soft but insistent tapping from the front of the house causes Ryder to raise his head. "Is that someone at our door?"

"I don't know. Ignore it. Maybe they'll go away." I take his face in my hands, pressing soft caressing kisses to the corners of his mouth.

"Chief Blackthorn," a man's voice calls, as the tapping continues.

"I'd better see what it is," Ryder says, moving out of my arms. He slips into his pants, ties them low around his hips, and pads to the door.

I heave a defeated sigh knowing that, for now at least, bliss must give way to the realities of our urgent situation.

Ryder returns to the bedroom, combing his long fingers through his tousled hair. "Liam and Adahy are here," he says. "They're having breakfast at the main house, but they have a report for us. We should dress and join them, love."

I groan. "Oh, all right. Do you mind if I shower first?"

"Of course not. I'd join you," he says suggestively. "But I'm afraid we'll not make it to the meeting if I do. I'll shower down the hall."

I smile at the lovely visual. "All right, but I'll probably take longer than you, so don't wait for me. I'll meet you there." I scoop up my underdress from the floor and head for the bathroom.

Memories of my night with Ryder send shivers through my whole body as the spray of the shower warms my skin. My mind wanders back to the overpowering magic of last night. The way I felt in Ryder's arms was indescribable—in mere mortal language. It's still unfathomable to me that I'm actually married to the most amazing man I ever met.

But it's only for a few days, a cruel voice reminds me, *then you'll never see him again, never be held by him, never be loved by him—ever again.*

The pain of that knowledge slams into me like a fist to my midsection. Gasping, I wrap my arms around myself to stave off the agony. I lean back against the cold marble wall and slide to the floor. Long shuddering sobs of unutterable sorrow rack my body. Tears of grief flow down the shower drain like grains of sand sifting through the hourglass of my rapidly fleeting time with Ryder.

I arrive late and red-eyed for the meeting. Ryder holds my chair for me while the others stand. "Shall I fix a plate for you?" he asks.

"No. I'm not hungry. Please everyone, be seated. Shall we begin? I understand our trackers have a report."

Adahy stands. "We do, Your Majesty." He methodically lays out for the others what Ralston and I already knew about the heavily armed Noir encampment. I tune him out after a minute or two. I know how the story ends, and I'm weary of hearing about it.

After the trackers' report, the others discuss arming the Royal Guardsmen and the role the Enclave and Unicoi armies will play in the battle.

Ryder speaks up. "Commander Greystone will coordinate the efforts on Unicoi's behalf. I'll brief him today and consult with the men in Old Unicoi about sheltering the royal family and perhaps supplying us with additional firearms. I shall travel to Old Unicoi directly from here."

My head whips around to him. "I thought you were coming back to the palace with me."

"Time is short, love," he says, "and we've much to accomplish."

"But can't Adahy and Liam go to Old Unicoi to arrange things?"

He takes my hand, peering deeply into my eyes. "We are asking a great deal from Alexander, Jaden, but we are also offering a great deal. It's important that I be the one to deliver the news that he'll soon be reunited with his wife and son, and to seek his pledge of help."

"Then I'm going with you," I say. The thought of Ryder leaving me right now is unbearable.

"Jaden, I would advise against that," Father says guardedly. My eyes stay glued to Ryder.

"You know you cannot," he says. "You must return to the palace and continue with the wedding arrangements, attending to your normal responsibilities as if nothing is amiss. An unplanned excursion to Old Unicoi would raise many suspicions. It's your duty as queen, my love."

Sufficiently chastised, I duck my head. "All right. I'll go home alone. But when will you return?"

"As soon as humanly possible. I swear it."

I quietly move my chair away from the table and hurry from the room so as to be spared the additional embarrassment of weeping in public.

EIGHT

On our return to the palace, we find it teeming with frenzied activity in preparation for the royal wedding. Within moments of our arrival, it's clear I'll have blessedly little time for a pity party on my agenda today. As Ralston and I cross the threshold, Jennifer Osborne practically accosts me.

"Your Majesty, thank goodness you're back," she says, forgetting to curtsey. "At least a dozen items require your immediate attention, and I'd like you to view the progress on the remodel of the Queen's Suite, if possible. I believe you'll be quite happy with it."

Though my mother made significant contributions to planning my wedding before she died, Jennifer has taken over all responsibility for the myriad of festivities leading up to and including the wedding ceremony itself. She has legions of help, but the strain appears to be wearing on her. Orange stains mar her otherwise immaculate pastel blue jacket, and clumps of hair straggle from her normally pristine bun.

"All right, Jennifer. Give me a few minutes to change, and I'll take a look at what you've got." Her frazzled enthusiasm is gratifying, but I wonder what she'd think if she knew all her hard work was about to be obliterated in a bloody battle.

"Thank you Your Majesty," she says with a grateful smile. "Shall we meet in your office in, say, thirty minutes?"

Ralston touches my arm. "Don't forget Your Majesty, you have another important matter to attend to before dinner." He raises his eyebrows, and I realize he's reminding me that I need to update Asher this afternoon.

"Oh, right," I say. "I'll see you in a half hour, Jennifer, but we'll have to work quickly."

"As you wish." She makes a small dip and scurries off, high heels rat-a-tatting on the marble floor.

Ralston and I make arrangements to meet in my office later. He'll be my cover again while I shift to Arumel for my first update with Asher.

I quickly change into a gown of royal purple satin and secure a small tiara atop my head. Retrieving the polycom from its hidden compartment in my jewelry chest, I select the directory, touch Asher's name, and type a little message: *Will be there in approx 2 hours for update. Okay? J.*

In a surprisingly short amount of time, I receive a one word reply. *Yes.* I replace the polycom in its plain black case, stuff it back into the chest and lock it securely.

Jennifer waits for me inside my upstairs office. When I enter, she hops to her feet, remembering the curtsey this time. She issues a blustery apology for her appearance, blaming the orange stains on the lobster bisque tasting she conducted earlier in the day.

"It will be perfect for the Wedding Eve Dinner as long as the servants don't spill," she says.

We sit facing my desk, and Jennifer opens her enormous file. At this point, dealing with open wedding issues is a senseless irritation for me. Substituting snap-dragons for freesia in the flower arrangements doesn't seem to rise to the level of needing the queen's authorization, but it's obviously terribly important to Jennifer.

"Only a few additional items require your approval, Your

Majesty." She withdraws several sheets of paper from the file.

"You know what, Jennifer? I really don't have time to look at any more flower arrangements, seating charts, or hors d'ouvere selections. Going forward, you have my permission to make any and all wedding decisions. I'll put it in a royal decree and plaster it to the palace walls if you like."

Her face flames red. "Are you quite certain, Your Majesty? I want everything to be completely to your liking."

"I know it'll be awesome." I stand, ready to dismiss her.

"Will you at least see the renovations to the Queen's Suite?" She rises quickly.

"All right, but let's hurry. I have another meeting."

As we step across the threshold to the Queen's Suite, unbidden memories of Mother lying on her death bed flutter across my mind, but the rooms have been so utterly transformed that the bleak image has no place to roost and quickly moves on.

New window coverings have yet to be installed and the bed is missing, but the overall extravagance of the suite is spectacular. The walls are a soft green with gold accents. The intricate design of the chandeliers is extraordinary. The ceiling of the bed chamber has been painted with a lush pastoral scene complete with a robin's-egg-blue sky and fluffy white clouds—two things residents of Domerica have only heard about. My stomach clenches with the realization that Ryder and I will never share this room.

I whirl around abruptly, startling Jennifer. "Are you all right, Your Majesty?" she says.

"Yes. It's all incredibly lovely, but I have to go. Thanks for the tour." I lift my long skirts, and practically sprint from the room.

Ralston waits for me in my office, with Patrick standing sentry just outside the door.

"I shouldn't be long," I say, after closing the door. "There's not much to tell them except that everyone's on board with the plan."

"No rush, my dear," Ralston says. "I'll manage things here."

I open my TPD bracelet. "See you soon," I say, before clicking the latch. Z*zzt*.

Once again, Asher answers the door before I have a chance to knock. His eyes skid across my queen getup. "You're looking awfully regal tonight," he says coolly. "We'll meet in my apartment, unless you'd prefer one of the offices."

"Your place is fine," I say.

We take a chilly ride in the elevator to the third floor. Asher's in some kind of mood and doesn't speak a word until we step inside his apartment.

"Do you want something to drink?" he asks.

"No thanks. This shouldn't take long." I stroll into his black and while living room. "Hey, you replaced your rug." A new white shag rug sits in place of the previous one that I bled all over after a berserk black knight nearly sliced my hand in two during the attack on my travel party.

He folds his arms and props up against the wall. "Kinda had to. Red didn't go with the rest of the décor." His voice holds no humor.

"I wish you'd let me reimburse you for this. It's the least I can do for all your help that night."

"Don't worry about it."

"What's wrong, Ash? Am I catching you at a bad time or something? What's with the cold shoulder?"

"How was the wedding? Did you really go through with it?"

I roll my eyes. "Is that what this is about? You're pissed because I married Ryder?"

"I'm blown away that you'd actually marry the poor schmuck

61

when you know you can't stay with him."

"I don't have to explain myself to you. I've got enough shit going on in my life right now, without you throwing some kind of jealousy-fueled, judgmental tirade at me. If you can't handle these meetings in a professional manner, I'll ask Narowyn to assign me someone who can." I stomp to the door and fling it open.

"No. Wait, Jade, please."

I wheel around. "What?"

"I'm sorry for acting like a jerk. I shouldn't have let my personal feelings get mixed up in this. I realize you're going through hell, and the last thing I want to do is add to that."

"Why don't I believe you?"

"No really. Please. Let me stay on as your contact. I give you my word, I won't lose it again."

I shake my head. "I don't know, Ash. This whole thing sucks so bad. I was hoping having you here would make things a little easier. At least you're my friend … or I thought you were."

"I am. Don't ever doubt it. Please, come in and sit down." He takes my arm lightly. "Do you want a soda or something? I've got Coke Lite."

"You mean Diet Coke?"

"It's called Coke Lite here, but I'm sure it's the same thing—without all the preservatives." We stop at the kitchen and he takes two cans from the fridge.

My mouth waters. I haven't had a soda for weeks. "Okay, but I swear Ash, if you bring up Ryder again, I'm out of here."

"Deal." He hands me a frosty, silver and red can, and we head back to the living room.

"There's not a lot to report," I say, flopping down on the white sofa. "We met with Father, Ryder, and General LeGare at my brother's place. There was some debate, but in the end, everyone agreed that Ralston's plan probably has the greatest likelihood of success. So they've all gone off to meet with their own people to set the wheels in motion."

I take a few gulps of the sweet bubbly liquid.

"Good," he says. "Sounds as if things are coming together well on your end."

"Yeah, so far. I really won't know much more until Ryder and Father return to the palace. So it'll probably be a couple of days before you see me again."

"Don't run off just yet. I have some good news for you too. Urick's in."

"What? Wow, that was fast. How'd he manage it?"

"The members of the Transcender force are kind of fearless … and maybe a little nuts," he says, grinning. "Anyway, Urick and this guy named Roper from his team discovered this hole-in-the-wall about five miles outside of Warrington Village where the Noirs were rumored to hang out. People go there to bet illegally on fights."

"You mean like fist fights?"

"Well, it's more like dirty cage fighting—fists, elbows, feet, whatever. So they got some information that the Noirs have recruited some of the fighters to join their band of thugs. Urick and Roper showed up there last night, and Urick basically obliterated two of the toughest guys. The Noirs approached him afterwards about enlisting with them."

"That's awful. He had to fight to get in?"

"It's all right, Jade. Urick loves that kind of stuff. He grew up on a warring earth. He used to fight for recreation. The point is, now we have someone on the inside, and Narowyn and Captain Watterson feel much better about the whole plan. Urick will bring back intelligence, and he'll be on the scene to protect you when you make your shift to Arumel."

Asher's practically jubilant as he tells me this. His mood swings are making me dizzy.

"That's awesome, unless he gets himself killed first," I say. "Those guys sound really nasty."

"Don't worry. Urick can take care of himself. I'll fill you in once we get his first report."

"Okay, great. I'd better get back now." I take the last gulp of my Coke Lite. "Ralston's holding down the fort, and the whole palace is on wedding crack preparing for the onslaught of our foreign guests in a few days. Someone's likely to come looking for my permission to use Fargen-shaped urinal cakes in the men's room."

We get to our feet, and I lift my sleeve, exposing my bracelet.

"Next time, just shift straight to my place," he says.

"I'll do that, thanks."

"And Jade, I'm sorry about before—about harshing on you and all."

"It's all right, Ash."

"Was it nice? The wedding I mean?"

I squint at him like *you're really brining this up?*

He holds out his arms innocently. "I'm just asking as a friend."

"It was okay for a spur-of-the-moment gig."

"Well congratulations," he says, planting a chaste kiss on my cheek.

"I'll be in touch," I say, and Z*zzt*, I'm off.

"Goodness, that took no time at all," Ralston says when I appear back in my office.

"Like I said, not much to report. Asher had some news, though. That guy on the Transcender Police Force has already joined up with the Noirs."

"So quickly?"

"Yeah well, this guy looks like he belongs on the brut squad except for his choir boy face. But maybe that's his best asset. He comes across as trustworthy."

Ralston sets aside the book he was reading. "A useful quality for both a law enforcement officer and a spy. I'll program this new information into the QP. It should improve our likelihood of success." He checks his watch. "Now I believe it's time for you to make your appearance in the dining hall, Your Majesty." He rises gracefully from his chair.

I groan loudly. "Oh man, Rals, I'm tired. Can't we just eat up here tonight and say our meeting ran over, or something?"

"No, my dear, we cannot. You have not dined in the formal hall for three nights in a row. Those present at court are already grumbling about the conspicuous absence of the soon-to-be-wed queen. We must not provide them with grounds to suspect that something is amiss."

"All right, but I'm leaving right after dessert. No boring after dinner small talk tonight. I haven't seen the Skorplings in a while, and I don't have much time left with them. I'm thinking of having them for a little sleep-over."

"As you wish, Your Majesty." He opens the office door. "After you," he says, bowing deeply.

NINE

Fred and Ethel are hyper-excited about spending the night in my room. We have a rousing game of hide and seek. Afterward, I let them both style my hair in exchange for promises that they'll turn in early—mostly because I'm too tired to play anymore.

In the morning, we feast on a breakfast of fruit, Fred's favorite muffins, and egg casserole. I drop off my furry friends at the nursery before making my way to the gown room. The final fitting for my new wedding outfits is scheduled for ten o'clock. My plan is to get it over with quickly and take a long ride on Gabriel.

A uniformed butler greets me as I arrive at the gown room and informs me that the fitting has been relocated to the east ballroom. That seems a bit odd to me, although it might be kind of fun. The east ballroom is a gorgeous space used for smaller dance parties. It has a golden mirrored ceiling and walls, sparkling crystal chandeliers and a shiny wooden dance floor. The butler escorts me down the short corridor.

When he swings open the doors to the ballroom, I'm convinced there's been a mistake. The whole room is completely transformed into something appropriate for fashion week in Paris. A brightly lit runway skirted in blue velvet sits in the center of the dance floor, with folding chairs for spectators arranged on either side. A blue curtained dressing area has been erected in the back, and a young man in formal attire sits in the orchestra area playing a complicated concerto on a grand piano.

Uh oh. I pick up an unpleasant vibe that someone may be expecting me to model my new gowns. *No way that's gonna happen.*

Jennifer Osborne hurries over grinning hugely. "Oh, Your Majesty, isn't it lovely?" she says with a curtsey.

"Uh, yeah, it is. But *what* is it?"

"I hope you don't mind, but everyone's been working so hard to prepare for the wedding celebrations. I invited the young ladies in waiting to view your fitting as a kind of reward for all their efforts. Cook has prepared some refreshments for them."

She gestures to a long table covered with a white cloth and laid out with silver platters, tiered crystal serving stands, and cake pedestals loaded with the most luscious looking desserts I've ever seen.

Really? Nobody can take a crap around here without asking the queen's permission, and yet Jennifer sets up this whole party/fashion show without even telling me?

"That's really thoughtful of you, Jennifer," I say, biting back my annoyance, "but I'd planned to have a quick try-on and then go out for a ride. In addition to which, I'm not comfortable parading around in front of a bunch of people, and I doubt they'd find it very entertaining."

Her face crumbles just as the ballroom doors fly open and dozens of smiling, chattering young women burst inside. When they see me, all conversation ceases, but the smiles remain as they curtsey and hover near the door.

Jennifer looks pleadingly to me. "What shall I tell them, Your Majesty?"

I blow out a long sigh. Well, hell, I'm not going to be responsible for spoiling everyone's good time, but I'm also not prancing around like Kate Moss while everybody else sits and gawks. Then an idea strikes me. Jennifer won't like it, but tough. I'm the queen and she brought this on herself.

I take her arm and move us over to one side of the room. "Look, Jennifer, here's what's going to happen. You tell everyone to get something to eat and make themselves comfortable. While they're doing that, send some butlers over to the gown room and have them bring back a bunch of those rolling racks of my gowns and Mother's old gowns. Anyone who wants to try on dresses and model them for the crowd is welcome to do so."

Jennifer's features contort into a troll doll mask of disapproval. "But they're maids, Your Majesty. You want them to wear your gowns?"

"They'll be careful with them, I'm sure. It'll be fun." *I'm never going to wear them again anyway.* "In the meantime, the seamstress and I will take care of my fitting in the dressing area back there—in private—and everybody will be happy." I pat her shoulder reassuringly.

She looks scandalized, but having no choice in the matter, she agrees. "As you wish, ma'am."

While Jennifer instructs the butlers, I locate the seamstress and we quietly slip into the temporary dressing area to work on my gowns. My heart dips when I catch sight of the luminescent wedding gown that was once my mother's. I miss her so much and wish she were here. All things considered, though, I suppose she'd be an additional loved-one to worry about when the shit hits the fan on Saturday. Maybe it's best she is not here to suffer through all that is to come.

When the racks of evening gowns are wheeled-in by a small army of butlers, a loud squeal of excitement fills the room. I catch myself smiling with amusement as the ladies race each other to have first choice of the fairytale dresses. The rumble of their shoes on the dance floor sounds like a small Fargen stampede.

The seamstress and her assistants efficiently help me into and out of the new gowns created for my wedding events. They are beyond gorgeous and most fit me to a tee, with little or no need for alteration. My favorite is the floor length beauty designed for the Wedding Eve Dinner. It's indigo satin, with a deep v-neckline and a wide drop-waist sash fringed in silver. It hugs my every curve, and the slit up the front of the skirt is just high enough to make things interesting.

After the seamstress secures the last straight pin into the fitted waist, I change back into my riding clothes, anxious to get to the stables. When I step out into the room, though, I'm immediately swept up in the party atmosphere, and my attention is captivated by the amateur high-fashion models breezing up and down the runway.

The piano player—the only male still in the room—must think he's died and gone to heaven. He's switched to playing sultry tunes for the girls, most of whom are dressing and undressing out in the open without a thought as to who might be watching. The guy's got to be hoping this day will never end.

Once my eye is drawn to the dessert table and a mound of gooey looking chocolaty squares, all thoughts of the stables are pushed aside. I grab a plate and decide to hang around a few minutes longer.

Jennifer is seated near the back of the room, and I take the empty chair next to hers. She sips punch and seems to be enjoying herself as she oversees the jubilant girls playing queen-for-a-day. Some of them put on quite a show, and I find myself giggling and applauding along with the other spectators.

Half-way through my triple-chocolate, frosted fudge brownie, the doors open a crack and Ralston pokes his head inside. He doesn't spare a glance for the girls, but stiffly motions for me to join him.

I set my dish on an empty chair, and hurry to the door. "What is it, Rals? What's wrong?"

He flaps a sheet of paper in the air. "I've been summoned to headquarters. They wish to have a signed copy of your contract filed with the agency's legal department prior to your wedding day. In addition, they wish to question me regarding the matter of a mini QP which seems to have gone missing on the day I departed IUGA."

"Oh god, Rals. You can't go. We have to figure out something else."

"But I must go, my dear. Otherwise *the jig is up,* as they say. May we discuss this in your office?"

We quickly take the stairs to my office and lock the door. "What are we going to do, Rals? Do you think they already know you're helping me?"

"No, I do not. Otherwise I believe they would simply have removed me from the palace and sent another agent to pick up your signed contract."

We sit at the small conference table. "I'm confident I can handle the issue of the contract rather easily," he says. "The stolen QP may be more problematic. It was checked out to a friend and fellow agent. I swore to him I'd return it to the equipment room that afternoon. The record keeping in that section is notoriously bad. I assumed this whole thing would be over by the time they discovered it missing."

"Can't you just deny ever having it?"

"I do not wish to place my friend in a bad situation. I must find a way to return it without them knowing I've had it these past several days."

"What happens if you get caught?"

"You must go to Arumel at once. It's too dangerous for you to attempt to proceed without me *and* the quantum predictor."

"Don't say that, Rals. Just don't let them catch you, okay?"

He pats my hand. "I'll do my best, old girl."

"So how will you handle the contract issue? I can't sign that thing electing to stay in Domerica."

"No. You cannot, and you will not. You shall sign a contract stating that you have elected to join the Transcenders in Arumel. We'll make certain Narowyn Du Lac has a copy of that contract and that she files it with the Office of Records in Arumel City."

"But what will you tell IUGA?"

"It's best if I do not disclose that to you at present. It's important that you have plausible deniability."

"Plausible what?"

"Never mind. All it means is that, in this situation, what you don't know can't hurt you. You must trust me on this."

"Okay, if you're sure you know what you're doing."

"I'll run my plans through the QP before I do anything. Rather ironic isn't it," he says with a tilted smile, "relying on a bit of stolen technology to get me out of the sticky predicament created by the theft itself. Poetic justice, don't you think?"

"Only if it works. When do you leave?"

"They don't expect me until tomorrow. I'll use the remainder of the day to prepare the contracts for your signature and run a few scenarios through the quantum predictor."

"Okay. I'm going for a horseback ride, but I'll be back in an hour or two if you need me."

"Fine. Don't worry if I'm not in attendance at dinner tonight. I'll see you in the morning before I depart."

* * *

Patrick joins me in the stables as I'm saddling Gabriel. "Your Majesty," he says bowing. "Where are we off to this afternoon?"

"We're riding to the lake," I say, tightening the saddle's flank cinch.

"Then we will require a few more men," he says.

"Ah, Patrick," I wheedle. "Let's just go by ourselves. It's not that far."

"No ma'am. You know it is not safe. If you wish only the two of us to ride, we must stay within the palace grounds."

I scowl at him, even though I know he's only trying to protect me. "All right, we'll stay within the grounds, but I want to go all the way to the high meadow today."

"As you wish."

Gabriel snorts and prances as I mount up. He's as excited as I am to be out in the open country breathing the freshly ionized air and putting acreage between us and the palace. We gallop for a time, the wind whipping through my hair and the sweet smell of pommera blossoms tickling my nose. It doesn't take long before the momentous cares of the upcoming days slip from my shoulders and a lightness of spirit descends on me.

We slow to a trot, moving as one unit through the outrageously gorgeous landscape. I've grown to love this richly luxuriant land, especially the distinctive silvery light of the soaring dome that imbues every object with radiant glow.

When we reach the upper meadow, I slide off Gabriel's back and walk to the edge of a nearby brook. Dipping a cupped hand into the icy water, I raise it to my lips. Gabriel saunters over to join me, drawing deeply from the little spring. Patrick hovers in the background, allowing me my space.

"Patrick, come and sit for a minute," I say.

He dismounts and leads his horse to drink from the stream. I perch on a large stone near the bank. Patrick goes down on one knee facing me.

"What may I do for you, Your Majesty?"

"You've seen some unusual things the past few days—my hasty marriage to Chief Blackthorn, the secret meetings at my brother's estate. I'm sure you've wondered what triggered these events."

"It is not my place to question you."

"I know that. You're the best bodyguard—and friend—I could

have hoped for. Nevertheless, I'd like you to know what's at the root of these actions. We've become aware that Dome Noir plans to attack Warrington Palace on my wedding day. Their soldiers are already hidden away in a series of caves in the Northern Hills. The goal is to kill me and as many other members of the royal family as possible, with the ultimate objective of taking over Domerica."

He gazes at me a moment with his earnest, honey-colored eyes. "How did you discover this?"

"Do you remember Eve?"

His face brightens and he nods. They met a few weeks back when Eve went AWOL from the Transcenders to help us rescue the kidnapped Skorplings. She saved Patrick's life that day, using advanced medicine from Arumel to treat a serious wound to his arm.

"The information originally came from her people. But we've confirmed the facts ourselves. General LeGare knows, but you're the only other member of the Royal Guard to be informed, and you must keep it in the strictest confidence. The bulk of our defense will be handled by the Enclave and Unicoi armies."

"I will fight for you. I have sworn to protect you with my life," he says.

"I have complete confidence in you. I'm going to need you, especially on the day of the attack."

Deep furrows crease his forehead. "Surely you do not intend to be here at the palace on the day of the attack."

"Yes, I do. It's important that the wedding appears to be proceeding exactly as planned, or our defense strategy won't work."

"What do you wish me to do, Your Majesty?"

"For now, just keep quiet about this. Make note of any new people you think might be spies, and tell General LeGare. We'll take care of them first. If you're a religious man, Patrick, pray this all works."

"I shall, Your Majesty." He stands and offers me his hand. "We'd better return before the rains begin."

One more person added to the circle of intrigue. I hope I've done the right thing in bringing him on board.

* * *

At dinner, the palace groupies seem unusually animated. The entire castle is buzzing with stories of the uproarious party/fashion extravaganza of earlier today. Hilarious tales are making the rounds about the risqué antics of some of the guests. The accounts make it sound a little like *Maids Gone Wild,* but I suspect most of it didn't really happen. Things seemed pretty tame when I left, and Jennifer was there to supervise.

I'm not sure if I come off looking good or looking bad for throwing open my closet to the household staff, but at least it was a memorable day for those who attended … and also for those who only heard the stories.

Back in my room, Maria helps me out of my formal dinner clothes. "Why weren't you at the bridal fitting party today?" I ask.

"The party was really for the young, single women. Now that I'm engaged, I feel more … settled." She holds up my robe and I slip into it.

"I understand that, it was a little frivolous, but fun. By the way, have you've set a wedding date yet?"

Her cheeks flush a pretty shade of pink. "It is in June. It will be a very small affair, but I would be honored if you and Chief Blackthorn would attend."

"Thank you, Maria. We wouldn't miss it," I say, regretting the lie. Sitting at my dressing table, I remove my earrings and crown. Maria replaces them in my jewelry chest and begins to brush out my hair. She's an expert at pampering, and I admit it feels wonderful.

"Are you nervous for your wedding day?" she asks.

"Maybe a little." *But not for the reasons you think.* "How about you? Are you nervous for your wedding?"

"Oh, I am nervous." She gently draws the brush down the length of my hair. "But not for the wedding. For what comes after."

I glance at her in the mirror. She pauses, her lips trembling slightly. "I've never been with a man before. They say the first time is very painful."

Rotating in my seat, I take the brush from her and hold her hands in mine. "Listen, Maria. It's nothing to be afraid of. It's not that bad. Really."

Her eyes register shock at my admission of not being a virgin.

I laugh lightly. "It's all right. Chief Blackthorn and I are already married."

"You are?"

"Yes, we were married two days ago in Unicoi."

"But why?"

"Well that's complicated. Mostly it has to do with politics, but it's a big secret. You can't tell anyone, understand? Not even your fiancé."

"Oh, I would not." She makes the sign of the cross. "As God is my witness."

She swivels me back to face the mirror and resumes smoothing out my tresses. "My congratulations to you. And truly, it is not so bad?"

"No, it …"

I'm interrupted as the door to my room swings wide, and Ryder stands framed in the entrance, dusty, unshaven, and utterly splendid.

I leap from my chair and run to him. Arms, lips, and barely controlled passion crash together in a fervent embrace. He smells of the springtime wind, damp earth, and deep longing. Maria hastens out of the room, discretely closing the door.

"I missed you so badly," he says. Fiery kisses sear my neck, teeth graze my earlobe.

"Me too," I whisper, grasping madly at the laces on his tunic.

"Allow me to shower and make myself acceptable for you," he says, helping me with the laces.

"No. That can wait. I want you the way you are. Don't leave me, even for a second."

Grinning, he yanks the tunic off over his head. "As you wish, Your Majesty."

TEN

A knock at my door startles me awake, and I realize from the rosy glow of the room that it's morning. I raise my head from Ryder's chest, causing him to stir.

"Who is it?" I call.

"It's Ralston, Your Majesty."

I clap my hand to my mouth. "Oh no, I forgot he has a short trip planned. I need to speak with him before he goes."

Ryder nuzzles a kiss to my shoulder. "Perhaps this would be a good time for me to have that shower I've been in need of since yesterday."

"Good idea." I snag my robe from the foot of the bed. "Just a minute, Rals."

Ryder gathers his discarded clothing and makes for the bathroom.

"Good morning," I say, opening my door. Ralston stands just outside, dressed in travel duds, valise in hand.

"I'm sorry to disturb you." He glances into the empty room. "I understand Ryder has returned. But I have the contracts for you to sign, and I felt we should speak before I depart."

"I'm sorry, I overslept. Come in and sit down. Ryder's showering, so we'll have a few minutes alone."

He takes a seat in an armchair facing the faux fireplace and sets his bag on his lap. Removing his gloves, he opens the case and draws out a sheaf of papers.

He spreads the papers across the coffee table in front of us. "I have three copies of the contract, one for you, one for the Transcenders, and one for IUGA. Sign each of them in the space where it says you have elected to permanently join the Transcenders in Arumel." Pointing to a signature line, he passes me his pen.

"There are four copies here, Rals. Do I sign them all?"

"Oh, pardon me." He folds up the fourth copy and slips it inside his jacket. "Just these three," he says.

I cock an eyebrow at him, but he shoots me a *don't ask* look, so I just do as I'm told. After all copies are signed, he gives two of them to me and places the third inside his valise. "Put those in a safe place where no one will happen upon them. Now that you have a roommate, you must be more circumspect about where you keep your more unusual possessions." He gestures to my TPD bracelet.

"I know, Rals. I'm being cautious."

"I recommend that you deliver one of those contracts to the Transcenders today and inform them as to what has transpired. If I do not return to the palace by tomorrow evening, you should assume IUGA has detained me and an attack may be imminent. Go to Arumel at once, Jade. You cannot risk staying to see what happens. Remember a ninety-eight percent probability exists that you will die in an attack unless our plan is in place."

"Yeah, yeah, I remember. But did you run your own plans through the QP thing last night?"

"Yes. For the most part, it appears things will go smoothly at headquarters. But I can't be one hundred percent certain. You must be prepared for the worst."

He tugs on his gloves and rises. "Give my best to Ryder. With any luck, I'll see you tomorrow, old girl."

"Be careful." I hug him quickly and close the door after him.

To my disappointment, Ryder emerges from the bathroom fully clothed. I prefer him a little more casual.

"Do you have time to eat breakfast with me this morning?" he asks.

"I thought we'd spend the whole day together," I say, curving my arms around his waist.

He tilts his head. "Your wedding is three days away, the delegations from Dome Noir and Cupola Vita arrive tomorrow, and the queen has nothing on her agenda for today?"

Geeze, talk about a buzz kill. "Yeah, I've got a few things to do, but still ..."

He tucks a fly-away strand of hair behind my ear and kisses the lobe softly, sending a pleasurable tremor through me.

"Commander Greystone is due here in an hour, love. He needs to have the lay of the palace grounds and familiarize himself with the area where his warriors are to be positioned. After that, Alexander's men from Old Unicoi are scheduled to arrive with wagons of firearms for General LeGare. Alexander is overjoyed at your offer of amnesty, by the way. He sends you his profound thanks."

"Well, I'm grateful for his help. Plus, we know he didn't assassinate Damien. But it sounds like you're the one with a busy day. Maybe we can plan a private dinner up here for this evening. Just the two of us?"

"Are you not expecting your father this afternoon?"

"Oh man, I forgot about that." I huff out a long breath. "I guess you're right. We both have a lot to do today." I curl my fingers around his neck and pull him in for a stolen kiss. "Let me shower quickly, and we'll have a nice breakfast together."

"Or we could just skip breakfast," he says, a playful light in his eyes.

* * *

With only a few days remaining in Domerica, I spend some time in my office taking care of some unresolved matters. Several copies of my formal proposal for the resumption of trade with Dome Noir are stacked neatly in one corner.

Ralston recommends that I go ahead and deliver my presentation to the two dickhead princes, as if I don't know their real intentions. It's not going to be easy pretending everything's cool, knowing they consider me a dead man walking.

The more pressing piece of business at the moment, though, is writing my last will and testament. I don't care a bit about what happens to my jewelry and other stuff; it was never really mine to begin with. But I do care what happens to Fred and Ethel and Gabriel after I'm gone. I pull a few sheets of the queen's stationery out of the top drawer and begin to write.

Thirty minutes later, I'm still scribbling away when the door to my office opens and Lady Lorelei Bartlett's lovely face appears. "May I come in, Your Majesty?"

"Of course, Lorelei." I quickly flip over my make-shift will and motion for her to be seated. "What brings you to the palace today? There's not a problem with your upcoming journey?" I ask, referring obliquely to her impending trip to Old Unicoi.

"No, there is no problem. I have come here to beg you to reconsider your decision and to join the rest of us in Old Unicoi. The country needs you. It is not necessary for you to risk your life this way."

Though her frame is slight, her bearing conveys strength and conviction. Yellow hair falls in shiny waves around her stunning face. Intelligent, cornflower blue eyes stare directly into mine, and I'm struck by what an extraordinary queen she will make.

Once again, I have to wonder about this thing called destiny. Is it real? And could it be so inconceivably complex as to have orchestrated all circumstances in the universe to ensure that this remarkable woman will ascend to the throne of Domerica during its darkest hour?

I'm convinced IUGA's got it all wrong. Destiny can't be outsmarted. It'll find a way despite the best efforts of misguided men to control it.

"Thank you, Lorelei, but I'm committed to seeing this through. Father and General LeGare assure me the invaders will be overwhelmed by our forces. So, really there is little danger in my staying."

"Then Jacob and I feel we should be here also, to support and protect you."

I shake my head. "You know I can't agree to that. The queen and the heir apparent must be separated during a time of danger. You need to be as far away from Warrington Palace as possible."

"Is there nothing I can say to change your mind?"

"No."

Her eyes probe mine once again, and she blinks away a trace of sorrow. "Then I shall trouble you no further."

I rise, and we share a gentle embrace.

"This is a very brave thing you are doing, cousin." She kisses my forehead. "Please be careful."

I dig deep for my most reassuring smile. "Don't worry about me, Lorelei. I'm certain everything will go according to plan."

She curtseys and glides gracefully from the room.

I return to putting the finishing touches on my handwritten will. When it's done, I fold it neatly and slide it inside a thick, cream-colored envelope. The desk clock chimes, reminding me that the day is rapidly slipping away, and I still need to sneak in a visit to Arumel.

Without Ralston here to cover for me, I don't see how I can just disappear for a time. I never know when Jennifer, LeGare, or someone else will drop by my office unannounced. Then it occurs to me that maybe I can just text Asher on the polycom and deliver the contract to him later.

I hurry to my room and lock my door. I dig the polycom out of its hiding place in my jewelry chest. Flopping onto my bed, I open the directory and find Asher's name. When I press the key, a message box pops up and I begin typing.

Ralston summoned to IUGA. May be trouble. Can't meet today.

I press Send. In a few seconds, I receive a reply.

Why was Rals summoned?

I respond.

They want my signed contract. They know about the missing QP.

I watch the screen intently for a beat. Then two. Then *Zzzt!* Asher materializes next to my bed.

"*Yeek!*" I chuck the polycom into the air, and it crashes to the floor.

"What the hell, Ash! What are you doing here?" I scoop up the phone and toss it on my dressing table. "What if I'd been with someone?"

"I figured you wouldn't be scripting me if you were with somebody. This is bad, Jade. IUGA may already know Ralston has sold them out. They have ways of retrieving information from automatons."

"I know it looks bad, but Ralston says it'll be okay. He's figured out what to do about the contract, and he's going to try to sneak the QP back in like it's been there all along. He ran his ideas through the predictor. He says it looks good."

Ash shakes his head doubtfully. "What exactly is he planning to do?"

"He wouldn't tell me—*plausible deniability* or something like that. But he had me sign copies of the contract saying that I elect to join the Transcenders in Arumel. I have a copy for you."

I hustle to the jewelry chest and take out a copy of the contract. "Rals says you should file this with the Office of Records in Arumel City right away." I hold it out for him.

He snatches it from me, clearly agitated. "For the love of God, Jade, you should have told me about all this immediately. We need to send someone over to IUGA headquarters to quietly find out what's going on. I hope our plan hasn't already tanked."

"Well, I'm sorry I couldn't get in touch sooner. Things are pretty chaotic around here, you know. I can't be popping in and out of dimensions at the drop of a hat. Now you've got me scared. Is this going to blow up on us?"

"Don't worry about it. I'll go myself and see what I can do. When is Ralston supposed to return?"

"He said if he's not back by tomorrow evening, we should assume they're detaining him and that an attack may be about to happen."

"All right, we need to settle on a Plan B right now, in case he doesn't return."

"Rals says I should go straight to Arumel, since I'm ninety-eight percent dead if I don't."

"That's good advice, Jade. I assume that's exactly what you intend to do?"

"I—" A loud rattling at my door causes Asher and me to jump.

"Jade, are you there?" It's Ryder. "Open the door."

In a panic I turn to Asher, only to find dead air where he just stood. My heart pounding wildly, I sprint for the door and fumble with the lock.

Ryder steps inside and scans the room. "What were you doing in here? Why was the door locked?"

"Oh, I was just trying to steal a few minutes of privacy. I haven't had a moment to myself all day." My cheeks grow hot, and I hope I resemble a blushing bride and not a red-faced liar.

"I thought I heard voices. Is someone else here?"

"No! I was just … going over our vows, rehearsing in the mirror, you know." I glance at my dressing table where the polycom sits in plain sight.

Ryder's mouth twitches in amusement. "That's charming, love, but as you are aware, we'll probably not have an opportunity to recite our vows on this Saturday at least."

I shrug. "I know, but it doesn't hurt to be prepared."

"I came to tell you your father is here. We're meeting in General LeGare's office in a few minutes. Do you wish to join us?"

"Yes. Let me freshen up a bit, and I'll be right there."

"Don't be long, love." Placing a finger under my chin, he tilts my face to his. "I've missed you today." He presses a sweet kiss to my lips before sweeping out the door.

My knees nearly give out. *Holy crap, that was close.* Thank heaven Asher dematerialized without a word. I would have been so busted.

I snag the polycom off the desk and lock it back in my jewelry chest. On reflection, it was kind of a good thing that Ryder showed up when he did. It saved me from having to tell Ash that I'm not running off to Arumel if Ralston doesn't return on time. I intend to follow through with the plan—despite the dire predictions of my probable demise.

ELEVEN

Our session with LeGare lasts until nearly seven o'clock, but the news is all good. The plan is coming together remarkably well, and everything's falling into place. Ryder and I hurry back to my room to quickly dress for dinner.

Maria helps me into my dress and secures a silver crown on my head. We decide to skip the makeup for tonight, since Ryder and I are already a few minutes late. She gathers up my dirty laundry and wishes me good evening.

A moment later, Ryder steps out of the bathroom dressed in formal attire, his shiny hair pulled back and tied with a black ribbon. His golden skin still glows from the shower. The breath quivers in my lungs, and I'm reminded of the first time I ever rested my eyes on him. I believed an angel had fallen to earth.

"Am I presentable?" He runs a hand along the front of his coat. "My suit became wrinkled in my bag."

"Uh, *presentable* doesn't quite capture it. You're well … *yum.*"

His lips curve appealingly. "Shall we join the others?"

"Give me another minute." I turn back to my dressing table and hastily apply some mascara and lip gloss. Call me vain, but I don't want my man out-dazzling me tonight.

The size of the dinner crowd has grown considerably since yesterday. New guests arrive daily to take part in the pre-wedding celebrations, and a festive mood fills the halls of the palace. When Ryder and I step into the dining hall, we're greeted with enthusiastic applause and cries of *Long Live the Queen*.

Glasses of champagne are immediately placed in our hands, and we're surrounded by a throng of cheery faces. An air of excited anticipation prevails throughout the evening as the ladies and lords chatter about tomorrow's expected arrival of the royal wedding parties from Dome Noir and Cupola de Vita. I'm glad to see Drew and Adelais among the guests. They've been invited to stay at the palace tonight and be a part of the welcoming reception tomorrow. I'll need all the moral support I can get for that little show.

Though the upheaval of the past days has made me tired and stressed, the exuberance of the crowd carries me through dinner, and I actually enjoy myself. By the end of the evening, though, it's liberating to be back in my room with Ryder. We change out of our formal clothing and enjoy the quiet relief of being alone together.

I sit at my dressing table to remove my crown. The hairpins have dug so deeply into my scalp I'm concerned they may need to be surgically removed. Gingerly extracting them one-by-one, I pile them onto a silver tray. Ryder stands behind me observing the process with a mixture of curiosity and amusement. Once I've finished, I reach for my brush.

"Would you like me to brush your hair?" he asks.

"Seriously?" I've never had a man brush my hair before, but it sounds kind of sexy.

He takes the brush from my hand. "You seem to enjoy it so much when your maid does it. I'd like to offer you that pleasure."

Ryder brushing my hair is one of the most sensual experiences of my life. Every stroke of the brush sends tingles through my entire body. Every touch of his hand against my neck stirs me to my core. When he's finished, I take over the brush and return the favor for him. His silky hair sifts gloriously through my fingers as the brush glides smoothly through his shoulder length tresses. He closes his eyes, enjoying the indulgence and allowing me to gaze at his beautiful face.

For once the time passes slowly for us, like a lazy dream I never want to end. We fix tea and talk for hours, but not a word is spoken of the approaching battle or what the future may bring. I ask him to tell me about his mother, who I never got to meet. His eyes sparkle when he speaks of her and his childhood in Unicoi. His stories of training to become a warrior are mesmerizing. Being the son of the great Chief Blackthorn, he felt compelled to excel in every field, while striving to forge his own identity.

I have to improvise when he asks about my childhood. I share a few vague experiences based on the stories I've heard and what I imagine Princess Jaden's life was like. But I neatly steer the conversation back to him by asking about the years he spent with Ralston as his teacher.

My new husband is still mostly a mystery to me, but as I lay beside him, I feel in some ways as if I've known him my entire life. If there's any truth to this *perpetual contract* thing, I guess I've known him much longer than that. I send up a silent prayer that I'll be fortunate enough to know him again … maybe in another lifetime.

* * *

Morning arrives too quickly, bringing the ships from Dome Noir and their deadly cargo in with the tide. And so, the games begin. My remaining time with Ryder and my Domerican family is slipping away too swiftly. Fortunately, the swirl of activity involved in preparing for the welcoming reception is enough to keep my thoughts keenly focused on the duties at hand.

As Ryder and I are finishing breakfast, a uniformed butler appears at my door and informs us that the royal wedding parties from the other domes have arrived at the palace. I'm not expected to greet them until the formal ceremony, but my breakfast turns to concrete in my stomach just knowing that my would-be murderers are now under the same roof.

Maria brings several young maids with her to assist me in dressing for the reception. Ryder makes a hasty retreat to dress in one of the guest rooms. The maids help me into a long-sleeved, shimmering white silk gown. Then two of them hold up a stiff mantle of woven-gold for me. It's sewn with hundreds of tiny crystal beads and I slip inside, careful not to snag my gown. The maids lace it securely and tie it in the back. Maria positions a full-length mirror in front of me so I can view the effect. Dazzling light bursts in countless colors from the crystals, rendering my face and body radiantly incandescent. It's by far the most stunning outfit I've worn since coming to Domerica—and the most uncomfortable.

The ladies in waiting style my hair and anchor a heavy jeweled crown in place. Then Maria directs two of them to fetch the queen's Robe of State. I'm staggered when they return carrying a gold-trimmed, crimson velvet robe with a white fur collar and a train as long as a football field.

"I'm supposed to wear that?" I ask, incredulous.

Maria stares at me as if I've lost my marbles. "Absolutely. The queen wears it to all formal functions of state."

"Oh, yes, well, I didn't realize this was *that* formal," I say, attempting to recover from my gaffe. I'd never seen the robe before today.

The taut line of her mouth displays disappointment at my lack of royal acumen. "We will place it on you once your guard has arrived to escort you to the reception."

As if on cue, a knock at the door signals my escort waits outside. The ladies scurry over with the miles of red cape and secure it on my shoulders with a large jeweled clasp.

It weighs a ton. Between the robe, the oversized crown, and the daunting ceremony ahead of me, I feel the heaviness of the entire dome pressing down on me. Maria opens the double-doors and I draw in a fortifying breath, willing my feet to move forward.

Once I'm positioned in the center of the escort and the young maids have straightened out my train in the hallway behind me, I signal to the captain. *Let's do this thing.*

One hundred percent of my concentration is required just to walk upright dragging the gigantic sea of velvet behind me. I become vaguely aware that my route to the Grand Hall is lined on both sides with Royal Guardsmen dressed in formal white uniforms. As we clear the threshold, a band strikes up a very loud rendition of the national anthem.

The hall is crammed with gaily dressed people. A fragrant mixture of fresh paint, women's perfume, and nervous perspiration permeates the air. Reassured that I'm not the only one sweating, I trek slowly down a long red carpet leading to two enormous thrones placed side by side on a raised dais.

My eyes rake the crowd for Ryder, while my brain attempts to work out how I'm going to sit down with this highway of fabric attached to my back. As we near the dais, Ryder steps forward and offers me his hand. My escorts back away, and simultaneously four ladies in waiting separate from the crowd and adjust my cape so that I may be seated. *Oh, so that's how it works.* Only when Ryder and I are safely ensconced in our thrones do I give myself permission to breathe again.

The reception is structured in accordance with some arcane royal protocol which requires that the lesser nobles be presented first, so that the big splashy entrances of the more important personages are saved for last.

Unfortunately, that means we have to sit through the introductions of a couple of dozen random people I've never heard of before the dishonorable princes of Dome Noir will show their faces. A page stands next to my throne and announces the name of each guest who then steps forward and curtseys or bows, while I nod and say something inane, like *Thank you for coming.*

My fur and velvet cape is slowly suffocating me, and my stiff overdress digs brutally into my ribcage, so I'm thankful when the highest ranking members of the Cupola de Vita party are presented, and I know we are nearing the end of the ceremony. Duke Ferdinand

and Duchess Isabella walk arm in arm down the center of the red carpet followed by two servants, each carrying a large, ungainly object covered by a blue cloth.

Duke Ferdinand is extraordinarily handsome and normally works it like a rock star at these types of gatherings. Today, though, his arrogance has abandoned him. He looks pale and stressed. I wonder whether it is due to a rough sea voyage or a guilty conscience. I hope it's the later. I always liked Ferdinand. He alerted me a while back when he believed my Uncle Harold didn't have my best interests at heart. I'm disappointed to know that he's unofficially aware of the Noirs' evil scheme and hasn't seen fit to warn me.

"Your Majesty," he says, "so good to see you. May I present my sister, Duchess Isabella." She curtseys prettily and Ferdinand continues, "King Rafael observed a day of farewell celebration in Cupola De Vita to honor the glorious passing of your mother, Queen Eleanor. We shall all miss her. My uncle also sends his deepest regrets that urgent matters of state prevent him from attending your nuptials in person."

"Thank you. Are you well, Ferdinand?"

"I confess to being rather unwell, ma'am. My sincere apologies." His dark eyes penetrate mine for a moment, conveying something I can only interpret as remorse. "But we bring you gifts." He steps aside and removes the cloths covering the large objects held by the servants. "Saddles for you and Chief Blackthorn tooled by our premier saddle makers."

The saddles are amazingly fine. Ryder and I glance at each other with appreciation.

"In addition, King Rafael has sent you a case of his private collection wine and a cask of highest quality extra virgin olive oil, pressed from trees on the grounds of Castillo de Angeles."

"Thank you, Ferdinand. And you, Isabella. Welcome."

My stomach buckles when the page announces our final guests of the day, His Royal Highness Prince Gilbert Auguste and His Royal

Highness Prince Jean Louis of Dome Noir.

Prince Gilbert practically swaggers down the red carpet like he already owns the place. Prince Jean Louis trails behind like a timid lamb.

Gilbert bows with a flourish. He's tall and elegantly dressed. "Your Majesty, what a great pleasure it is to see you again—this time as queen. The passing of the beloved Queen Eleanor came as a shock, but we are delighted to have the honor of joining you on the joyous occasion of your wedding to Chief Blackthorn." He half-bows to Ryder.

Ryder nods stiffly in return.

"As you know my father's poor health has prevented him from being here," Gilbert says. "I beg that you accept the humble presences of my brother, Jean Louis, and myself as his most ardent emissaries."

Swallowing down the acid I'd like to spew in his face, I reply, "I hope your father's health improves. But naturally, we're pleased that you and Jean Louis have come in his stead."

"Thank you, Your Majesty."

Jean Louis bows, but says nothing and doesn't make eye contact with me. *Either he's a gutless coward or he has more of a conscience than his brother.*

"Please pardon our zeal," Gilbert says, "But we wish to present you and Chief Blackthorn with a few small gifts from our country." He glances over his shoulder, and several servants carrying two enormous chests make their way down the red runner. They place the chests on the carpet in front of our thrones and open the lids. Audible gasps go up from those who are close enough to see the contents. One chest is chock full of golden and jewel-laden treasures. The other contains silks, laces, and exotically embroidered fabrics.

Obviously pleased with the crowd's reaction, Gilbert beams. "Modest tokens of our great esteem, Your Majesty."

"Your gifts are impressive and most generous," I say. *He can afford to be generous when he expects to own everything in Domerica in two short days.* "Thank you, and welcome to Domerica." The words leave a bitter tang in my mouth.

The two black-hearted princes take their places in the crowd, and Jennifer Osborne signals that it is time for me to rise and bring the ceremony to a close. I stand, carefully avoiding tripping over my robe.

"Chief Blackthorn and I are grateful to each of you for sharing in the happy occasion of our wedding. Our special thanks to those of you who have traveled great distances to be here. Please enjoy the remainder of the afternoon."

The band immediately strikes up an earsplitting march. My military escort positions itself on the carpet and the ladies in waiting scramble to assist me with my train while Ryder and I pass down the runner and out the door. I catch sight of the expansive staircase looming large in the distance, and my whole body groans.

No freakin' way am I climbing up that thing in this outfit. I bring the procession to an abrupt halt.

Jennifer rushes to my side. "What is it, Your Majesty?"

"We need to make a small detour," I whisper. "I'm not lugging this rug behind me up those stairs."

Her eyes swell with disbelief.

"The sitting room to the right of the stairs will do just fine as a temporary way station." I ignore her incredulity. "We'll be comfortable there while the rest of the crowd disperses."

"Yes, Your Majesty." She quickly instructs our escort and rearranges the line of royal Guardsmen so that our new destination is the sitting room not the staircase.

Ryder's eyes dance and he presses his lips together to suppress a smile. When we reach the room's entrance, our escort stands aside allowing us to enter. I'm forced to walk all the way to the other end of the room so my ladies in waiting can haul the entire train inside.

Jennifer closes the double doors behind. "Are you ill, Your Majesty?"

"No," I say crossly. "I'm hot and dehydrated and tired of wearing this ridiculous throwback to the dark ages. Make a note that I would like this robe to be placed on display in a museum—never to be worn at functions of state again." I yank at the clasp and my velvety prison falls to the floor.

"Yes, ma'am," Jennifer says.

The sitting room we landed in is one of my favorites. It has floor-to-ceiling windows that overlook my mother's rose garden which has been meticulously well-tended in preparation for the wedding. It's gratifying to see it so lovely in full bloom.

"I have a wonderful idea," I say to Ryder. "We have nothing scheduled until dinner. Why don't we ask Father and Drew and Adelais to join us for lunch in here? It appears there's room enough to set everything up." The idea of a small family lunch makes me feel so much better.

He nods, smiling. "That would be nice."

"I'll see to it right away, Your Majesty," Jennifer says. She motions to the maids to gather up the puddle of robe and follow her.

"Thanks Jennifer, and thank you ladies," I say as they cart the heap of velvet from the room.

"Ugh, I thought that reception was never going to end," I say, wrapping my arms around Ryder's waist, "and did you see how smug Prince Gilbert looked?"

"It must have been difficult for you to be civil, but you handled yourself beautifully." He pulls me closer.

"Ow!" he cries moving away. "I believe your dress just stabbed me."

I groan a laugh. "What do you think it's been doing to me for

93

the last three hours? Help me get out of it, please."

I turn my back to him, and he loosens the laces of my golden cage.

"This dress is outrageously beautiful, but I think it's going to the museum along with the robe. I've never been so uncomfortable in my life."

He slips the rigid garment off my body and tosses it on a chair. My silk gown is crushed and sweaty but I feel free. "Whew, that's better. Help me with the crown too?"

"Whatever you say, Your Majesty. I'm at your service."

"You know, you're already remarkably good at this husband thing."

TWELVE

Ralston still has not returned to the palace by evening, and my fears begin piling up like cars of a derailed freight train.

What if IUGA found out he stole the QP to help me? What if they've already dismantled him? What if the Noirs are surrounding the palace right now preparing to attack?

"Is everything all right, Your Majesty?" Maria asks as she attempts to style my hair for dinner. "You're quite fidgety this evening."

"Sorry. I'm a little nervous with all our foreign guests in the palace and the wedding events beginning tomorrow."

"Yes, there is much excitement, but I will not have you ready on time if you do not settle down."

"All right, just give me a minute." I close my eyes and inhale slowly, relaxing my shoulders as I exhale. "I'm better now," I say, opening my eyes.

She smiles her approval and quickly goes to work making up my face. I'm dressed and waiting when Ryder arrives for me.

"You haven't heard from Ralston have you?" I ask him.

"No. Shall I send someone to inquire after him?"

I shake my head. "Not just yet."

My appetite is squelched as much by my growing anxiety as by my unsavory tablemate, Prince Gilbert. I maul my roasted squab with a fork, watching the door for any sign of Rals. Gilbert has a natural charm, but I find it difficult to make small talk with a guy who's plotting to execute me, no matter how attractive he is.

I try to catch Ryder's eye, but he's deep in conversation with the powdered and perfumed matron on his right, *Lady-something-or-other*. Her wig is slightly askew, and her teeth are grayish yellow, but she bats her eyes at him as if she's a blushing debutant.

A butler appears at my elbow and bows. "You have a message, Your Majesty."

I snatch the neatly folded piece of paper and read it quickly: *Your Majesty, Do you have a moment to speak with me?" Your humble servant, Constantine Ralston.*

Without thinking, I rise from my seat. A chorus of chairs scraping the floor rings out as the dinner guests prepare to stand also.

"Please remain seated," I say. "Ryder, will you excuse me for a moment? Ralston's returned and I need to speak with him."

"Certainly. Do you wish me to accompany you?" he asks.

"No. I won't be long." I tip my head to Prince Gilbert who stands to hold my chair.

Ralston waits for me in a small parlor on the first floor. "Rals. Oh my god, I was so worried." I hug him briskly.

"I know, my dear. I'm sorry to have caused you concern, but I had rather a close call at headquarters. If it hadn't been for Asher Steele, I believe I would have been ... what's the term? Ah yes, toast."

"I'm so glad Asher found you."

"As am I. My interrogation was only minutes away when he located me and offered his help. He managed to secretly shift into the equipment room and place the QP between two cabinets as if it had accidently fallen there. I had some difficulty convincing my superiors to conduct another search before drawing any conclusions. I argued that, due to the many irregularities in that department, a second search was not unreasonable. The much maligned Supervisor of Equipment strongly protested, but she was overruled. The missing QP was discovered, and I was cleared of suspicion."

"That's such a relief, Rals. I should have contacted Ash earlier. I'm just thankful it turned out all right. So what happened with the contract?"

He waves his hand dismissively. "That was no problem whatsoever. But how are things here? I understand your guests from Dome Noir have arrived."

"The reception today was brutal. Be glad you missed it. I had to wear this hideous robe that weighed more than a small pony. And Gilbert was so arrogant. It was all I could do to keep from skewering him with my katana. Anyway, I'm happy you're back. Only one more day and then ... well, we find out if that QP really works. Are we going to be okay without it?"

"As long as no major variables change, we should be just fine." He retrieves his hat and traveling cloak from the chair. "Now you'd better return to your guests. We do not wish to arouse any suspicions."

"All right. You coming?"

"No I believe I'll retire to my room. I shall join you for tomorrow's festivities, my dear. The Transcenders expect to have a final briefing with you at some point after brunch and prior to the wedding eve dinner. Asher said he will await word from you on the timing."

"Okay. We need to concoct another cover story. I'll need at least an hour with them. See you mañana, Rals."

I return to the dining hall in time for dessert and after dinner toasts. When the evening finally comes to a close, I'm exhausted and anxious to spend time with Ryder. But I have something important to do first.

Once we're back in my room, I turn to Ryder. "I know it's late, but I must deliver something to Father tonight. Will you be all right without me for a while?"

He takes my hand. "No, I'll miss you terribly, but I'll manage. Is it all right that I stay here?" He gestures to the room. "Prior to the wedding, I mean. Your guests may look askance at such an arrangement not knowing our marital status."

"Who cares what they think? What are they going to do, kill me?" Ryder visibly winces.

"Sorry, bad joke. I need you here with me. We can't be bothered by some possible backwash when we're in the middle of a maelstrom."

"You're right, love." He kisses my forehead.

I open my desk drawer and draw out the envelope I put there yesterday. "Back in a flash," I say.

Father opens his door almost immediately when I knock.

"Jaden, come in," he says, beaming. He's remarkably relaxed in light of the impending battle. "To what do I owe the honor of this visit?"

"Do you have a few minutes? I need to ask a favor of you."

"Of course. Sit down, sweetheart. How can I be of assistance?"

We sit near the twinkling fireplace.

"My handwritten will is in here." I give him the envelope. "Not to be melodramatic, but I wanted to put a few things in writing just in case something unexpected should happen on Saturday."

Two lines form between his brows. "Sweetheart, this is absurd.

If you fear for your safety, you must go to Old Unicoi. Please. No valid reason exists for you to place yourself in such peril. I do not understand your decision to remain at the palace."

"I know you don't, Father, and I'm sorry." I ache inside, realizing that when the princess's body is found he'll probably blame himself, as will Ryder, for not physically carting me off to Old Unicoi.

"It's complicated," I say, "and I really don't think I can adequately explain it to you. So, even though I acknowledge your wise counsel, I ask you to accept my judgment. And I'd be most grateful if you would see to it that my wishes are carried out should it come to that."

He holds up the envelope. "May I?"

I nod silently.

Opening the flap, he withdraws the one page document. After reading it to himself, he raises his eyes to mine. "Your horse and your Skorplings?"

"Yes. I really don't think of them as *possessions*, but it matters very much to me what happens to them."

"I'm touched you would consider leaving Gabriel to me. He's as fine a horse as I've ever known. But I'm curious about your bequeathing the Skorplings to your cousin, especially after the falling out you had with your Uncle Harold. Is this to make up for removing Osrielle from the line of succession?"

"No. It's because I know she loves them almost as much as I do, and she has a gentle heart. She'll play with them every day, and she'd never do anything to harm them. It's Uncle Harold I'm worried about. That's why I put in all that extra stuff about their care, housing, and ownership."

Father scans the page again, smiling. "Immediate imprisonment for anyone placing the Skorplings in a cage?"

"Well, I felt the need to spell out certain things. It has to be clear that they belong to Osrielle, not Harold. I don't want him trying to sell them. I'm leaving Osrielle more than enough money to cover their care and feeding for several lifetimes."

"Yes, you've been quite generous." He passes a hand over his whiskered chin. "And I see you've set aside a rather large sum for the care and feeding of your horse also."

"I know you don't need the money, Father, but he is rather fond of pommeras."

He refolds the paper and tucks it inside the envelope. "So that's it? Your three animals? That's all you wish to pass along?"

"They're what I love most. I don't care about the other things." My hands tremble and my throat closes in on itself.

"Well then, if you are set in your decision to remain at the palace, rest assured that your husband and I will not allow harm to come to you. We have a very strong defense planned. I foresee little bloodshed if the Noirs are reasonable in surrendering under our terms."

"I know," I say, choking down the tide of emotion that threatens to overwhelm me. I feel a strong bond with my Domerican father, and I'll miss him tremendously.

He sits silently for a moment, studying my face. Then he pushes out of his chair. "Jade, what is this about, really?"

I stand and hug him fiercely. "I just love you so much."

"I love you too, sweetheart." He puts his hands on my shoulders and holds me away from him. "Jaden, look at me."

My reluctant eyes meet his. Tears trickle down my cheeks.

"You're leaving again, aren't you?"

My heart swoops. *How can he know?* "What are you talking about? I'm not going anywhere."

"Yes, you are. I can sense it. I knew when you returned last month that you might not stay."

"That's completely ridiculous." I wipe away my tears. "Ryder and I just got married. We have our whole lives ahead of us." My words sound unconvincing even to me.

"Jaden, I'm no fool. I don't know where you were for those twelve months you disappeared, but do not think for a moment that I believe the story that you lived with Outlanders until the Cleadians discovered you."

"What do you mean? That's absolutely what happened."

"Don't insult my intelligence, sweetheart. You were healthier and more robust than I'd ever seen you, and you returned possessing the skill to wield a samurai sword. Outlanders certainly could not have fed and trained you so well."

"But, where else could I have been?"

He shakes his head slowly. "I have not the slightest inkling, but I suspect the real story may be even more remarkable. May we sit for a moment?"

I perch on the edge of my chair, and he reseats himself, tilting toward me. "The universe is a mysterious place, Jaden, and what lies beyond is more enigmatic still. I'm not a mystic, but any educated man knows that the world we see before us is not the sum and substance of this existence. Do you suppose I honestly believe heavenly angels were responsible for these domes? And that only the *chosen* were saved from annihilation? Or that Cleadians are descendents of settlers from Nova Scotia? Good lord, Jaden, I know beyond doubt that your hand did not miraculously repair itself in the forest." He reaches out and takes my right hand.

"I'm a doctor. You suffered a grievous injury. The cut was clean through." He traces the scar with his fingertip. "I've never seen such extraordinary healing."

I lower my eyes. "I ... I don't know what to say."

"If you cannot tell me where you were or where you are going, please tell me this—will I ever see you again?" He squeezes my hand, his eyes pleading.

I peer up at him through wet lashes and slowly move my head from side to side. "No. It will appear as if I'm dead. So I can't really return to Domerica. Ever. But I want you to know it's not really me. Check her hand. You won't find a scar."

The whole truth may be too much for him right now, but maybe part of it will help to ease the pain when I'm gone.

"Will you be somewhere safe?"

"Yes. It may be the only safe place for me in the universe right now. Don't worry about me, Father. And please don't tell Ryder. I want him to move on with his life. Maybe even marry Erica when the time is right. Promise me, please."

He swipes teardrops from his cheeks. "I shall make you that promise if you will make one in return."

"What is it?"

"If the opportunity ever presents itself, you will pay me a visit. Even if only for a short time. Just to let me know you are well. I swear to tell no one."

"I promise," I say, choking back a sob.

He pulls me out of my chair, and we hold each other tightly. "I'm going to miss you, Father."

"And I you, daughter. Every day. For the rest of my life."

My conversation with Father leaves me sick at heart, but a tiny part of me is soothed knowing that his grief will be tempered by the slight hope of seeing me again.

On returning to my room, I find Ryder sprawled across my bed in pajama bottoms, sleeping soundly. I quietly slip into my nightdress and climb up beside him, pulling a giant satin throw over us. The temptation to wake him is strong, but I let him sleep. We're both going to need all our strength to get through these next two days.

THIRTEEN

It's wedding day minus one, countdown to the apocalypse. My last full day with Ryder. My last twenty-four hours in Domerica. Everything must run like clockwork from here on out, or this whole plan could crash and burn. Solid determination and crushing fear take turns using my insides for a punching bag.

Before brunch, I arrange for copies of my *Proposal for Resumption of Trade with Dome Noir* to be delivered to Prince Gilbert and Prince Jean Louis, with a request that we all meet in my office at three o'clock. I have no intention of attending the meeting—Ralston will take it in my place—but it will provide a nice diversion so I can visit the Transcenders for our final briefing.

The moment Ryder leaves for an update from General LeGare, I lock myself in my bathroom with the polycom and send a text to Asher to expect me at three.

No one has to tell me keeping up appearances is important at this point, but my patience wears thin as three ladies in waiting—four if you count Maria—*ooh* and *goo* all over me attempting to make me dazzling for the garden party brunch.

"All right, enough!" I say. "I look fine. Where's my dress?"

The ladies recoil at my cranky outburst, making me feel a little guilty.

Even I have to giggle, though, when Maria sweeps into the room with my new gown floating like a cloud in her arms. The dress seems befitting of a barbeque in *Gone With The Wind*. Off the shoulder with a lavender sash, embroidered yellow flowers cascade prettily down a full chiffon skirt. Maria makes an opening for me and I gingerly climb inside. The ladies efficiently button, tuck, and tie me in.

They work in concert to fluff out the billowing skirt to its maximum mushroom cloud shape. Maria finishes the look by securing a tall golden crown to the top of my head. A check in the mirror reveals that I bear a striking resemblance to Glinda the Good Witch from the Wizard of Oz. I didn't remember the dress being this dramatic at the fitting, but now I have no choice but to grin and wear it.

Ryder arrives to escort me downstairs. "You look wonderful," he says, kissing my cheek.

"Are you sure? It's not too much, is it?"

"Not at all. You are lovely as an orchid freshly in bloom."

I link my arm with his. His warmth and strength instantly fortify me, and I know I'll make it through all this … for him.

Brunch isn't horrible. Instead of being stuck sitting with Prince Gilbert again, the outdoor setting makes it easier for me to wander among the tables and visit with Father and Drew and the others whose company I will miss. Ryder and I hold hands and stroll among the guests, pausing to receive congratulations or good wishes for our future. The pleasant afternoon keeps my internal demons at bay, at least temporarily. Soon, though, Ralston reminds me of my three o'clock meeting, and I'm forced to focus once again on pressing realities.

I kiss Ryder and promise to keep the meeting short. Ralston and I cut through the bustling kitchen and make our way up the back staircase to my office.

"Try to get Gilbert and Jean Louis out of here by four o'clock if possible," I say, "so I can reappear without scaring the bejesus out of them."

"I shall do my best, but why don't you land just outside the door to be safe?"

"Good idea." I punch the coordinates for Asher's apartment into my TPD bracelet. "See you soon."

Zzzt.

I land in the center of Asher's white shag rug. When he glimpses me in my garden party dress and golden crown, his eyes light up with glee.

"Do-Not-Say-A-Word," I warn him. "I know I look ridiculous, and I'm not in the mood."

He dips into an exaggerated bow. "You look enchanting, Miss Beckett. But where's your magic wand?"

I glower at him. "Don't press me, Ash. I can turn you into a toad without one. Is Narowyn here?"

"She and Captain Watterson are waiting for us in her office," he says, still grinning like an idiot. "Shall we take the elevator, or would you care to ride in your bubble?"

"Ha ha. Let's go." I push past him to the door.

Captain Watterson shakes my hand as I enter Narowyn's first-floor office. She kisses me affectionately on both cheeks, but her face is taut with worry. "Jaden, how are you? How are things progressing in Domerica?"

"Everything's good. Outside of Ralston's little scrape at IUGA, we've had no surprises." I swivel around to Asher. "Thanks for helping out with that by the way."

"No problem," he says, eyes still brimming with suppressed hilarity.

"Please, let's be seated," Narowyn says. "Jaden if you'll bring us up to date on everything on your end, Captain Watterson will go over his final plans for tomorrow."

"Sure. The Noir princes arrived by ship two days ago with a large wedding party and several trunks. Unbeknownst to them, their every move was being watched. Before they reached the entrance to the dome, a number of the wagons carrying trunks were diverted to the north. Our trackers followed them to a hidden tunnel entrance we didn't know about before. We assume the trunks are full of firearms, but we didn't intercept them because we thought it would set off some alarms, if not trigger an immediate attack."

Watterson pipes up. "Wise move. Better to let them have the weapons than to alert them that we're onto their plan."

"In any event, we'll seal up that tunnel prior to their planned attack," I say. "Just to make certain no one escapes if things go awry with our plan."

"Do you have any reason to believe they will?" Narowyn asks.

"No. According to my father, the Enclave army is ready to move tonight. A distant section of the palace fence will be temporarily removed to allow them to slip inside. They'll hide in the trees on the outer edge of the palace grounds. Ryder tells me the Unicoi Army will arrive before dawn and take a position in the forest on the opposite flank. We have surveillance on the Noirs' camp and will be notified as soon as they're on the move."

"You're confident no one in the palace will be alerted to the arriving armies?" Narowyn asks.

"We're taking every possible precaution," I say. "The area where the soldiers will hide is well-wooded and not visible from the palace. Also, the outdoor lighting on the grounds will conveniently suffer a malfunction in the early morning hours. With no moon or stars, it'll be pitch black outside. I'm convinced we've got it covered."

"That's all well and good, but the battle will surely be engaged the moment the first of the Noir soldiers enter the grounds," Watterson says. "Is the Royal Guard prepared to hold them off until the order to attack is given?"

"General LeGare swears they are. He's told only his most trusted and long-serving men, but we were able to obtain rifles and some explosive devices from Old Unicoi. Those will be distributed to the men in the morning. The Noirs won't be expecting that. It should be enough to deter them until they're all inside the grounds."

"Good," Narowyn says. "It seems as if all is in order. Captain, would you please go over your plans for Jaden."

"Certainly. According to Urick, everything in the Noir camp is progressing as we initially understood. The attack is scheduled to take place in the early afternoon when the wedding guests are seated and the ceremony is about to begin. We'll have a team on the ground to assist your man Ralston with the placement of the princess's body, and with his escape.

"I didn't know you were helping us with the princess's body," I say.

"We worked that out at IUGA headquarters yesterday," Asher interjects. "The agent helping Ralston got a little nervous when Ralston was called in for questioning. The agent said he'd get the body to Warrington Village, but no farther. We've arranged to transport it by wagon to the palace in the morning."

"Okay. A little glitch, but it sounds like you handled it," I say, hoping it's not enough to throw off the prediction model.

Watterson continues the briefing. "Urick will make certain he leads the assassination party to you in the tower room. Keep your polycom turned on to vibrate mode. He'll send you a warning once they've entered the palace. It's the only notice you'll get. You can count on him to do whatever it takes to keep you unharmed until you're able to make your shift. You understand the shift must be instantaneous with your fall? You've not a fraction of a second to waste."

"I understand."

"Once the princess's body is discovered, Ralston will meet us by the parked wagon inside the palace stables. We'll secure him with a harness to one or two of the men, and transport him back here using a team shift."

"Got it," I say. "Anything else?"

Narowyn moves to the edge of her chair and leans in toward me. "Jaden, I'll be here waiting for you when you make your shift. The complaint against IUGA has been prepared and will be filed with the IGC Court the moment you arrive. We're asking for emergency relief to insure your safety."

I nod solemnly. "I appreciate it. And thank you all for everything you're doing for me and for the people of Domerica."

I get to my feet and Watterson shakes my hand again. "Don't worry about a thing on this end."

Asher hugs me. "I'll see you tomorrow, Jade. Take care of yourself."

"You too, Ash."

Narowyn kisses each of my cheeks and then folds me into an embrace. "Be safe, little sister."

I assure her that I will.

"Well then, until tomorrow." I click my bracelet, and Z*zzt*.

Landing just outside my office, I practically plow into Patrick, who seems to be guarding my door.

My heart climbs halfway up my throat. I didn't expect a witness to my reappearing act. "Patrick! What the hell?"

"I'm so sorry, Your Majesty," he says completely flustered. "I did not see you. Where did you come from?"

"Never mind. Why are you here?"

"I was told you had a meeting with Prince Gilbert and Prince Jean Louis. I wished to be nearby in case you needed me."

"Oh yeah, right. Thanks. I had a little wedding thing to take care of. Um, wait here."

When I open the office door, Ralston and Prince Gilbert are shaking hands. Everyone is smiling, so I guess things went okay. The three men bow when they see me.

"Hi," I say stupidly, still rattled by my near collision with Patrick. "I'm sorry I missed the meeting. I trust Professor Ralston answered all of your questions."

"Yes," Gilbert says. "This is a strong proposal. We will present it to our father immediately upon our return to Dome Noir. I'm certain he will be persuaded."

Yeah, right. "Wonderful." I manage a near smile. "Professor, may I speak with you a moment?" I ask, prompting the frog princes to take their leave.

"We shall see you at dinner tonight," Gilbert says. He lifts my hand and kisses it.

I resist the urge to ball it into a fist and shove it down his throat. "Yes. Lovely."

As usual, Jean Louis speaks not a word and avoids eye contact altogether. He shuffles out behind Gilbert like an obedient puppy.

Once the door is closed, I collapse in a chair. "I nearly landed on top of Patrick just now."

"Oh my. Did he witness your reappearance?" Ralston asks.

"He doesn't really know what he saw. I hope he writes it off as a trick of the light or a hallucination or temporary insanity or something."

"I wouldn't worry about it, old girl. What did the Transcenders have to say?"

"Just that everything's set on their end. They said they're bringing the princess's body in from town for us."

"Yes. I encountered a bit of a problem with that, but this should work out well. They'll have all the necessary credentials to gain entrance to the palace grounds, and to anyone conducting a routine inspection, the wagon will appear to be laden with flowers for the ceremony."

"This change in a variable doesn't screw up our whole scenario, does it? I mean from a prediction standpoint?"

"I can't be certain, but this is such a minor detail. It should have no impact at all."

"That's good. But these little glitches worry me. They seem to be adding up. Anyway, I assume you know that once the body is discovered, you're supposed to meet the Transcenders in the stables to be taken to Arumel?"

"Yes, we discussed it. I believe all will go swimmingly, my dear." He reaches over and squeezes my hand.

"I hope for both our sakes you're right."

* * *

The door to my room stands open, and I'm expecting to find Ryder inside. Instead, the fashion brigade, led by Maria, waits impatiently for me. The top of my dressing table is crammed with pots of makeup, containers of perfume, and a truckload of hair pins. *Yikes.*

My gorgeous indigo dress lies spread across the bed, and a new diamond and platinum crown perches atop a pedestal near my dressing table. I love having so many beautiful things, but right now I'd kill for a pair of yoga pants and tank top.

After the ladies work their magic on my face, hair, and body, Maria leads me to the full length mirror. I have to say, I'm pleased with what I see. The slinky gown and the smoky eye shadow make me appear kind of bad girl sexy, which is more to my liking than the Good Witch look from earlier today.

When Ryder arrives to collect me for dinner, his eyes sweep over me appreciatively. "I've never seen you more beautiful." He uses his fingertips to slide a wisp of hair away from my shoulder, and he touches his lips to the nape of my neck sending chills down my spine. The ladies titter in the background.

"Are you ready?" he asks.

"Do not forget your gloves," Maria says, laying a pair of above-the-elbow, black satin gloves across my palm.

"Nice touch," I say and slip them on.

Ryder and I walk arm in arm to our last supper together.

FOURTEEN

It's nearly midnight when we finally say goodnight to the last of our guests. I embrace Adelais lovingly, knowing it's the last time I will ever see her. "Have a safe journey," I whisper.

Drew will escort her as far as Warrington Village where all those escaping to the safety of Old Unicoi will gather and caravan to their destination under heavy guard and the cover of night.

Ryder and I climb the steps to my room in silence. Once inside, he slips out of his dinner jacket and drapes it across the back of a chair.

I remove my crown, which mercifully is held in place by combs instead of hairpins. My freed hair cascades down my back. I shake it out and then reach for the knot of my sash.

"I'd like to do that," he says softly.

"Yes," I whisper.

With slow sensuous fingers, he unties my sash, allowing it to fall to the floor. He presses a tender kiss on my right shoulder, while sliding down my strap. He repeats the gesture on my left shoulder. Lacing his fingers into my hair, he tilts my head back exposing my neck. His warm lips whisper across my throat, light as butterfly wings. Hot blood surges through my veins, and my breath comes in short bursts. I clutch the front of his shirt for support. I want him desperately, but I also want to savor every second of this night.

He raises his heavy-lidded eyes for a moment, and then presses his eager mouth to mine. The sweetness of his lips and tongue, the fierceness of his embrace ignite passion and pleasure in me. My hands find their way beneath his shirt and up his chest. His belly quivers as I run my fingertips downward. For me, there is only the solidness of Ryder—heartbeat, flesh, muscle, and heat. I block out all else and lose myself completely to him … my once and future love.

* * *

I'm not certain of the time when I awaken in Ryder's sheltering arms. The room is abnormally dark, so I assume the lights on the palace grounds have already been tripped as planned. The glowing crystalline logs in my fireplace provide the only illumination. I carefully slide from the bed so as not to waken my sleeping husband. Pulling a shawl from my chair, I wrap it snugly around my shoulders and wander out onto the balcony. Inky blackness envelopes me, and though I see nothing, I envision the fully armed Enclave soldiers filing quietly through the gap in the fence, taking their position on the grounds. My ears strain for any tell-tell sound, but the night is eerily still.

"Do you see anything?" Ryder moves softly behind me and rests his hands on my shoulders.

"No. Do you think they're already here?"

"Most likely. It will be dawn soon."

His words turn my blood to ice.

Soft lips brush across my ear. "Come back to bed, love," he whispers. "We've not much time left."

Noisy commerce wakes us shortly after sun-up. Final preparations for the royal wedding day are underway. A non-stop parade of delivery wagons clatters through the palace gates—one of them bearing the princess's body, if all has gone according to plan. A loud hammering echoes across the courtyard, as last minute tasks are being completed.

The Grand Arboretum, already decorated with thousands of twinkling lights and cartloads of flowers, teems with workers installing the white satin runner leading up to the gazebo. Graceful white canopies flutter serenely overhead as the men work, blissfully ignorant of the battle to come.

Ryder dresses early and slips out to make certain all is ready for the arrest of the two princes and their covert transportation to Wall's Edge Prison.

Maria and two maids arrive at eight to help me prepare for the private royal breakfast.

"I'm not wearing my new dress," I tell them. "Please take it back to the gown room."

Maria raises her chin. "Just what do you intend to wear, Your Majesty?"

"What I have on," I say gesturing to my riding clothes.

"But you cannot …"

My stern look silences her, and I turn to the two maids. "Take the dress and all the rest downstairs and wait for further instructions."

They bustle out the door leaving us alone. Maria wheels around ready for an argument.

"Please sit down," I say. "I have something to tell you."

She lowers herself warily into a chair. "The wedding is still on, is it not?"

"Well, yes and no. For all intents and purposes, it will appear as if the wedding is taking place exactly as planned. But a rather large army of black knights is inside the dome, and likely on its way here, with plans to attack the palace as the ceremony is about to begin."

Her eyes expand in fear. "Why are you still here? You must get to safety at once."

"Not just yet. I plan to have the two princes from Dome Noir arrested in about an hour for planning the attack. I wouldn't miss that for the world."

"No." She raises a shaky hand to her open mouth.

"Yes." I pull the hand away from her mouth. "So, here's what I want you to do. Find your fiancé. Is he here on the grounds today?"

"He is helping to set up the food tables."

"Good. Find him and the two of you leave now, before the guests arrive. Get as far away from the palace as possible. Go someplace south of here, Warrington Village, maybe. The Noir army will be coming from the north, and you don't want to run into them."

She gapes at me but doesn't move a muscle.

"Did you hear me? You've got to get going. Now!"

"But what about you? What about everyone else?"

"Don't worry. The palace is heavily guarded, and we've called on the Enclave and Unicoi armies for help. I'll be fine, but some incidental casualties are inevitable. I don't want you to get hurt, Maria. Understand?"

She nods slowly as if trying to process the information.

"Come on, then. You have no time to waste."

Springing from her chair, she surprises me with a strong embrace. "Oh thank you, Your Majesty. Thank you for saving us. Are you certain you will be safe?"

"Yes, yes. Just one more thing," I say.

"Certainly, anything."

"What's the name of that girl who tucks in the Skorplings at

115

night—the one who plays ball with Fred sometimes?"

"Katie?"

"That's it, Katie. Is she here today?"

"Yes. The entire staff is here for the wedding."

"All right. Now go on, and not a word to anyone else."

She takes my hand. "I pray you come to no harm, Your Majesty." Then she darts out the door.

"Was that blur I just saw Maria?" Ralston asks, stepping inside my room.

"Yes. I told her to get the hell out of here for her own safety. I hope she doesn't blab to anyone else, though. We don't need Chicken Little running around shouting *the sky is falling.*"

"She's a bright girl. I'm certain she'll be discreet." He closes my door. "Do you have everything ready for me?"

"Yes. Wait here a second."

I haul a bag out of my closet that I had packed earlier with a full set of clothing identical to what I'm wearing.

"Here it is." I set the bag at his feet.

"Very good. Now the rest." He holds out a hand.

I sigh heavily, and tug off my wedding ring, kissing it softly before placing it in his open palm.

"And the necklace."

"Can't I just keep this one thing? Please."

"You know you cannot." He wiggles his fingers impatiently.

I unhook Ryder's wolf head necklace and drop it into his palm, feeling as if I just turned over half of my heart.

He stuffs the jewelry into his pocket. "Now I have something for you," he says withdrawing a pair of glasses from inside his jacket.

"What're those?"

"My extra set of glasses. As you may recall, they are capable of identifying other automatons. Put them on."

I do as he tells me.

"Now look at my eyes."

When I look up, a tiny red light flashes in the outer corner of the left lens. A small readout appears: *nonhuman – automaton, IUGA ID# D7829.* "Oh yeah, cool." I say.

"More than cool, they may save your life. Once your guard is in place inside the tower room, put these on to determine if any of them is a spy. They are all supposed to be long-serving members of the Guard, but someone may slip through. It occurred to me last night that is a variable we did not make provision for."

"You think that might actually happen?"

"It is a slim possibility. LeGare will send only his most trusted men, and I doubt IUGA would use agents in actual combat. But should you discover an imposter among your guard, make certain the others restrain him immediately. Accuse him of high treason or of threatening you—something to get him shackled right away."

"I will, but an automaton? Do they restrain him like they would a regular man?"

"If he cannot be restrained the normal way, remember all automatons employed by IUGA have one point of extreme vulnerability, a manufacturing weakness, if you will. A nerve center of sorts exists at the base of the back of the neck." He turns around and places his hand on the spot. "A hard blow to this site will immediately disable the subject. Recovery is not possible without a complete reboot."

"Okay, got it, a hard blow to the back of the neck."

"By the way," he says, with his back still toward me, "another way to identify IUGA agents is by this small tattoo on the inside of the right earlobe." He folds back his right lobe, and I see a small gray mark.

"It looks like a miniature barcode," I say squinting.

"Yes, for inventory control. But I suspect if you are close enough to see it, you may already be in peril. Use the glasses."

"I will. Thanks. So, I guess we won't see each other again until we meet up in Arumel?"

He places a fatherly hand on my shoulder. "That is correct, my dear. Will you be all right?"

"Well, I'm not happy about it, obviously. But I suppose I'll be all right ... someday."

We hug each other warmly.

"Bon chance, old girl." He picks up the bag and leaves.

I toss Ralston's glasses into a small carved tray on top of my desk and take a sheet of my stationery from the top drawer. After scribbling a hasty note and placing the queen's seal on it, I fold it and tuck it in my pocket. My jewelry chest stands open, and I rummage through the contents until I find what I'm looking for—a simple gold ring with a modest square cut ruby. I slip it on my finger and lock the chest securely.

The back stairway is nearly deserted as I hurry down to the Skorplings' nursery. Katie's inside, fastening the last of the buttons on Ethel's new dress.

"You look beautiful," I say to Ethel. "Come here." She crawls into my arms and gives me a fuzzy hug.

"Jay weh-ing," she says.

"Yep, the wedding's today. Fred come here, let me look at you."

Fred climbs onto my shoulder. His gold embroidered, satin suit is a perfect match for Ethel's tiny dress.

"Jay," he coos and immediately tugs at my hair.

Katie curtseys. "May I help you with something, ma'am?"

"Hi Katie. I wanted to see these guys, and I need a word with you, also."

"Yes, ma'am," she says, shyly glancing at the floor.

I hug Ethel and kiss her furry head. "You know I love you very much, but go and play for a bit." The moment I set her down she scoots across the floor to her playhouse.

Fred topples from my shoulder into my arms, taking Ethel's place. "Ball, ball," he says.

"Katie will play ball with you in a minute. Give me a big hug."

His arms circle my neck, and he bestows a small wet kiss on my cheek.

"I love you, buddy. Now run and play." He hops down and races straight for his ball. He flings it against the wall and bounces up and down with glee.

Taking Katie's elbow, I steer her away from the Skorplings. "Listen Katie, I need you to do something for me. You must stay inside the nursery with Ethel and Fred until the wedding is over. Understand? No matter what kind of commotion you hear outside, stay put and keep the door locked."

Her thin brows draw together. "But the wedding …?"

"I know. I'm sorry you won't be able to attend, but I have a reward for you for keeping the Skorplings inside." I slide the ruby ring from my finger and hold it out for her.

She pales and takes two steps backwards. "Oh no, Your Majesty. I couldn't. People will think I stole it."

"No they won't. I've taken care of that. See?" I pull out the note and hand it to her.

She opens the folded paper and reads out loud. "*To whom it may concern: I have ordered Katie to stay with the Skorplings in the nursery until the wedding ceremony is over. In recognition of her excellent service, I have made a gift to her of my ruby ring. Jaden Victoria Hanover Beckett, Queen of Domerica.*"

Her eyes grow large, and I shove the ring at her again. This time she takes it and drops it and the note into the pocket of her apron. "Thank you, Your Majesty. Thank you so much."

"You're most welcome. Just keep the Skorplings here as I've asked, and you'll have earned that ring."

She nods vigorously.

"Love you guys," I say, blowing kisses to Fred and Ethel.

"Lock this door behind me," I tell Katie.

"Yes, ma'am." She curtseys deeply.

The hallway's crawling with harried servants as I make my way to the kitchen, keeping my head down. Most of them don't notice me, but a few drop a quick bow or curtsey my way and then continue on with their appointed tasks.

Leaning around the door of the noisy kitchen, I snatch two pommeras from a bowl on the sideboard and head out the back door to the stables.

A few stable boys are busily polishing the queen's carriage. I slip around them to Gabriel's stall in the rear.

"Hi boy," I say, running my hand along his sleek coat. "Brought you a treat." I flatten my hand and offer him a pommera. Gabriel pulls it into his mouth with his soft lips. "One more," I say when he finishes the first.

"I'm going to miss you so much." I rub his forehead and the spot between his eyes. "Father will take good care of you. I promise."

Wrapping my arms around his neck, I breathe in his earthy

scent. How I wish I could ride him one last time, but I'd be late for the royal breakfast. So I kiss his nose and rush out of the stables, tears burning my eyes.

FIFTEEN

The back stairway is deserted as I jog up the steps two at a time, hoping Ryder will be waiting for me. I'm disappointed to find my room empty. Emotionally, I'm prepared for my confrontation with Gilbert and Jean Louis, but it feels like pure Red Bull running in my veins instead of blood. I can't sit for more than a few seconds, so I pace up and down my balcony while I wait.

After thirty minutes or so, Ryder bursts through the door, out of breath but smiling. "Time to go, love," he says. "All is in place. I believe you will be pleased."

We walk hand in hand to the private dining room on the first floor where the breakfast is scheduled to take place.

A lavish buffet is laid out on a sideboard at the head of the room, and the table has been set with the finest royal china and crystal. Four white-gloved butlers stand at attention, ready to serve the guests.

"Where are the men?" I ask quietly as a bead of cold sweat snakes down my back.

Ryder tilts his head toward a side door. I open it and peek inside. The large adjoining room is crammed with dozens of Royal Guardsmen armed to the hilt. The men bow when they see me. I smile and salute the captain, then quietly reclose the door.

"Nice," I say.

"All you need do is signal me, and I will bring them in," Ryder tells me.

"Perfect. Once everyone arrives, we should be good to go." I pour myself a cup of tea and take my place at the head of the table.

The first guests to arrive are Duke Ferdinand and his sister, already dressed in their wedding finery. Ryder and I welcome them in. As a butler is seating them, Prince Gilbert and Prince Jean Louis arrive. They've brought along their elderly uncle, the Grand Duke of something or other. While this is unexpected, it's not a problem. I greet them and invite them to be seated. The doors are closed behind them.

After everyone is settled at the table, I stand.

"Good morning to you all," I say, smiling. "Thank you for joining Chief Blackthorn and me on this most momentous day. I have a few words to say before we eat."

I turn to the side of the table where the princes are seated. "Prince Gilbert, Prince Jean Louis, and monsieur Grand Duke, I wish to inform you that you are all under arrest." I nod to Ryder. He opens the door for the Guardsmen who quickly file into the room and surround the table.

Prince Gilbert leaps up from his chair. "This is outrageous! You have no authority to arrest us. This is nothing short of an act of war against Dome Noir."

"Sit down, Gilbert." I glare at him.

He doesn't budge. "I shall not be seated. I demand you call off your guards at once."

"You're hardly in a position to demand anything," I say. "Sit down and shut up or I'll have you bound to that chair and gagged."

He grudgingly sits.

"If I may continue, you are all charged with plotting to

overthrow the government of Domerica, conspiracy to murder the queen as well as other members of the royal family, and a whole host of other high crimes and misdemeanors which will be read to you in their entirety once you are locked away in Wall's Edge Prison."

"That's absurd," Gilbert says, though he remains seated. "Who has spread these lies against us? We wish to confront our accusers."

"Spare us the theatrics, Gilbert. We know all about your plans to attack the palace today. In fact, your soldiers are riding into a trap as we speak. Unfortunately, you will not be able to witness it because you'll be miles away inside a prison cell. Your soldiers will either surrender to me or face certain death."

I turn to the Duke and Duchess. "Ferdinand, I'm sorry to place you in the middle of this, but here you are, and I have no choice but to insist that you pick a side. You may either swear your allegiance and that of Cupola de Vita to Domerica right now, or you will be placed under arrest and removed to Wall's Edge Prison along with these vipers."

Ferdinand stands. "Your Majesty, I will gladly pledge my allegiance and that of Cupola de Vita to Queen Jaden of Domerica. I give you my word that King Rafael will honor this pledge." He bows grandly, and for the first time since arriving in Domerica, he smiles at me.

"Thank you, Ferdinand. What about Duchess Isabella?"

He holds out a hand for his sister, and she rises demurely. "I too pledge my allegiance to Queen Jaden of Domerica, Your Majesty," she says softly and makes a small curtsey.

"All right then." I face the princes and their uncle. "Gentlemen, please stand and remove your coats."

None of them makes a move to rise.

"Guards," I say.

The captain signals, and the Guardsmen nearest the princes draw their swords threateningly. The old Grand Duke rises with dignity and removes his coat. Turning to his nephews he says, "Gilbert! Jean Louis! *C'est fini.* Stand and take your punishment like men."

They both rise warily and shuck off their coats. On the captain's order, Royal Guardsmen place black hooded robes on each of the men and shackle their wrists behind them. All three are gagged and the black hoods are pulled low over their faces. Guardsmen surround the prisoners on all sides and usher them through the back door to a waiting carriage.

"Make haste," Ryder says to the captain. "Report back to the queen as soon as they are secured inside the prison."

"Yes sir," he salutes and quickly departs.

Ryder turns, grinning, and gathers me up into a fierce embrace. "That was most satisfying," he says triumphantly. "I must leave you now to join my men. Promise me you will be safe."

"I promise." I raise my face to his, and he kisses me softly. But I wrap my arms around his neck and bring him in closer. This will be our last kiss, and I want to be able to remember it ... forever.

He crushes me against his hard chest. I feel his heart racing. His moist lips are like warm honey on mine. Every ounce of love I hold inside me flows through my kiss and into him.

"I love you desperately," I whisper hoarsely.

"And I you, with all my heart," he says, eyes shining. "This will soon be over, and we shall be free to live and love in peace."

Then he's gone...

A dense, black emptiness shrouds me so completely that nothing can penetrate it—no thought, no sound, no vision. I feel nothing inside but the throbbing chasm of what I've just lost. I wrap my arms around my middle just before my knees give way, and I crumble to the floor.

The anxious cries and gentle hands of worried servants register vaguely in my brain, but I've nothing to give in response. Then

Patrick Stillwater's clear voice breaks through the fog, and his strong arms lift me from the rug.

"We must get you to safety, Your Majesty."

He discreetly carries me up the back stairway to my room, while I cling to his neck and weep into his leather armor. Gently placing me in one of the armchairs facing the fireplace, he kneels beside me.

"What may I do for you, ma'am?"

I sniff back my tears and swallow hard. "I'm all right now. Thank you for your kindness."

My unchecked emotions quickly turn into anger with myself for falling apart like some freakin' damsel in distress. "Where's my sword, Patrick?" I straighten my clothes in an attempt to recover some dignity. "Update me on what's happening outside."

He strides to the corner of the sitting room and gathers up my sword. "Guests have been arriving for the past hour or so," he says.

I take the katana and strap it to my side.

"They are being seated as we speak. Once the fighting begins, they will be ushered to the Grand Ballroom inside the palace. The Enclave and Unicoi armies are in place, and we've been informed that the Dome Noir soldiers are on the move. Their arrival is expected within the next hour."

"Where are the other men? Please check on the guard that's supposed to be posted around my room, and find out why they're not here yet."

"I cannot leave you alone, Your Majesty."

"Well then, send somebody else to check. We can't just sit around and wait. They should be here by now. Maybe something's gone wrong."

He appears reluctant, but I've given him an order. "Lock the door behind me. I shan't be long," he says.

Once Patrick is out of the room, I hurry to my jewelry chest and remove the polycom from its hiding place. It takes some fiddling before I figure out how to set it to vibrate mode. Then I shove it in the pocket of my riding pants. Next, I take out the black velvet pouch containing the pentagram key to the tower room and tuck it my other pocket.

As I'm locking up the chest, Patrick returns with several additional Royal Guards.

"General LeGare made some last minute adjustments to the palace detail," he says. "Ten Guardsmen were arrested this morning on charges of spying. More men had to be assigned to guard the brig, necessitating further changes, but additional reinforcements will be here shortly."

Damn! Last minute changes aren't good. Anything could impact our plan.

"All right, we'll just have to make do until then," I say. "Take care of things down here while I run up to the tower room to get a better view of the grounds. Maybe we can see something from up there."

After Patrick stations the additional guards in various spots around my rooms, he follows me to my closet. I climb up through the hatch in the ceiling, and he clambers up the ladder behind me, his sword banging against the side rail. After we emerge inside the tiny storage room below the tower, I shove aside the rolling rack of dresses concealing a small wooden door, and use the pentagram key to unlock it.

An electric lantern sits on the bottom step where I left it. I switch it on to light the steep staircase. We make our way up the steps and emerge into the brilliant light of the glassed-in tower room, the highest point in the palace.

The wedding guests being seated in the Grand Arboretum are clearly visible from here. In the adjoining gardens, servants work to arrange vases of flowers, gigantic ice sculptures, and dozens of silver platters of food on mile long tables.

I scan the woods to the east and west for traces of the hidden armies. Nothing is visible to the naked eye. Sliding open the top drawer of the Bombay chest, I take out a small telescope and a pair of opera glasses the princess had placed there.

"See if you can spot either our guys or the bad guys." I give the telescope to Patrick, and he moves along the bank of windows surveying the countryside.

I raise the opera glasses and check out the guest area. People are talking and laughing, seemingly oblivious to the impending melee.

"I see no sign of soldiers in the distance, ours or theirs," Patrick says. "But many Royal Guardsmen have taken positions on either side of the palace. Most likely that means that the Noir army is rapidly approaching. The guests will soon sense that something is awry. We should go down to your room." He lays the telescope on top of the chest.

"You go ahead. I need to get something up here."

"I will wait for you at the bottom of the steps." He makes a slight bow and leaves.

I set the opera glasses next to the telescope and open the bottom drawer of the chest. A sketch pad lies to one side. I slide it out and flip through the pages until I find what I'm looking for. The handsome face of a young Ryder Blackthorn stares up at me. The princess made this sketch and wrote a short poem for him many years ago on the day they met. I rip out the page and replace the pad in the drawer. Then I carefully fold the sketch in thirds, making certain that the creases don't run through Ryder's face. It's the only memento of him I'm taking with me. I slip it inside my shirt and tuck it next to my heart.

SIXTEEN

I find Patrick pacing stiffly at the foot of the tower room stairs.

"Leave this door open in case we need to come back up here," I say. "It's a much better vantage point from the tower."

"Perhaps, but you must not be seen. We are not certain of the range of their rifles." He motions to the hatch. "After you, ma'am."

We climb down the ladder into my closet, and I wander into the sitting area of my room. "Please take a seat away from the window, Your Majesty," Patrick instructs. "There is nothing to do now but wait."

I drop into one of the armchairs near the fireplace, my nerves raw as hamburger. I detest being stuck in this room, not knowing what's happening out there. "How will we know when the Noirs finally get here?" I ask.

"The sounds of gunfire may be our first indication, or perhaps the sound of the wedding guests making their way inside the palace."

Goosebumps prickle across my skin. "Yeah, it's going to be chaos down there—a lot of frightened people."

"They will be safe inside the palace, as will you." Patrick says.

Someone pounds on my door. A spike of adrenaline shoots through me like a storm of needles.

A voice calls out. "Stillwater? It's Luskin. General LeGare has sent us."

Patrick opens the door to two Royal Guardsmen armed with long rifles. They step inside and both bow to me.

"I'm Luskin, ma'am," the taller one says. "This is Cartwright. We're riflemen. General LeGare wants us stationed on your balcony."

"That way." Patrick jerks his head toward the French doors, and the soldiers tromp outside.

"Do you know those guys?" I ask him. "Because I've never seen either of them before."

"Yes. Luskin's been around longer than I have. Cartwright is fairly new."

"I understood only long-serving members of the guard were going to be assigned to me."

"Perhaps General LeGare made an exception because he is skilled with a rifle. If you are uncomfortable with his presence, I will send him away immediately."

"Not yet," I say. "He might be handy to have around."

I sidle over to my desk where Ralston's glasses sit in the tray. Slipping them on, I try to appear nonchalant while I take a turn around the room. I attempt to make eye-contact with each of the soldiers. They seem a bit confused or flustered by my actions, but, so far, no little red flashes.

The soldiers, Luskin and Cartwright, are positioned at the balcony rail with their sited rifles at the ready. "Hey, Cartwright," I say.

He lowers his rifle and spins around. "Yes, Your Majesty?"

Instantly red flashes in my upper left lens. *Nonhuman – automaton, IUGA ID# S1772. Shit! He's IUGA.*

"You any good with that thing?" I ask, nodding toward his rifle.

"Yes, ma'am," he says with a touch of pride. I reach up with my fingertip and press the small silver emblem on the side of my glasses, surreptitiously snapping his photo. A wary look crosses his face, like he's pretty sure he's just been made.

"All right, carry on." I step back inside, my mind frantically sifting through my possible options. I've no doubt he's an expert with that rifle, and he's probably here to use it on me. Even if he's not here to kill me, he's an IUGA agent so they now know we're on to their plan.

I grab Patrick's arm and drag him into a corner of the sitting area not visible from the balcony. "That Cartwright guy's a spy," I say in a harsh whisper.

His expression conveys confusion and disbelief. "How do you know this, Your Majesty?"

"It's hard to explain, but these glasses." I rip them off my head. "They can identify spies."

He stares at me, eyes still dubious.

"No really, Patrick." I quickly make up an explanation and hope he'll believe me. "Eve's people gave them to me. Remember, she had all that special medicine that healed you? They have other special things too, like these glasses that identify spies. I know he's here to harm me." I shove the glasses into my back pocket.

"Go after him and take him out," I say. "I don't care how you do it, but get that gun away from him before he uses it on me."

"Yes ma'am." He draws his sword.

I open my mouth to tell him about the vulnerable spot on the back of Cartwright's neck, but before the words reach my lips, the first shots ring out on the palace grounds. The battle is engaged.

Patrick sprints for the balcony, signaling to one of the guards to follow him.

The next thing I see is Patrick's body being blown backward, simultaneous with a loud crack. *Goddamned Cartwright shot him!*

I dive behind an armchair, clamping a hand over my mouth to keep myself from crying out.

"Stop!" I hear Luskin's voice followed by another loud crack.

I peer around the side of the chair in time to see Cartwright advancing through the French doors, rifle at shoulder height. He points it at the two guards in front of him.

"Drop your weapons. Now!"

Their swords clang loudly to the floor. He wheels to his right, aiming his rifle at the guard stationed in my bedroom. "You too."

The sword falls from the man's trembling fingers. He raises his hands above his head and cowers pitifully in the corner.

"Your Majesty," Cartwright calls. "Come out now. You and your men will not be harmed."

Yeah, right. If I stand up, we're all dead. But what do I do? My sword's useless against his rifle. I grasp a heavy brass paperweight from the table in front of the fireplace. Two options occur to me: hurl it at his head or use it as a distraction. I'm a lousy aim under the best of conditions, so I opt for the distraction and chuck the paperweight into the kitchenette.

My brilliant ploy doesn't fool him for a second. He whirls around and aims his rifle in the direction of my hiding place. "There you are. Come out, or I will begin executing your men."

I peek around the side of the chair again, and he takes a potshot at my head. The bullet barely misses me, thudding into the chair. Amazingly, the formerly cowering Guardsman from the bedroom springs into action, rushing Cartwright from the rear. He leaps onto the automaton's back and places him in an impressive chokehold.

The two remaining guards quickly retrieve their swords and assail him head on.

Cartwright parries their sword blows with his rifle, while the scrappy guardsman on his back tries to choke the life out of him. Unfortunately, the kid doesn't know what I know—automatons don't need oxygen. The guy's never going to pass out.

I draw my sword and jump into the fray. It's clear he's been programmed for combat, though, and he succeeds in knocking one guard's sword from his hand. I swing my katana wildly at the robot's arms, but he maintains his grip on the gun, not feeling the cutting blows.

This frontal assault is getting us nowhere. The automaton's too strong, and unless we can completely cut-off an arm, we're not getting his gun. I fling my useless katana to the side, and dropping to my hands and knees, I sweep-kick the robot's feet out from under him. Both he and the piggy-back guard crash to the floor. The rifle clatters out of Cartwright's hands.

Scrambling to my feet, I make a charge for the weapon. Cartwright thrusts himself up from the floor and attempts to intercept me. I hold out a hand to fend him off, while reaching for the rifle with my other hand.

"Stop!" I shout as the robot lunges for me.

In a surreal moment, Cartwright's body sails backward across the room as if propelled by some invisible force. He slams against the wall and falls face first to the floor.

Too occupied to question my inexplicable good fortune, I seize the gun and dart to the downed automaton. Mustering every ounce of strength in my body, I slam the rifle butt into the base of his neck. His body convulses once and becomes deathly still.

I drop the gun and rush to Patrick. Kneeling at his side, tears pour down my face as I press against the gaping hole in his chest. "Help me get his armor off," I shout to the others as his life blood seeps into the fabric of my riding pants.

Gentle hands grasp my shoulders. "There is nothing you can do, Your Majesty. He is beyond help. We must get you to safety." The gray haired guardsman's eyes are kind, but steely with purpose.

"I can't leave," I say, wiping my bloody hands on my thighs. "Besides, where would I go? The palace is under siege."

"Only three of us are left, ma'am. We cannot adequately protect you."

"Get reinforcements from the second floor," I say. "Tell them we've been attacked. I'll hide in the tower room until you return with more men."

His jaw clenches as he scoops the rifle from the floor and faces the other men. "Do either of you know how to use this?"

They both shake their heads.

"Well, do the best you can," he says, handing it to the older of the two. "Guard her with your lives. I won't be long."

"Where is the tower room?" The younger guard looks to me expectantly.

"This way," I say, heading for my closet.

"We'll stay down here," the guard with the rifle says as I step on the first rung of the ladder. "Once you're inside, close and lock the hatch. We'll roll the ladder to the other corner."

I nod and start my ascent up the ladder. Near the last rung, I'm almost knocked to the ground when a loud explosion rocks the palace. *Shit!*

The guardsmen exchange worried glances. "Be careful, ma'am," one of them calls to me. "They may have breached the palace walls. If you hear fighting, stay quiet. We'll do our best for you."

"Thanks," I call, scrambling up through the ceiling hatch. I slam it shut and trip up the steep staircase to the tower room. When I reach the bank of windows facing the front of the palace grounds, I'm unprepared for the sight of the all-out melee taking place below.

The palace gates have been secured, but the Noirs aren't surrendering the way they were supposed to. Instead, they're fighting viciously. In the Grand Arboretum, overturned tables and broken chairs lie scattered alongside mangled bodies and body parts. The pillared gazebo has become a stage for a brutal standoff between Royal Guardsmen and black knights. My gut flails at the appalling carnage.

Falling to my knees, I dry heave until my insides throb with pain. How could Ralston's prediction model have been so wrong? Or did he just sugar-coat everything for my benefit? What if our grand plan doesn't work after all and we're all goners?

The polycom vibrates loudly inside my pocket, nearly sailing me out of my skin. It's Urick's signal. When my heart slides back down my throat, my brain registers that the assassination party is on its way. An icy-hot shudder racks my body. *This is bad.* Only two guards and Urick stand between me and a crazed death squad.

Using the window sill for support, I hoist myself to my feet. The dual sights of the sickening battle in front of the palace and the frightened wedding guests clawing and shoving their way inside the back doors are too horrifying to witness. I move near the door to the walkway and turn to face inside the room, steeling myself for the final act to come.

Tense, trembling seconds tick away. I barely dare to breathe.

The crack of a door bursting open below me makes my blood jump. All my nerve ends stand at attention. The thud of boots tells me the Noirs have made it inside my room. Only a few heartbeats now before they reach me. I test the knob to make certain the door will open easily. Sounds of soldiers clanging through the hatch in my closet send fresh tremors of fear through me.

A soldier's head emerges from the stairwell, but it's not who I expected.

"Charles! What are you doing here?" LeGare and another Royal Guardsman bound into the room.

135

"I came for you, Your Majesty. We heard you'd been attacked. Come quickly, we must get you to safety."

"But I can't. I need to stay here," I say, confused. This was not in the plan. This didn't show up in any predicted scenario.

"You cannot stay here. The Noirs are on our heels." He urgently takes my arm and a small seed of hope sprouts in my soul. *Maybe I can go with LeGare and be safe. Maybe I can live through this and stay with Ryder after all.*

But my tender dream is ground into dust when four black-armored soldiers, led by Urick, trample their way inside the room, guns raised.

"Drop your weapons," Urick shouts at LeGare. Against such hopeless odds, he and his man immediately surrender their swords.

"Take care of them, the queen is mine," Urick orders his men. He aims a large pistol at my head and cuts his eyes sharply to the walkway door—my signal that it's time to go.

I back up slowly and twist the knob, never taking my eyes from Urick's. I tentatively place one foot on the rotted walkway, and release the door knob. My hand is poised on the latch to my TPD, and I glance quickly at the ground below, preparing to jump. A sudden burst of activity in the room makes me jerk my head around. A knot of Unicoi warriors explodes up and out of the stairway. Loud battle cries and swinging broadswords quickly divert the Noirs' attention away from killing me to staying alive.

Gunshots ring out as Ryder breaks through the fray and races straight for me. I pivot to scramble back inside the room, but an unexpected jolt makes me stumble. The wood under my foot cracks and begins to give way. In a split-second I realize what is about to happen. But it's too late. Ryder lunges for my hand and our eyes meet at the exact moment the walkway splinters and disintegrates beneath my feet.

"Nooo!" It's the keening of my soul ripping in two. I clutch wildly at my bracelet and manage to click the latch before I slam into the

earth, but not before the sight of Ryder tumbling from the tower behind me is engraved forever upon my heart.

SEVENTEEN

In the space of a single pulse, I land in Narowyn's office. Her eyes flare when she sees my bloodied clothes. "Jaden," she gasps. "What's happened?"

"Going back." I fumble with coordinates on my bracelet and double click the latch. Z*zzt*, I touch down at the base of the tower. The princess's body lies eerily alone, splayed in the grass as if she's just fallen there. A group of men I recognize as Transcenders is gathered around another body fifteen feet away. One of Ryder's boots protrudes grotesquely from the huddle.

"Ryder!" I shout.

Asher detaches from the cluster of men and intercepts me, using his body to shelter me from view. "Jade, you've got to go. Soldiers are coming. You'll be discovered."

"I don't care," I shriek. "I need to see him."

Narowyn appears at my side and places a hand on my shoulder. Quick as lightning, we're back in her office.

I roughly shrug off her hand. "Let me go!"

"No. You must not." She lifts my arm and smoothly slips the bracelet from my wrist. "Be reasonable, Jaden. The lives of your

Domerican family, and possibly the fate of the entire country, depend upon your following through with this plan."

I consider snatching my bracelet away from her, but I know she's right. Instead, I crumple into a chair and cover my face with my hands. Unspeakably black thoughts invade my head, and all reason threatens to abandon me.

"I think he's dead," I cry. "I think I killed him."

She gathers me in her arms and gently strokes my hair. "Let us not presume the worst, my dear." Her voice quavers. "We'll know soon enough."

I raise my eyes to hers. Unchecked tears spill down her cheeks. *She knows he's dead. Of course he's dead. He fell fifty feet.*

"Send me back in time," I frantically plead. "You've got to send me back in time so I can save him."

"You know that's impossible, Jaden. You cannot go back to a time you've already lived."

Shaking my head slowly, I mutter, "No, no, no. There has to be a way. This wasn't supposed to happen. He wasn't supposed to die. He's supposed to live a long life and save that godforsaken planet. He's having a child in a few months. He can't just die like that."

She pulls in a shaky breath. "We must get you out of these clothes, my dear. We'll hear soon enough."

I focus on my bloody riding pants. "Patrick's blood," I say. "He's dead too. Everyone I love ends up dead."

"You're not responsible for these deaths, Jaden. IUGA is. None of this would have happened if they hadn't tried to control events for their own nefarious ends. Let us place the blame where it rightfully belongs."

She walks to a glass-shelved corner cabinet and removes two glasses and a crystal decanter filled with dark amber liquid. She pours a small amount of liquid into a glass and gives it to me. "Drink it. It will calm you."

"What is it?" I ask as she pours herself a glass.

"Very fine brandy."

She takes a long draw and I do the same. It blazes through my already tender insides, stealing my breath. "*Yeow!* That burns."

"Oh. I'm sorry. I should have warned you." She takes my glass. "Jaden, dear, we have some time before the others return with Ralston. Why don't you shower and change while we wait? I'll show you to your quarters."

"I don't want to shower. I want to know what's going on. I'm about to crawl out of my skin with worry."

"I understand. But sitting and stewing will not make the time pass more quickly. You might as well do something to take your mind off things until we receive an update."

"All right. Do you have something I can wear?" I ask, realizing I have nothing but the clothes on my back.

"Yes, dear. We've put together a few things for you until you can make your own purchases. Come with me."

I follow her as if in a trance, up to the third floor and down a hallway. She opens a door leading to an apartment and gestures me inside. The floors are light oak, the walls are cream-colored and devoid of decoration. The place smells strongly of new paint and cleaning products. I wonder vaguely if anyone lived here before.

"This is your apartment," she says. "It's very neutral at the moment, but you will have the opportunity and the funds to decorate it any way you wish."

I nod without a word. I don't freaking care about interior design at the moment. Someone's taken a sledge-hammer to my life. The left over bits and pieces don't seem to matter much right now.

She shows me to the bedroom. "I selected some dresses for you and put them in your closet. You'll find underthings and pajamas in the dresser drawers. The bathroom is fully stocked, but should you need anything, let me know, and I will get it for you at once."

"Thank you," I say. My voice sounds detached and alien, as if it's coming from someone else. The weight of my fear and desolation threatens to crush me. Tears well in my eyes again and I tremble uncontrollably. "Narowyn, can I ask a favor?"

"Of course, dear. What is it?"

"Will you wait for me while I shower? I don't want to be left alone in this strange apartment. I'm so scared."

She wraps her arms around me with no thought for my bloody clothes. "I am here for you. Take all the time you need. I promise I will not leave you for a moment."

I close the door to the bathroom and turn on the shower. The room is large and modern, but if I focus on this sterile, unfamiliar place as my new home, I'll go stark raving mad. I grit my teeth and try to anesthetize my brain to any and all thoughts.

Sitting on the edge of the bathtub, I yank off my boots. The blood on my pants has partially congealed and the fabric sticks to my legs as I pull them off. I don't allow it to affect me. I stay numb. But when a folded piece of paper topples from my shirt to the floor, I come completely unglued. Peering up at me is the face of a youthful Ryder Blackthorn.

Clutching the sketch to my breast, I lie on the cool tile floor and weep my heart out—for him and for myself and for the utter senselessness of it all.

EIGHTEEN

True to her word, Narowyn waits for me, even though I take well over an hour to shower and dress. I find her in the kitchen. Trays of sandwiches, vegetables, and cookies have been set out on the counter.

"I thought you might be hungry," she says gently.

My first impulse is to refuse, but I haven't eaten all day, and the brandy is burning a hole in my stomach. "Thanks. That's kind of you. Would it be okay if we filled our plates and ate in your office? I'd like to wait there for news, if that's all right."

"Certainly." She removes two white plates from the generously supplied cupboard and hands one to me.

I place two sandwich quarters on top along with some carrots and cucumbers and a huge oatmeal cookie.

"I have ice water in my office if that suits you. Or we can have tea sent in if you prefer."

"Water's fine," I say.

We carry our plates down the elevator to Narowyn's office and seat ourselves in her comfortable chairs.

I nibble on my food and stare at the floor, forcing my mind to remain blank and not wander into places where it shouldn't go.

"Forgive me for bringing up a point of business on a day like today," Narowyn says as I crunch on a carrot. "But I thought it might put your mind at ease to know that while you were showering I had our lawyers file the papers with the Inter-Galactic Confederation Court, setting out all of IUGA's offenses and requesting an emergency restraining order."

"Okay. Thanks."

"If necessary, we will amend the complaint later to include any new information we receive."

"Well, here's some information you might want," I say. "Patrick was killed by an IUGA agent—an automaton. The thing was posing as a Royal Guardsman in an effort to get at me."

She shakes her head. "Simply outrageous. In direct violation of Confederation articles. They'll most certainly deny everything, but we will include it."

"I got a photo of him if that helps."

"Goodness, how did you manage that?"

"Ralston gave me his extra set of glasses. That's how I knew the guy was IUGA in the first place. They're in the pocket of my pants."

"I imagine that will be most helpful to our case."

The door to Narowyn's office swings open, and Captain Watterson, Urick, and Asher file in.

I toss my plate aside and jump to my feet, the unspoken question on my lips.

Asher's stormy green eyes meet mine, and he shakes his head sadly. "I'm sorry, Jaden, he's gone."

I inhale sharply and fresh tears follow the trail of the thousands before them. "What about the rest of my family?"

"Your father and brother are fine," Asher says. "Everyone who went to Old Unicoi is safe. Lady Lorelei's ascension to the throne was automatic when the princess's body was discovered. She's on her way back to Warrington Palace."

"I'm afraid the clean-up's going to take a while," Captain Watterson says. "The palace was badly damaged by explosives, and the casualties were higher than expected. All in all, though, it could have been worse."

"Where's Ralston?" I ask.

The three men exchange uneasy glances. "He didn't show up, Jade," Asher says.

"*What do you mean, he didn't show up?*" My voice sounds like the screech of a mad woman.

"We waited as long as we could. We believe IUGA has him," he says.

This is more than I can handle in one day. "*Nooo*," I wail. "They'll destroy him."

"We'll find him," Urick pipes up.

"How will you find him?" I scoff.

His wolf eyes fasten on me. "You do not need the details. But I assure you we'll find him."

For some reason, I believe him. "All right. Please let me know when you do," I say more calmly.

He bobs his head once.

"What's going to happen to Domerica now?" I ask.

"Shall we sit for a moment?" Narowyn says, waving a hand toward the chairs.

Everyone but Urick finds a seat. "If you will excuse me," he says. "I have a missing automaton to locate."

144

"Of course. Thank you, Urick." Narowyn says. He slips quietly out the door.

"Jaden, we believe Domerica is currently in a strong position vis-a-vis Dome Noir, in light of the capture of the two princes and the Grand Duke," Narowyn says. "The opportunities for avoiding war and remaining a top world power are great. But whatever happens must be allowed to unfold of its own accord. We must be cautious regarding the extent of our interest in Domerica."

"What's that supposed to mean?" I ask.

"Currently, as Transcenders, we are given great freedom to visit other realms and conduct our research as we see fit. We must not open ourselves up to an accusation of meddling in the affairs of that country. It's exactly what we've accused IUGA of doing."

I scowl at her. "I have no intention of meddling in the affairs of Domerica. I'm interested in its welfare. I think that's understandable."

"It certainly is," she says. "I do not mean to imply you would do anything inappropriate. But remember you have signed a contract agreeing never to return to Domerica."

"What're you talking about? You think that contract's still valid after everything IUGA has done?"

"That is for the court to say, not me. Try to understand, the IGC is a court of equity. We must go to the court with *clean hands*. We cannot provide IUGA with grounds to state that you also breached the contract, or worse, that you violated the Transcender Code of Conduct."

Raising my palms to my temples, I snap, "Okay, I get it. I can't go back to Domerica right now."

"I'm sorry, dear. It's only that you still have much to learn about this universe and the Transcenders' place in it. We operate under a strict code. But you will have ample time for all of that once you have returned from your trip to Connecticut."

The mention of my home is like a soothing caress to my battered heart. "Will I get to go soon?"

"Oh yes," Narowyn says. "In fact, you must return next week. The thirty-day time period you were allotted at the beginning of your agreement with IUGA expires in four days. You must return home or your life there will resume without you. That is the way the contract was originally written."

"The sooner the better," I say. "Do you have a cover story for me yet?"

"Yes, it's all arranged. But let's discuss it tomorrow. It's late, and I'm certain you're exhausted. You should rest now."

I grip the arms of my chair, irrationally alarmed at being left alone.

"Is that all right, dear?" she says.

"Yes, but please don't make me sleep in that apartment tonight. I ... I can't be by myself right now."

"Stay with me," Asher offers. "I have two bedrooms, and TV, and ice cream. I'd be glad for the company."

"Really? Could I?" I love Asher's place, and at least it's familiar.

"Come on." He stands and offers me his hand.

I take it gratefully. We say goodnight to Narowyn and Captain Watterson, and I follow Asher back to the third floor. We pass two people in the hall, but I just look away. I'm not fit for polite conversation tonight.

Asher's apartment is two doors down from mine. "Guess we're going to be neighbors," I say.

"I'll try not to play my music too loud," he says with a crooked smile.

NINETEEN

Asher and I sit on his white sofa eating mango mint chip ice cream out of the carton and watching a mindless sitcom about a blended Arumel family. The mom's a rocket scientist, the dad grows orchids, and the kids are adorably obnoxious. The family has an automaton that's treated like a treasured old uncle and a dog from another planet that walks on its hind legs and understands only French. It's kind of like *Modern Family* meets *The Jetsons*.

The parts I understand are kind of funny, and for a minute or two here and there I almost forget the reality of my screwed up life—newly widowed after only five days of marriage, my husband lying dead a million light years away and me forbidden to go to him, Ralston MIA and probably nothing but a mangled heap of circuits by now.

Eventually shock and bone-deep exhaustion overtake me and I doze off, my head resting on the arm of the sofa. The white noise of the TV in the background is my lullaby. I don't know how long I've slept when Asher shakes me by the shoulder.

"Here," he says, handing me a blue t-shirt.

"What's this?"

"Something to sleep in. Your room's the last door on the right. See you in the morning."

I drag myself down the short hallway, my body so heavy it feels like I'm wearing a lead coat. Not bothering with the t-shirt, I pull down the sheets and stuff myself inside fully clothed. Blessed sleep slowly claims my tortured mind.

"Jaden, Jaden, help me." It's Ryder. He's imprisoned inside a thick glass ball, high on a mountain top in Domerica.

I reach for my katana, but it's not at my side. I frantically scour the area for a rock or something to use to break open the ball. I find nothing. I beat on the outside with my fist, but it does no good. Then, without warning, the ball begins to roll down the slope of the mountain, picking up speed as it goes. I scramble after it, but my boot heel catches on a rock, and I tumble head over heels down the steep incline, then out into starlit space, then beyond space into darkness so dense, so impenetrable I cannot see. I cannot breathe. I cannot survive.

I shoot straight up in bed gasping for air. For a moment, I can't remember where I am. Then it all floods back to me. Grief billows out of me filling the room with intense bleakness. The pain is so suffocating I'm sure it will kill me. I want it to kill me. But I don't want to die alone.

Scrambling out of bed, I fumble my way down the unlit hallway until I find Asher's room. "Ash," I utter into the darkness.

"Jade, what is it?"

"I don't know if I can make it through this."

"Come here," he says softly. I find his arms, and he wraps me up firmly. "You are a strong woman. You will make it through."

"I'm sorry to be so pathetic."

He scoots over and makes a place for me on the bed. "Shh. Just lie down. Try to sleep. I'm right here."

"I think this may kill me," I say, clinging to him.

"You're not going to die. I'm right here."

The presence of another living, breathing human lying next to me helps me feel less vulnerable. Gradually, my fear subsides, and

I'm able to relax into a shallow, dreamless sleep.

When I wake, Asher's gone. For a moment, I teeter on the brink of despair, remembering that Ryder's dead and I'm still alive. But then I catch sight of sunlight streaming through the bedroom's white curtains. The simple beauty of the natural golden light touches me. It's been a while since I've seen pure, unfiltered, sunshine. It's so normal, yet so profoundly miraculous. This is something good about still being alive. This is something I can cling to, rather than dwelling on what I've lost. So I resolve to begin a mental list of things to be grateful for. Unsullied sunshine, not refracted by a dome shell is number one on the list.

I climb out of bed and attempt to straighten out my slept-in dress. The problem with linen is that it prefers to be wrinkled. *To hell with it.* Why fight the natural order of things? I pad into the bathroom and use Asher's comb to tame my rowdy hair. A quick check of his cabinets fails to turn up any mouthwash or toothpaste, so I'll just have to be careful not to breathe on him.

I follow the sounds of puttering in the kitchen. Asher hands me a mug of coffee with milk and sugar when I enter.

"Mornin', sleepyhead," he says. "How about some breakfast?"

"Mmm, this coffee's great." I gulp it greedily. "What are you making?" I notice sliced mushrooms, tomatoes, and onions on a red plastic cutting board.

"Omelets are my specialty ... and I have a bit of contraband here you might be interested in."

"Oh yeah, what's that?"

He extracts a white paper package from his freezer and unwraps it for me. "Bacon," he says with a sinful grin. "The food engineers haven't come up with a decent substitute, so I smuggle in a little whenever I can."

My eyes widen. "Would you really be in trouble if someone found out?"

"Nah. Arumel has laws against raising animals for food, that kind of thing. But no one cares about a bit of bacon from another world."

"Okay, what can I do?"

"Just enjoy your coffee."

I climb up on a counter stool and watch Asher work. He seems to know his way around a kitchen. The smell of frying bacon is familiar, comforting, mouthwatering. Item number two for my list of things to be grateful for: *bacon*.

"Thanks for last night, Ash. I had a nightmare and woke up scared."

He glances up from his frying pan, eyes soft and sympathetic. "You're not a bad bunkmate except for the thunderous snoring."

"Oh god, did I really snore?"

He smiles and shakes his head. "Nah. Just keeping things light."

I sigh. "Don't know what I'd do without you."

He concentrates on the sizzling bacon for a moment.

"Hey, Narowyn wants to meet with us later to talk about your trip to Connecticut," he says. "And, if you're up to it after that, I thought I'd take you over to the Urban Bazaar to pick up a few things for your place."

"What's the Urban Bazaar?"

"It's in a park in the artsy section of town. Every Sunday, some of the locals get together and sell their wares at discount prices. A couple of the prints in my living room came from there."

My heart and soul are so terribly crippled right now, it's hard to imagine doing even normal tasks, but my head knows that getting out will probably be good for me. "Okay. Maybe for a little while."

The omelet is divine. My hollowed-out stomach appreciates the warm food. We sit in silence for a few minutes enjoying the meal.

"What do you think happens when people die?" I say quietly.

Asher looks up from his plate with guarded eyes. Maybe the subject is too heavy for breakfast conversation. But I'm struggling for answers.

"This is just so different from when my mom, well both my moms, died," I explain. "It's the same gut-wrenching sense of loss, but with Ryder what kills me is not knowing where he is or what's happening to him right now. I worry about him. Is he safe? Can he see everything now? And if so, does he understand why I did what I did? Or does he hate me for lying to him? It's maddening."

Asher takes a sip of coffee and swipes his napkin across his mouth. "I wish I could help you, Jade. Most people in Arumel believe that we're eternal, and when we die we just move into a non-material kind of dimension until we're born again. Reincarnation is pretty much universally accepted here, and the Transcenders' studies of other earths prove that certain people are found together in lifetime after lifetime. Well, you already know about *perpetual contracts*."

He takes a bite of omelet and chews it slowly. "So, do I believe you'll see him again? Yes. But exactly what happens when we die—the actual mechanics of it—I don't have a clue. Maybe all the different Ryders that currently exist are just small sparks of the same larger energy. Each is similar yet distinctive. Maybe his spark was just absorbed back into that larger Ryder energy. But then maybe I don't know what the hell I'm talking about."

"I wish it wasn't so damn mysterious," I say. "I want to understand more, but I realize no one can really know for sure. Thanks for talking to me about it, though." I take the last bite of my breakfast and pick up my plate. "I'll help you with the dishes. Then I'd better head back to my place for a shower."

"I got this," he says. "You go ahead. Can you find your apartment from here?"

"I think so, since it's about ten steps down the hall. But if I get lost, I'll be back." I kiss his stubbly cheek. "Thanks again."

* * *

Wiping a swath of steam away from the bathroom mirror, I stare at my reflection. Amazing. I still look the same, but everything else in my life is changed completely and irrevocably. The hot shower was nice, but now depression hovers over my shoulder waiting for the green light to plunge me into the pit of despair. I halfway consider giving in to it as I rummage through the contents of the bathroom drawers and can't even find a damn toothbrush. But then I stumble onto a treasure—a hairdryer. *Yes!* I do a little happy dance.

It's been a month since I had the use of a hairdryer, and after twenty minutes or so, I have one more item for my gratitude list: *glossy straight hair.*

The closet's a different story, though. The dresses Narowyn picked out for me are long, loose, and as drab as the rest of my apartment. Not quite like the queen's closet I'd grown used to, or even the modest array of jeans, cute tops, and dresses I have back home in Connecticut. Narowyn's always so put together, I wonder why she chose these Amish-looking clothes for me.

Oh well. I take the least objectionable dress from its hanger and slip it on over my head, careful not to disturb my perfect hair.

TWENTY

A brisk knock at my door reminds me that Asher said he'd pick me up for our meeting with Narowyn. I quickly shove my feet into the beige flats she purchased for me and sprint to the door, but it's not Asher who waits on the other side.

"Jade!" Eve hugs me affectionately. "I'm so sorry for everything that's happened to you. It's so freaking unfair. You must be a total wreck. Your hair looks really nice though."

I have to smile at the sight of my only other friend in Arumel. "Thanks, Eve. Come in," I say, taking a step back from the door.

"I just got home from doing my community service and heard you were here." She steps inside dressed in an adorable spring frock that elicits a tiny pang of envy in me. Her spiky white-blond hair forms a shimmering halo around her sweet face. "I came right over to convey my condolences and let you know that I'm here for you."

"That's so nice. I'm glad you came by. I'm going to need friends like you to get me through this. You want something to drink?"

"No, I can only stay a minute." She scans my apartment. "So, this is the new place, huh?"

"Yep."

"It's really ... white."

I glance dolefully at the rooms behind me. "Yeah, it's kind of bare right now."

"Well, it has a lot of potential. We should go shopping!" Her large blue eyes light up.

"I'm taking her shopping. You're grounded," Asher says, coming through my open doorway. "How was the gig, Shorty?" He yanks at a spiky piece of Eve's hair.

"Not my favorite way to spend the morning," she says. "An Elder Care Center. Some sweet old codgers, but mostly it was kind of boring—they like to play video games all day." She turns to me. "It's part of my punishment for helping you with the Skorplings and healing Patrick's arm. How is he by the way?"

I drop my eyes and take in a quaky breath. "He was killed in the battle yesterday."

"Oh god, Jade. That's awful." Her eyes fill with sorrow. "What happened?"

Asher jumps in and saves me from having to explain. "Jade and I are late for a meeting with Narowyn. You two will have plenty of time to catch up later."

"Oh, sorry. Well, I'm on the second floor, Jade. Let's talk. Just stop by anytime." She waggles her fingers and then startles me by evaporating before my eyes.

"Geeze, isn't there some kind of rule against disapparating in the Chateau?" I say.

Asher smirks. "Out of courtesy, most people don't do it. But Eve's, you know ... young." He gives me a little *after you* gesture to the hallway.

"Hey Ash, I know Narowyn's waiting, but I couldn't find a toothbrush, you don't happen to have an extra, do you?"

"Actually, toothbrushes haven't been used here in years. Come with me, I'll show you." I follow him to my bathroom. He pulls open the top drawer and takes out a stainless steel object about the size of a marker. "This is for your teeth."

He holds it up and flips off the cap. A flat square head on a slim rod protrudes from the top. "Just push the button." He demonstrates by using his thumb to push a black button on the side, and the square head illuminates with neon blue light. "Run this along your teeth, gums, and tongue. Then rinse and you're done."

"Are you sure it'll work? I haven't brushed since sometime yesterday, and my teeth feel distinctly mossy."

He snorts a little laugh and gives the wand to me. "Try it."

I press the head to my front teeth. It has a texture like smooth bumps, and it tickles my gums a little. Once I'm finished, I rinse out my mouth with some water from the bathroom glass. Running my tongue along my teeth, I'm amazed at how clean they feel.

"Hmm, cool," I say. "I like it, but I miss the minty taste."

"You'll get used to it. But look, it does much more than clean your teeth. He shows me a small readout on the side. "While you're using it, sensors inside analyze your breath and saliva and take your body temp. It warns you if you're low on any vitamins or minerals, and it gives you a heads up when it detects the presence of viruses or disease-causing bacteria. You never have to get another cold." He smiles, replacing the cap.

"That's amazing. This little thing does all that?"

"You'll discover lots of amazing things in Arumel, Jade. But let's go. We're late."

Narowyn comes to hug me as we enter her office. "How are you today, dear?"

"Numb. Grief-stricken, but holding up, I guess."

My TPD bracelet sits atop her desk, and she hands it to me. "I'm sorry to have taken this from you, but I felt it was best under the circumstances."

It's comforting in a small way to clip the familiar bracelet back on my wrist. "Don't worry about it. It was probably the right thing to do at the time."

"Well, I hope this isn't too taxing for you, but I'd like to discuss the plans for your visit home. I have everything right here." She slides a manila file from the stack on her desk. "Let's sit down, shall we?"

We take seats in the office sitting area, and Narowyn opens her file. "As you probably know, most Transcenders have what we call *cover stories* for our loved ones back on our home earths That way our long absences are easily explained, but we can still visit them occasionally. Some have shared the truth with their families, but I wouldn't recommend it in your case. Your family would likely find your gift disturbing, if not completely unbelievable."

"That's putting it mildly," I say. "A cover story would be good."

"All right, then, since you are graduating high school in a few weeks, it seemed a natural choice to assemble a cover for you involving attending college in a foreign country. Accordingly, we arranged for you to be enrolled, on the books at least, at Oxford University in Oxford, England. More specifically, you will be enrolled in the Humanities division and working closely with a professor in the Rothermere American Institute."

I raise my eyebrows. "Oxford University? That's kind of swanky isn't it?"

"Not really. You're currently an accepted student at Yale University. The schools are comparable," she says. "In addition, you'll be receiving full financial support including grants and scholarships, or bursaries as they are called in the UK. So your father should have no objection to your change of schools."

"Oh, he'll object all right. The longest and farthest I've ever been away from him was six weeks of summer camp in the Poconos."

"Do you foresee a problem?"

156

"Uh yeah. I foresee all kinds of problems. What happens if my dad or my brother decides to pay me a visit? That's not out of the realm of possibility, you know."

She flips to a sheet in the middle of the file. "We've made provision for that. We've leased a small flat for you near the school. Nothing fancy, but adequate for short visits. You'll probably wish to spend a little time there yourself to become familiar with the school and the town."

"I'll have a flat in England?" I ask in astonishment.

"Yes. It's nothing more than we've done for the others." Her lips curve up. "We're a small but tight-knit family. We want to make certain all your needs are taken care of. What else troubles you about the arrangement?"

"Well, what if my dad wants to see my grades or something?"

"That's easy enough. Your father will receive all the normal parental correspondence distributed by the school, and if you desire, we can arrange for transcripts to be sent home also."

"Sounds like you've thought of everything."

"I believe we have. We've done this before. But it is entirely up to you to make your father comfortable with your decision. Do you believe that is possible?"

"Yes. He won't like it, but he won't stand in the way of such an incredible opportunity."

"Good." She folds her hands on top of the file. "Now let's discuss your actual visit home. Precautions will need to be taken for your safety. We considered placing a teacher in your school, but Asher tells me IUGA already has someone there."

"Right, Mr. Nordgren, my physics teacher. I didn't know he was IUGA until Ralston took me to his house right before Asher helped me shift back to Domerica. He probably knew I was walking into a death trap back there."

"Even more reason you must be watched over around the clock. With that in mind, Asher has very generously offered to return with you to Earth 7Y12."

That surprises me a little. "Okay, but how's that going to work? I mean who's he supposed to be?"

She fingers the pearl necklace at her throat. "In discussing it with Captain Watterson, we agree it would be optimal if you introduced him as your new boyfriend."

"Boyfriend! No freakin way." I glance at Asher. He's bent over, elbows on knees, looking a bit sheepish. "No offense Ash, but I just lost my husband." My voice cracks, and tears prickle my eyes. "I won't do that."

"I understand your feelings, dear," Narowyn says, "and if that is your final decision, we will consider another option. But please hear me out first. Asher would be your *boyfriend* in name only. By describing him as such, it will not appear suspicious that you spend most of your waking hours together. And since no one there knows of your great loss in Domerica, nobody will think ill of you."

The whole idea makes me squirm in my chair. "I'll think ill of me. It's disrespectful. I won't tarnish Ryder's memory that way." I grab a tissue from the box on the table next to me and blot my eyes.

"But it's only for your protection, Jaden," Narowyn says. "I suspect your Ryder would want you to do whatever was necessary to stay safe. If you are that adamantly opposed, though, we will send Urick instead."

The tears caused by this uncomfortable discussion are quickly staunched by the absurd visual of Urick in Madison, Connecticut. That makes me want to laugh out loud.

"Seriously? Urick? And he would be what? The head of the local Hell's Angels chapter?"

"He'd be your new neighbor. There's a vacant unit in your townhouse development. He would need to be close by."

"Oh please. People are going to believe that *Thor the Thunder God* just relocated to Madison? I'm sorry, but he's just not the townhouse type. Or the small-town Connecticut type. How about if Asher becomes my new neighbor, and we're just friends? Maybe he's gay or something."

She bites her lower lip, clearly not enchanted with the idea. "But we were hoping Asher could join you for Senior Celebration and other graduation activities where you will likely be most vulnerable."

"He can still do that as my friend. It's really nobody's business what our relationship is. I'll invite him to everything."

"Will your father find that acceptable?" she asks.

"Sure. I've always had guy friends."

She shifts her eyes to Asher. "Is that satisfactory to you?"

He shrugs noncommittally. "Whatever."

"All right then, that's the way we'll handle it." She closes the file. "You may stay through your graduation. After that, the story will be that you are attending summer orientation at Oxford and must leave at once to get settled into your new flat. Does that meet with your approval?"

"Yes, of course. It's more than I dreamed possible. Thank you for everything. Both of you." I flash Ash an appreciative smile.

I can hardly believe it. I'm really going home.

TWENTY-ONE

The next few days pass in a dull fog. Asher and I do a little shopping in the Urban Bazaar and a local galleria, but I feel a little like a zombie just going through the motions. I'm not really into buying pretty things. Eve brings by some decorative pillows and a colorful throw for my couch to give my apartment a homier feel. Still, I end up spending a lot of time in the common areas of the Chateau or out on the serene grounds. It's not that I feel like socializing, I just need other people around me.

During the daylight hours it's easier to keep my mind on other things—familiarizing myself with my new home, figuring out the voice control system in my apartment, and preparing for my trip. I even eat a few meals in the main dining room with the other Transcenders. Everyone has been kind and sympathetic.

But at night it's impossible to keep the demons at bay. After dark I sit at my window hugging my knees, engulfed by a loneliness so profound it seems to fill my entire apartment. My sleep is sporadic and fitful.

Narowyn stops by frequently. Sometimes she brings baked goods or drops off things I'll need when I get home, like applications for a passport and a student visa. To the outside world it will look as if I'm traveling back and forth from London the normal way. She watches me closely during her visits, concern etched on her brow.

On Monday afternoon she delicately broaches the subject of my mental health.

"Jaden, with all you've been through, I wonder if you would consider having a few sessions with a therapist—someone who can help you cope with your grief and assist you in adjusting to your new life?"

"I'll be okay," I tell her. "A few weeks at home is exactly what I need, and once we find Ralston, I know I'll feel much better."

Her brow softens, but her eyes remain doubtful. "Even though I'm a trained psychologist myself, when I separated from my first husband, I found it beneficial to speak with a grief counselor—a professional. She helped me sort through my feelings of sadness and guilt."

Her words strike a raw nerve. Even though my rational mind knows I'm not responsible for Ryder's death, part of me still believes I could have prevented it somehow. I replay over and over again those horrific last minutes before Ryder's fall. What could I have done differently? Maybe if I'd reacted more quickly we'd both be alive and well in Domerica right now ... or maybe we'd *both* be dead.

"Listen Narowyn, I appreciate your concern, but I'm going home soon. If I'm not feeling better by the time I return to Arumel, I'll arrange to see someone."

This seems to pacify her. "Very well, dear. But I will give you one piece of unsolicited advice—take it in small bites. Don't try to swallow the enormity of what has happened to you whole. It is too much for the human psyche to process all at once."

* * *

On Tuesday evening, Narowyn and I are in her office going over the final details for my trip when Captain Watterson and Urick walk in.

"We found your man, Ralston," Watterson says to me with a satisfied smile.

"You did? Fantastic! When can I see him?"

"Well, it's not all good news, I'm afraid. He's been partially disassembled. His limbs are missing. We don't even know what condition his components are in or if his memory module has been corrupted."

"What does that mean?" I ask.

"It means he may no longer be the Ralston you knew," Watterson says.

"Where is he?" Narowyn asks. "Are we in a position to acquire him?"

The captain rubs the back of his hand across his jaw. "He was transported two days ago to a remote automaton parts facility IUGA maintains on Earth Z772. It could be a bit of a tricky situation locating him. Urick and his team will go in tonight and evaluate the advisability of a rescue. If the automaton's no longer viable, we won't risk bringing him out, since what we're doing may not be considered exactly within our jurisdiction."

"Wait a minute. I want to go with you," I say.

"Out of the question." Narowyn replies. "You have no training for such a mission, and you have important business to take care of tomorrow."

"If someone's going to decide whether or not Ralston's worth rescuing, I want to be there," I say. "I'm the only one who can know if he's still himself."

Narowyn presses her lips together firmly, clearly wishing I wasn't always such a pain in the ass.

I change my tact and focus on Watterson. "Please take me, Captain. I promise I won't get in the way."

"It's Urick's mission," he says. "It's his call … assuming the chief approves."

We all turn to Urick who lurks unobtrusively in the corner.

He gazes at me a thoughtful moment. My eyes hold steady with his.

"She can come," he says.

"Thank you," I say quietly.

Narowyn exhales loudly and checks her watch. "We still have much to go over," she says with slight annoyance. "Your shift to Connecticut tomorrow needs to be specially orchestrated and carefully controlled by Dr. McDonald since you are traveling back in time."

"Fine, I'll get up as early as you like."

"All right. Then you'd best go now and get a uniform." She turns to Urick. "Jaden has no firearms training as yet, but she can handle a sword, and she's an expert in Tae Kwan Do. Please be careful, both of you."

"Thanks Narowyn," I say, following Urick to the door.

"Jaden, we'll reconvene at seven a.m., sharp," she says.

"Yes ma'am."

I hurry to keep up with Urick's long strides as we take the short hallway to the kitchen and exit through a back door. Once outside, Urick places a hand on my shoulder. "I'm taking you to the barracks." *Zzzt.*

A fraction of a second later, we're standing in what looks like a locker room.

"Oh," I say, a little shaken. "I thought we were walking."

"We have no time to waste." He shuffles through a closet of black uniforms. "Here, this should fit you." He holds out a hanger on which a plain, one-piece uniform identical to his is hung. "Change in there." He nods to a door with a woman symbol on it.

Inside the women's locker room, I quickly put on the uniform. It's close-fitting but made of light, stretchy fabric that gives with my

163

every movement. I drape my dress over the hanger and slip my feet back into my ballet flats.

Urick waits for me outside the door, holding a pair of black boots and a short sword in a scabbard. He squints at my shoes.

"You have large feet," he says, shoving the boots toward me.

"Uh, thanks." This guy's got as much personality as a bowl of warm spit. I kick off my flats and shove my feet inside the boots, then buckle the scabbard around my hips.

"The team has received its instructions," he says. "I don't have time to go over them again for you. Just follow my lead, and if I need your help, I'll ask for it."

"Yes, sir." I salute him stiffly.

He turns and strides down a dimly lit hallway, and I scamper along behind him. We enter a room that looks vaguely like a classroom. Several people in similar unadorned black uniforms are present inside. They all wear side arms instead of swords. I wonder if that means they're expecting a fight. When they see Urick, they gather around the long table at the head of the room.

"This is Miss Beckett," he says to the three men and two women standing at the table. "She is Ralston's master. She will help us determine his condition."

They stare at me. Some nod soberly. I haven't met any of them before. I consider taking issue with Urick's description of me as Ralston's *master*, but I sense these people don't give a crap about such subtle nuances.

The men look distinctly like special ops—tall, broad shouldered, closely cropped hair, hard expressions. The women are as different as night and day, but both gorgeous in a kick-ass way. One has blonde hair, clipped short on the sides, long and spiky on top. Her cheekbones are so high they seem to want to crowd her blue eyes right off her face. The other has skin dark as midnight, pale gray eyes, and long, dark hair pulled back into a cruel ponytail showcasing her perfect features.

Urick doesn't bother giving me their names. Instead, he goes to a shelf and takes down two boxes. "Security level is plus-five. We need gloves and mesh." He places the boxes on the table, and people reach inside pulling out gloves and things that look like black bags made out of mosquito netting.

I slip on a pair of stretchy fabric gloves—one size fits all—and take one of the mesh bags. "What's this for?" I ask.

"The facility has facial recognition security," the blonde woman says. "The mesh blocks the camera's ability to record features." She places the bag over her head and draws the mesh down to completely cover her face.

The rest of us do the same.

"This is our destination." Urick jots some numbers on a whiteboard, and we all flip open our TPD bracelets and plug in the coordinates.

"Are we ready?" Urick asks.

"Yes, sir," the team members say in unison.

"Let's go."

We click our bracelets and *Zzzt*.

The seven of us land simultaneously in front of a large security fence surrounding an enormous darkened warehouse.

"Search the perimeter first," Urick says.

Two piles of debris as tall as houses sit on a strip of land adjacent to the fence. "Roper, Travis, Nila, take the far pile," Urick says. Two men and the dark pony tail quietly jog off.

Urick removes an instrument from his belt and flips it on. The readout lights up, but I can't make out what it says. He studies it for a second and silently gestures for the rest of us to follow him. We stand at the foot of the junk heap. At first glance, the mound appears to be composed of a grisly assortment of human body parts. Closer inspection and tell-tale protruding wires reveal that they're actually robot limbs. I don't know how we'll ever find anything in this mess.

"Kai," Urick says to the guy standing next to me, "use your illumometer and you two go that way." Kai unclips a similar instrument from his belt and fires it up. He and the blonde woman inch their way around the pile. Kai swipes the instrument up and down over the debris as they go. Urick and I do the same walking in the opposite direction.

After we've gone several yards around the perimeter, the guy named Roper quietly appears next to Urick and whispers something to him.

He turns to me. "They found him. Let's go."

I latch onto Urick's arm. In an instant, we land next to the second scrap pile. It also consists mostly of worn out robot parts, but there's other stuff here as well—old shoes, soda cans, beat-up computers, and something that looks like it might have been a bicycle at one time.

My heart pounds low and hard as Roper leads us to an armless, legless torso that's been pulled away from the heap. It's clothed in a stained, white undershirt. The face is obscured by the darkness, so Urick holds his lighted instrument near the head to give me a better look. I move closer and push a wisp of hair away from the robot's forehead.

Oh my god, it's him! The sight of Ralston's battered face and broken body is like a kick to my gut. I crash down on both knees and raise the mesh covering my mouth a split second before vomiting violently into the grass.

Urick moves next to me and sweeps the hair away from my neck. He applies pressure to the base of my skull with his thumb and forefinger. The nausea quickly recedes, and he helps me to my feet.

"Him?" he asks quietly, tugging the mesh back down around my chin.

I nod.

Urick unclips a thin metal rod from the side of his hand-held instrument. He leans over Ralston and inserts the rod behind his ear.

After he presses a few buttons, Ralston's head begins to rock slightly. His eyes flutter and flash open. He stares blankly at the sky.

"Ralston?" I say crouching beside him. I graze his cheek with my fingertips. "Ralston, can you hear me?"

He blinks twice and rotates his head toward me. "Is that you, old girl?" His voice is reedy and feeble.

"Yes, it's me. We've come to rescue you."

His mouth forms a broken smile. "Not much of me worth saving, I'm afraid. But thank you, my dear."

I turn to Urick. "He sounds fine. Let's get the rest of him and go."

Urick shakes his head. "This is enough." He pushes a button on his polycom and summons the remainder of the team. They land beside us at the scrap heap.

"Found him," Urick says. "Time to go."

Roper and Travis lift Ralston from the ground, while Urick removes a nylon harness-looking thing from his belt. The men work quickly to strap Ralston's torso onto Urick's back.

"We'll shift as a team," he says to me. "Hold on to someone."

Urick's people gather behind him. The three men clamp their hands on Ralston's body. The rest of us grasp onto each other and the men. In an almost blinding flash of light—Z*zzt*—we land back inside the barracks once again.

The team efficiently unharnesses Ralston from Urick's back and places him on the long table. Seeing him in the stark light of the classroom is even more disturbing than finding him at that macabre body parts warehouse.

"What can we do with him in this kind of shape?" I ask,

suppressing another bout of nausea. "Why didn't we get his arms and legs? He can't function without them."

Urick focuses his golden eyes on me. "Miss Beckett, please change your clothes while I debrief my team." His voice is strained.

I get the impression Mr. Etiquette has just chastised me for speaking out of turn. "Okay, but I'll be right back. And I need to know what the next step is."

He doesn't respond, and the rest of the team stares at me like I'm an insolent brat. I skulk out the door and head back to the women's locker room.

I change back into my dress, rinse out my mouth with water, and finger comb my hair. After ten minutes or so, I figure Urick's had enough time to dismiss the others, so I find my way back to the classroom.

Urick's tilted back in a chair, hands clasped behind his head, feet up on the table next to what's left of Ralston. It strikes me as a disrespectful pose, and though my chest burns I don't comment. We never would've found Ralston if it hadn't been for this surly Viking.

I sit in the chair facing him, averting my eyes from the pathetic heap on the table. "Look Urick, I'm sorry if I embarrassed you in front of your team."

"I'm not that easily embarrassed." His eyes focus on some distant point in the room.

"Well, thanks for finding Ralston. I owe you a solid. What's that instrument you used?"

"An illumometer. It tracks imprints."

"Oh yeah, I heard about those. I think IUGA used one on me."

He continues to gaze ahead.

"So what about Ralston?" I say. "What happens now? Can we get him new arms and legs?"

"Not my issue. My assignment was locate and rescue."

"All righty, then." I push up out of the chair. "Is it okay if I leave him here until I figure out what my next step is?"

"Sit down." He aims his full golden stare at me. "Narowyn will be here in a few minutes. She'll decide what we do next."

"You told her we have him?"

He nods curtly.

I flop back down in the chair. *Oh joy!* I'm stuck here with the Mute Brute until Narowyn shows up.

We sit in uncomfortable silence until I can't stand it any longer. "So, Urick, where are you from originally?"

After an extended pause, he replies. "Earth M238, a country named Demonstadt."

"Asher told me it's a warring planet. What exactly does that mean?"

"It means a state of constant war exists among the major countries."

"Constant? You mean like there's never been peace?"

"Not for more than a month or two."

"But why? Why do the people put up with that?"

"It's all they've ever known. Entire national economies are driven by supplying the wages of war. The major world powers would collapse if peace persisted for any significant period of time."

"That's so bizarre. Were you a soldier, then?"

He unclasps his hands and leans forward. Before he can answer, or tell me to shut up, Narowyn walks in. "Where is he?" she asks.

We both stand and Urick gestures to the lump on the table.

She examines Ralston's mutilated torso. "Good lord, this is terrible."

My hopes plummet to the basement. "Is there anything we can do?" I ask.

She looks to Urick. "Have you checked his AIN?"

"Yes. The model's over forty years old."

She shakes her head. "And his memory module and processor are not damaged?"

Urick shrugs. "He recognized her right away. He formed coherent sentences. We won't know for sure until the techs check him out."

Narowyn turns her attention to me. "Jaden, it's late. You should try to get a good night's sleep for your journey tomorrow. We'll do everything we can here. The Automaton Identification Number indicates this model is very old. Replacement parts may not be available. Every effort will be made to locate them, but if we cannot, we may have to transplant his memory into a later model."

"What does that mean?" I ask.

"It means we'll restore him as best we can. Inside he'll be the same Ralston you've always known. But he may look a bit different on the outside. Do you trust me to handle this while you're away?"

"Yeah, as long as he's going to be okay. I mean, I don't care what he looks like if he's the same old Rals."

"That's all I need to hear. We'll do our best with what we have to work with." She rests a hand on my shoulder. "Get some rest now, dear, you look tired."

I start for the door, but Urick loudly clears his throat freezing me in my tracks.

"Uh, there is one other thing," he says.

"What is it?" Narowyn asks.

"The lower half of Miss Beckett's face may have accidentally been exposed." He gallantly neglects to mention it was because I barfed all over the place.

Narowyn's eyebrows pop up. "Oh dear. Well that may present a bit of a problem. I suppose we'll just have to deal with that if and when it arises. No sense concerning ourselves about it until then."

She waves me on. "I'll see you in the morning, Jaden. Don't worry about things here."

TWENTY-TWO

Back in my apartment, my nerves are still wound up tight from the night's little foray into covert operations. I scour my kitchen for something good to eat, since I lost my dinner on the ground outside the automaton facility. If there was ever an occasion for junk food, this is it. But people in Arumel are focused on eating healthy vegetarian fare, and so far I haven't come across anything resembling Doritos on this earth. I settle for a jar of peanut butter and a bag of cut-up veggies which I take with me to the living room.

Kicking off my shoes, I curl my legs under me on the couch and suck peanut butter off a celery stick, while I reflect on the night. Ralston's been rescued, even if a bit worse for wear, and I'm going home tomorrow to see my family and friends. For the briefest of moments, I experience a tiny glimmer of hope that I might feel happy again one day. But then Ryder's image flutters across my mind, and I'm drenched in sorrow once more.

"TV on," I say, and the television lights up. "Good evening, Jaden, the pleasant software assistant's voice says. "What would you care to watch?"

"Something happy."

"Movie or series?" she asks.

"Movie, and turn the volume to low." I snuggle into the pillows, and eventually the TV lulls me to sleep. I spend the night on the couch. Why bother climbing into bed? The emptiness of it only makes me feel lonelier.

In the morning, I shower and sort through the meager selections in my closet wondering what to wear for my journey home. It doesn't much matter since I'll have to change into my own clothes as soon as I arrive. I tug one of the non-descript sack dresses off its hanger and slip it on over my head.

Small shivers of excitement ripple down my arms when I think about seeing my dad, my brother, and my best friend, Liv. I pull a colorfully embroidered cross-body bag that I bought at the Urban Bazaar from my dresser top. My polycom is already inside, and I tuck the sketch of Ryder into the zippered compartment before slipping the strap over my head. On my way out the door, I turn off all the lights. Our apartment doors have no locks, which still seems a little strange to me, but I guess it's a sign of trust and safety inside the Chateau.

Narowyn's already working at her desk when I show up at seven on the dot. "Come in," she says smiling. "I've just received some excellent news."

I take a seat facing her. "What is it?"

"Last night the IGC Court granted our request for an emergency injunction and temporary restraining order against IUGA. As we expected, the agency denied any involvement in the violence that took place in Domerica. We presented enough evidence, however, to persuade the court that we have a viable case against them."

She passes a copy of the court order to me and summarizes its contents. "Based on the preliminary papers we filed, the court has ordered that neither IUGA nor anyone working on its behalf may maintain a presence in Madison, Connecticut while you are there. In addition, they and their agents may not approach you or have you under surveillance in any way while you are in Arumel City."

"That's great. IUGA must be completely pissed that I'm still alive. What do you think their next move will be?"

"I assume they'll lay low until this matter has been fully resolved by the court. It would be too risky to do otherwise. The hearing on our lawsuit should be scheduled soon. I can't imagine they'd dare take any action prior to the hearing."

She opens a fat file on her desk. "By the way, this order means your physics teacher will no longer be employed by your school when you return."

"Good. He was kind of a hard grader." Something else occurs to me. "Hey, he still has my cell phone. Is there a way we can get that back?"

"Well I can petition to have your personal property returned to you, but it may take the court a few weeks to rule. Since you're going home today, you may prefer to purchase a new one."

"Oh man, that sucks. Those things cost a minor fortune."

She smiles indulgently. "Perhaps I haven't explained matters thoroughly yet, Jaden, but you needn't worry about money now. You have access to all the funds you need, or in this case, want." She pulls a thin blue leather case from her file and extends it across the desk. "Here is your banking information and cash card."

I open the case and inside I find information relating to a checking account in England and a savings account in Arumel, along with a shiny new ATM card. "Barclays?" I say, reading the logo at the top.

"Yes one of the largest banks in England. Since, for outward appearances, you're going to school there, it made the most sense. Your card will work at cash machines in the U.S. and all around the world, really."

"We've deposited fifty-thousand British Pounds Sterling in your checking account and one hundred thousand Confederation Dollars, known as CDs, in savings. That should last you for a while, but most of us also carry a decent amount of local currency with us when we travel inter-universally." She passes me a letter-sized envelope. "Inside you'll find five one-hundred pound notes and ten U.S. one-

174

hundred dollar bills. Upon your return, you'll begin receiving a salary."

The size of the numbers she just threw at me makes my mouth go dry. "Wow, thanks," is all I can manage to squeak out.

"You're most welcome, dear."

Next, she takes a small accordion file from her larger file and slides it across the desk. "This is all your paperwork regarding Oxford University. Envelopes with the proper postmarks are inside—one congratulating you on your acceptance and another outlining your financial aid package. I've also included the address of your flat in Oxford along with photos and keys."

Narowyn closes her file and rests her elbows on the desk. "Now, do you have any questions for me?"

My head swims with all these new details, and I'm feeling a little like James Bond with the polycom inside my purse, a fat white envelope stuffed with cash, and a file full of falsified documents.

"I think you've pretty much covered it. What about Asher? Is he all set?"

"Yes, we went over everything last night while you were on your mission. Oh, and in that regard, we've already quietly sent out inquiries regarding replacement parts for your Ralston. Asher will provide me periodic updates on your stay in Connecticut, and I'll keep him posted of our progress on Ralston's repairs."

She rises from her chair. "You have your polycom should you need to reach any of us in an emergency, and I advise you to wear your TPD at all times. It's vitally important."

"I will." I gather up my bank case, the accordion file, and my envelope of moolah and stuff them inside my bag.

"Asher and Dr. McDonald are waiting for you in her lab. God speed, dear." She kisses both cheeks.

"Thanks for everything, Narowyn. See you in a few weeks."

I locate Dr. McDonald's laboratory on the first floor and knock lightly. A grinning Asher swings open the door. "Hey are you ready for this?"

"I guess so," I say.

A woman wearing a white lab coat and a strange set of goggles, whirls around to face me, and immediately staggers backward.

"Whoa!" she says, ripping off the goggles. "You gotta warn people when you walk into a room."

"Excuse me?"

Asher gives a small chuckle. "Jade, this is Doctor Lucrezia McDonald. Doctor this is …"

"Ah, this gal's corona has already introduced her. That's quite a nimbus you got going on there." She wipes her hand on the side of her lab coat and extends it to me.

"I'm sorry, I'm a little confused," I say, shaking her hand.

"I just mean your energetic imprint. Narowyn warned me yours is pretty intense. Like supernova status. Here put these on." She shoves her weird goggles into my hand, and I do as she asks, positioning them over my eyes.

"Now take a gander at Asher," she says. When I do, he appears to be glowing with a rich yellow light.

"Oh, cool. You look like an angel," I say.

"Now look at your own arms," she says.

I glance down at my outstretched arms. Dancing flames of orange and red light swirl around my hands and arms, leaping and licking like something alive.

"Yikes!" I shake out my hands, but the shimmering light remains. "That's so creepy." I yank off the goggles and rub my arms. "What is that stuff?"

Dr. McDonald laughs heartily. "It's only light energy. Everyone has it. But for some reason you seem to have more than your share. I'd love to know why." She studies me with a squinting gaze, then briskly claps her hands. "No time for that today, though. We have work to do. May I have your bracelet, please?"

I slip off my TPD and give it to her. "What are you going to do with that?"

She carries the bracelet to a table that holds a microscope, a giant suspended magnifying glass, and a number of other instruments most of which I don't recognize. "Oh, I need to make a few adjustments for this little excursion back in time."

Holding the bracelet behind the magnifying glass, she picks up a miniscule screwdriver and pops off the back plate. "Time travel is an art really. The folks at IUGA have made some strides, but their methods are still rather primitive. And the Garugians, forget it. They don't have a clue."

She gingerly extracts a tiny circuit board and places it under the microscope. "Course it's easier for Transcenders. We don't have to fool with all the machines and other falderal associated with inter-dimensional travel."

Taking a small instrument from the table, she says, "This should only take a sec. We already adjusted Asher's."

Asher and I watch in silence as she works.

"Okie dokie. That should do it." After replacing the circuit board in the bracelet and securing the plate in back, she opens the medallion on top and punches a few virtual keys.

"All set. You two come with me." She hands me my bracelet.

I snap it on, and Asher and I follow the slightly eccentric Dr. McDonald to a darkened room in the back of her laboratory.

"Stand up against the wall there." She gestures to one side of the room, and we position our backs to the wall. "This is going to shake up your system a little, so as soon as you land, pop this little pill." She

177

hands each of us a tiny blue pill. "It'll settle your stomach and stabilize your inner ear. But don't go swimming for at least an hour." She chuckles, and I can't tell if she's joking.

"Brace yourselves. When I say *three,* click your latches." She holds up her fingers. "One, two, three."

Asher and I simultaneously click the latches on our bracelets and *swhoosh!*

The feeling is completely different from the usual exhilarating shift through dimensions. Instead of the incandescent streaming stars sensation, it feels as though my entire body is being powerfully sucked through a long, black tube the size of a hotdog. A dark, unholy terror begins to build inside me, but within a few seconds, my feet hit solid ground.

The world swings violently to and fro. My lungs feel flattened, and I drop down on all fours gasping for air. Asher's cool hand touches the back of my neck, and his fingers place a small pill between my lips.

"Swallow this," he says hoarsely. Grasping my shoulders, he eases me down to the floor. I lie on my back, eyes clamped shut.

In two or three minutes, I'm able to open my eyes without feeling as if I'm falling off the edge of sanity. Plain white ceiling doesn't help me get my bearings. The opaque globular light fixture looks familiar, though. *Ah, home.* The thought gels in my mind. *I made it home.*

Turning my head to the right, I see Asher lying on the floor next to me—hands crossed over his belly, face waxen, eyes closed. "Asher?" I say softly.

He groans. "Can I trouble you for that other pill?"

"Oh sorry." I dig the pill out of my pocket. "Here it is." He opens his mouth and I place it on his tongue.

"Thanks, Ash. I really appreciate—"

"Don't talk," he mutters.

"Okay. Sorry."

Gathering myself into a sitting position, I prop my back against the couch and survey the room. Something seems a little off, but I can't put my finger on it. The clock on the DVR reads 11:10. I'm not completely certain of the time Ralston and I left here, but I believe it was around eleven on Saturday morning, exactly thirty days ago. If everything went the way it was supposed to, we've arrived back here on the same day, just a few minutes after my departure.

"Are we in the right place?" Asher asks. His eyes are open, and he looks a little less like day-old oatmeal.

"Yeah, this is my house, but something's different. Or maybe it's that my brain was just squished down to the size of a peanut." I raise both hands to my head to make sure it's back to its normal size.

Asher props up on his elbows. "That was one of the more unpleasant experiences of my life."

"Ugh, same here. Hey, do we need to do that again when it's time to go back to Arumel?"

"No, everything adjusts if we're going the other way. We'll end up in real time."

"*Whew*. That's good to hear. Are you ready to stand up yet?"

"Yeah, I think I'm fine now." Using the coffee table for support he hauls himself to his feet and offers his hand to help me up.

I spot my laptop on the table. "The time of day seems about right, but let's check the date on my computer." I open up the lid and the screen lights up. I type in my password but instead of my home page, my last Google search comes up.

"Zambia?" Asher says. "Were you planning an exotic vacation?"

I quickly exit out—as if I needed another reminder of Ryder and the constant throbbing in my heart. "No. I was searching for something, but I won't be needing that information after all. Looks like we're here on the correct date."

Asher pulls out a chair. "Mind if we sit for a minute? I'm still a little woozy from the trip."

"Sure." I rest my elbows on the table and prop my chin on my hands.

"So, what's in Zambia that you won't be needing anymore?"

I sigh. "I'd just located Ryder's *mirror* on this earth when Ralston showed up to whisk me back to Arumel. He's doing volunteer work in Zambia, but he lives here in Connecticut. I don't know what I'll do if I ever run into him. It would kill me."

"That's not very likely, especially since you'll be living in Arumel."

"I hope you're right. This *mirror* stuff can really screw with your head. I guess Narowyn tried to warn me."

"She's usually right about those things."

"How about you?" I ask. "Does anyone in your family have a *mirror* in Arumel?"

He shrugs. "Don't know. Never bothered to find out. If I saw one of their *mirrors* on the street, I guess it would be weird. But really it'd just be someone who bore a strong resemblance to my family member."

"What about your father? I mean, he was killed when you were so young. Haven't you ever wanted to see if he's alive in Arumel?"

He shakes his head. "Even if he was, it wouldn't be my dad—the man who raised me. I wouldn't have anything to say to him."

I chew on my lower lip for a minute. "I guess you're right. Although in some ways I felt closer with my Domerican father than I do with my real dad. He was more open and seemed to be a more authentic version of himself. You know what I mean?"

"Not really. Do you think he would have been that way had he known you're not his real daughter?"

"Who knows? I almost told him before I left, but I couldn't bring myself to do it, so I guess I must've believed it would make a difference. It was just so hard not to get caught up with all of them. I was living an illusion and telling myself it was real. I know that now."

"You were sort of forced into pretending to be the princess." He rubs my shoulder reassuringly.

"Yeah, but I've changed my approach now. I hope none of my family members have *mirrors* in Arumel. And, if they do, I don't want to know about it. Ever."

"Not even Ryder?"

"Especially not him. I couldn't go through all that again." The intense grief tries to claw its way up my throat and out into the open, but I shove it down hard. I'm home, and I'm going to enjoy the short time I have here.

"At least you don't have to worry about running into your own *mirror* in Arumel City, like I do."

"You have a *mirror* in Arumel?" I'd never thought about that before.

He nods smiling. "A lot of Transcenders do. Some people have actually met their *mirrors* and become friends, but I studiously avoid bumping into mine."

"That would be so bizarre," I say, shaking my head. Then something clicks in my brain. "Hey, I think I know what's different here. That rocker's usually in the other corner." I point to a wooden, cane-bottom chair.

Asher frowns. "Do you know for sure where it was when you left?"

I close my laptop. "Hell, I barely know my own name at the moment. Everything else looks the same, so it's probably just me. I'm going to go get changed and put these papers away. Then we're going

181

to check out your new digs."

Asher stretches his back and gets up from the table. "Okay, but when will your dad be home?"

"Not for hours. Help yourself to anything you want in the kitchen. The powder room's down the hall. I'll be back in a few minutes."

TWENTY-THREE

I've never been so happy to see my own bedroom. I throw open the door to my closet and search through my clothes. Everything looks fresh and new to me after being away for so long. I find my prettiest sundress and slip it on. It caresses me like an old friend. I shove my feet into my favorite purple flip-flops with the crystals on top, and smooth down my hair before rejoining Ash in the living room. He doesn't comment on my outfit, but I can tell by the way his eyes shine that he approves.

"Ready?" I ask. "Do you know where this place is?"

"Apparently, it's just around the corner." He tosses a key ring in the air and catches it with one hand. "Follow me."

The day smells gloriously like sunshine and new grass and home. We amble along the sidewalk checking numbers on the adjacent townhouses. "Twenty-six, twenty-five, this is it," Asher says, turning up the short walkway. He unlocks the white wooden door that looks exactly like all the other front doors in the neighborhood and we step inside.

The tangy scent of the musty air assaults my nose.

"Unbelievable!" Asher says, surveying the living room. "Who lived here? Hobbits?"

A small laugh escapes my lips before I have time to clamp my hand over my mouth. I've seen worse decorating, but only in a frat house. The carpet is putrid green, and the walls are painted a dark maroon. The furniture can only be described as early Brady Bunch, and not in a good way.

"I don't think I ever saw anyone come or go from here," I say. "It smells like the place hasn't been lived in for quite a while."

I trundle along behind Asher as he wanders through the other rooms shaking his head and groaning. "Oh hell no." He pulls a fuzzy zebra spread off the bed in the master bedroom.

"C'mon, Ash, it's only for a few weeks. Man up."

He glares at me. "I'd have nightmares sleeping under that thing. Gutting the place is probably out of the question, but at a minimum it needs fresh paint, and carpet, and some new furnishings."

"Just when do you plan to accomplish all that?"

"While you're at school, obviously. Now, help me open some windows and get the air circulating."

While I unlatch and raise the windows, Asher tugs the sheets off the bed. The mattress doesn't look too bad. No suspicious stains or crawly bugs.

"We'll need to buy some new bedding for tonight, and a coffee maker, and a few supplies," he says. "Is there someplace we can get all that?"

"Yeah. There's a Target not too far from here. Let me get my wallet, and I'll drive us. Maybe we can stop at the Apple store and pick up a new phone for me."

"Sure." Ash piles the dirty linens on top of the washer in the small laundry closet before we head out the door.

As we approach my house, I catch sight of someone standing on my front porch, bent over to the side, peering into the living room window. A flash of platinum blonde hair makes my heart leap for joy.

"Liv!" I run to my best friend and throw my arms around her neck.

She gives me a brisk one-armed hug before laying into me. "Where have you been? I've been calling and calling all morning. I thought you'd forgotten our shopping date."

Shopping date? That seems like lifetimes ago.

"Sorry, Liv." I launch into a lame explanation when Asher steps onto the porch, hands tucked inside his jeans' pockets, signature sexy smile at full wattage. Liv forgets I'm alive.

She does a quick up and down scan of the deliciously hot package that just crossed into her zone of conquest. In a heartbeat, she seamlessly shifts from *pissed-off pit-bull* to full *shameless vixen*.

"Oh, so this is what you've been doing." She holds out a long-fingered, perfectly manicured hand for Asher. "I'm Liv, Jaden's best friend, and you are?"

Asher shakes her hand. "Asher Steele. I'm new in the neighborhood."

She wheels around on me thrusting out her lower lip. "You could have at least answered my calls and told me what you were up to."

"I lost my phone," I say. "And, to tell the truth, I had forgotten about our shopping trip, so I promised to take Ash out to get some supplies for his new place. He doesn't have a car."

"Great!" she says, beaming a full-frontal smile all over Asher. "He can come with us. It's always nice to have a man's opinion when searching for sexy new party dresses."

"I don't need a party dress, Liv. It's just Senior Celebration. Plus, I'm sure Asher's got a lot to do this afternoon. He's not completely moved in yet."

"Every girl needs a new dress for her graduation," Asher says. "I don't mind going as long as we can stop for supplies later. It'll give me a chance to see some of the town."

I flash him a *thanks a lot* scowl. The last thing I want to do is go party dress shopping. "Okay. Come in for a minute while I grab my wallet."

"I'll go with you," Liv says, following me downstairs to my room. When we step inside, she shuts the door and grasps me by the forearms, buzzing like neon. "OMG where did you find him! He's the most gorgeous man I've ever seen. Those eyes are incredible, and that mouth. *Sa-woon!* Have you kissed him yet?"

"I told you, he just moved in around the corner. He's a nice guy."

"Nice guy? Sweetie, are you sick or something?" She lays a cool hand against my forehead. "That man is smoking hot. You need to stake a claim on that before someone else does."

"I just like him as a friend." I snag my wallet from the dresser. "Let's go. I want to be back early. I have some stuff to talk over with Dad before his date tonight."

"Yeah, like your upcoming wedding to the new neighbor." She giggles, but the reference to a wedding scrapes the open wound in my heart. It takes all my will power not to break down. I turn my back to Liv and pretend to touch up my lip gloss in the mirror. If she only knew what I've been through.

"I'll meet you upstairs in a sec. I need to get one more thing," I say, swallowing down my tears.

"Okay, but hurry. I might just steal Mr. Tall Drink of Water away if you take too long."

Once she's out of the room, I pull my embroidered purse out from under the bed. Fishing out the white cash envelope, I remove five of the crisp, new Benjamins and stash them in my wallet. Narowyn didn't say what I should use the money for, so I guess it's up to me. Maybe a little retail therapy will make me feel better.

Liv takes her own car, and we agree to meet at Asiye's Boutique in the heart of town. The place is a treasure trove of awesome evening wear, and Liv is as animated as a five-year-old choosing a new Easter dress. She flits from one rack of bright, glittery gowns to the next. "Oh I love this!" she cries, or "What do you think about this color for me?" or "Sexy or slutty?"

In no time, she has an armload of gem-colored frocks and two sales ladies trailing her to the dressing rooms. Liv and I have known each other since second grade and even back then she had an extraordinary flair for fashion and a zest for spending money.

Her joyful enthusiasm is heartening, but even so, I can't seem to muster the desire to try on anything. My heart is in mourning, and besides, none of these dresses can compare to what I had in Domerica.

Asher seats himself in a comfortable armchair near the dressing area, stretching out his long legs and crossing his ankles. He picks up a magazine from the table and begins leafing through it. I wander over and slouch down in the chair on the other side of the table.

"Can't find anything you like?" he asks.

"Nah. I'm just not into it today."

"Don't you want something new for graduation or your senior party?"

I shrug. "Not really. I wish Liv could have seen my closet back in Domerica. I wonder what they'll do with all those beautiful gowns now that I'm gone, and Mother's gone. I wonder if the gown room even survived the explosions." Dark thoughts of Domerica and the chaos that might be occurring there creep into my head like parasitic worms eating away at the pleasant afternoon.

Asher's translucent eyes seem to read my thoughts. He closes his magazine. "Wait here," he says and disappears into the store.

Liv prances out of the fitting room in her first dress—a short, tight, navy lace number that shows off her killer body to its best advantage. She's always had a knack for transforming otherwise sensible men into panting piles of dumbass, but this dress will definitely set more than a few IQ's diving.

Her face falls when she notices her audience has dwindled to one. "Where's the Man of Steele? I want his opinion on this."

"He said he'd be right back," I tell her. "But personally I think it hurls."

Her mouth twitches preparing to spew some sass my way, but instead she laughs and admires herself in the three-way mirror. "Honestly? I look *amazing* in this dress."

"Yes you do, so why do you need anyone else's opinion?"

"I don't know. I guess I just like to hear it from a man."

That tickles my gag reflex. "You did not just say that."

Asher walks up carrying a few dresses. "Whoa," he says when he sees Liv. "You can stop right there. That one gets my vote."

She grins and does a couple of hip sashays for him. "What've you got there?"

"Oh, some things for Jade to try on. I tired her out working on my place, so I volunteered to find a few things for her."

"That's so sweet," Liv gushes. "Go try them on Jade. But you," she points a shellacked nail at Asher, "stay right where you are. I have more to show you." It sounds like a promise. She scampers back to the dressing room.

Asher holds up a gorgeous silver dress for me. "You'd look hot in this." He raises his eyebrows. "Try it on? Please."

Truthfully, the dresses he chose are kind of cute, and I'm touched by his thoughtfulness. "Okay. Give 'em here."

Liv spends the next hour modeling for Ash and anyone else who happens by the dressing area. In the meantime, I try on the dresses he picked out for me in the privacy of my little fitting room.

The silver dress is a bit too sexy and festive for my current frame of mind. Next, I try on a short black sheath with a sweetheart neckline. It looks nice on my frame and meshes more with my mood. If I have to go to a party at least this dress will allow me to express my mourning for Ryder in a discreet way. I decide it's perfect, and I skip trying on anything else.

Liv settles on two dresses—the navy lace for Senior Celebration and a more conservative gray silk for the graduation ceremony. We carry our dress bags out into the bright sunshine.

"Now all we need are shoes and purses and maybe some long earrings," Liv says. "Let's hit Caio Bella and see what they have."

"It's getting kind of late," I tell her. "Asher's got to get some bedding and supplies from Target, and I still have to pick up a new phone."

She screws up her mouth. "Oh, okay, you go take care of that stuff. I'm going to look for accessories for us. If I see anything to die for, I'll snag it for you."

"All right, but nothing too expensive." I fully expected her to bail on us. She's not exactly the Target type.

"Call me when you get your phone." She tosses a careless arm around my neck and kisses my cheek. "Are you okay?" She asks in a semi-concerned tone. "You seem a little down."

"Everything's good. Just tired from studying for APs and all."

"You study too hard," she scolds. "We've got partying to do! Nice to meet you Asher. Hope I get to see more of you," she says, a trace of suggestion in her voice.

"Likewise," Asher says.

Target's crowded as usual on Saturday afternoon, but we fill a cart with sheets, towels, and kitchen supplies and wait in one of the endless lines.

For once, there's no line at the Apple store, and Asher and I both purchase new iPhones.

"You'll have to show me how to work this thing," Asher says back in the car, eyeing the thick instruction booklet.

"I will. It's pretty simple. You'll love it. There're lots of cool apps you can get for it too."

"Apps?"

"Never mind. I'll show you."

Dad's car is in the driveway when we pull up to my house. I'm anxious to see him. "You ready to meet my dad?" I get my dress from the back seat while Asher gathers his Target bags.

"Sure. You've already been subjected to my family. I'm looking forward to it."

We drop our bags near the stairs in the living room.

"Dad?" I call.

"In here, sweetheart."

We follow his voice to the kitchen. My heart nearly leaps out of my chest when I see him standing at the counter pouring himself a smoothie. Although he's in his usual green hospital scrubs, the rest of him looks like my Domerican father, close-cropped beard and all.

"Father?"

He looks up. "Hey, too old now to call me Dad?"

It's definitely Dad's voice, but he did *not* have that beard when I left.

"Uh, no. Sorry. This is our new neighbor, Asher Steele." Dad and Asher shake hands.

"He's renting the place around the corner."

"Oh yeah? Welcome to the neighborhood, Asher. Where're you from?"

"Boston," Ash says without blinking an eye. "I have a summer internship with Sikorsky before finishing up my degree at Northeastern."

"Ah, good school. When do you graduate?"

"Next spring."

"Well, I hope you enjoy our little hamlet. It's quite a change from Boston."

"Yes it is. Thanks, Mr. Beckett."

I'm completely thrown by Dad's altered appearance, and I stammer a little. "Um, I know you're going out tonight. But I was wondering if you're going to be around tomorrow. I have some, uh, college stuff to discuss with you."

"Yes. I actually have a day off tomorrow. First one in three weeks. Lisa and I plan to catch a movie in the afternoon, but I'll be here all morning." He cups my chin in his hand and raises my face to his. "Anything wrong, sweetheart?"

"No, no. Nothing's wrong, but … well, let's just talk tomorrow."

"All right." He checks his watch. "I need to get ready for my date. You'll find chicken, pasta, and some leftover salad in the fridge for dinner."

"That's great, Dad. Is it okay if Ash stays?"

"Sure. Just don't be up too late. You've got exams next week. Got to keep up that GPA or Yale may rescind their offer." He winks and heads for the stairs.

I whirl around to Asher. "Something weird's going on," I whisper. "My dad does not have a beard."

From the hallway Dad calls, "Oh, and Jade?"

"Yeah, Dad?"

"Remember to feed the cat."

"Uh. Sure thing."

I clutch Asher's arm. "And we don't have a cat."

"Are you sure, Jade? You're not just shaken up by the time travel, are you?"

"Ash, I think I'd remember if I had a pet."

He makes a little circuit through the kitchen scanning the floor. Inside the laundry room door, he bends down and comes up holding a white porcelain bowl with *Brady* printed on the side between two painted paw prints.

"Brady? He named the cat after Tom Brady?" I say. "Oh man, Ash, I don't know what's going on, but we need to contact Narowyn. Something's terribly wrong."

"Don't worry about it," he says. "I'll go back to my place and try to get her on the polycom. Dr. McDonald showed me how to do it. It's a little tricky because of the time element. If I can't reach her, we'll have to go back together. I can't risk leaving you here alone, especially when we don't know where *here* is."

"Okay, but hurry. This is creeping me out."

TWENTY-FOUR

Dad kisses me goodbye before leaving for his date. It's uncanny, but he seems exactly like himself—only with facial hair. I'm too nervous to sit still, so I remove a few things from the fridge and begin preparations for dinner. I put the water on for the pasta and take a sauté pan from the cabinet for the chicken breasts.

Asher appears in the kitchen doorway as I'm drizzling olive oil in the pan. "Did you get her?" I ask.

"Yep. I have some answers. Turn that off, and let's sit down for a minute. I'll explain the whole thing to you."

I switch off the burners, wipe my hands on a kitchen towel, and join Asher on the couch.

"So what's up?" I ask. "Do we need to go back and try again?"

"Narowyn says *no*. According to her we're just experiencing a temporary cosmic wrinkle."

"What's that supposed to mean?"

"She says it's a phenomenon that occurs occasionally in time travel. You can—"

"*Yeow!*" I squeal as a ginger-colored ball of fur lands lightly in my lap. The feline intruder doesn't seem to notice he's scared the stuffing out of me. Purring loudly, he rubs affectionately against my neck.

Asher chuckles softly. "This must be Brady." He runs a hand over the cat's sleek head. Brady leans into his touch.

I hold him out and study his face. Kind of cute. The second I let go of him he hops to the floor and scuttles off to the kitchen.

"Dinner's going to be late tonight," I call after him, "and don't get into my chicken." Turning back to Ash, I say, "Okay so you were about to explain this comic wrinkle thing to me."

"Right. Apparently we landed in the correct existence. Narowyn confirmed that with Dr. McDonald. But we're just a shade off center. That's why everything seems normal with just a few subtle exceptions. It has something to do with quantum physics and the fact that all possibilities exist at any given time. What we're seeing are shadows along the edges. The slight variations are the decisions that could have gone either way."

"I'm not sure I understand. So at some point my dad considered growing a beard, but decided against it? And what we're seeing is what might have been?"

"Exactly. He must have thought about getting a cat, too."

"I asked to get one last year, but he said *no*."

"Well, in a discarded scenario he obviously said *yes*."

"All right so what do we do to fix it?"

"Nothing. Narowyn says we just go with it, and eventually, it'll straighten itself out. According to her, it's impossible to ride the edges for any significant period of time, because the universe pulls you back to the center. It's like gravity. Anyway, she claims we'll be back on track in no time."

A shiver passes through me. "It's just so weird. What happens if we get stuck in this shadow land? I mean what about my real life?"

He pushes a limp strand of hair away from my forehead. "I don't

194

think that's going to happen. We should give it a little more time."

The touch of Asher's fingertips on my skin, feels uncomfortably intimate. I know he didn't mean anything by brushing the hair out of my eyes, but I spring to my feet.

"Okay then. We'll just wait it out. Come help with dinner, and let's see what that cat's up to."

"Just one other thing," he says. "Narowyn sent a couple of people to keep an eye on you, but they haven't located us yet, since we're kind of in *no man's land*. She wants us to be extra careful until things are back to normal."

"She told me she didn't think IUGA would try anything here since the court issued its restraining order."

"Apparently Captain Watterson picked-up some intelligence that IUGA's director is really pissed about the screw-up in Domerica and about the court's order. We just need to be super cautious."

"Fine, but if the Transcenders can't find us, I doubt IUGA can either."

He shrugs. "You may be right."

We busy ourselves in the kitchen. Our chicken and pasta meal turns out to be pretty tasty, thanks to some fresh basil I clipped from the plant on the window sill and Asher's impromptu pesto sauce. Gotta love a guy who cooks.

After the cat is fed and the dishwasher loaded, we schlep the Target bags over to Asher's place and make up his bed with the fresh linens.

He brews some coffee, and we talk over the day. "You'd better call Liv tonight before you turn in," he says. "She obviously doesn't like being ignored."

"That's putting it mildly. She's been my best friend since forever, and it was nice spending time with her today because I really missed her, but I feel like a big gulf has opened up between us. I took a sharp turn onto a different road, and now I have to keep all this stuff from her. She used to be the one I talked to about everything."

"Yeah, I get it. Arumel's about the only place I don't have to pretend," he says.

"Have you ever thought about telling your family you're a Transcender?" I ask.

"Nope. Mom would think it has something to do with the devil. Amber would just be pissed that I got the bonus DNA and she didn't. Anyway it'd be too hard to explain."

I snort a small laugh. "I hear ya. Every time I visualize telling Liv about Domerica and about Ryder or about being a Transcender, I realize it would be a disaster. I wish I had someone to talk to, though."

He lays his hand over mine. "You can talk to me, you know. About anything." His eyes are soft and sincere, but I can't make out if there's something more than friendship underlying his offer.

I withdraw my hand. "Thanks Ash. You're a good friend."

"Hey, why don't I stay at your place tonight, to be on the safe side? Your dad will never have to know."

"That's so sweet, but I'm looking forward to being in my own room tonight." *Alone.* "I could use your help in the morning, though. This Oxford thing's going to be a tough sell for Dad."

"Right, okay then, let me walk you home. And, Jade, don't worry about your dad, we'll figure out a way to win him over."

Back in my room, I change into my ratty old pajama pants and a gray tank top. I sit cross-legged on the bed and slide my embroidered bag over. Rifling through the things stashed inside, I locate all the Oxford information and stack it on top of my dresser, for the morning. Next, I take out the blue leather Barclays bank case. A shimmering ball of warmth forms deep in my belly as I thumb through the information and realize that I'm semi-loaded. According to Narowyn, I'll never have to worry about money again. That's a good thing, and I mentally add it to my gratitude list.

Closing the bank case and tucking it back in the bag, I stare for a moment at the zipper compartment. I conduct a little mental tussle with myself before unzipping it and reaching for the next item. I know it's probably not in my best interest, but whether I want to admit it or not, it's the reason I opened the bag in the first place.

Tears trickle down my cheeks as I carefully withdraw the folded sketch of Ryder. "I miss you so much, love," I whisper to the small square of paper. The sight of his eyes and mouth, so faithfully captured by Princess Jaden, crushes my heart. "I'll never forget you, I swear."

Slipping the paper beneath my pillow, I press my face to the soft cotton case that smells so familiar. The tears I've held inside all day are finally allowed to flow freely, and I cry myself to sleep.

* * *

Dad sleeps-in late in the morning. Being that it's Sunday and his day off I guess he's entitled, but I'm nervous as a double espresso. I wish he'd get up so we can get this over with.

I spread out the Oxford materials on the coffee table, and Asher and I rehearse what I'm going to say several times.

"Got anything to eat around here?" Asher asks. He's on his second cup of coffee, and I haven't offered him any sustenance at all. My stomach's a turbulent acid lake, so the thought of food hadn't entered my mind.

"I'm sorry, Ash. Let's fix some breakfast. Maybe the smell of frying bacon will get Dad out of bed."

"You know you're going to have to give him a few minutes to wake up before you hit him with all this."

"Yeah, yeah. I'll let him eat first. That ought to put him in a good mood. Let me see if we have any of those refrigerated cinnamon rolls. He loves those."

I open the fridge and find the blue cylinder of dough in the door. Each time I make these I swear I'm not going to eat any because of the generous helpings of sugar and chemicals concealed inside each decadent swirl, but the smell never fails to override my good judgment.

Ash and I are a great team in the kitchen once again. Watching him expertly flip the hash browns to crisp on the opposite side, I feel a surge of affection for him. He could be my best friend in Arumel if it wasn't for my sneaking suspicion that he wants more from me. I know I'll have to confront that issue sooner or later, but my plate's overflowing as it is. So, it's going to have to wait.

Brady the cat rubs against our legs as we finish setting the table. A few minutes later, we hear Dad padding down the stairs. He's surprised not only by the lavish breakfast spread on the table, but also by Asher's repeat appearance in our home.

"Well, what have we here?" he asks running a hand over his bed-head.

"Oh hey, Dad. I … we made breakfast for you."

He scratches his whiskered chin and nods at Asher. "You haven't been here all night, have you?" I can tell he's only half-joking.

"Nah, I got here about an hour ago. Jaden kicked me out early last night but said I could come back for breakfast if I knew how to cook hash browns."

Dad's eyes light up. "We have hash browns?"

"And cinnamon rolls," I say, holding up the plate of frosted pastries.

"Let's eat!" Dad takes his chair at the head of the table and begins filling his plate. "Jade, do you mind getting me a cup of coffee?"

"Coming right up."

Breakfast passes pleasantly. Asher asks Dad about his work at the hospital. Dad shares a few funny stories of his days as an ER nurse, before he moved over to Cardiology. Brady begs for food under the table, and Dad slips him a few nibbles of bacon.

After we've eaten our fill, Dad clears up his plate and announces he's heading upstairs to shower.

"Wait a sec. I have something important to discuss with you. Remember?"

"Oh yeah. Sorry sweetheart. Something about college?"

"Yes. Come into the living room, I want to show you some stuff."

Dad and I sit on the sofa facing the coffee table. Asher perches in an armchair across from us. The colorful brochure of Oxford catches Dad's eye and he picks it up.

"Oxford University?" he asks. "You thinking of some kind of summer program?"

"Uh, no. I'm thinking I may want to go to Oxford instead of Yale for college."

He laughs mildly. "Isn't that a bit unrealistic, sweetheart? For starters, you haven't even applied. But England? It's so far away. What put this idea into your head?" His eyes flicker to Asher, like maybe he's the culprit.

"Mrs. Colgate, one of the placement counselors at school, told me about a new program Oxford started at the Rothermere American Institute." Ash and I made that up earlier this morning. "Anyway they're looking for American students and she encouraged me to apply. And, well … they accepted me."

"What! When did all this happen? You didn't mention it to me." Brady chooses that moment to hop on Dad's lap and rub up against his terry bathrobe. "Bad timing, buddy," Dad says, setting him on the floor.

"Jade, you can't be serious. Oxford University?" He shakes his head slowly. "I'm sorry, sweetheart, but I could never afford to send you there. The only reason you're able to go to Yale is the package of loans and grants they put together for you."

"But Dad, Oxford's paying for everything, even my housing and plane tickets. See?" I slide the financial aid information in front of him.

He squints at the papers and furrows of worry rumple his forehead. "Hand me my reading glasses, will you?"

I pass him the glasses, and he scans the papers. "I'm not sure I understand this. What's a bursary?"

"It's a scholarship," I tell him. "The way it was explained to me, none of it has to be repaid. That's better than what Yale is offering."

He leans back against the couch and goes over the papers once again, this time more thoroughly. "This does look mighty attractive," he admits. "Would you live on campus, then?"

"They've reserved a small flat for me in the foreign student housing section." I hand him photos of the apartment. "They say it's very secure and other American students live there."

After examining each of the photos, he tugs off his glasses and slumps back. "This is all so sudden, Jade. The idea of being an empty-nester wasn't so bad when I thought you'd be down the road in New Haven. But Oxford? Are you sure about this? You wouldn't know a soul. I'd hate to think about you being there all alone."

I cut my eyes to Asher. We cooked-up an answer for this also.

"Actually, Mr. Beckett, my great aunt lives in the town of Oxford," he says. "I stayed there often as a kid. I'm sure she'd be thrilled to have me for a visit, and she'd love to meet Jaden. I thought Auntie Millie and I could show her around a little."

Dad raises an eyebrow. "That's quite a coincidence." His voice carries a tinge of suspicion.

Asher shrugs. "My whole family's from England. I'm a first

generation American. My own father's an Oxford man."

I cast a cautionary look his way, like *don't get too cute.*

"I guess I'll be a little scared—my first time out of the country and all," I say. "But it's such an amazing opportunity, I think I'll regret it if I don't go for it."

Dad gathers all the papers together. "I'd like to look these over tonight and think about it a little more. Also, I'd like to have a chat with Mrs. Colgate at your school."

Uh oh. "Um, Dad wouldn't you rather talk with the people at Oxford. They'll probably know more about this than Mrs. Colgate."

"Good idea. What's the name of the person you spoke with?"

"Tell you what, why don't I just get in touch with her tomorrow and set up a time for you two to speak?" Narowyn will know what to do.

"Okay. That will be fine. How about tomorrow evening? Oh, wait, Drew'll be home from school tomorrow and we're having dinner at Lisa's. Better make it Tuesday. Are they ahead of us or behind us time-wise?" He looks to Asher.

"They're five hours ahead of us, sir," Asher says.

"All right. Tuesday morning then, Jade. See if that works."

"Will do. Thanks, Dad."

He gazes at me and shakes his head. "Hard to imagine my little girl being so far away."

Asher flashes me an amused look.

"I know, Dad, hard to imagine. Sometimes I can't believe it myself."

TWENTY-FIVE

Asher and I spend the afternoon at the Ikea in New Haven picking out furniture, rugs, and other household items for his place. He's talented at selecting furnishings, but after a few hours in the crowded, maze-like store, I'm feeling trapped in a bad rendition of *No Exit.*

"I gotta get out of here before I start hyperventilating," I tell him. "Maybe you can come back tomorrow when I'm at school."

"Just a couple more minutes. All I need is a coffee table, and I'm done."

I plunk down on one of the sofas. "Okay, but hurry. I'll wait here."

He returns in ten minutes with his list of items. We make our way through the labyrinth of kitchen gadgets to an enormous warehouse filled with towering shelves of brown cardboard boxes.

"How're you planning to get all this home? It's not going to fit in my Kia," I say.

"They'll get it all together for me and deliver it for a small charge. Let's go check out."

Asher gives the cashier his list, and she efficiently enters everything into the computer and presents him with a total. He slides his Barclays card out of his wallet and swipes it through the terminal. The girl hands him a receipt and promises everything will be delivered tomorrow.

Once outside, I check my phone. Three missed calls from Liv. I punch redial.

"Where are you?" she squeals. "I have something humongous to tell you. You're never going to believe it."

"I'm with Ash. We just got out of Ikea. What is it?"

"Come to Ashley's. I'll tell you when you get here. And bring Mr. Steele along. I look really cute today." She clicks off.

"You in the mood for ice cream?" I ask. "Liv wants us to join her. She says she has something big to tell me."

"Sounds intriguing. Let's go."

Ashley's Ice Cream is crammed with people when we arrive. A table full of teenage girls turns to gawk at Asher as we wedge our way inside. The smell of sugar and vanilla caresses my nose and reminds me of Sundays as a kid.

I crane my neck in search of Liv. "Ash, do you mind waiting in line while I find her? Oh, and if I'm not back in time, I'll have a Coffee Oreo cone."

"Yes, ma'am."

I spot Liv at a table in the rear of the store sitting with our friends Julie and Drake. She animatedly waves me across the room, but her face falls as I near the table. "Where's the new boyfriend? I thought he was coming with you?"

I hug Julie and say "hi" to Drake. "He's in line, and he's not my boyfriend. We're just friends," I announce to the table.

"Better not say that, I might believe you and make my move," Liv says.

203

"Be my guest. But I don't think you're his type."

"Oh, I'm his type all right," she says, "judging from the way he looked at me in those dresses yesterday. I felt the male pheromones pulsating from way across the room."

Her unwavering self-confidence where matters of the opposite sex are concerned is enviable.

"Sit," she commands. "You're never going to believe what Julie's mom told her."

I slip into the empty chair between Julie and Drake. "What?"

Julie scoots in closer. "Mr. Nordgren got canned. He's not coming back to school."

"Really?" I fake a surprised expression. "That's so weird. How did your mom find out?"

"She's best friends with Connie Logan, the lady who handles personnel matters for the district."

"What happened? Why'd they fire him?" I ask.

Julie shrugs. "They're being really closed-lipped about it."

Drake speaks up for the first time. "I heard he was having an affair with a junior."

I roll my eyes. Drake's one of those guys who thinks everything that happens on earth is in some way related to sex. Or maybe he just wishes it was.

"Oh yeah? What junior would that be?" I ask.

"I don't know. That's just what I heard," he says defensively.

"Well, it's more likely that he left for health reasons or something," I say. "They have to be careful what they say about that."

Liv peers over my shoulder and her face lights up with a rosy glow. She tosses her hair appealingly. That can only mean Asher's standing behind me.

"Your Coffee Oreo cone," he says, passing it to me.

"Thanks." I glance up sheepishly. "Sorry I didn't make it back."

"Don't mention it." He takes a healthy bite of his Carmel Ripple.

"Ash, this is Julie and that's Drake. Guys, this is my neighbor, Asher Steele."

Julie shyly waggles two fingers. "Hi."

Drake says "Yo."

"Asher, come sit over here," Liv coos at him.

"Sure." He saunters over and glides into the chair next to hers.

She focuses all her attention on him as if they're the only two at the table. Leaning in, she whispers something close to his ear. He responds in a low tone, effectively excluding the rest of us from the conversation.

"So, Liv tells me you're going to Yale," Julie says. "That's so cool."

"Uh, well, I haven't made a final decision yet." I glance cautiously at Liv, but she seems completely engrossed in Asher's company. "I'm also considering Oxford University," I add quietly.

"What!" Liv shrieks, obviously not so swept away by Asher's charm as to prevent her from eavesdropping. "You're thinking of going where?"

"Liv, calm down. I was going to talk to you about this when we were alone."

"That's totally not fair. I chose Trinity College, so we could be close to each other," she complains.

"You chose Trinity because your mom went there," I say.

"Don't make me feel guilty about this. It's an incredible opportunity."

"But you can't move to England. We'll never see each other." She thrusts out her lower lip, her eyes wet bright. I sense show time coming on—probably more for Asher's benefit than mine.

"Can we save the theatrics for later, please? My dad hasn't even said *yes*. Anyway, I thought you'd be happy to have a friend to visit in Europe."

The idea appeases her for a second. "It might be okay. I could see where Will and Kate live ... but I can't believe you didn't tell me about this sooner." Clearly she's ready to launch into one of her *it's all about me* rants, but mercifully her phone rings.

"Oh, I have to take this," she says checking the screen. "I'll be right back." She shoots me a stony medusa glare before scurrying out the back door.

Provided with the perfect opportunity for escape, I scoot out of my chair. "Tell Liv we had to go," I say to Julie. "Asher needs to stop by the walk-in clinic for his medication. It closes at five."

Looking mildly surprised, Asher nods to Julie and Drake. "Nice to meet you." He follows as I flee out the front entrance.

"The walk-in clinic?" he says once we're alone.

"It's all I could think of. We had to get out of there. Liv was about to cause one of her famous public scenes. You don't want to get in the middle of one of those."

"She does seem kind of high-strung."

"That's a gross understatement. Oh, and a little heads-up, she's kind of into you, in case you hadn't noticed. Just be careful. She can be a bit callous where men are concerned."

"Thanks for the warning, but I don't find her all that attractive." We toss what's left of our cones in a trash can and slide into the seats of my sweltering car. I crank up the AC.

206

"You expect me to believe that? Liv's every school boy's wet dream and everyone knows it, including her."

"Well, I haven't been a school boy for a while, and I tend to like women who run a little deeper."

"She can be deep, once you get to know her." I'm not sure why I'm defending her. "Don't judge. She has a really good heart."

He grins. "Hey, you trying to set me up or something?"

"No. And by *no*, I mean I don't know. You could do worse."

"I'll keep that in mind."

We make the short ride home in silence. I stop at the curb in front of Asher's townhouse.

"I'm going to take a bath and relax for a while," I say. "Do you want to come over later for dinner?"

"Yeah. We're supposed to stick together, remember? I'll get in touch with Narowyn about having someone call your dad on Tuesday." He opens the passenger side door.

"Thanks, Ash. Oh, and ask her about Ralston, please. I'd like to know what's happening with him."

"Sure. Remember to lock your doors." He thumps the car roof with his hand.

"Yes, sir."

I park next to Dad's car in the driveway.

"Jade, we're in here," he calls as I step through the front door.

He and his girlfriend, Lisa, are sitting on stools at the kitchen counter. She looks pretty in a turquoise and white wrap dress. Thoughts of Mom involuntarily float through my mind. I hope she'd be happy for Dad.

Dad's pouring red wine into two stemmed glasses. "Hey, we're thinking of going out for Italian tonight. Want to join us?"

"Thanks, but Asher's coming over. We'll probably just order pizza."

"You two are spending an awful lot of time together," he says. "Is he your new beau or something?"

"Nah. He just doesn't know anybody else in town. I'm introducing him around a little. I think he kind of likes Liv."

Dad rolls his eyes. "Heaven help him. Don't forget I'm picking up Drew tomorrow around six. Dinner at Lisa's at seven."

"Oh yeah. Sounds good."

"I heard about your acceptance to Oxford," Lisa says. "Congratulations. That's such an honor. You must be thrilled."

I wish some of her enthusiasm would rub off on Dad. "It'll be an amazing experience, if I get to go."

Dad swirls the wine in his glass but doesn't comment.

"Invite your new friend along for dinner tomorrow, if you like," Lisa says. "It's very casual."

"Okay. I'll ask him. I'm going to take a quick bath before he gets here. Have a nice dinner you guys."

My phone rings as I'm pouring scented bubble bath into the stream of steaming tub water.

"Hey Liv. Sorry we had to leave so quickly today."

"I can't believe you just walked out on me." Her voice is rich with righteous indignation. "I told you I wanted to talk."

"Asher had some things to do before five. What can I say?"

"We need to discuss this Oxford thing now."

"No, Liv. I'm taking a bath, I'm tired, and I don't really need you yelling at me because I got this great opportunity."

She *humphs* into the phone. "What are you doing tonight? Are you going out?"

"No. We're staying in. Probably order pizza. School night, you know."

"Who's *we?*"

"Ash and me."

Silence on the other end.

"Liv?"

"Were you serious when you said you're not interested in him as a boyfriend?" The bite has vanished from her voice.

"Yes."

"And you're not just saying that because of that guy you're stalking on the internet?"

"Liv! I'm not doing that anymore." The reminder pricks my heart. "What's your point?"

"Can I come over for pizza tonight?" Her tone shifts to one of conciliation. She's obviously decided that seeing Asher is more important than being angry with me.

"Tell you what, you can come over and have pizza with us if you promise not to bring up the subject of Oxford."

"But, Jade—"

"No *buts*. We'll talk about it some other time. Not tonight."

"Okay. So, what should I wear?"

"Seriously? It's pizza on the couch. Later." I click off.

I love Liv because of our long history, but sometimes she's just so *high school*.

After I'm bathed and changed, I order a couple of pizzas for us.

Ash arrives early and fills me in on his conversation with Narowyn.

"Everything's all set for the call on Tuesday. She wants to handle it herself. She'll use the polycom and ping it through a cell tower near Oxford. Just tell your dad that Mrs. Du Lac from Oxford Admissions will call at ten a.m. our time. She does a completely authentic British accent."

"Well, let's hope her powers of persuasion are as remarkable as her accent," I say. "Did you ask her about Ralston?"

"Yep. She says they tested everything, and his primary and secondary memory components seem to be intact. But they've had no luck in finding new limbs. She went ahead and ordered a whole new shell."

"A what?"

"A new body. A later model. Narowyn says they tried to get as close to his former appearance as possible, but he's going to look different, Jade. There's no way around that."

I release a long breath, contemplating how weird that's going to feel. "I'll be okay. It'll be like he had cosmetic surgery or something. I'm just glad he's all right."

Liv struts up my front steps right behind the pizza delivery guy. In her white halter top and short leather skirt, she's dressed more for clubbing in Manhattan than TV night at the Becketts'. Her ice-blond hair has been flat-ironed to a perfect sheen.

She slides past the acne-faced delivery kid and into the living room. He's so flummoxed by her startling appearance that he forgets to collect for the food, and I have to chase him down the sidewalk to pay.

Judging from the look on Asher's face when I return, he appreciates Liv's outfit nearly as much as the delivery guy did. We put the pizza boxes on the coffee table and pile our paper plates with the greasy wedges. I grab Diet Cokes for Asher and me, while Liv sneaks a little of Dad's red wine. We settle in the living room for a *Scandal* marathon.

Brady Cat and I make ourselves comfortable on the couch. Ash and Liv sit side by side on the floor in front of us. I'm not sure how Liv is able to sit in that skirt without revealing all, but she manages. The two of them seem to have a nice rapport, and I feel good not having to worry about moving the conversation along … or participating at all, really. I feed tiny bites of sausage to a purring Brady.

At some point after the third episode, I doze off stretched out on the couch. When I open my eyes, Asher and Liv are sharing a rather vigorous kiss. Something thuds unpleasantly at the bottom of my stomach, and I'm not sure why. Does it remind me of the kiss Asher and I shared? Or is it Ryder's warm mouth I'm thinking of? Asher opens his eyes and catches me staring. He pulls his lips away from Liv's.

"Well, look who's up," he says grinning.

"Hey." Liv stands and smoothes down her skirt. "Asher's going to show me his place. Is that okay? We didn't want to wake you."

"Uh, sure." It feels weird, seeing them leave together, but I guess I kind of orchestrated this. "See you at school tomorrow, Liv. 'Night, Ash."

TWENTY-SIX

I brush my teeth and climb into bed. For a few minutes I stare at the ceiling and mentally prepare myself for going back to school tomorrow. In nearly every way, I'm a different person than I was before. Only the weekend has passed for my teachers and classmates, but for me it feels like a month of years. And what a momentous time of upheaval and transformation it was.

Unbidden images of Ryder falling from that walkway flash through my mind, causing my insides to shudder. I curl into a fetal position and wrap my arms around myself. I know in time I'll be better equipped to parse through the memories of my time in Domerica. But getting through these next few weeks of school and the multitude of special activities for seniors has to be my top priority. *Take it in small bites* Narowyn told me. *Don't try to swallow it whole.*

I close my eyes and try to sleep. Unconsciously my thoughts drift to Asher and Liv and what they may be doing at his place. I reach over and flip on my lamp. Why am I thinking about them?

Is it jealousy? Do I subconsciously wish for a relationship with Asher? Am I upset that Liv is more interested in him than me at the moment? Or do I have a sick desire for Asher to stay locked in the chains of unrequited love for me, while I play the tragic heroine who'll never recover from her husband's death?

I try to objectively imagine Ash and me together at some point in the future—when I'm not such a jagged mess of emotions. It doesn't sit right in my heart. If I really wanted to be with him, wouldn't I feel it somewhere inside? Even now, going through all this grief and pain? I know I would. So that's not the reason.

And I don't think it's because I crave Liv's undivided attention. She's been wearing on my nerves all weekend. That only leaves option number three, and I really don't want to be that person.

I suppose it's normal to want people to love you. Hell, Liv needs to have everyone's undying adulation around the clock. Asher may have kissed Liv to make me jealous, or he may really be interested in her. Either way, I need to be honest with him about my feelings.

I reach under my pillow and withdraw the folded sketch of Ryder. The charcoal lines of the drawing are beginning to fade a bit from sliding it in and out from under my pillow. Sighing deeply, I wonder for the thousandth time why it couldn't have been different. Why couldn't we have just lived happily ever after? I replace the sketch in its secret spot. "Goodnight, love," I whisper to the darkened room.

* * *

My stomach is nervous and jittery as I dress for school. You'd think it was my first day of kindergarten, rather than the home stretch of my high school career.

"Breakfast," Dad calls down to me.

"Be right there." I grab my book bag and trudge up the stairs.

Dad's in the kitchen scooping scrambled eggs in to a bowl. "Morning," he says when he sees me.

"Dad, you shaved!" I peck his whisker-free cheek.

He chuckles. "I shave every morning, sweetheart. You kids may find that unshaven look sexy, but the Hospital Administration considers it poor grooming."

Oops. That must mean we've navigated across the little cosmic ripple and are back to normal.

"Well, you look good," I say, trying to recover from my slip.

He glances down at his same old faded scrubs. "Thanks. Glad you're so upbeat today. You excited to see Drew?"

"Yeah, I've kind of missed him. Anyway, I'm just having toast this morning. My tummy's a little iffy."

"You're not coming down with something, are you?"

"Don't worry, it's nothing. I'll see you tonight at Lisa's." I snag a slice of toast from the plate.

On my way out, I peek into the laundry room. Brady's bowl and litter box are gone. *I'm going to miss that cat.*

My usual spot's free in the senior parking lot. Inside, Liv's already waiting for me at my locker.

"I think I'm in love," she gushes, hugging her books to her chest.

"That's great, Liv. Asher's a really nice guy."

"Oh, I'm not in love with *him.* We went dancing last night after we left you, and I met this guy, Antonio. He's so Latin and *sooo* hot. You've got to see him, Jade." She fumbles in her purse. "I tried to take a picture of him with my phone. I was going to put it on Instagram, but it didn't come out very well."

"What the hell, Liv? You just dumped Asher?"

"Oh he didn't care. He danced with tons of other girls. I mean that one kiss was totally toe-curling, and after he showed me his place, I was like ready to get all cozy. Only, he was like *let's go somewhere.* So I took him to Marou."

She shoves her phone in my face, and I see a blurry photo of a black-haired dude with long sideburns and huge, soulful eyes. I smile and shake my head. *Why am I even surprised?* "Yeah he's a hottie all right. Can't wait to meet him."

The first period bell rings, and we hurry off to class. We take our usual seats, and I listen to my classmates chatter about going off to college while Liv flirts with the two football players sitting behind us. Others in the class are dozing off, surreptitiously texting under the desk, or finishing homework for other classes. It strikes me as surreal to be back in this setting when only days ago I was caught up in an epic battle, attempting to save my family, myself, and my adopted country. Although I know in my heart the activities taking place in this tiny classroom have significance and meaning for my classmates, for me it's all trivial and irrelevant when compared with what I just went through and what lies ahead of me.

The rumor that I'm considering Oxford gets around quickly. I halfway expect the placement office to call me out on the lie. But Narowyn says if anyone bothers to check, my acceptance and enrollment will appear perfectly legit on the Oxford records. Besides, the placement counselors are too harried focusing on students who didn't get accepted anywhere to worry about me.

Physics class is weird. Mr. Nordgren's replacement, Mr. Sherman, is a sour-faced old guy with exactly three strands of white hair plastered to his shiny scalp. He says we're woefully behind on studying the AP exam materials, and he loads us up with a ton of homework. Just what we need when we've already mentally checked out of high school.

At first, I'm completely annoyed, until it dawns on me that I don't care about the exam because I'm not really going to college. But then that realization is itself unnerving. I always pictured myself as a college grad. Narowyn says I'll be in Transcender training, but I don't know exactly what that includes. I hope my education doesn't hit a brick wall in Arumel. There's still so much I want to learn.

After seventh period, Liv invites me to hang out with her and Antonio at her house. I take a pass, though. I promised Ash I'd come straight home from school. Plus, he needs to know that Dad is beardless again and all traces of Brady have evaporated.

Asher's waiting on my front steps when I drive up.

"Hey. You been here long?" I ask.

"Nah. I came over early to get away from the paint fumes. The place looks a lot better, though. How was school?"

"It was okay." I unlock the front door for us. "Nordgren's replacement is kind of a Physics Nazi, though. I have a bunch of homework—but it's only a few more weeks." I drop my book bag near the stairs, and we head for the kitchen.

"Brady's gone," I say, examining the contents of the fridge.

"What do you mean?"

"I mean we're back to normal. Dad's clean-shaven and Brady and all his stuff have disappeared. It's so bizarre." I pull out the leftover pizza and set it on the counter.

"Guess Narowyn was right about that cosmic wrinkle thing. Normal's good," he says.

"Yeah, but I'd kind of gotten used to the little fur ball."

"You talking about your dad's beard or the cat?"

"Ha, ha. By the way, we're going to Lisa's for dinner tonight and you're invited. Dad's picking Drew up at the airport and they'll meet us there."

"All right. Sounds good." Ash puts slices of pizza on napkins for us, and I grab two sodas.

We carry our food and drinks to the living room. "So, I hear you and Liv went dancing after you left here."

"Yeah, I wanted to see what Madison night life was like, and you seemed kind of tired." He leans back on the couch and props his feet on the coffee table. "We had an interesting time."

"Look, Ash, I'm sorry about Liv. It's not that she's totally unfeeling. She just has a short attention span. Are you okay?"

He grins. "Thanks for worrying about me, Mom. I'm fine. I

216

realized kissing her was a big mistake as soon as we got to my place. She made it clear she was interested in more, and, well, I thought about the fact that I'm only here for a few weeks. It wouldn't be fair."

"You're a nice guy," I say, clinking my soda can on his.

"That's what I keep telling you." He treats me to a slow sexy smile.

I'm not sure if he's flirting or just being Ash, but I concentrate on picking the pepperoni off my pizza.

"How are you holding up?" he asks. "It must be hard seeing all those people and having to act like nothing's happened to you."

"I have my ups and downs. It hasn't all sunk in yet. It makes me crazy not knowing what's happening in Domerica, though." I twist at my TPD bracelet.

"Try not to dwell on that, Jade. You can't be anywhere but here right now. Narowyn made that clear. She won't be very happy if you defy her orders."

Whether from frustration, exhaustion, or the constant gnawing pain, I don't know. But something inside me snaps and the floodgates fly open sending a river of dammed up tears streaming down my face.

Asher tosses his pizza on the table and puts a steady hand on my shuddering shoulder. "Whoa, damn, Jade, I'm sorry. Did I say something wrong?"

I sniff hard. "No, it's not you. Everything's just catching up with me. I'm sick of pretending everything's okay when it's not, and … I think I'm just tired. Maybe a nap before dinner would do me good."

"You sure you're going to be okay?

"Yeah, I'm sure. I'll be fine. How about I pick you up for dinner at six-thirty?"

"All right. I'd better check on the painters anyway. Just don't answer the door. Okay? And call me if you need me."

"I will," I snuffle.

TWENTY-SEVEN

Dinner at Lisa's turns out to be a kind of graduation/welcome home celebration for me and Drew. It's great to see Drew again. His skin is tan, and his sun-kissed tawny curls are impeccably disheveled, as usual. He and Asher hit it off right away, and Drew challenges him to a ping-pong tournament at Lisa's outdoor table.

Lisa has prepared all our favorite foods, plus baked two cakes— a towering death by chocolate layer cake for me and a coconut, pineapple, macadamia nut concoction for Drew. She's probably mostly trying to impress Dad, but I respect the woman's efforts.

Ash and I are the first to leave the little party. Mental exhaustion weighs heavy on my shoulders, and thoughts of my snug bed beckon to me. Lisa puts leftovers into plastic containers to send home with an appreciative Asher. Dad and Drew promise to be along shortly.

Asher's front porch light burns soft yellow illumination across his threshold as we pull into his driveway. "You going to be okay sleeping with all the paint fumes?" I ask.

"It'll be fine. I left the windows open, so it shouldn't be too strong. Let's have dinner over here tomorrow. The new carpet will be laid, and I'll have all the furniture arranged. We may have to order Chinese, though. It'll probably take me most of the day to put everything together. By the way, does your dad have a power drill I

219

can borrow?"

"Yeah. You want me to bring it over?"

"Nah. You go inside and lock the doors. I'll put this food in the fridge and come over in a few minutes to get it."

"Sure. See you in a bit."

When I reach home, I park at the curb so Dad can pull into the garage. I unfasten my seatbelt and reach for my phone and purse on the passenger seat. My driver's side door abruptly swings open, and something cold and heavy clamps hard around my neck.

"*What the—?*" I reach up to my throat, but my arm is roughly yanked away by a man dressed in black. He drags me out of my seat and shoves me up against the car. A gloved hand grasps my wrist and claws at my TPD bracelet.

Years of Tae Kwan Do training click in immediately. I wrench my arm away and rotate out of his grasp. Using the car as leverage, I kick out hard. My foot rams into the man's groin area. The impact causes him to stagger back, but other than that, he seems unfazed. His face remains placid—nearly devoid of expression. I don't understand. Titanium athletic cup?

I step away from the car and assume a fighting stance, with my weight on my back foot. He lumbers toward me. This time I give it all I've got—a spin kick to the jaw, my personal specialty. His head jerks violently to the side, but he remains standing. *Shit! He should be flat on his face.*

All at once I get it—the guy's an automaton. It's the only explanation. In seconds he recovers and comes at me again.

To hell with this. I reach for my bracelet and double click the latch. Nothing happens. So I scream my lungs out for help. I barely see the blur of his fist before it connects with my cheek. *Yeow!* The pavement rushes up to meet me, the air slams out of my lungs, and my entire body feels broken.

I will myself to get up, but the robot drops heavily onto my torso, pinning my arms to the ground. He yanks the TPD bracelet from my immobilized wrist and hurls it across the street. Reaching to his side, he unsnaps his gun holster. Adrenaline sizzles in my veins, and my brain kicks into overdrive.

I'm not going down like this. I struggle to flip over on my side and twist out from under him. *I know how to do this.* But it doesn't work—not even a little. He withdraws his gun slowly, and aims it at my forehead.

Mustering the energy from every cell in my body, I give it one last herculean try. *NO!* I roar, freeing my hand and shoving it in his face.

Incredibly, he does a double backward somersault through the air and scuds across the pavement.

What the hell? I don't know what just happened, and I don't care. I push up from the ground and make a stumbling run for it.

Help! I shriek. The kitten heel on my shoe snags on a manhole cover, and I go down hard. My head slams against blacktop rattling my teeth. The Northern Lights explode behind my eyes.

My aching brain knows I've got to get out of here, but my body isn't responding. After a second or two, the sound of thudding footfalls reaches my ears. I brace for the worst. *I'm going to die. Please be there for me, Ryder. Please find me.*

A hulking body looms above me, and Urick's face comes into focus. "You all right?" He clutches a long wicked blade in his right hand. In his left, he holds the head of the robot that attacked me. He pitches it to the curb, and extends his hand for me.

Unsteadily, I clamber to my feet. "God, Urick, I'm so glad you're here," I gulp for air. "That thing almost killed me."

"I will take you to Asher. Then we will remove this bot to Arumel. We must report that IUGA has tried to harm you once again."

For the first time I notice Urick's not alone. The ebony-skinned beauty with the brutal ponytail clacks up in stiletto knee-high boots and holds out my bracelet.

"Here. You'll need this," she says.

I make a meager effort to reach for it, but my arms feel like spaghetti. She lifts my hand and places the bracelet on my wrist.

"She's in shock," Ponytail says to Urick. "Her skin is cold as ice."

Urick sheathes his blade and lifts me in his arms.

Running footsteps echo in the street behind us. "Holy Sweet Jesus. What happened?" Asher asks, taking in the scene.

"A bot. Must be IUGA's," Urick gestures to the headless corpse lying in the gutter.

"Get her inside." Asher says, scooping up my keys from the pavement. He unlocks my front door, and Urick carries me into the living room.

He lays me down and props pillows under my feet. "She's in shock," he tells Asher. "He put a dog collar on her."

Ash sits next to me and unclamps the metal thing around my neck. "Goddamned bastards." He holds it out for me to see. It's a flat ring of shiny silver metal that does sort of look like a dog collar, only it has a flashing red plastic square in the center.

"What is that?" I run my fingers along the scratches on my neck.

"It's a nasty little device that sends a low level of electrical current over the surface of your skin. Prevents you from shifting."

"Oh," I say, shivering uncontrollably.

"God, you're freezing." He grabs a woolen throw from the back of the couch and wraps it snugly around me.

"She needs a doctor," Urick says, "and we need to get the remains of that bot out of the street."

"Do what you need to," Asher says. "I'll call for an ambulance." He hands the dog collar to Urick. "And, let Narowyn know about this."

Urick and Ponytail slip out the front door.

"Jade, I'm so sorry. This is my fault. I never should have let you out of my sight."

I open my mouth to tell him it's okay, but blackness swirls around me, and I allow myself to surrender to it.

* * *

My temples pound as if giants are taking turns clobbering my head with tree trunks. A deep moan rumbles up from my chest and rattles out through my throat.

"What is it, sweetheart?"

I open my eyes, but it's like I'm looking through wax paper. "Dad?"

"Yes, sweetheart. I'm here."

"My head hurts."

"I know. You've suffered a concussion. The medication will kick-in soon."

"Where am I?"

"The hospital. St. Ignatius. Do you remember what happened?"

"I don't know. Someone attacked me."

"Asher's giving his statement to the police right now. Thank god he came along when he did and scared the guy off."

"Yeah," I say, not really remembering the sequence of events. "That was lucky."

"The police will want to take your statement a little later when you're feeling better. Did you get a look at the guy?"

"No. It was pretty dark." I touch my fingertips to my tender cheek and swollen eye. "Is anything broken?"

"No, just contusions and abrasions and one hell of a shiner." He lifts up my chin to get a better look. "Anyway, they want to keep you overnight because of the concussion and because you were in shock when you arrived. Drew's here and Lisa. Let us know if you need anything."

"Thanks." I close my eyes and sink down into the soft pillows.

It seems like no time has passed when Dad gently shakes my shoulder to wake me.

"Jaden, the police are here. Do you feel up to speaking with them for a few minutes?"

"Uh, okay." Dad gives me a cup with a straw, and I sip some water.

Two uniformed officers, a man and woman, come over to the side of my bed. They introduce themselves. Their names bypass my brain. One of them asks me to tell them in my own words what happened.

I keep it basic because the whole thing is like a bad dream that I don't really want to remember.

A man in black dragged me out of my car. He grabbed for my bracelet. I fought back but he hit me, knocking me to the ground. Then Asher ran up, and the guy high-tailed it out of there. I didn't really get a good look at his face.

I skip the part about the gun and the robot's head being severed from its body, and Urick and Ponytail showing up.

"Did he get away with anything? Your bracelet? Your purse?"

"No. I don't think so."

The only time I get tripped up is when they ask me about the marks on my neck.

"Did he put something around your neck or try to strangle you?"

The stocky sandy-haired officer asks.

Not knowing what Asher has told them, I just wiggle around the question. "Uh, I really don't remember. He might have done something after I hit my head on the ground. It gets kind of fuzzy past that point."

She nods sympathetically. "We'll need you to come to the station in the next few days to sign your statement and look at some mug shots."

I promise to do that and they leave. Dad resumes his seat at my bedside, and mercifully, I fade off to sleep again.

The night passes in a haze of semi-conscious misery. My left cheek throbs nonstop, and my headache fades to a dull thudding, but never really goes away. Every time I drift into a deep sleep, someone wakes me to check my vital signs or give me more medication.

In the morning Dad brings in clean clothes for me and informs me that I'll be discharged later today. He plans to take the afternoon off work to make sure I'm comfortably settled in at home.

"You'll need to miss a few days of school, sweetheart. It's important to rest physically and mentally after a head injury like that."

"No worries, Dad. I'll get my assignments online, and Liv will take notes for me. Oh, and I forgot to tell you, the lady from Oxford is going to call you this morning at ten. Do you have your cell phone?"

"Yes. Don't give it a second thought. I'll be sure to take the call. What's her name?"

"Narowyn Du Lac."

He uses one finger to type it into his phone. "The British sure have some odd names." He pats my sheet-covered leg. "Sweetheart, I've asked Dr. Rivera to come by and see you this morning. She's a … therapist who specializes in PTSD."

"Post traumatic stress disorder? Dad, c'mon. I really don't

need—"

"I know you don't think you need to see anyone, but this was an extremely violent and upsetting thing that happened last night. Hell, I probably need a therapist. The point is, I'm not sure you can predict how it will affect you later. Also, I just think it would do you good to talk to someone. It hasn't been that long since we lost Mom, and this is a stressful time as it is, with graduation coming up and you thinking about moving. I probably should have set this up for you long ago."

"That's not true, Dad. I hope you don't think I've lost it or something."

"I don't, sweetheart … but I admit I've been concerned about you since your mother died—particularly over these last months when you seemed to have developed a kind of an internet obsession for someone you hardly know."

"Wait, Dad. You don't have to worry about that anymore. It's all in the past. I promise."

"That's good to hear, but I wish you'd speak with her anyway. Please. For me?"

He's so concerned that I don't want to upset him by refusing. "Okay. But just this once."

"That's all I ask." He smoothes my hair with his palm. "I need to work for a few hours, but I'll be back to get you discharged around two."

TWENTY-EIGHT

After picking at the food on my hospital breakfast tray, I shower and change back into civilian clothes. My TPD bracelet's not with the rest of my things, so I assume Asher's holding it for me. I feel a little naked without it.

A check in the mirror tells me it's a good thing I don't have to go to school for a few days. I look seriously wrecked. When I don't show up for first period, Liv and I exchange texts:

Where r u?

St. Iggies. Don't Freak. I'm fine.

WTF?

Long story. Come by the house after sch?

K

I hang out on the bed and flip through television channels for a couple of boring hours. Mid-morning, Asher walks in carrying a huge arrangement of spring flowers. "Hey, Ash. Those are gorgeous. Thanks."

He sets the vase on the windowsill and hands me my TPD

bracelet.

"God, I can't believe you're still speaking to me," he says, the muscles in his jaw tense. "I'm so sorry Jade. I shouldn't have left you alone."

"It was only two minutes, Ash. You couldn't have known." I snap on the bracelet and immediately feel more secure.

"But that's what I'm here for—to anticipate those things and protect you. Narowyn will probably kick my ass back to Arumel. This was an epic fail on my part."

"No! She can't send you back. I need you here. You're the only one who knows what's going on."

He slumps down into the bedside chair. "I'll tell her you said that, but I'm not sure what she'll decide to do."

"Look, everything turned out all right, and now we have direct evidence that IUGA is trying to kill me. It's kind of a good development."

"Nice try, but that got screwed up too." He slides further down in his chair. "When Urick and Nila got back to your car, the whole scene had been cleaned up."

"What? What do you mean?"

"No robot and no gun, that's what I mean. All we have is the dog collar, which probably can't be traced back to IUGA."

Oh man, that really sucks."

"Yeah. Anyway, Narowyn's going back to court today and taking Urick with her to inform them what happened. Not sure what that'll accomplish. IUGA will just deny everything. She also sent a bunch of additional people to help watch over you. Urick's entire team arrived last night. You'll probably see some familiar-looking new janitors at school. Don't act surprised."

"We should let them know I'm taking a few days off school. Dad says I need to rest. Also, he set me up to talk with some shrink.

He's afraid all this may send me over the edge."

Asher leans forward, elbows on his knees. "You know, Jade, that's not a bad idea. You've been through a hell of a lot lately."

"Not you too!"

He holds his hands up defensively. "I'm just saying ..."

Then, as if staged, the door opens and in walks an attractive young woman wearing a beige sheath dress topped by a white lab coat. She smiles brightly.

"Hello, I'm Dr. Rivera." She holds a clipboard in one hand and extends her other hand to Asher.

He stands and shakes it. "Asher Steele."

"Nice to meet you. And you must be Jaden Beckett," she reaches out to shake my hand also. "I believe we have an appointment." She turns to Asher. "We'll only be an hour or so. You're welcome to come back then."

Ash fumbles out of the room and closes the door quietly. Dr. Rivera pulls the bedside chair around so she's facing me.

Right away, I notice her killer shoes with red soles. Louboutins, *nice*. She's not exactly the gray-haired doctor I was expecting. In fact, she looks about fourteen years old.

"How are you feeling today, Jaden?" she asks.

"How old are you?" I reply.

"Thirty-one. How old are you?" she says, without skipping a beat.

"I'll be nineteen in three months."

She makes a small note on her clipboard.

"I was so sorry to hear what happened to you last night. Can you tell me a little bit about the incident?"

"I'm sure it's all there in your notes," I say, gesturing to her clipboard. But I repeat the short version of the story for her anyway.

"Wow, that sounds awful. Can you tell me a little about what you were feeling while this was happening?"

"Yeah—scared, afraid I was going to die. I tried to defend myself, but nothing worked."

"How did that make you feel? I understand you're an expert in Tae Kwan Do."

She's asking better questions than the police did. "I am, but he must have been wearing protective gear because nothing I tried had much of an impact on him. Before I could run, he clocked me."

"You must have felt pretty helpless, then?"

I can't very well tell her that martial arts are useless against robots, so instead I say, "Look, I feel like under normal circumstances I would have been able to handle the guy. It was just a combination of things—he took me by surprise in front of my own house, he had on some kind of a cup or something, and I was tired."

"That's certainly understandable." She makes another note. "So, did this incident change the way you look at your neighborhood now? I mean do you feel safe there?"

"Yeah, I do." *Especially now since I know Urick's whole team is watching over me.* "I don't know what this guy was doing there last night, but I think it was just a fluke. I feel the neighborhood's a pretty secure place."

"I'm glad to hear that." Dr. Rivera leans back in her chair. "Jaden, I believe your father wanted me to speak with you just to let you know that after this kind of event it's normal to experience a certain amount of fear and anxiety. You may find yourself going over the event frequently in your head, or feeling some trepidation when you drive home at night. You may even occasionally have nightmares about the event. The only time this is a concern is if it becomes acute or if it continues for more than a few weeks. It's very important to take care of yourself physically and emotionally during this time."

"Okay, I understand."

"Everybody deals with trauma in different ways. Your father told me he had a very difficult time after your mother died, and I believe he's a bit worried about you."

"I know what he's concerned about. And he doesn't have to worry anymore."

She tilts her head, eyes curious. "Can you tell me what you believe he's worried about?"

I sigh and stare at the ceiling. *I don't know why Dad's forcing me to do this but if it makes him feel better, fine.*

"A little over a year ago, I lost touch with someone I cared about very much—a guy. I started searching for him on the internet, and I guess I got a little over zealous in some of my efforts to find him. Some people complained. But that's all over now. I'm not looking for him anymore."

"I see. Do you feel comfortable telling me why? Did something happen?"

"Yeah, I found him again, that's what happened." Tears sting my eyes, and I cover my face. "We were reunited for a few weeks. We were together, you know, as a couple. Then he died."

"Died? Oh my, that's so heartbreaking." She takes the tissue box from the table and places it next to me on the bed. "What a tremendous loss for you."

I pluck a few tissues from the box and blot my face. "Dad doesn't know any of this, and I don't want you to tell him."

"Of course not. Anything you say to me is strictly confidential. I'll never tell him anything unless you ask me to, or unless I fear you may be a danger to yourself or someone else. I don't perceive that as a concern here. Is it?"

I sniff and clear my throat. "No, I'm not going to hurt myself, if that's what you mean. But I don't want Dad to know any of this."

"Understood, but can you tell me a little more about his death?"

"It was a horrible accident," I snuffle. "He fell from a fifty-foot tower. The walkway was rotten, and it broke away under his feet."

"How awful. I imagine it was devastating for you."

"It was, I loved him," I say. "He was everything to me."

"I'm so sorry." Her eyes burn with compassion. "Have you been able to speak with anyone about this, Jaden?"

"A few people know, but not my family. My dad and I have never really been that close. He wouldn't understand."

"I hear what you're saying, but you may find that people understand more than you might think. What has gone on since this happened—in terms of a funeral or saying goodbye or communications with his family?"

"I couldn't go to the funeral." I sob unabashedly now, twisting the tissues in my hands. "Or say goodbye. And he doesn't have any family but a sister, and she can't stand me."

"Oh dear." Dr. Rivera sighs softly and allows me a moment to collect myself.

"Jaden, I appreciate you speaking with me today and sharing your experiences. I would love to be able to help you with this. Grief is something I understand well, both personally and professionally. Often the tendency is to keep these feelings inside, but I urge you to express your feelings of sorrow and seek support from others during this time. One of the best ways to cope with grief is to talk about it."

"I don't have time to wallow in it, and please don't suggest a support group. That's not my style. I've got a lot going on in my life right now, and I don't want people asking a bunch of questions. It's a private matter I have to deal with alone."

"Fair enough," she says. "But grief is a process you have to work through to get beyond. Would it be okay if I put together some things for you? I have a number of excellent books and articles on the grieving process. They may help you to understand some of the confusing emotions you're experiencing, and they may also help you realize that no matter how isolated you feel, you're not alone in this."

At this point I just want Dr. Rivera to leave. I've already said too much, and I don't want Dad or Asher walking in on this scene. "That would be all right, I guess."

"Good. They'll be waiting for you at the front desk when you're discharged."

"Fine." I dab at my face with the crumpled tissue.

"I'm going to give you my card, and I want you to call me at anytime if you have any questions or just want to talk." Dr. Rivera stands and reaches into the pocket of her white coat for a business card. She lays it on my table, and moves the chair back into place beside the bed.

"You seem like a very strong young woman, Jaden." She smiles warmly. "I look forward to possibly seeing you again, and I hope you begin to feel better physically and emotionally."

"Thanks," I mumble.

* * *

Dad and Drew show up at two o'clock with a wheelchair for my trip to the car. Dad stops at the front desk to pick up the bag of materials Dr. Rivera left for me, and Drew pops a couple of wheelies on our way out the door. I giggle, but we garner a few dirty looks from the hospital staff.

Once we reach home, Drew borrows the car and disappears to visit friends. Dad makes a little bed for me on the couch. He fixes us glasses of iced tea and eases himself down into his armchair, propping his feet on the ottoman.

"You feel well enough for a little conversation?" he asks. "Or would you rather get some sleep?"

"I'm good right now. What's on your mind?"

"I just wondered how your meeting with Dr. Rivera went."

"It went well. She was very sweet to leave those materials for me."

"She has a good reputation. Do you mind telling me what was in the bag?"

"Just some books on dealing with grief, that kind of thing."

"That's great, sweetheart. Do you think you'd like to set up regular meetings with her … at least until you go off to school?"

"I don't know, Dad. Let me look through what she gave me. I'll consider it. And, speaking of school, did Mrs. Du Lac call you today?"

"She certainly did." He takes a long draw on his tea. "It seems Oxford is very impressed with Jaden Beckett. The Du Lac woman made a compelling case as to why this would be the optimal education choice for you. She actually had me wishing I was eighteen again and going off to college. It sounds like a truly remarkable place."

"Really? So, does this mean I can go?"

He rocks his head from side to side noncommittally. "*Eh*. I'd still like to mull it over a little more. What bothers me most is that she says you'll need to be there shortly after graduation to get settled in your flat and attend the summer orientation program. I don't know if I'm prepared to let go of you that quickly. Are you sure you don't want a summer vacation?"

"Dad, the whole thing will be like a vacation. I mean, I know I'll have to work, but I'm looking forward to seeing England."

"If it's what you really want, sweetheart, I don't see how I can stand in your way. Just give me a day or two to get used to the idea."

I take that as a resounding *Yes.* "Yay. Thanks Dad. It is what I want."

* * *

Liv comes by around three-thirty with the new heart-throb, Antonio, in tow. He's smolderingly hot in a dark, brooding sort of way. He sits quietly in Dad's chair while Liv dishes nonstop about what went on at school today, the latest celebrity gossip, and other similarly inane subjects. I'm actually relieved when, after an hour, she says they have to leave. Somehow the quality of Liv's chatter has lost its appeal for me.

Dad heads out to pick up my prescriptions and shop for dinner. I haven't heard from Asher since this morning, which seems odd, so I try his cell phone. No answer. I'm worried that maybe he was right about Narowyn sending him home.

With nothing better to do, I doze until Dad gets back and begins preparations for dinner. After two more failed attempts to reach Asher, I consider using my polycom to call Narowyn and find out what's going on. Fortunately, I'm saved from the trouble by a knock on the front door.

"I'll get it," I call. Pain shoots through my skull when I get up too quickly.

Asher stands under the glow of the porch light.

"Where've you been?" I say. "I've been worried sick."

He moves to one side and gestures to the street. It's twilight in Madison, but it's still light enough for me to see a shiny new, red car parked at the curb.

"Is that yours?"

"Yeah. Narowyn summoned me back to Arumel this morning. I thought she was going to reprimand me. But we went over everything, and she decided on a few adjustments in our strategy. She's going to speak with you about that tomorrow so keep your polycom handy. Then she sent me back here to buy a car."

"A car? Not what I would've predicted, but I like it. Can you even drive that thing?"

"Yeah, I had to learn for some of my explorations. Even have an international driver's license."

"What kind of car is it anyway?"

"A Tesla. It's electric. Narowyn insisted." He grins.

Dad comes out of the kitchen wiping his hands on a paper towel. "Is that a new car, Ash?"

"Yeah. Just brought it over to show Jade."

"Well, come in and stay for dinner. It's only stir-fry, but we've got a bushel of it. Drew should be back any time now."

"Thanks, Mr. Beckett."

TWENTY-NINE

It turns out the "adjustments in strategy" Narowyn wants involve Asher driving me everywhere, except school—hence the car. She also tells me that if I still want to stick around Madison until graduation, I need to have her approval *in advance* for any activities outside of school.

"So I'm under house arrest until I graduate?" I ask her.

"That's not what I said. Of course you may attend your Senior Celebration, and all the school-organized graduation activities, as long as Asher accompanies you. We went back to court today asking for sanctions against IUGA for violating the court's order. The justices refused to grant our request due to lack of evidence. This is the only way we can be certain you are safe."

I'm not happy about it. I don't like being constantly under guard again, but I'm not in a position to argue with her. I fume for a silent moment.

"If there is another event which is especially important to you," she says, "you may request to attend. It will require some shifting of resources, but it may be possible to arrange."

That makes me feel guilty. Urick's entire team is already here babysitting me, and I'm just being difficult.

237

"Don't worry about it. The adjustments you want are fine. I appreciate everything you're doing, Narowyn. And thanks for being so persuasive with my dad. He's on board for the whole Oxford thing now."

"Don't mention it. Oh, and I'm happy to inform you that Ralston's new, ah … *body* has arrived. He should be up and operating normally by the time you return."

"That's great news. Please tell him I miss him."

"I will, dear. Be safe."

* * *

Even though I'm essentially confined to quarters, the days leading up to graduation fly by quickly. With all the end-of-year activities at school—yearbook day, the internship luncheon, awards assemblies, and sports banquet, I have more than enough to keep me busy and to help keep my mind off Ryder.

Narowyn gives her blessing for me to spend time at Asher's place as well as mine. His townhouse is comfortable and inviting now that it's been redecorated, and he's a better cook than Dad, so I find myself there as many nights as home.

Despite my many protestations, everyone, including Dad and Drew, believes that Asher's my new boyfriend. I've gotten tired of correcting people, and my own words have a hollow ring, since all the evidence points to the contrary. Truthfully, I'm thankful every day for his company. He's the only one who really knows what I'm going through.

He still acts flirtatious with me all the time, but it's not uncomfortable anymore because I understand that's just him. And he's always respectful of my moody bouts, when I sink into the deep, dark cellar of grief where no one can reach me.

The books Dr. Rivera gave me have helped a lot in that area. I have a couple of face-to-face sessions with her, but find it frustrating that I can't be completely honest. We agree that, going forward, I'll call her on an *as needed* basis. I'm thankful Dad introduced me to her because, even though she seemed very young at first, the books she gave me and her wise insights have had a real impact on me. You'd think I'd have learned by now that age is no indication of ability.

One of Dr. Rivera's best suggestions is to put my gratitude list in writing and carry it with me for when I'm feeling down. It helps me to be more optimistic about the future, and reminds me that I can still find small patches of joy in life—like watching old movies with Ash. He subscribes to all the premium cable channels, and we spend hours catching up on the latest series while we play Words With Friends. He's addicted to American TV, but many nights he's content to sit and read while I study for exams.

One night at dinner, I even decide to confide in him about the weird thing that happened when the automaton attacked me in the street.

"I know you're going to say I need to start seeing Dr. Rivera five times a week. But you know when that automaton had me pinned to the ground and he pulled out his gun? It was the weirdest thing. I shoved my hand in his face and screamed at him. Then a big rush of energy seemed to gush out of my arm. I swear that's what sent him flying down the street."

He inclines his head to one side. "What? You mean you hit him with some kind of super-charged martial arts move?"

"No. I didn't touch him. It felt more electrical or like a force field or something. I know it sounds hokey, but do you think my illuminosity could have made him short circuit and spaz out like that?"

"I guess it's possible. You should tell Dr. McDonald about it. Maybe she'll have an idea what it was all about."

"Okay, but don't say anything to Narowyn. I was pretty freaked-out that night. It might have just been my imagination."

Ash agrees to keep it just between us, and I trust him completely.

The night of Senior Celebration, Ash and I plan to meet Liv and

Antonio at the Madison Pavilion so we can all sit together. Makeup covers the faint traces of bruising still left over from the attack, and I feel kind of pretty in my new black dress. But it just doesn't seem right to be going to a party when I'm still so broken up inside.

When we walk into the ballroom, the air is electrified with the nerves, excitement, and exultation that accompany closing one phase of life and opening a new one. The formal program is blessedly short, the dinner barely passable, but the band turns out to be awesome. Soon, everyone crowds onto the dance floor to party away the pent-up energy. I'm not feeling it, though, and I ask Asher if he would mind taking me home early.

"It's kind of sad," I say. "I just don't belong here anymore."

"Not a problem," he says, "but you'd better let Liv know we're leaving or you'll never hear the end of it."

When I tell Liv that Ash and I are ducking out, she waggles her eyebrows suggestively. "I want details tomorrow," she whispers.

Once we're in the car, Ash puts on some nice jazz music. "Want to talk about it?" he asks.

I shake my head, staring out the window. My thoughts aren't clear even to me. It would be difficult to convey to someone else my anxiety about not belonging anywhere. I'm grateful for this amazing gift I have, but now that I know the world is something much more wondrous and dangerous than I could ever have imagined, my place in it has become even more uncertain.

We park in the driveway, and Ash walks me to my door. "Sleep well," he says, kissing my cheek.

"Thanks for being so great, Ash. See you tomorrow."

Dad looks up from his book as I lock the door behind me. "Didn't expect to see you for hours yet. Did you have a good time, sweetheart?"

"Yeah, it was fun. I have a little headache, though. I'm going to take some Advil and turn in early. G'night, Dad."

I sit on my bed and stare at the sketch of Ryder. "A lot of changes are coming my way, love. I hope I'm up to the challenge."

* * *

Waking on the morning of graduation day, I feel excited and more than a little freaked out. This is really it. The end of life as I knew it. In a few short days, I'm off to England and then on to Arumel to begin a new chapter. It's frightening to think of leaving the small, comfortable way of life I've always known. But it's clear I've outgrown this existence and it's time to move on.

In the auditorium, amid a sea of red caps and gowns, my emotions hover close to the surface. I sit and listen to the nervous chatter going on around me. My own throat aches with the realization that this is the last time I'll see most of these people.

We're seated alphabetically, so I'm among the first group to receive diplomas. When my name is called, my family and friends hoot and cheer and applaud.

I have an odd tightness in my chest on my way to the stage. *Please don't cry. Please don't cry,* I tell myself. The toe of my shoe catches on the very last step and I stumble slightly. A titter goes up from the audience, and I'm sure my face turns the exact shade of my cap, but I don't shed a tear.

And then, after little more than an hour, it's over.

Dad snaps dozens of pictures after the ceremony. "Your mother would be so proud of you," he whispers to me.

Drew slathers a bunch of grief on me for my fumble-footed stage entrance. Asher hugs me warmly. "Congratulations," he says simply. We all head back to the townhouse for a cookout organized by Dad and Lisa.

The next few days, my last in Madison, are beyond hectic. It's astonishing how time-consuming making preparations to abandon one life and start another one can be. Narowyn grants me special permission to visit my mother's grave before I leave town.

Asher drives me to the cemetery in his little red Tesla, while Urick and Nila follow in a black SUV. I place a bouquet of roses on Mom's grave and say my silent goodbyes, wondering if she can see me or sense me from wherever she is. I hope she knows how much I miss her and how scared I am inside.

When we climb back in the car, I inform Asher, "We have one unauthorized stop to make before heading home."

"What? Where?"

"I'll show you. It's on the way."

"Okay, but Narowyn's not going to like it."

"She'll get over it," I tell him.

* * *

"Dad?" I shout when I walk through the front door.

"In here," he calls from the kitchen.

When I stroll into the kitchen with a small ginger kitten in my arms, he laughs. "What've you got there?"

"This is Brady," I tell him. "After your favorite QB."

He takes the kitten from me. "Hey buddy, whose cat are you?" He scratches Brady's head.

"He's yours, Dad. I didn't want you to get too lonely without me."

"Are you serious?" He looks mildly astonished and slightly horrified, but he's still smiling.

"Yep. I got him from the shelter. The little guy needed a home, and I figured the two of you could keep each other company. Asher's out getting you a litter box and food and everything else you'll need."

"You're really something, Jade. You know that?" He rubs his cheek against little Brady's head.

"Yeah, I know. I'll miss you too, Dad."

Asher and I are booked on a flight to London leaving from JFK airport. Dad insists on driving us there, even though the trip is nearly two hours. This little complication contributed to our decision to actually take the flight instead of just shifting from Madison to Oxford. In reality, it's a good development because now we'll be able to leave our things at my flat in England instead of having to stash our suitcases here. Urick and Nila have orders to shift to Oxford and meet us there later.

I say my goodbyes to Drew and Liv at the house. Liv helps me pile my luggage in the car and promises to visit me soon. Asher shakes hands with Drew, and we begin the trek to the airport.

Dad's eyes are wet when he parks in the passenger unloading area. He hugs me closely. "Take care of yourself, sweetheart. If you decide you hate it there, call me. I'll send you a ticket home, no problem."

"Thanks, Dad. Don't worry about me. I'll let you know I made it safely, and I'll send pictures, so check your phone."

"Love you, Jade."

"You too, Dad." Ash and I wave as we roll our suitcases inside the terminal.

I giggle with glee when I find out we're ticketed in first class. The flight attendant takes our drink orders the moment we're buckled in our seats. She smiles engagingly at Asher and calls him "Mr. Steele," in a British accent.

"This is awesome," I say. "We can watch movies and everything."

"Yeah, it's pretty nice, but be prepared for a long, boring flight," Asher grumbles. "Transcender travel is much more efficient."

After takeoff, I find my Oxford travel book and start flipping through the pages. "The first thing I want to do when we get there is see Hogwarts."

"You mean Christ Church College?"

"Yes, but it will always be Hogwarts to me."

"There's much more to it than just the great dining hall," he says, an edge of weariness to his voice. "We'll squeeze everything we can into two days, then I'll be ready to get home." He leans back in his seat and closes his eyes.

For the first time, I fully realize how much Asher has sacrificed to make all of this possible for me. I place my hand on his arm, and he opens his eyes.

"Ash, I've never told you thanks for everything you've done. I hope I haven't seemed too self-centered or ungrateful. I've been dealing with a lot, but I'm truly and deeply grateful for the sacrifices you've made so I could be with my family and go to graduation. You've gone above and beyond."

"Don't worry about it, Beckett. I'm just irritable because I hate to fly." He closes his eyes once again, and I let him have his space. He's more than earned his rest.

THIRTY

Charming is the only word to describe the town of Oxford. The buildings are stately and ornate, the homes straight out of a Victorian picture book. Delicate spring flowers bloom along the boulevards and in quaint planters and window gardens. The taxi drops us in front of the elegant wrought iron railed stairs to my new flat. Of course "new" is a relative term. The building was erected in the 1700s. It resembles a small palace from the outside, though I know I have only a few rooms on the ground floor.

When we step inside, we're greeted by a dank musty smell typically found in neglected old museums or abandoned houses. The rooms are dark with low ceilings, and the furnishings are from another century. It's not quite as cheery as the appealing façade would lead one to believe. I have to remind myself that I'm not really going to be living here.

We unpack our things and decide to nap for a couple of hours before setting out to see the sights. The bedroom has two smallish twin beds. Asher stretches out on top of one of them, his feet dangling over the end. He drifts off to sleep right away. I'm too wired and restless to doze, so I wrap up in a crocheted afghan and settle into a chair facing the living room window. The neighborhood is pretty and appears to be populated mostly with students or the elderly.

I put in my earbuds and pull up a playlist from my phone. For a while after Ryder died, I couldn't listen to music at all, especially love songs. They were painful reminders of what I'd lost. Now though, the old familiar songs are comforting, reminding me of my high school years and home.

The gentle rhythm of the comings and goings in the neighborhood and the soothing music soon lull me into a hazy, dreamlike state. I'm completely taken by surprise when *Zzzt!* Urick and Nila land with a loud thud not two feet from where I sit.

"Holy shit!" I grasp the arms of my chair to keep from falling out.

They seem as startled to see me as I am to see them.

Urick dips his head. His eyes furtively survey the room. "Sorry. We did not expect you to be here already."

I collect myself a bit. "Um, we got here about an hour ago. Asher's sleeping."

"Not anymore," Asher says, padding into the room in stocking feet. "Don't you guys knock?"

"We didn't know you were here," Nila says. "Narowyn wanted us to be on location when you arrived."

"Well, you're late. So does that mean we're all staying here?" Asher asks.

Urick nods.

"Okay," Asher says testily, "but there're only two beds unless the couch folds out."

"We do not require beds," Urick says. "We will take turns on watch."

"Whatever you say. Jade and I are going out to do a little sightseeing and grab some lunch. You two want to come?"

Urick shakes his head. "We will be around."

"Okie dokie. Well, Jade, let me put on my shoes and we'll go."

We hail a cab that takes us to Tom's Gate, the front entrance to Christ Church College.

"Wow, this is huge," I say, taking in the enormous size of the complex.

Asher digs out his Barclays card and buys two tour tickets for us.

The tour takes most of the afternoon with the gardens and the many buildings. The highlight for me of course is the Grand Dining Hall. Once we leave Christ Church, we make a stop at the American Institute so I can familiarize myself with the place where most of my classes are supposed to be—just in case friends or family members visit sometime.

"I know a great place for dinner, Asher says on the cab ride back to the flat. "The White Horse Pub. It sort of epitomizes what Oxford is all about, and you'll get to sample some real British ale."

"Okay, sounds great. Shall we invite Urick and Nila?"

He looks dubious. "Do we have to?"

"No, but they'll be following us anyway. It seems only humane to feed them."

"All right, but I doubt Urick will say two words all evening."

Nila beams when we ask them to join us for dinner. "That sounds great. Doesn't it Urie? I can't wear this uniform, though. Jaden, do you have something I can borrow?"

"Yeah, I brought a few fun things from home."

She chooses a white, sleeveless, embroidered dress that I bought for an outdoor concert last summer. When she steps out of the bedroom, she looks like Queen Bee herself. Shiny sable hair falls attractively around her bare shoulders, softly framing her flawless face. Her long arms and legs are buff without being bulky, and the creamy white dress is stunning against her dusky skin.

247

"Are these boots okay with this?" she asks, referring to her signature black, stiletto knee-highs.

"Oh yeah. You look amazing," I say. Asher doesn't say a word, but the way he's looking at her, I may need to wipe drool off his chin any minute.

The pub is within walking distance of my flat. Nila and Urick follow behind Asher and me. It takes a few minutes after we step inside for my eyes to adjust to the darkness. The strong smells of fried fish and beer hang low in the air, and the sounds of lively conversation and clinking dinnerware greet our ears.

"Care for a table, luv?" The hostess asks Asher with a gap-tooth smile. Her hair is a shade of red that brings raw steak to mind.

"Yes, ma'am. Four, please."

As we follow her through the dining room, all heads turn to gape at Nila and Urick—the Cimmerian Goddess and the Viking King.

After we're seated, Asher orders pints of Wychwood Hobgoblin ale all around. Everything on the menu looks great, but I've already decided on the fish and chips.

A harried waiter delivers our drinks and takes our food orders. I cautiously sip the amber colored ale. It bites my tongue and makes my eyes water. I decide to switch to lemonade for the rest of the evening.

"So Jaden," Nila says once our food is served. "I hear you're a third degree black belt in Tae Kwan Do."

"That's true," I say.

"I practice Akido. Want to spar sometime?"

"Well, since I haven't worked out for a month, and you look like you could kick my ass without breaking a sweat, I think I'll take a rain check on that."

She laughs a rich infectious laugh, showing off her perfectly straight, white teeth. Surprisingly, she laughs quite a lot during the evening. Her style's not nearly as severe as I'd originally assumed. Flashes of a quirky sense of humor and quick wit reveal themselves throughout our dinner conversation. Her manner is confident and easy with both Asher and me—in stark contrast to Urick who sits practically mute with his back to the wall and one eye always on the door.

After the server has cleared away our dinner plates and we're contemplating the dessert choices, a young man in shorts and a t-shirt approaches our table.

"Can I have your autograph?" he says to Nila, laying a pen and a paper cocktail napkin on the table.

"Now why on earth would you want *my* autograph?" she asks.

"Well, besides the fact that you're the most gorgeous woman I've ever seen, I figure you must be famous because you've got a bodyguard." He nods to Urick.

She grins at him. "Why sure, you can have my autograph." She signs the napkin with a flourish and holds it out for him.

"You can put your phone number on there too, if you want," the kid says with a sheepish smile.

"Honey, I'm sure we're not even in the same calling zone."

The guy takes the napkin and reads aloud, "*Tomae Gozen.* Cool name."

"That's me." Nila says.

"Thanks for this!" He snakes his way back through the crowded dining room, waving the napkin at his pals.

"Tomae Gozen?" Asher says.

"I know who that is," I say.

"Girl, you do not. Nobody knows who that is," Nila says.

"Only the most famous woman samurai who ever lived—on this earth at least," I tell her.

"Shut your mouth." She leans across the table. "And how do you know that?"

"Actually, I used to carry a katana back in Domerica. I studied Kendo for a while."

"Kendo?" Her voice raises an octave. "Shit, girl. Now we definitely gotta spar. You sure got a lot more going on than those other Chateau-dwellers." She glances nervously at Ash. "Sorry, no offense."

He treats her to one of his special smiles. "None taken," he says.

We linger over dessert and return to the flat around midnight. With a belly full of fried food and lemonade, I feel contented, exhausted, and ready for sleep even though it's only six o'clock back home. Nila tells Urick she'll take the first watch, and Ash decides to sit up with her for a bit. Urick disappears somewhere into the night.

THIRTY-ONE

In the morning, Asher suggests we go out for an authentic full English breakfast. It sounds wonderful to me, but Urick and Nila decline. I let Asher order and I'm shocked when our food is delivered. It's a full breakfast all right—eggs, sausage, bacon, baked beans, hash browns, roasted tomato halves, and toast.

"Do people really eat this much so early in the morning?" I ask.

"Most important meal of the day," Ash says, stuffing an entire sausage in his mouth.

"I hope we're going to walk this off later."

"I thought we'd rent bicycles. It's a great way to see all the quaint side streets and hidden shops."

"Sounds fun." I shovel my sausages off onto Ash's plate.

"Hey, have you let your dad know that we made it here safely?"

"Yeah. I called him last night and told him all about our day. But that got me thinking. My cell won't work in Arumel so how am I supposed to communicate with people back home?"

"We'll program your cell number into your polycom and you'll use that."

"Okay, but how will that work when we pick up time going back to Arumel? Will there be a big time gap in my communications? I don't want Dad to be worried."

"You'll do what Narowyn did when she called your dad about Oxford. For a while, you'll need to call or text backward in time, but eventually you'll catch up. I'll show you how to do it before we rent the bikes. I got kind of good at it when we were in Connecticut."

"That sounds a little weird."

He shrugs. "Not that much different from calling someone in another time zone. You'll have to finesse it a little in the beginning, but you'll be texting and emailing in real time well before you go home for a visit."

"I can email too?"

"Yeah, after we program your polycom, just sync it to your computer in Arumel and it'll work the same way."

"If you say so." I'm constantly amazed at how much I don't fathom about parallel worlds.

We get in a half day of bicycling around Oxford's neighborhoods before Asher's polycom rings. After a short conversation, he says, "A Garugian has been sighted on a Confederation earth. Urick and Nila need to leave immediately, which means you and I must return to Arumel now."

Urick and Nila wait for us while we drop off the bikes. I stuff everything I can fit into my embroidered bag—my favorite dress, a pair of flip-flops, a photo of Dad and Drew, and two books Dr. Rivera gave me. Then, *Zzzt,* we're off—Asher and I to Arumel City, Nila and Urick to hunt Garugians.

The shift back to Arumel seems normal, even though we recoup the time we lost traveling back to Madison. It's early evening when we land in the downstairs foyer of the Chateau du Soleil. I feel slightly disoriented, and shake my head briskly, to clear out the cobwebs.

Narowyn comes to greet us as we arrive. She embraces Asher warmly and plants kisses on both my cheeks. "Welcome home, you two," she says. "Jaden, we've all been rather anxious for your safe return. Ralston, in particular, is looking forward to seeing you."

"I can't wait to see him. Where is he?"

"We thought it might be best to ease you into your first visit with him now that he looks quite different. Why don't you and Asher put away your things, freshen up if you like, and join us in the library. We've put together an impromptu reception for the two of you."

Ash and I take the elevator to the third floor. "Want me to come and get you?" he asks as I turn toward my apartment.

"Nah, I'll just see you in the library. I'm going to shower before going down."

"All right. Catch you later."

When I open the door to my apartment, a shuddering gloom gusts through me like an icy wind, bringing back memories of the first time I set foot inside this apartment—covered in Patrick's blood, only minutes after witnessing Ryder's fall. Although I've done a few things to make the place cozier, it still feels alien to me—the frozen tundra of my exile. I wonder if it will ever feel like home.

I slip the embroidered bag from my shoulder and pull out my wrinkled sundress. At least this is familiar. I shake it out and take it with me into the bathroom, hoping to steam away the creases while I shower.

Thirty minutes under a stream of hot water does wonders for my outlook. A warm excitement fills me up when I think about being reunited with Rals. I've missed his quiet, nurturing support these past weeks. I'm going to need him now more than ever to help me adjust to this new existence.

I dress quickly and take the elevator downstairs. The library is one of my favorite rooms in the Chateau. One wall is floor to ceiling windows, specially treated to block out harmful UV rays. All of the other walls are lined with bookshelves, which I was pleased to see hold real hardbound books—some very old and rare.

The room now brims with vibrant, chattering people, sipping from crystal goblets and munching exotic finger foods. As I enter, Narowyn steps forward to greet me and the crowd erupts with applause. This enthusiastic reception surprises me. I'm not a queen or princess here. I'm just an ordinary member of the household, and that's all I want to be. I smile and nod, feeling a little shy.

Narowyn slips an arm around my waist, and several people step forward to welcome me home. I haven't spent enough time in Arumel to recognize everyone, but it's reassuring to find a few familiar faces in the room.

"Ah, here is someone I believe you've been waiting to see," Narowyn says.

She turns me in the direction of an attractive man in his mid-forties with wavy, sandy-colored hair and a raffish smile.

"How are you, old girl?" he says with a slight British accent.

My jaw falls slack. I know the voice, *but it can't be*. "Ralston?"

"It is I," he says. "What do you think?" He holds out his arms and does a full three-sixty.

"No. This is just wrong," I say.

His expression falters, and I can tell he's completely crushed. "You don't like the new me?"

I put my hands to my burning cheeks. *God, I can be such an ass sometimes*. "No. It's not that … It's, well, you're just so … handsome."

A trace of his smile returns, and his pale blue eyes look meaningfully into mine.

"Your eyes?" I say.

"Yes. They're mine. The technicians were able to salvage them, and my voice box, as well as my memories. I hoped that would help mitigate the shock of the change in me."

"Oh god, Rals, I'm sorry. Come here."

I wrap my arms around his neck and close my eyes. He smells wonderfully like his old cologne.

"I've missed you, my dear," he says.

"Same here." I release him and appraise the new look once more. Appearance shouldn't make a difference, I know. But there's comfort in the familiar, and this is going to take some time getting used to.

"How are you holding up?" he asks.

I lower my eyes. "I have my ups and downs." This isn't the right time or place to go into detail, and I need a minute to get over the shock of Ralston's transformation. "We'll talk a little later. Okay?"

"Of course. Please ..." he gestures to the room. "Get some food and say your *hellos*. I shall be right here."

I snag a glass of sparkling water from the tray of a passing waiter and wander to the buffet table.

"Jade! You're home." Eve bounces up behind me and hugs me enthusiastically, sloshing water all over my dress. "It's been like a tomb around here. But I'm off restrictions now. Let's do something fun this week."

"Sure, that'd be great." I blot the front of my dress with a cocktail napkin and link my arm in hers. "Walk with me for a few minutes, okay? I've forgotten some of these names. You can remind me."

"Absolutely. And I'll give you the inside scoop on everyone as we go."

I huff a nervous laugh. "Just be subtle about it, all right?"

We smile our way around the room, and Eve whispers names to me as we approach different knots of people. She also offers juicy little tidbits here and there as we mingle with the crowd.

"Frank has a huge aquarium in his apartment," she says, "and I swear he eats his own fish. Oh, and Judy over there—the tall blonde—she only dates automatons."

"Do people really do that?"

"People who're afraid of certain kinds of involvements, if you know what I mean. She's been sniffing around Ralston ever since he arrived."

After an hour or so, Asher makes his appearance. He says a quick hello to Narowyn and hurries to my side.

"I'm so sorry, Jade. I fell asleep. I've traveled backward and forward through time so much lately, my internal clock is completely screwed-up."

"Don't worry about it Ash, Eve's taking good care of me." She clamps a possessive arm around my waist.

"Have you seen Ralston yet?" Asher asks.

"Yes. Have you?"

He shakes his head scanning the crowd.

"He's so pretty now, he'll be impossible to live with," I say.

"Where is he? I've got to see this."

"I need to talk to him anyway. I'll walk you over."

"I'm going to get some food," Eve says. "Can I fix you a plate, Jade?"

"No. I'm good. I'll see you later, though."

Ash is almost as blown away by Ralston's new look as I was. "Rals you look ten years younger, my man." He slaps him on the back.

"I feel ten years younger too." Ralston runs a hand over his thick thatch of hair. "None of the nasty tics I had with the older model."

"Hey, Rals. Can I speak with you for few minutes alone?" I say.

"I'd be delighted, my dear. There's a lovely little sitting room just across the hall. Shall we?"

I set my empty glass on a tray and follow him to a homey, lamp-lit room. We close the door and sit in two arm chairs near the fireplace. It's weird, I feel kind of timid in his company. I don't think I've fully accepted that he's really the same old Rals I know and love.

"Jaden, I was so very sorry to hear about Ryder. You must be devastated," he says softly.

"Yeah, I'm pretty wrecked about it. Patrick's dead too. Did you know that? An automaton from IUGA somehow got assigned to my protection team. Without your glasses, I never would have known, and we all would've been killed."

"I only know some of the details, but it must have been terrifying for you."

"It was nothing compared to watching Ryder fall from that tower. I felt helpless. I couldn't get to him in time. What was he doing up there, Rals?"

He shakes his head slowly. "I wish I could tell you. As you know, none of the probable scenarios placed him in the tower room. Some alteration must have occurred after we were forced to give up the QP."

"I can't help but think I could've done something to save him." I lower my eyes. "He died trying to rescue me, and I wasn't really in danger."

"His death is not your fault, Jaden. You sacrificed everything to ensure the well-being of your family. You executed your part of the plan perfectly."

I look up with a tinge of resentment that he doesn't have the same old amiable, avuncular appearance anymore. But his eyes convey his deep concern. I suppose I'll get beyond his new looks soon enough.

"What happened to you?" I ask. "Why weren't you at the stable to meet Asher and the others?"

"Oh, well, that is a rather unpleasant story. It must have been IUGA's plan all along to be rid of me as soon as they were certain you were dead. I was ambushed the moment I set foot in the stable. My arms and legs were summarily removed to prevent my escape. What was left of me was whisked away to the graveyard facility where you discovered me."

"I'm so sorry, Rals," I rest my hand on his arm.

"Not to worry." He pats my hand. "I'm in better condition now than before, and we're together. It's more than I could've hoped for."

"Hey, you don't wear glasses anymore?"

"No. Everything's built-in on this model. It's quite remarkable." He grins, and I see some of the old Rals in him.

"So, do you like it here?" I ask, betraying my own misgivings.

"Oh yes. I have a flat-mate—I believe you've met Gil, the only other automaton in residence?"

"Yes, I met him before. Seems nice."

"He can be a bit tedious at times, rather an unimaginative chap. But not bad company. Now that you're here, though, I'm hoping to pursue some more agreeable pastimes."

I smile. "Like whipping my ass at chess, you mean?"

"That, among other things. I assume you'd be up for some advanced fencing instruction and additional tutoring in French, perhaps?"

"Fencing, yes. French, not unless forced. I'm glad you brought it up, though. It doesn't feel right, my not going to college. I don't want my education to just stop right here. Maybe you can help me with that."

"When do you begin your Transcender training?" he asks.

"I don't know. Soon I think."

"Why don't you see what Narowyn has in store for you, and we'll fill in the rest."

"Okay. That'll work." I try, but fail, to stifle a yawn.

"You must be tired, my dear."

"Yes, and time-zone loopy from all the traveling. Also, I need to go upstairs and send a message to my dad. I phoned him from Oxford, but I promised to send photos. Ash showed me how to do it on the polycom."

"Then you should retire to your apartment, if you like. I'll make your excuses to Narowyn and the others. I'm certain they'll understand."

"Really? You don't think Narowyn will mind?"

"Heavens no. She knows what you've been through."

"Thanks. See you in the morning." Even though it feels weird, I peck him on the cheek.

"Goodnight, old girl."

THIRTY-TWO

Back in my apartment, the melancholy sets in again. The place has as much charm as a Motel 6.

After changing into my pajama bottoms and a tank, I stare at the photo of Drew and Dad for a few minutes before placing it on the bedside table. I'm grateful that they're still in my life, even if I can't live near them. Especially now that Ralston feels a little like a stranger to me.

I dig out my polycom and type out a text to Dad, attaching photos from our tour of Christ Church College. I program it the way Asher showed me so that it will arrive two days after my departure from Madison. I hit the send button and cross my fingers that it works.

The computer monitor sits prominently in the center of my desk. I've never fired it up before, but I figure this might be a good time to sync my phone to it so I can send and receive emails.

It takes me a minute to locate the "on" switch. Once the screen lights up, a multitude of unfamiliar icons swim before my eyes. I check the drawer for a keyboard or mouse, but find nothing. I touch one of the icons and a woman's voice says, "Good evening, Jaden. How may I help you?"

I recognize her—same lady who works the TVs. "Uh, I'd like to sync my polycom with the computer and set up an email account."

"Of course," she says. "You currently have two active email accounts. By synchronizing your polycom with your computer, you will have the ability to share files between the two devices."

"Really? What are my active email accounts?"

"Jaden Beckett at Transcender Society Headquarters, or Jaden Beckett at Oxford University. Do you wish to set up another account?"

"No. I think those are good. Do I have the ability to exchange emails with people on other earths?"

"Yes, if the other earth possesses the appropriate communications satellites. Would you care to see a directory of communications compatible earths?"

"No. That's okay. Is earth 7Y12 one of them?"

"Yes. Would you care to send an email to someone on 7Y12?"

"Not right now. But what about sending emails back in time? Can I do that too?"

"This computer is not equipped with that capability. If your polycom possesses time transversing capability, once the devices are synchronized, your computer can triangulate with your polycom to transmit antedated emails."

"Okay, cool. So how do I sync the devices?"

"Type this code into your polycom and press send."

The code J7268954 appears on my computer screen. I type it into my poly and send it. The polycom screen lights up and a small brain icon appears with all kinds of colorful synapses firing inside.

After about a minute the brain is replaced with the message "Synchronization Successful."

"You have successfully synchronized your devices," the

woman's voice says. "May I help you with something else?"

"Not tonight," I say, amazed that it was so easy. "Oh wait, before you go, what's your name?"

"Vasa," she says.

"Vasa? Does that stand for something?"

"Yes. Voice Activated Software Assistant."

"So what else can you control in my apartment?"

"Computer, television, music—"

"I have music?"

"Yes. Each room is equipped with surround sound, and you have access to the entire library for the Chateau. Would you care to see the menu?"

"Not tonight, but we'll do it soon. What else?"

"I can adjust the lighting and the thermostat, run your major appliances, and take telephone messages. Simply say a command."

"That's great. Thanks, Vasa."

"You're welcome, Jaden. Goodnight."

The monitor shuts itself off. That was kind of spooky-cool. I may not be a princess here, but there are some perks.

I try to wrap my brain around how far an email would have to go to reach Dad on a completely different earth. But then again, maybe that's not how it works. Maybe he's really very close, being in a parallel dimension. It overwhelms me to realize how much there is to know about my new life. The learning process begins tomorrow.

My bed is soft and the plush comforter inviting. I squish the pillows up behind me. "TV on," I say.

"Hello again, Jaden, what do you wish to watch?"

"Find me something funny and light."

"Movie or series?" she asks.

Before I can answer, someone tap-taps the knocker on my front door. "Who is it?" I call, sprinting out of bed.

"Jaden, it's Eve, I have someone here to see you."

Visitors? When I open the door she appears to be alone, but she scoots to one side, and a yellow haired dog with floppy ears and liquid brown eyes waggles inside.

"Callie!" I crouch and scratch her fluffy head. "Hey, girl. What are you doing here?"

She slathers my face with wet kisses.

"She showed up at the front door a few minutes ago. We figured she was here to see you because she hasn't come back to the Chateau since you two spent the day together."

"This is great. Can she stay the night?"

"Sure. The people at the Community Animal Center will know where she is. All of the animals have chip implants that transmit their location and vital signs to the Center. The caregivers always know where they are and that they're okay."

"Oh, cool. Thanks for bringing her up."

"You two have fun. Ta," Eve says.

Callie follows me to the bedroom. She leaps into the center of my comforter, circles twice and flops down. I climb up beside her and pull her into my arms. The wonder and joy I feel at her unexpected appearance is almost mystical. She licks my cheek and settles in my arms. Pure dog energy seeps into my soul.

"This is good," I say nuzzling her fur. "This is a good omen."

* * *

Callie wakes first and nudges me with her wet nose.

"Morning, girl. You probably need to go outside." She hops out of bed and waits, tail wagging, for me to do the same. I change into a pair of slouchy linen pants and yank on a sweater over my tank top.

When we reach the first floor, I follow the sounds of voices and the aromas of cooking to the main kitchen. I'm surprised to see a half dozen fellow Transcenders working with the kitchen staff preparing breakfast. It smells divine like sweetness and spice. My stomach gurgles when I spot a tray of gingerbread muffins on the counter.

"Is it okay if I have one of these?" I ask the skinny redhead standing at the counter cutting up fruit. I search my still drowsy brain for his name.

"Sure, Jaden. Help yourself," he says with a sunny smile.

"Thanks Jeffrey." I pluck his name from the air just in time. The muffin is warm and I wrap it in a cloth napkin. "Do you know if there's anything to feed my friend here?"

"Yeah, sure. We always have food for the animals in the pantry. It'll be on your left."

"Great. See you later."

Callie and I pad into the pantry. I pick up a couple of bowls and a can of organic veggie dog food, and we head out the back door. The morning air is cool and clean with a piney, fresh scent. Callie sniffs around the grounds while I empty the can of food into one bowl and fill the other with water from the outside tap.

I perch on a picnic bench and nibble my muffin while Callie eats. The Chateau grounds are gorgeous and meticulously maintained, reminding me of pictures I've seen of some grand chateaus in France. Trees line the circumference of the property. Sparkling white pathways crisscross vast expanses of lawn. Precisely trimmed hedges surround garden areas containing comfortable benches, playful fountains, and well-tended flower beds. The grounds crew is already hard at work, mowing, trimming, pruning, and sweeping.

A few attractive cottages dot the property. I know Narowyn and her husband live in one of these, and some of the married Transcenders live in the others. A large greenhouse hugs the southern border of the grounds and the Transcender police barracks is just visible in the distance.

"Jaden?" My survey of the estate is interrupted by a vaguely familiar voice. I turn to find a tall, sulky-looking girl with milk-white skin, jet-black hair, and an eyebrow stud, standing behind me. I remember her from my first visit here. She's the only Transcender I would characterize as unfriendly.

"Hi, Monica," I say.

"Narowyn asked me to find you and tell you to meet her in her office at ten. Okay?"

"Sure. Fine. Did she say what it's about?"

"Didn't ask. Not my business." She's perfected the *I don't give a crap* slouch.

"All righty then. Thanks for delivering the message."

"One more thing," she says, picking at her black nail polish, "are you and Ash, like, together?"

"What are you talking about?"

"I mean, the two of you seem awfully cozy."

I shake my head in disbelief. "Seriously? It's only been a month since my husband died."

"That doesn't really answer my question." She raises her dark brows.

"Uh, yeah, it does, and for future reference, my love life is also not your business."

Curling her lip at me, she whirls on the heel of her Doc Martens, and trudges off.

Callie looks up at me with knowing eyes. "Yeah, she's weird," I say, picking up the dog bowls. "Are you coming with me or going back to the center?"

She nudges my hand with her nose and I figure that means *I'm with you* in dog speak.

THIRTY-THREE

Once I'm showered and dressed for the day, Callie races me down the three flights of stairs to Narowyn's office.

"Stay here, girl," I say when we reach Narowyn's door. She lies down on the rug. Inside, I find Narowyn working at her conference table.

"Oh Jaden, come in. Please sit down." She nods to the chair next to hers. "I pulled some things together for you. How did you sleep the first night back in your apartment?"

"I slept okay. Callie, my dog friend from the center, stayed with me last night. It was nice to have company."

"She's a sweetheart. Are you comfortable in your apartment, then?"

"Truthfully, no. It still reminds me of the day Ryder died, and it's awfully bare."

"Oh dear. Well, we didn't want to do too much to it before you arrived, but let's make it a top priority now. Would you like some decorating help, or would you prefer to do it yourself?"

"Maybe Asher will help me. He's much better at that stuff than I am."

She shuffles through the papers in front of her. "I'm certain he'll be happy to lend you his considerable skills."

"I'll ask him."

"Fine. Now, I want to go over some of the household rules with you."

"Household rules?" I bristle at the term.

"Not many, really. We have a household staff which tends to all the common areas and the grounds of the Chateau. Your apartment will be cleaned once a week by the staff, but other than that, each resident is responsible for keeping his or her apartment tidy and in good repair. In addition, each resident is assigned a tour on kitchen duty. It normally turns out to be one week every other month. This varies depending on exploration schedules and the like. Do you know how to cook?"

I shake my head. "Not really."

"Then this will be an excellent opportunity for you to learn. In addition, while at home, all residents are encouraged to eat a minimum of one meal a day in the main dining room. We feel this fosters camaraderie, the free exchange of information, and a collegial atmosphere. Most of us choose to share the evening meal together. It's always quite enjoyable. Of course you are welcome to eat all your meals in the dining room if you wish."

"Do I have to sign up in advance or anything?"

"No. We always have enough food, and we give away anything we do not consume."

"All right. What else?"

"Other than respecting the comfort and privacy of others, that's about it for household rules." She slides a document across the table to me. "Everything is written down here. You'll have a generous allowance for decorating and upkeep of your apartment. Any special requests requiring a major remodel must go through me, as must any complaints."

I scan the paper. Basically it reiterates what she just told me. I think I can live with the rules.

"Also, I wanted to give you this." She presents me with a beautiful black leather bound volume. My name is embossed in gold on the front cover along with the Transcender motto: *timeas non plures semitas vitae*, which translated means *fear not the many paths of life*.

"This is beautiful. What is it?"

"It's the Transcender Handbook. It contains our mission statement, our code of conduct, and special governmental regulations relating to Transcenders."

"I flip open the book. What kind of special regulations?"

"Essentially, they cover things like the use of advanced medicine or weaponry on other earths, bans on importation from other earths, those types of things. You should familiarize yourself with all of them. This will be your bible." She taps the book with her finger.

"Okay. I'll read it tonight."

"Excellent. Lastly, I have a tentative schedule here for your training. You are to begin tomorrow, if you are up to it. I hope to have you ready for your first exploration in a few months."

That sends a little shiver through me. "I'm up to it. What does it entail?"

She places a schedule in front of me and I read down the list:

Firearms Training, 9:00 10:00 a.m. M, T, W, Th, F
Spontaneous Shifting, 10:10 11:10 a.m. M, T, W, Th, F
Study of Alternate Earths, 11:15-12:15 p.m. M, T, W, Th, F
Cartography, 12:20-1:30 p.m. M, W, F
Science of Transcending, 12:20-1:30 p.m. T, Th

"This looks great," I say. "I hoped to get in some additional fencing training from Ralston. We can do that in the afternoon."

"Indeed, and I wonder if you'd object to Ralston training a few others in fencing and perhaps sharing his knowledge of other governments with us?"

"That's completely up to him. I don't own him. He's his own man. Or I think he is. Now that you bought him that great body and all, you don't plan to force him to do chores or anything like that do you?"

"We don't force anyone, Jaden. But as a member of the household, I would expect him to want to do his share."

"I'm sure he will. It's just that he's more of a teacher than a house servant."

"Understood," she says indulgently. "Now let's go over your schedule."

We don't have the opportunity, though, because the office door opens and Captain Watterson says, "Narowyn, I have some gentlemen here who wish to speak with you."

"Of course, please come in." Narowyn rises from her chair.

Watterson steps inside followed by two uniformed men. They look like police, but obviously not part of the Transcender force.

"Mrs. Du Lac, I'm Lieutenant Michaels of the Arumel City Police. This is Officer Ross." The lieutenant is tall, athletic, and a good haircut shy of being handsome.

"Nice to meet you," she says, shaking his hand. "This is Jaden Beckett. She has recently relocated to Arumel."

He turns to me. "Ah yes, Miss Beckett. I'm familiar with the circumstances of your relocation."

I don't have a clue what he means by that.

"What can I do for you, Lieutenant?" Narowyn says.

"Ma'am, we're looking for some stolen property, and we received a tip that it might be here at the Chateau du Soleil."

"Really?" Narowyn's voice is a blend of surprise and indignation. "What stolen property?"

"An automaton. Model X-226, IUGA Registration No. D7829. It's valued in excess of one hundred fifty thousand CD, making the theft a first degree felony. Our information indicates you currently own two automatons?"

"Yes, we have two in residence."

"Do you have paperwork for them?"

"Of course."

"May we see it?"

She narrows her eyes a moment as if considering this. Then she goes to a nearby filing cabinet and takes a brown folder from the second drawer. "You will find everything in order."

The lieutenant takes the offered file and flips through the documents inside. He raises his eyes to Narowyn. "One of these is quite new."

"That's correct."

"May I ask why you made this recent purchase?"

"Because we desired a second automaton," she says dryly.

His jaw tightens. "I see. May we have a look at them?"

"You may. Captain Watterson, would you kindly locate our two automatons and bring them to my office?"

"Yes, Chief." He bows slightly and leaves the room.

"Lieutenant, exactly where did this tip of yours come from?" Narowyn asks.

"The automaton is the property of IUGA, ma'am. We were told it had a previous connection to Miss Beckett and that it may have found its way here."

Holy shit! My stomach caves in on itself.

"This is quite outrageous. Since when do you go about invading the privacy of law abiding citizens on a baseless tip from IUGA? You know full well they have a vendetta against Miss Beckett. She has filed a major lawsuit against them, alleging among other things that they facilitated a plot to have her assassinated."

"I'm aware of that ma'am. But this tip came from the IUGA director himself."

This bit of news seems to intrigue Narowyn. "Oh really? How interesting that Director Canto is personally involved in a case relating to a missing automaton."

Captain Watterson returns with Gil and Ralston trailing closely behind.

"Gentlemen, thank you for coming," Narowyn says. "Here they are Lieutenant. What now?"

Officer Ross removes an instrument from his belt that I recognize as an illumometer. He pushes a button and the readout lights up, crackling with loud static.

Ross squints at the readout, taps the instrument against his thigh and checks it again.

I try to swallow, but it feels like a wad of toilet paper is stuck in my throat.

Ross holds the instrument first in front of Gil and then in front of Ralston. "I'm picking up some kind of interference in here," he says, confused. "I can't get a reading."

Narowyn touches my shoulder. "It may be Miss Beckett. Her illuminosity is rather powerful. Jaden, why don't we stand over here?"

I follow her to the other side of the room. She places a reassuring hand on my shoulder. My breath stalls in my chest while Officer Ross tries again. The static on the instrument dies down, and he uses it to scan both Ralston and Gil from head to toe.

Turning to Michaels, he shakes his head. "Neither of them is our guy."

"You want to check me, just in case?" Watterson says, holding his hands up in the air.

Michaels ignores the sarcasm. "It appears our tip was inaccurate, ma'am. My apologies."

"Do you wish to search the premises?" Narowyn asks.

"No, thank you, Mrs. Du Lac. It's not necessary. As I'm sure you're aware, that instrument would've picked up something had the robot been anywhere on your property. Sorry to have inconvenienced you, ma'am."

"Please tell Chief Prescott I'd appreciate the professional courtesy of a phone call if he intends to pursue any such spurious tips in the future." Narowyn's voice has an icy edge. "I will not be so accommodating the next time."

"Yes, ma'am, I'll let him know." The lieutenant salutes her, and the two men quickly leave.

Gil speaks first. "My goodness, what was that all about? My tension sensors are registering off the charts."

"Sorry to have involved you in this, Gil," Narowyn says. "It's nothing for you to be concerned about. You may return to what you were doing before you were summoned."

"Yes, ma'am. I'll just be on my way." He starts for the door. "I'll see you at home Constantine." He gives Ralston a small wave before slipping out. Narowyn closes the door behind him.

Ralston's cheeks flush slightly, and he studies the rug.

"Let's sit for a moment, shall we?" Narowyn resumes her seat at the conference table. Ralston and I join her there. Watterson pulls out a chair, flips it around, and sits with his arms resting on the seat back.

"So they have discovered you are missing," she says to Ralston,

273

"and the Director himself seems to have taken an interest in getting you back. I find that rather curious."

"Perhaps," Ralston says, "But I imagine they're anxious to locate me because of what is contained in my memory storage. I know too much. If the information were made public, it could be quite detrimental to the agency."

"Well, if they view you as a threat, why did they toss you outside on that scrap heap?" Watterson asks. "That whole pile was slated to be carted off to the public refuse center the next day."

"I do not know. I'm afraid my circuits had already been disabled when that decision was made," Ralston says.

Narowyn fingers the crystal beads at her neck. "The Director's personal involvement is intriguing. In any event, I suspect we've not heard the last of this."

Watterson stands and rotates his chair back to its original position. "I was just on my way to a briefing. Anything else, Chief?"

"No, that will be all for now. I understand Urick's team was successful last night."

"Yes. One less Garugian terrorizing the multiverse."

"Very good."

After he leaves, Narowyn turns to Ralston. "I'm sorry you were subjected to that. I trust you knew you were in no danger of being discovered."

"No apology necessary," he says. "I'm aware that my imprint changed along with my shell."

"Good. Now, I need to finish up a few things with Jaden. But at some point, you and I should speak about the possibility of your taking on some instructional duties here at the Chateau."

Ralston stands and bows. "I'm at your service."

Once we're alone again, I ask Narowyn, "How worried should I be about this? I mean, IUGA tried to make it look like I stole Ralston. Could I be in trouble?"

"It's nothing for you to worry about, dear. We may need to address the issue of Ralston's ownership at some point, but I'm confident that IUGA will be on the losing end of that battle. In fact, we have an important hearing in our case coming up next month. You and I will meet with the lawyers beforehand to prepare. They'll answer all your questions at that time."

"All right."

"Let's return to your training schedule, shall we?"

I look over the schedule again. "Okay Firearms Training I understand. What's Spontaneous Shifting?"

"It's important that you learn to shift to and from certain familiar locations without the aid of your TPD. It requires some training, but should eventually become second nature. Your Cartography class includes instruction on reading and constructing three-dimensional, interstitial maps. The kind you have in your bracelet. Also an important part of our work."

"The Study of Alternate Earths sounds self-explanatory," I say. "But what's the Science of Transcending?

"It's the study of how it all works from a scientific perspective—mostly physics and quantum mechanics."

That sounds intimidating. "But I don't know much about either of those things."

"Your professor may need to work with you to bring you up to speed, but you should be able to grasp it easily enough."

All thoughts of becoming stagnant or letting my education slip have vanished. Now, I'm just hoping to keep up.

"In your spare time you can work on decorating your apartment and seeing more of Arumel," she says. "We have many fine museums and gardens. The Creighton Zoo is a must. It houses many formerly extinct animals not found anywhere else on earth—including a herd of wooly Mammoths, and a few of the smaller dinosaur species. You'll not lack for interesting activities here."

"I'm sure you're right." I gather my things, preparing to leave.

"Give me a moment and I'll get you an electronic notebook." She steps out of the office and returns two minutes later holding what looks like a clear rectangle of glass, about five inches by seven inches.

"Here you are, dear. It's mainly for your textbooks and class notes, but certain games and videos have been included. Additionally, you may download whatever else you wish."

"Great. Thanks." I turn it over in my hand, baffled as to how a clear piece of glass can do all that.

"Will you be at dinner tonight?" she asks.

"Yes. I'll see you then."

With all the earlier commotion, it appears Callie decided not to stick around outside Narowyn's door. I take the stairs to the third floor and meet Asher in the hallway. He's wearing gym clothes with a towel draped around his neck. Sweat-drenched locks of hair cling to his forehead and neck.

"Good workout?" I ask.

"Yeah. You'll have to come with me sometime. Gym's on the second floor. He eyes my armload of things. "I see you got your schedule and your handbook."

"Yep. All set to start training tomorrow."

"Great. You'll be ready to get out in the field before you know it."

"Narowyn says a few months. We'll see. Anyway, I'm glad I bumped into you. Do you have some time this afternoon to take me shopping for my apartment. I mean, it's kind of pathetic in its current vanilla condition, and I could use your *je ne sait quoi*."

He laughs. "Stick to English, Jade. What you want is my *savior-faire*."

"What I want is your mad decorating skills."

He pulls the towel from his neck and mops his forehead. From the looks of his arms and legs he must work out often. "Sorry, Jade, I can't this afternoon. I have another commitment. But what about tomorrow? What time do you finish up?"

"I'm done at one thirty."

"We can virtual shop from your apartment, if you want. You know, try things out holographically. I always like to see things in person, though—touch the fabric, test the sturdiness, that type of thing. How about we grab a late lunch downtown? After that, I'll take you to this amazing place, Trope's Home Furnishings. It's no Target, but I think they'll have everything you need."

I laugh. "Sounds great. You going to be at dinner tonight?"

"Yeah. It's lasagna night. Wouldn't miss it," he says with a grin.

"Okay, see you then."

Since I have nothing to do for the rest of the afternoon, and after seeing Asher's toned body, I decide this might be a good time for me to resume my workout program. The Chateau's gym is large, bright, and well-equipped.

After warming up on a treadmill, I decide to do a circuit or two on the machines. They're pretty much the same as the ones at the YMCA in Madison, except these have clear overhead screens attached. The screens display the weight resistance, number of reps, current heart rate, and calories burned. It's kind of cool until, in the middle of my routine, I hear a little ding, ding, ding and a flashing red message appears on the screen. A man's voice authoritatively informs me I'm not lifting my arms high enough.

If I wanted to be nagged, I'd hire a personal trainer. After a minute, I figure out how to disable the obnoxious screens, and do the rest of my workout in peace. By the end of my second circuit, I'm winded and beat. I'm more out of shape than I realized. I down a glass of cucumber water and trudge through the outside door in search of Callie. She's nowhere to be seen on the grounds. I call a few times, but nothing. I hope I wasn't just a one night stand for her.

After a hot shower, I sit cross-legged on my bed and open up my new Transcender Handbook. Page one contains the Transcender Mission Statement: *To enhance quality of life for all and encourage multiuniversal cooperation through the nonintrusive study of parallel societies and ecosystems.* Sounds lofty.

The Transcender Code of Conduct begins on page two. My eyes begin to glaze over as I scan down a dozen rules relating to being a Transcender. I toss the book aside and slump back into my pillows, feeling a little crabby. I've only been out of high school for a week, and I'm definitely not ready for more rules.

"Vasa, put on some music please."

"Good afternoon, Jaden. What type of music do you prefer?"

"I don't know. Something soft. I'm ready for a nap."

"I have a collection of piano instrumentals with gentle sounds of the ocean in the background."

"Hmm, sounds perfect."

THIRTY-FOUR

The main dining room is already half full by the time I arrive for dinner. As the newest member of the Transcender community, I still feel awkward when I'm in a large group. The room is bathed in a soft golden glow of candlelight and dimly-lit chandeliers. I crane my neck for a sign of Asher or Ralston, but neither of them has arrived yet. Urick and a few members of his team are seated on one side of the long plank table. I consider taking an empty seat next to Nila, but Narowyn calls to me from the head of the table.

"Jaden, please come and sit next to me."

I'm relieved at the invitation, and I plant myself in the empty seat on Narowyn's right.

"I'd like you to meet my husband," she says. The gentleman on her left stands and extends his hand to me. "Hugh, this is Jaden Beckett. Jaden, this is Hugh Du Lac."

"Nice to meet you," I say. "I've heard so much about you." This is the first time I've seen Narowyn's husband at the Chateau.

"We're happy you're finally here," he says, shaking my hand with gusto. "Narowyn did not have a moment's peace or a good night's sleep until you arrived safely back in Arumel."

"Hugh exaggerates," Narowyn says, her eyes betraying slight

embarrassment. "But we are happy to have you with us again."

Asher makes an entrance looking extra gorgeous in a loose silk shirt the same pale green as his eyes. He whispers something to the woman seated on my right, and she graciously gives up her seat to him. "You look beautiful," he says, kissing my cheek.

Gil and Ralston trundle in moments later and sit together near the end of the table. Ralston catches my eye and nods. Once everyone is seated, Narowyn rises and the room grows silent.

"Good evening. It is wonderful to see you all tonight. This is a special evening. We are blessed to welcome our newest sister, Jaden, back into our household after her extended visit home. In keeping with our house tradition, before we begin our meal, I'd like to ask Jaden to share a few words of gratitude with us on any subject she desires." She smiles at me, eyes shining. "Jaden, if you would be so kind ..."

I'm jolted as if she just threw a glass of cold water in my face. Narowyn reseats herself, and all eyes turn to me. My brain scrambles to compose a few cheesy lines about how great it is to be in my new home with my new brothers and sisters, and yada, yada, yada. But *No!* I refuse to be that person, even if I was blind-sided.

"Thank you, Narowyn," I say, looking into the faces around the table. "Most of you don't know me well. But you probably do know that I recently lost a beloved husband. And though we were not married long, I found it difficult in the beginning to dwell on anything other than the enormity of my loss. But one morning I awoke to sunshine streaming through the bedroom curtains. The simple beauty of that brilliant light sliced through the pain and darkness, and for the briefest moment, I experienced a small spark of hope.

"Since then, I try to find something hopeful to hold onto each day—something that touches me or brings me joy. I've made it a practice to jot these things down on what I call my *Gratitude List*. It's a deeply personal compilation, but I'd like to share it with you."

I tug the somewhat tattered list from my dress pocket and slowly begin to read.

> "Gratitude List:
> *Sunshine through white curtains.*
> *A good hair day.* (This draws a few snickers from the table.)
> *Crisp, salty bacon.* (A few groans.)
> *Warm hugs.*
> *A father's love.*
> *A purring kitten.*
> *A friend from childhood.*
> *A brother's lame jokes.*
> *Freshly baked cinnamon rolls.* (Some *mmms* from the group.)
> *A kind and generous savior.* (I nod to Narowyn.)
> *Financial security.* (A chorus of quiet *amens* from the table.)
> *Someone who lets me be me.* (I cut my eyes to Asher.)
> *Old movies late at night.*
> *Guardian angels.* (I tip my head to Urick's team.)
> *A high school diploma.*
> *Sweet love songs.*
> *Familiar blue eyes.* (I smile at Ralston.)
> *A dog's goodness.*
> *An awesome and frightening ability.*
> *A fading sketch of someone I love.*"

Quiet applause and murmured expressions of appreciation arise from the table.

"Thank you, Jaden," Narowyn says, "for sharing part of yourself with us tonight. Your list was quite moving, and I feel as if I know you better than I did before."

More applause. I tuck the list into my pocket. It wasn't so bad really, opening my soul to a bunch of strangers. In a weird way, it made me feel more at ease. My own version of group therapy, I guess.

Narowyn signals for the food to be served, and the sounds of silverware clinking against china and friendly conversation mix with heavenly food aromas and suffuse the room with intimate warmth. Asher seems in high spirits. He talks about the fun we're going to have on our shopping excursion tomorrow. Hugh Du Lac turns out to have a wry sense of humor. His droll comments make Narowyn laugh softly, and they hold hands under the table. I feel a tinge of envy at their close relationship.

The spinach and cheese lasagna is delicious. I'm still getting used to the meatless diet, but when the dessert plates are finally cleared away, I feel stuffed and a little drowsy.

After we say "goodnight" to Narowyn and Hugh, Asher escorts me out of the dining room. "Is one-forty-five okay for tomorrow, or will that rush you too much?" he asks.

"It's perfect. Want to come over for tea and teach me the Transcender Handbook tonight?"

"Tempting, but I'll have to pass. See you tomorrow."

I'm a little disappointed until I catch sight of Ralston in the hallway, with Callie by his side. "This girl was waiting patiently for you." he says.

I bend to hug her, and she licks my face. "I hoped she'd come back tonight."

"I think you've made a friend for life. Actually, I think you made a few friends this evening. Your recitation before dinner was quite lovely, especially the part about the blue eyes."

"You knew you'd be on the list, Rals. You up for some tea tonight?"

"I wish I could, but I promised Gil a game of chess this evening. He's down two games, and he's really rather competitive."

"Well, I'm glad you've made a friend too."

"Yes. It's a symbiotic relationship, he's teaching me the ins and outs of life at the Chateau, and I've shown him a few adjustments to his program that make him a bit more … shall we say, *human*."

"I probably wouldn't mention that to Narowyn, if I were you."

"I had no intention of doing so," he says with a mischievous wink. "Sleep well, my dear."

Although I'm still not completely comfortable with the dashing new Rals, I hug him affectionately. "See you tomorrow."

* * *

"Good morning, Jaden" Vasa says, "The time is now six a.m."

At first I'm disoriented by the voice speaking to me in my darkened room, but then I remember I asked Vasa to wake me early this morning so I could go over the Transcender Handbook.

I feed Callie and let her outside before parking myself at the kitchen table to review the Transcender Code of Conduct. It's a list of twelve rules and detailed explanations for each one. They are pretty much what I expected. The bottom line is simple: When visiting a parallel earth, be respectful, friendly, and observant, don't screw with the ecosystem, and don't bring back any souvenirs. Even I can't mess that up.

The last rule is the one that Eve got in trouble for violating when she used advanced medicine on Patrick:

> *12. To refrain from employing advanced technology, medicine, or weaponry on any parallel earth, except as needed to defend, protect, or assist an exploration partner or fellow Transcender.*

The second half of the book contains the regulations or the law behind the rules of the Code of Conduct. I study each one carefully. It's a lot of fancy wording, but basically it says keep to the code or there will be consequences.

When I finally finish the last page, my watch reads eight fifty-five. *Damn!* I'm going to be late for my first Firearms Training session. It's on the other side of the property in the Transcender Police Barracks. I slam my book shut and bolt out of my chair, ready to sprint across the grounds, until it dawns on me that I can just shift over. *Whew.*

"Vasa, lights off, music off, coffee off, please."

"Lights, music, and coffee off. Have a nice day, Jaden."

Mental note: don't ask for "lights off" until ready to walk out the door. Groping around in the dark hallway, it takes me a minute to locate the door knob, and I make my way out to the elevator.

Once outside the Chateau, I use my finger to pinpoint the barracks on the holographic map inside my TPD and double-click the latch. *Zzzt!*

I alight just outside the barracks and take the stairs to the main door. Inside, a large woman with styled blonde hair and reading glasses sits at a reception desk. She seems engrossed in her electronic reader, but looks up when she hears the door latch close.

"G'mornin'," she says. "May I help you?" Her accent is strongly southern.

"Hi. I'm Jaden Beckett. I'm here for firearms instruction."

She switches off her ereader and heaves her large frame up from the desk. "Well, I'm happy to meet you, Jaden." she extends a beefy hand. "I'm Eloise. I'll be your instructor."

"Oh. Nice to meet you too, Eloise." I was expecting one of those slick, black ops types with a buzz cut and badass attitude. In her flowy, white linen top and pants, Eloise looks more like she should have her own cooking show.

"Follow me to the armory, and we'll fix you up with a weapon." I hurry to keep up with her brisk strides down the hallway until she stops at a service window.

Jeffrey, the skinny carrot-top, sits behind the counter.

"Hey, Jeffrey. You know Jaden, here?"

Jeffrey breaks out a cheery smile. "Sure I do. Hi, Jaden." He waves a freckled hand at me.

"We need to get her set up with a pistol," Eloise says. "I'm thinking we might try a couple of the Colts, maybe a Sig, and a Kimber 1911."

"Yes, ma'am." Jeffrey buzzes us through the metal door next to his window. He unlocks a security gate to one of the rooms, and we follow him inside. The walls of the room are covered with hundreds of different makes and models of guns.

"Let me see your hand, Jaden," Eloise says. I hold out my hand, palm up.

She peruses the wall displays for a moment, and selects three different pistols. "These'll do, Jeffrey. Can you get us set up in the back?"

"Yes, ma'am. I'll meet you over there."

"The shootin' range is this way," Eloise says, jerking a thumb over her shoulder. After leaving the armory, we take another hallway to an outside door.

"So, how come I've never seen you at the Chateau before?" I ask her as we walk.

"Oh, I'm not a Transcender, hon."

"You're not?"

"No. I'm just the top shooter in the five-county area. Miz Du Lac wanted you to have the best." Her smile betrays a hint of pride.

A long, low building behind the barracks has been outfitted as a shooting range. It's brightly lit inside with several lanes partitioned off for target practice. We stop at a sleek, black counter opposite the front door. A rack of protective glasses sits on top. The back wall is plastered with used paper targets baring the name and the score of each shooter. Hall of fame, I suppose. A pegboard full of headphones covers the wall to the right.

"First, we'll go over some basic gun safety rules," Eloise says, picking up glasses and pulling down earphones for us. "Then I'll let you try out some pistols and see what you like. Personally, I like the Sig, but it's got a little too much bite for some folks."

I shake out my hands, a little on edge about the whole thing.

"Okay. Well, I guess we'll see." I never expected to have a job where I was required to pack heat.

Jeffrey steps inside carrying three gun cases and a set of targets. "Got the place all to yourselves today, ladies," he says, grinning. "I'll set you up in lane ten."

After Eloise goes over the safety rules with me, we put on our protective eyewear and super-soundproof headphones. She holds the first pistol in her palm.

"This here's a Sig Sauer P226 with a laser sight." She points out the various features of the pistol, and then holds it out for me.

"How's that feel? You like that weight? Is the grip okay?" she asks.

"Yeah, it seems fine." Like I have something to compare it to.

She hooks up a target to the pulley and pushes a button sending it gliding to the back of the lane. "Okay, let's see how she works. Use your laser sight, and you can't miss."

She's wrong. I line up the laser just where I want it, but when I press the trigger, the gun kicks, my hand jumps, and I miss by a mile.

"Here, grip it with both hands like this." Eloise takes the gun and demonstrates.

I plant my feet firmly, hold the pistol with both hands, line up my laser sight, and *bam*! I miss again. On my third try, I just nick the edge of the target paper.

"Hmm, that trigger feeling a little chunky to you?" she asks.

"Maybe a little."

"Let's try these others."

We spend the next thirty minutes testing and comparing the three pistols. They each have attractive features, but the Kimber just feels better in my hand. The trigger action is smooth, and I actually hit the target six times. Although none of them is a great shot, I find myself enjoying learning a new skill.

"I think we found a winner," Eloise says. "Remove the clip and make sure the chamber's empty like I showed you. You can lock it up in its case and take it home with you, if you like."

"Really?"

"Yes. "Some paperwork needs to be filled out, but we'll take care of that tomorrow. "Congratulations, Jaden. You got yourself a fine new weapon."

THIRTY-FIVE

Spontaneous Shifting is next on my schedule, and I have only five minutes to make it on time. It's probably not appropriate to take my gun with me, so I quickly shift back to my apartment. The closet seems the best place to stow the gun case, and I shove it to the back of the empty top shelf. Then I hurry downstairs to Dr. McDonald's laboratory.

"Whoa, there she is, Supernova Girl," Dr. McDonald says when I scuttle through the door.

"Sorry I'm late," I say, harried and not at all amused by the cutesy nickname.

"Not to worry SG, we're going to have a great time today."

SG? Is she serious?

"All right, Luci," I say, figuring two can play that game, "what're we going to do first?"

"Hey, you called me Luci." She laughs. "My dad used to call me Luci. I like it."

Crap.

"First off, I thought we'd have a little scavenger hunt. I made up a list of locations for you to shift to and things for you to bring back."

She hands me the list. "So, currently where are you able to spontaneously shift?"

"Where?" I shrug. "Nowhere."

"You mean nowhere, as in not anywhere?"

"That would be correct."

Squinting at me, she taps a finger against her temple. "Hmm. This is going to be a challenge, SG, and I love a challenge. Let's chuck the list for the moment and start easy." She takes the list from me and tosses it on her desk.

"Easy is good," I say.

She puts her hands on my shoulders and positions me facing the front of the room. "Okay, see that whiteboard on the wall behind the desk?"

"Yep."

"Your first shift will be from right here to over there."

She runs through the basics of spontaneous shifting for me. "Picture a specific place in your mind—in this case, that space in front of the whiteboard. Conjure up the feel of the place and combine that with the crazy streaming stars feeling of shifting, and *poof!* That's how it happens."

I already knew that, but my first go-round last year didn't work out so well. "I'll do my best, Luci, but last time I tried this, I ended up in a previously undiscovered jungle world being drooled all over by some unidentified species of carnivore. Are you ready to find me if something goes wrong?"

"You betcha." She flips open her bracelet. "You're on locator. If you don't land where you're supposed to, I'm hot on your trail. Now concentrate."

I hold the picture of the whiteboard firmly in my mind. Closing my eyes, I allow the feeling of shifting to flood through me. *Zzzt.*

When I open my eyes, I'm standing unsteadily on top of the desk in front of the whiteboard.

"Woohoo. That was great!" Luci bounds across the room and offers me a hand down. "You're a natural at this, SG. I think we're ready to try some things on the scavenger list."

She reads over the first few items and scratches her head. "You want to try your apartment first or the main kitchen?"

"Probably my apartment. I know it better than the kitchen."

"Okay, shift to your apartment and bring back a shoe from your closet."

"A shoe?"

She spreads her arms wide. "Whatever. Anything from your apartment will do."

I'm still not sure about this, but I'm willing to try. "Okay, here goes." I close my eyes and envision my bedroom. I summon up the comfortable feeling of lying on my bed and combine that with the streaming stars rush. *Zzzt!*

Incredibly, I land on my bed. *Yippee!* I bounce up and down for a few seconds, feeling proud of myself. Then I hop onto the rug and fish a shoe out of my closet.

Now for the hard part—getting back. I try to visualize Dr. McDonald's office, but I can't get a good feel for it. My mind keeps drifting back to the whiteboard from earlier. When in doubt, go with what you know, right? I concentrate deeply on the whiteboard, and *Zzzt,* I land back on top of Luci's desk, and triumphantly hold up my shoe.

"Got it."

"Bravo!" She applauds. "Want to try the kitchen now?"

"Why not?" I climb down from the desk feeling much more confident. Spontaneous Shifting is going to be a breeze.

"This time, shift to the kitchen and bring back some cookies" she says. "I'm getting kind of hungry. I like chocolate chip, but bring back whatever you like."

I laugh. Luci's a strange bird, but I'm kind of warming up to her. "All right. Give me a minute."

I shake out my arms and waggle my head back and forth to loosen up. Then I close my eyes and envision the kitchen. At first, my mind resists zeroing in on a specific spot, but I force myself to concentrate on the counter near the pantry. The flying through dimensions feeling fills me up and *Zzzt*.

"*Ouch!*" I bang my knee hard as I land in a confined, pitch-black space. A wave of claustrophobic panic washes over me. I don't have the slightest idea where I am. I frantically clutch for my TPD, but a door in front of me suddenly swings open, and light floods into the small space. I'm standing in the damn broom closet.

"Oops. We got a little off course on that one," Luci says, offering me her hand once again.

I clamber out of the closet with a vacuum cleaner hose wrapped around my leg. My shin and kneecap are pretty banged up, and a lovely purple bruise has begun to blossom.

"Oooh golly. That looks nasty." She untangles the hose and shoves it back in the closet. "You'd better ice that right away."

"Ya think?" I say, annoyed with the whole scavenger hunt game. "Just take me back to your office so I can get my shoe, please. It's almost time for my next class."

"No problem." She transports us back to her office in a flash. "We'll try something a bit different tomorrow. Maybe we'll work outdoors."

I limp out of her office and take the elevator to my apartment. Tossing my shoe on the rug, I open the freezer and scoop out some ice. My schedule says I'm supposed to be in "Classroom 3" on the first floor at twelve-twenty for the Study of Alternate Earths. That gives me ten minutes.

I rig up a make-shift ice pack and prop my leg on the couch for several minutes. Asher says it's considered bad form to shift locations while inside the Chateau, but I don't have time to wait for the elevator, and the stairs are out of the question. I chuck the ice in the sink, grab my electronic notebook, and use my bracelet to shift downstairs to the hallway where the classrooms are located.

When I open the door to Classroom 3, I receive two surprises. First, Ralston's roommate, Gil, is the instructor, and second, twenty or so people are already seated in the amphitheater classroom—most of whom I've never seen before.

"Miss Beckett, welcome. I wondered if you'd be joining us today," Gil says.

All heads turn to me. "I apologize if I'm late. I had a slight accident in my last class." I rub my swollen knee for emphasis.

"It's quite all right, please take a seat."

I slide into the nearest empty spot.

"This is your text-book." He places a small memory card on the desktop in front of me. "Do you have your tablet?"

"Yes, right here."

"Wonderful. Let's begin again."

I sneak a glance at the guy sitting next to me. His memory card is plugged into the side of his tablet, so I find the slot for my card and plug it in. The glass lights up like a screen, and the table of contents appears. A virtual keyboard sits at the bottom of the page for taking notes.

"As I was saying, we are aware of the existence of precisely one thousand seven hundred and sixty-two Archetypal Earths, or AEs," Gil says. "These earths share similar histories and are substantially the same in geography, technology, and political structure. You may study those earths at your leisure. In this class, we will concern ourselves primarily with the Outlier Earths, or OEs. They are by far the most interesting. While all earths began as Archetypal Earths, the outliers have, for one reason or another, deviated from the norm in one or more significant ways."

Gil spends the next hour going over the fundamentals of what constitutes an Archetypal Earth and pointing out instances of earths that don't fit the mold.

"Any AE can quickly become an outlier with the occurrence of a catastrophic event," he says. "Recently inhabitants of Earth 47CF, up until now an Archetypal Earth, embarked upon a major war—World War III. Though we do not know the final outcome as yet, the war will undoubtedly cause that earth to deviate politically and historically from the AEs, thus moving it into the OE category."

I type in notes, not really sure yet what's important and what's not.

"As another example," he says. "Ms. Beckett, our newest Transcender, is originally from Earth 7Y12, an AE. In her initial shift she found herself on Earth H87D, an OE. This earth had become an outlier, due in part to a natural disaster in the form of a catastrophic asteroid collision, and also due to the outside introduction of advanced technology in the form of enormous domes containing entire ecosystems."

Everyone turns to stare at me again, and I shrink a little in my seat. "She now finds herself a resident of Arumel City on Earth A1W5, also an OE, due to the existence of our eighth continent and our advanced social systems and technology."

I already knew that the country of Arumel is the counterpart of the United States on this earth, and that Arumel City is its capital and roughly equivalent to New York City. But this is the first I've heard that this earth has eight continents. Guess I have a lot of independent study to do.

After class, I apologize once more to Gil for being late and ask him about the other students.

"This class is open to the public," he says. "Most of the local colleges give credit toward graduation for completion of the course. Many of the students are more interested in seeing Transcenders in their natural habitat, rather than in the material itself. Prepare yourself to be approached by some curiosity seekers."

"Thanks for the warning," I say. "The thing is, I feel a bit behind everyone else because I don't know much about this earth or the history of Arumel. Can you recommend a book or something that will help me catch up?"

"I have some wonderful materials for you. Very rudimentary. I'll bring them to class tomorrow."

"That'd be great. See you then."

Cartography is just down the hall in Classroom 7, a smaller more intimate space. Ten students are in attendance, eight of whom are Transcenders. The class consists mainly of learning to read 3D maps. The professor says that later in the year we'll learn to construct them ourselves. I'm told I need to master both of these skills before heading up an exploration of my own.

After class, I collect my things and hurry back to my apartment. Asher's due in two minutes. I drop my school stuff on the dining table and shimmy out of my shorts on the way to my bedroom, leaving them in a heap on the floor. I yank a long lavender dress off its hanger and barely have time to pull it on over my head before Asher knocks at my door.

"Coming," I call as I shuffle my feet into sandals and grab my purse. I hope every day won't be as rushed as this one.

"Are you limping?" Asher asks when I join him in the hall.

"A little mishap in Spontaneous Shifting," I say. "Had a little run-in with a vacuum cleaner. It's not bad, really." I slide the strap of my embroidered bag over my shoulder.

"You still up for this today?" he asks.

"*Yeees!* I need this. It's been an intense day."

We take a community car downtown. It's still unnerving to ride in a car that drives itself, even though Asher explained on my first visit that the entire traffic system is satellite controlled by quantum computers. He claims there hasn't been an auto accident in years, but sometimes it feels like being on a carnival ride without tracks. Despite my apprehension, traffic flows smoothly all around us, and we move through the town at a decent clip.

The cityscape of downtown Arumel is awe-inspiring. Towering, futuristic buildings of glass and steel dominate the skyline. Each glittering structure is nestled in its own lush little park, creating the impression that the skyscrapers were conjured from the ground up by architect fairies. The streets and sidewalks are spotless and impeccably maintained. Asher tells me the locals call it the Emerald City, because of the glittering edifices and all the greenery.

We stop for lunch at a small sidewalk café. Our table occupies a shady corner under a cherry red umbrella. It's the perfect spot for people watching. Most Arumelans appear similar to people in my hometown, although they generally dress in flowy apparel like long dresses or loose pants and tunics. The younger people tend to experiment with more interesting, trendy designs. Uniforms are not an uncommon sight in town—some military, some law enforcement, and some community workers like sidewalk sweepers. Also, people in certain professions, like lawyers and judges, wear long robes in a variety of colors around town.

We order our meal from a touch screen menu built into the table. After only a few minutes, our pine nut and arugula salads, warm pistachio rolls, and tall glasses of iced raspberry tea are delivered to our table by a pretty, young woman. I notice she looks like the twin of the woman delivering food to the next table, and their sister appears to be totaling the tab for a table on the other side.

"Are they automatons?" I whisper to Ash when she leaves.

"Yeah, robots do a lot of service work in the upper-end restaurants and hotels," he says matter-of-factly. "So what style of décor do you have in mind for your place?"

I take a moment to process the idea of a fleet of automaton restaurant workers, before I answer him.

"Uh, I don't really know," I say. "Something colorful and pretty, maybe funky and a little unexpected. Does that sound stupid?"

"No. But it encompasses a lot. Do you have a favorite artist?"

"I guess I'm partial to the Italian renaissance painters like Botticelli. But I also kind of like Andy Warhol."

He grins. "I guess that's something to go on."

While we enjoy our crunchy salads, I fill Ash in on my first day of classes.

"Eloise taught me fire-arms, too," he says. "She's amazing. You'll get used to Dr. McDonald after a while. She's harmless and scary-smart. As far as Gil's class goes, if people ask you for autographs, or want to take photos with you, feel free to say *no*. They've been told that's not appropriate during class time."

"Okay, good to know."

As the pretty automaton server brings the bill to our table, I catch sight of a company of soldiers in white armor and helmets carrying long mean-looking rifles, marching straight for us on the sidewalk. For an anxious second, I'm sure IUGA has sent them for me. I grasp Asher's arm ready to bolt if necessary.

"Who are those guys?" I hiss. "Have you seen them before?"

He laughs out loud. "Relax, Jade. They're Imperial Storm Troopers. There's a Star Wars convention at the Civic Center."

The server ignores my outburst and swipes Ash's card. "Have a good day," she says brightly.

"Sorry, Ash. That was pretty lame. I guess I'm still a little paranoid after being attacked in Madison."

"Don't worry about it. It's good to be cautious. But you're safe here. Shall we walk over to Trope's? It's not far."

296

As we approach the door to the shop, a large shadow floats low overhead, and I duck reflexively.

Asher takes my arm. "It's okay, Jade. It's just an air taxi. This building has a port on its roof."

I look up to see the undercarriage of a small hovercraft as it lifts higher and then skates onto the top of the building. "Oh, cool. I've never seen one of those."

"You're so jumpy today." He opens the door for me.

"I know. I guess my little mishap in the broom closet has made me kind of skittish, and honestly, I'm feeling pretty out of place here."

"You'll get used to things soon enough. Try to relax. This will be fun."

The Trope's saleslady recognizes Asher as we step inside. "What may I do for you today, Mr. Steele?" she asks.

"We're shopping for my friend here," he says. "She's partial to classic Italian design but nothing too slick or traditional. She also leans toward the brighter colors."

The saleslady rubs her hands together enthusiastically. "Ah, we have just received some wonderful new imports. Come, I think you will be pleased."

We follow her to the "Eclectic Section," and Asher quickly goes to work pulling together accessories, small furniture pieces, and art that he thinks will work in my place. He doesn't give me much time to make up my mind about things. "Go with your gut reaction," he says. "If you don't instantly love it, you never will."

After two hours, we're finally finished, and none too soon. My head is swirling, and I can't say for sure what I actually ended up choosing. I sip on an espresso while Ash and the saleslady work out the delivery and payment details.

"Here." Asher hands me a carefully wrapped brown package. "I thought you'd like to take home that vase you loved so much."

"Oh, sweet. I didn't go over my budget, did I? This place doesn't look like it has Ikea pricing."

"Nah, you're good. They love Transcenders here, so they worked with us a little on some of the prices, and the vase is a gift from me."

"Ash, no," I say. "I can't accept it. It's too much. I've got some extra money …"

He clutches his chest dramatically. "You wound me. Of course you can accept it. It's a house warming present."

I lower my eyes. It doesn't feel right taking a gift from him. I don't want to send the wrong message.

He places a finger under my chin and raises my eyes to his. "Hey, you can accept a gift from me," he says softly. "It doesn't mean anything other than I want you to have it."

My lips twitch into a smile. "I do love it, Ash. Thanks … for everything. I never could have done this on my own, and the vase is exquisite."

"It was fun for me. I'm glad you asked me along." He checks his watch and tips his head toward the door. "We'd better get back to the Chateau. I've got to be someplace in about an hour."

I follow him outside. "Does that mean you won't be at dinner tonight?"

"'Fraid not. You'll have to fill me in if anything earth-shattering happens."

Unexpectedly, he grasps my arm and pulls me into a small deserted alley. "I don't normally like to do this in public when I'm in Arumel," he whispers, turning his head both ways to make sure we're alone.

He puts an arm around my waist, and for one frozen second I think he's going to kiss me. Instead, he says, "Do you mind if we shift back? I need time to shower and change."

"Sure. Let's go." I smile with relief.

"Hang on." *Zzzt.*

THIRTY-SIX

After dinner, I check the Chateau's front door several times before changing for bed, but Callie's a no-show. I feel kind of rejected and more than a little lonely, so I send out a few emails to people in Connecticut, not really expecting any responses tonight.

The quiet of the huge house is a stark contrast to the hustle and bustle of Warrington Palace, and it's hard to keep my thoughts from wandering to Domerica. The pain of Ryder's absence throbs deeply in my soul, and I fret about Lorelei and all she's facing as queen. The fact that I'm forbidden to set foot there, makes me a little crazy.

Nights are still the worst. I stare out my window at the darkened Chateau grounds and watch the lights of the Emerald City sparkle and dance in the distance. Air-taxis take off and land atop the skyscrapers, like fireflies in the inky sky. It's all so beautiful, but still so foreign to me. Sometimes it's hard to get my arms around which part of my life was or is real. I'm not really anchored to one specific earth or reality right now, leaving me feeling kind of displaced and homeless.

My mood drifts from melancholy to border-line depression, and I realize it's not wise to sit here and mope all night. Maybe some of Ralston's famous chamomile tea will help with my insomnia. It's late, I know, but how much sleep do automatons really need?

"Vasa, call Ralston." I say.

"Good evening, Jaden," Vasa says. "Calling Ralston." After several rings, she informs me that there's no answer. "Shall I leave a message?"

"No, thanks. I'll see him tomorrow." He and Gil missed dinner because they had gone out to the opera. They must be making a late night of it.

"Is there anything else I can do for you?" Vasa asks.

I consider striking up a little conversation with her, but quickly realize what a loser that makes me. "No thanks. Goodnight."

"Goodnight, Jaden."

It occurs to me that the main kitchen downstairs probably has a supply of chamomile tea. It won't be Ralston's special blend, but it may help make me drowsy. I might even happen upon a little company if I'm lucky. Surely I'm not the only one in the Chateau still awake at this hour. I throw my fluffy bathrobe over my tank top and pajama bottoms and pad downstairs in my slippers.

The kitchen's dark and deserted, and I'm nearly blinded when I flip on the overhead lights. I quickly shut them off, opting instead for the soft under-counter lighting. A bank of high-tech ovens— microwave, convection, and others I don't recognize—lines one wall, but I like my tea the old fashioned way, plus, I have all the time in the world. I fill the kettle with water and put it on the stove top to heat while I search the cupboards for tea.

Locating the drawer of teas is easy. Finding what I want isn't. Dozens of boxes of green tea, black tea, white tea, and rooibos are crammed side-by-side into the wide drawer. It takes me several minutes to locate the herbals and find the chamomile half-way back in the row. I have my choice of loose leaves or bags. Again, I go old-school and fill a silver tea ball with some of the fragrant leaves.

While I'm waiting for the water to boil, I stroll over to the small lounge adjoining the kitchen in hopes of finding another night owl or two. A lamp burns softly in the corner, but the fire has turned to

301

embers, and not a soul is present in the cozy room. Guess I *am* the only insomniac in the place.

Wisps of steam waft from the kettle spout, and I pull a blue and white chipped mug from the cupboard. For the first time, I become aware of a slight but consistent rasping noise coming from the direction of a work room off the rear of the kitchen. Maybe someone is awake after all, or maybe we just have really big mice. I follow the sound and peer into the dimly lit room with its tool-lined walls and scarred work tables.

I barely make out the silhouette of a man laboring at something under the lamp of a work bench. It's Urick. *Oh great. Mr. Taciturn.* Not exactly my first choice for stimulating midnight conversation, but I do like him, and maybe I can get him to tell me more about his weird home earth.

I head back to the kitchen and take another mug from the cabinet. After filling a second infuser with chamomile, I pour the now boiling water into both mugs. While the tea steeps, I locate a pitcher of milk and a bowl of raw sugar crystals. I like my tea sweet and milky, but I decide to leave Urick's plain. He doesn't strike me as the milk and sugar type. Hell, he'd probably prefer rust shavings in his tea, but he'll have to add his own. I grasp a mug in each hand and head fearlessly into the unknown.

Urick's head jerks up the second I enter the room. He acknowledges me with only the slightest glance and then goes back to his task.

"Hi," I say, setting his mug on the bench next to him.

"Good evening," he says without looking up. He's wearing a sleeveless tunic, and his arms are seriously impressive—huge biceps and ropy muscular forearms. He methodically works a papery cloth up and down the length of a shiny blade.

"What're you working on?" I ask.

He holds up a long curved weapon with a serrated tip and a razor sharp edge. The lamplight glints from its mirror finish as he turns it from side to side. "It's a Throkkin. Used in Demonstadt, where I'm from."

It's the same sword he used to sever the robot's head in Madison. "Looks heavy," I say, noting the unusual thickness of the grooved blade.

"That is what makes it so lethal." He goes back to his polishing. His hunched posture silently telegraphs *leave me to my work*, but I'm not ready to give up just yet. There must be a glimmer of personality behind all that splendid brawn.

I stare for a moment at a fearsome battle scene tattooed from shoulder to wrist on Urick's left arm. I've never seen his tattoo before because I've never seen him out of uniform. I recognize the piece from somewhere.

"I like your sleeve," I say.

He looks at his arms, then up at me, like *Huh? I'm not wearing any sleeves.*

I gesture my mug in the direction of his arm. "Your tattoo, your ink."

"Oh, thank you," he says quietly.

"It looks like a painting I remember from art class. Isn't that the Clash of the Amazons?"

"The Battle of the Amazons," he corrects. "Peter Paul Rubens."

"Oh yeah. Beautiful work."

He gazes at me a moment with his penetrating eyes. "You should not do this," he says finally.

"Uh, do what?"

"Play the temptress with me."

That makes me laugh, and I nearly spit a mouthful of tea across the room. "The *temptress*?" I choke. "You think I'm flirting with you?"

He half shrugs. "It is late at night, and you have no man. You have come here alone dressed only in your nightclothes."

I look down at my bulky pink robe with its embroidered blue bunnies.

"Great powers of deduction, Sherlock. I hate to break it to you, though, I'm not looking for a boyfriend or a quick bop between the sheets, and if I were, it wouldn't be with anyone as scary as you." I fold my arms across my chest and stare at him defiantly.

He tilts his head. "You think me frightening?"

The glint in his eyes tells me he'd like it if I say *yes*. "Well, maybe a little with that blade in your hand, but mostly I think you're just kind of cranky."

"Cranky?" Not what he expected. His face splits into a huge grin. It looks good on him. He has great teeth. "I suppose I can be."

"Look Urick, you've done a lot for me over these past weeks, and I appreciate it. I'm just trying to be friends here."

His smile fades. "A man and woman cannot be friends. They can come together for pleasure or for procreation, but not friendship."

I snort like any good temptress would. "Maybe it's like that in Demon-ville, or wherever you come from, but it's not like that on my earth, and it's certainly not like that here. Asher and I are friends."

He lowers his head, and looks up at me through thick lashes. "Asher would bed you in a heartbeat if you would allow it."

I open my mouth to protest, but if I'm serious about being friends with this guy, honesty's a good start. "That may or may not be true, but it's completely irrelevant to this discussion because *you* wouldn't."

He narrows his golden eyes at me, as if contemplating this. "No. I wouldn't," he says with conviction.

I should probably be insulted, but I'm not. I know Urick thinks of me as kind of an annoying kid sister, someone he needs to protect and defend. He's been doing that since the first day we met. Sort of the way Patrick did.

"Well all right then. Friends it is." I raise my mug in salute.

He responds with a curt nod and goes back to his work. I'm not sure if it's a nod of agreement, or a nod of dismissal, but I decide not to press the issue tonight. Instead, I slide the untouched mug of tea closer to him on the bench and turn for the door.

When I reach the threshold, he calls after me, "I like milk and honey in mine."

"Yeah, well, I'll remember that for next time," I say over my shoulder, smiling to myself. "Night Urick."

"Goodnight, Jaden." It's the first time he's ever said my first name.

Okay, this is good. I think I just made a new friend.

* * *

The chamomile works like a charm on me, and I sleep restfully through the night, until an insistent scratching at my door makes me roll out of bed to see what's up. I open up to find Callie waiting in the hall, her whole body wagging. Someone must have let her inside the Chateau. I'm glad she knows the way to my door.

"Hey, girl. Where were you last night? I missed you." I crouch down beside her. She flicks her wet tongue across my cheek, and prances inside to the kitchen, which appears to be a demand for food.

Once we've finished breakfast, I pull my gun case from its shelf. "I've got a busy day, girl, but I hope you'll stick around or at least come back tonight." We head downstairs, and I kiss her forehead before shifting to the police barracks.

Firearms Training goes surprisingly well now that I have a pistol that suits me. Eloise promises we'll do some outdoor practice tomorrow, to mix things up a little.

I feel apprehensive on my way to Luci's office for Spontaneous Shifting. A broom closet's one thing, but what if I land in some serious trouble today?

"Good morning, SG. How's the knee?" she says when I arrive.

"It feels okay this morning."

"Great! Well, I think I have this all figured out now. We're going to adopt a more gradual approach. We'll prioritize our locations, and the first few times you'll shift with your bracelet. Then, when you're comfortable, we'll try it without the bracelet and see how that works."

"Wait a minute, have you ever taught anyone Spontaneous Shifting before?"

"Well, no. Mathew, the guy who usually teaches it, is off on an exploration for three weeks. Narowyn asked me to sub for him."

I do an internal eye roll. That explains a lot. "All right. The gradual approach sounds reasonable. What do we do first?"

We agree that the main foyer of the Chateau is the best place to start, since I'll likely be coming and going mostly from there. I pick a spot next to a table with an enormous vase of flowers on top. This is my *home spot* for today's session. After we move the flowers out of the way, I practice shifting to and from various locations, always landing back by the table. I use my TPD bracelet until I'm sure I have the location and the feeling down. After that, I try it on my own. The method works fairly well. I overshoot the table a few times, but I always land in the foyer and don't have any calamities like yesterday. This is progress.

I arrive at my Alternate Earths class early to make up for being late yesterday. The classroom is still mostly empty, and I approach Gil at his desk.

"How was the opera last night?" I ask.

"Oh, delightful. I love *Carmen*, don't you?"

"Um, I've never seen it."

"You really should. Constantine was most impressed with our opera company. He says it's one of the best he's seen."

"That's nice. I'm glad you and Ralston enjoy some of the same things."

"I have the materials we discussed yesterday," he says, handing me another small black memory card. "Everything you ever need to know about Earth A1W5 is on that card. I hope you find it enlightening."

"Thanks Gil. Asher took me downtown yesterday, and I felt like a real country bumpkin. The more I learn about Arumel, both the city and the country, the quicker I'll adjust—I hope."

I take my seat, as my remaining classmates trickle in. Gil's lecture is fascinating once again. I'm mesmerized by the amazing and diverse parallel earths that exist out there. It's awesome to know I'll actually get to see some of them for myself.

Science of Transcending class is a different story. Five minutes in and I'm lost at sea. The professor is an elder Transcender named Martin. He has a long gray beard and nearly colorless eyes. He occupies the same corner of the dinner table every night surrounded by a small cult of followers. They usually discuss arcane matters, and the younger Transcenders hang on Martin's every word. I've always avoided that corner. Now I'm thinking maybe I should have sat in on a few of those discussions.

The class is fairly full of students—some Transcenders, some not. Most of the civilians are college students, but a few look like business people or professors. After the first class, I realize it's essentially a course in quantum mechanics, and it's pretty clear my high school science and math skills are not up to snuff. I'm going to need some serious tutoring help with this material.

I may have been born with Transcender abilities, but learning the ropes isn't going to be easy. After my second day of training, I'm feeling slightly beleaguered and distinctly inadequate.

THIRTY-SEVEN

My apartment phone is ringing as I step through the door after class. "Narowyn Du Lac calling," Vasa says.

"Thanks, I'll take it." I set my things on the hall table. "Hi Narowyn." I don't know where the mics for the speaker phone are, but each room seems to have one, and they work great for hands free.

"Jaden, I'm happy I found you at home. Do you have a few minutes to come by my office?"

"Right now?"

"Yes, if it's convenient."

"Okay, sure. I'll be there in five."

A man and woman stand chatting with Narowyn in her office when I arrive. They both wear dove gray robes similar to judges' robes. I've noticed people in town wearing them.

"Jaden, please come in," Narowyn says. This is Corinne Barker and Ted King. They are our lawyers in our suit against IUGA."

I shake hands with them both. "Nice to meet you."

"I'm afraid we've had an unpleasant development in our case," Narowyn says. "This morning IUGA filed counterclaims against the Transcenders, and you have been named individually."

Icy fingers of fear grip my insides. "What does that mean?"

"Why don't we sit down?" she says. "Corinne and Teddy will explain it all to you and answer your questions."

Ted is a tall slim man with a thatch of reddish-blond hair. He opens his valise and removes a stack of papers and an electronic notebook. We all take seats at the conference table, and Ted passes copies of a document to each of us.

"This is the counterclaim filed by IUGA," he says to me. "You may keep that copy. It contains a fair amount of legalese, but we'll summarize it for you."

"Essentially it alleges three things," Corinne says. "First, that when the automaton known as Constantine Ralston was in your service in Domerica, you unlawfully altered his program to obtain confidential proprietary information and to cause him to deceive his owner, IUGA."

Ted chimes in, "The second claim states you used this information to thwart the natural unfolding of events in Domerica, thus altering the fate of the entire Earth H87D."

"And third," Corinne says. "They accuse you of breach of contract. The complaint alleges that you signed an irrevocable contract promising to remain in Domerica for life, and to never return to either your home in Connecticut or to Arumel."

I slump back in my chair. "Am I in trouble?" I look back and forth between the lawyers.

Corinne smiles. Her make-up is flawless, and she'd be sort of pretty if her dark hair wasn't stiffly gelled to her scalp. "At this time we don't believe you have anything to worry about, but we'd like to ask you a few questions so we may file an answer on your behalf."

"Sure, ask away." I prop my elbows on the table.

"Did you at any time alter the automaton's program?" Corinne asks.

"Please call him Ralston," I say. "He's a good friend of mine."

She shoots Ted a look I can't decipher.

"No. I never altered his program. That's ridiculous. Even if I wanted to, I wouldn't know how. Ralston told me he rewrote his own program so he could exercise free will. He says lots of IUGA's automatons do it."

Ted makes a note on his tablet. "Do you know how he accomplished that?"

"No idea. You should ask him."

His eyebrows fly up. "Wait a minute, you know where he is?"

I glance at Narowyn to make sure I'm not talking out of turn. She nods giving me the go-ahead.

"Yeah. He's here at the Chateau. Well not all of him. The techs backed up his mass storage and transplanted his memory module, eyes, and voice box into another automaton body. The rest of him was returned to the refuse pile where we found him."

Ted leans back in his chair and tosses his stylus on the table. Amusement glimmers in his gray eyes. "Were you ever going to tell us about this, Nary? Or were you waiting to see how well we handle surprises in open court?"

Narowyn smiles at him fondly. "I didn't assume the information was relevant, Teddy. But I suppose with this new counterclaim, we'll need to involve him. Believe me, IUGA has no idea he's here. In fact they believe they've confirmed just the opposite."

"Is that so?" Ted says. "Well, we need to disclose his whereabouts in our answer. I trust you'll arrange for us to speak with the au... er, with Ralston after we're finished here? And I can't wait to hear the story of how he got here."

"You shall have as much access to Ralston as you wish," she

310

says. "And as for the rescue operation, that was well within Transcender Police jurisdiction. Captain Watterson can fill you in on that."

"Thanks, Nary," he says. He picks up his stylus again and refocuses his attention on me. "Jaden, we've already collected the facts on the plot to assassinate you and all the unfortunate events of that day in Domerica, so I won't ask you to go over all that again at this time. But do you know why Ralston turned against IUGA in the first place and decided to save you and your family instead of following through with IUGA's orders?"

"Look, I know you guys think he's just a machine." My chin quivers slightly while I speak. "But after you meet him, I hope you'll change your mind. He has a conscience, and he has the ability to love. He really does."

I swallow to loosen the log jam of emotion in my throat. "He loves me as a friend, and he knew that what IUGA was doing was morally wrong. They were attempting to kill me to save their own asses. He refused to be a part of that."

Corinne leans in toward Ted. "That's going to be difficult to prove in court."

He holds up his hand like *don't be such a downer.* "We'll see," he says.

"Regarding the breach of contract claim," Corinne says. "We have a copy of the contract Narowyn filed with the Arumel Office of Records. It clearly indicates that you chose to relocate to Arumel."

She slides a copy of the agreement over to me. "Is that the contract you signed?

I flip to the signature page. "Yes. That's my signature. This looks like the agreement."

"Do you know why IUGA is alleging that you signed a contract opting to remain in Domerica?"

I think back on the day Ralston had me sign three copies of the contract and he mysteriously kept a fourth unsigned copy for himself. He said he wanted me to have "plausible deniability." I guess this is what he was talking about.

"No. I don't know why IUGA is alleging that."

Ted jots a couple of notes on his tablet. "All right. I believe that's all we need for now." He looks to Corinne who nods in agreement. "We'll meet again at some point prior to the hearing. Do you have questions for us?"

"A few," I say. "What's the worst case scenario? How bad is this going to get?"

"No criminal charges have been filed as yet," Ted says. "But if IUGA wants to play hardball, it might file a theft charge with the local police after we disclose that certain vital parts of Ralston are present in Arumel. It sounds as if Captain Watterson has that covered, though. We'll interview him to make sure."

"The breach of contract issue should be disposed of easily," Corinne says. "As far as these other issues go, they have no plausible way to prove you altered Ralston's programs or unlawfully took information. I'm not certain whether Ralston's presence in Arumel works for us or against us. But it's possible the court will order him to be returned to IUGA."

"What? No!" Panic thrashes in my belly. "Narowyn, we can't let that happen."

"Teddy, she's right," Narowyn says, taking hold of my hand. "IUGA wanted him out of the way because of the damaging information he possesses. If they're allowed access to him now, all of that will be destroyed. It could severely impair our case."

"I'm well aware of that, Nary. I have some ideas on the subject. Let us speak with Ralston first, and then we'll talk strategy."

"That's reasonable." She pats my hand. "Ted why don't you tell us what our next step will be."

"We'll file your answer to the counterclaims on Friday, and

request a postponement of the hearing to give us time to prepare your defense."

"Do you think they'll grant the postponement?" Narowyn asks.

"They'll probably give us ninety days. That's standard. If their docket's jammed, they may push it back until sometime after the holidays."

"What'll the hearing be like?" I ask. "Is it a trial with a jury and all?"

"No," Ted says. "Hearings before the IGC Court are conducted in an entirely different manner. No right to a jury exists at the inter-galactic level. The hearing will be presided over by a five-justice panel. The justices are chosen from the best judicial minds in the galaxy."

"So they're not all human?" I ask.

"Since this matter involves events that occurred on different earths, we assume they'll all be human. In any event, both sides will present witnesses and make arguments to the court. Once everything has been reviewed, the Justices confer with each other and render a decision. Three of the five must agree on the final outcome."

"How soon will we know their decision?"

"Candidly, it can sometimes take months for the final judgment to be filed," he says. "All the justices will have an opportunity to read it and offer comments before it's released."

"But the final decisions are usually just and fair," Corinne adds.

Usually just and fair doesn't give me a lot of comfort. Both lawyers pass me their business cards.

"Call us if you think of anything else," Ted says.

"Thank you, Jaden," Narowyn says. "Don't fret about this. You're in good hands with Ted and Corinne."

Callie waits outside my apartment door when I return to the

third floor. Her wagging tail and happy eyes do nothing to calm my anxious nerves. We climb up on the couch together.

"Vasa, TV on," I say, hoping for some distracting, mindless entertainment.

"Good afternoon, Jaden. What do you wish to watch?"

"Just flip through the channels until I tell you to stop."

"Commencing scan."

When I see a show with a bunch of dogs romping in a field, I tell her to stop. "Look at this Callie." Her ears perk up, and she checks out the frolicking pups on the screen.

The film is a poignant and humorous documentary about a community dog named Buddy who adopts a little autistic boy in the city. It chronicles the ways Buddy has helped the little boy adapt socially and academically to public school. The love between the boy and his dog is sweetly touching, and I find myself tearing up as the closing credits scroll up the screen.

"We need to officially adopt each other," I tell Callie. She licks my ear in reply.

Something at the end of the credits catches my eye: *A film by Blackthorn Productions*. The feel of Ryder momentarily washes over me. Strange how just the sight of his name can bring his strong presence flooding back.

I shake off the temptation to dwell on missing him, and I pull out my tablet to look over this evening's homework. I have a couple of three-dimensional maps to study for Cartography, some reading in Alternate Earths, and an intimidating looking article on quantum entanglements for Science of Transcending. *Ugh.*

"Jaden, are you here?" Ralston calls from my front hall.

Callie bounds from the couch and meets him at the door. He looks handsome in black pants and a white linen shirt.

"Hey, Rals, come in. You look nice."

"Thank you, my dear. I hope I'm not intruding, but I've just come from meeting with Narowyn and the lawyers."

We take seats in my living room. The lines of his face are taut.

"How'd it go? Is everything okay?"

"They wish me to testify at the IGC Court hearing, which means revealing my existence to IUGA in the court filings. The woman, Ms. Barker, believes IUGA will ask the court to return me to their custody."

"I won't let that happen, Rals. I'll just tell them you can't testify."

"But I must. Don't you see? I must refute the claims they've made against you. Also, without my testimony, the Transcenders' case against IUGA will be difficult to prove. Mr. King and Narowyn both feel they can convince the court to allow me to stay with the Transcenders."

"But you don't believe that they can?"

"The point is, no one can be certain. I've come here to ask something of you. Something I have no right to ask."

"Sure, Rals. I'll do whatever you want me to. You know that."

He pinches the bridge of his nose. "I will not go back to IUGA. We both know what they would do to me. Accordingly, should the court order that I be returned to them, I'll need to make a quick exit from Arumel."

I gaze at him for a moment. "If that happens, Rals, we'll work it out. I promise. I can't transport you by myself. We had to use a team shift to get you out of that scrap yard. But I'll find a way to get you away from here."

He shakes his head. "You won't need to transport my entire body, just my memory. I'll show you how to extract it. If the court orders my return to IUGA, I beg you please, remove my stored memory and keep it hidden somewhere. Then, at some future date, if you can safely do so, perhaps you will transport me to a different world where I stand a chance at having a life again."

"Oh god, Rals, don't talk like that. Yes, absolutely. If it comes to that, I swear I won't let them send you back to IUGA. If I can't get all of you out of Arumel, I'll remove all your memory and keep it safe."

His eyebrows squish together. "I'm so sorry to place this burden on you, my dear. You could find yourself in considerable legal difficulty if you help me."

"Look, you've already saved my life once, and now you're risking your life for me again by testifying in this stupid lawsuit. You have my word I'll get you out, and I won't get caught."

His facial muscles relax. "Thank you, Jaden. This means so much to me."

"*You* mean a lot to me, Rals." I scoot close to him and put a comforting arm around his shoulder. I've finally gotten beyond the change in his appearance. I hope we don't have to go through that again.

"Shall we have a cup of tea to seal our pact?" I say.

"That's not necessary, old girl, and I really must be going soon. But first, tell me about your week. How is your training progressing?"

"Well, I enjoy Firearms Training very much. My instructor is a hoot. Cartography's boring and Spontaneous Shifting is a challenge. But I just love my Alternate Earths class. Your roommate is a great lecturer, and the subject matter couldn't be more interesting."

"Gil can be rather eloquent when he's passionate about something."

"Science of Transcending is kind of rough, though. It's mostly quantum mechanics, which I know nothing about. Rals, do you think you might have some time to tutor me during the week?"

"It would be my pleasure." He smiles warmly. "Narowyn has assigned me some duties, but I'm free most evenings."

"Great. Maybe we can get together tomorrow night after dinner?"

"That would be fine. Shall I come here?"

"Yes. I'll have all my new things in the apartment by then, and you can tell me what you think."

"Splendid." He gets to his feet. "Thank you so much, Jaden. You have put an old man's mind at ease."

"Old man? Oh please. You look like a young stud with that new chassis of yours."

His eyes twinkle. "Such talk. You must not forget to respect your elders, my dear." He pecks my cheek.

"Goodnight, Rals."

THIRTY-EIGHT

My classes go smoothly in the morning. I feel more confident and less klutzy in Spontaneous Shifting. I breeze through Cartography, and mercifully, I don't have Science of Transcending today. I reach my apartment in the afternoon with plenty of time to eat and prepare for the delivery of my new furniture.

I also take a few minutes to place a call to Joe, a zoologist and fellow Transcender, who works at the local community animal center. He agrees to help me get the ball rolling on adopting Callie.

"I'll email you the application to fill out," he says. "There isn't much more to it than that. The center has on record the amount of time she's spent with you, so there won't be any question of their approving it. You'll be charged a monthly fee for her healthcare, visits to the center, that type of thing."

"Fantastic. I appreciate your help, Joe. Do I get some sort of adoption certificate or something?"

He laughs. "Oh yes, suitable for framing, if you like."

Asher shows up early to supervise the installation of the furniture. He wants to be sure every piece goes exactly where he envisioned it. He doesn't say as much, but I know he's worried I might screw it up.

318

He directs the movers as to placement of the larger pieces, while he arranges the accessories himself. When everything's set up and the delivery people have removed the plastic and other packing materials, I'm ecstatic with the result.

"This is some serious awesomeness," I say, taking in the entire effect. "It reminds me of a boho chic Manhattan loft."

"You should have an open house so everyone can see it," Asher says.

"That's a fantastic idea. Will you help me shop for the food and stuff?"

"Who wants to shop? Let's do it the easy way. I know this little place that'll cater the whole thing. How about Saturday night?'

"You think they can do it on such short notice?"

"They'll do it," he says. "They've been trying to get an *in* at the Chateau for months. I'll set it up."

I hug him and kiss his cheek. "Thanks, Ash."

He wraps his arm around my waist and pulls me in close. "Anything for you, gorgeous." Laughing deeply, he releases me.

I know he's just kidding around, but sometimes I feel guilty about taking advantage of his talents and contacts. I don't want to unfairly benefit if he still has a "thing" for me.

"Ash, are you sure you don't mind? I mean you've already spent so much time helping me out."

"Don't worry about it. I enjoy it."

I decide to take him at his word.

* * *

I sail through my training the rest of the week. Already Ralston's tutoring in quantum mechanics has been a tremendous help in Science of Transcending. I think I'm beginning to understand the

319

main concepts now.

Saturday morning I wake early, excited for the first party in my new place. I spend the day cleaning and making sure my apartment looks perfect. Around four o'clock I go out to pick up fresh flowers and scented candles. Ash has taken care of everything else, including selecting the music.

By the time six o'clock rolls around, all is in place. Servers in black uniforms mill about my kitchen and dining room assembling food on trays and polishing glasses.

Luci is the first guest to arrive. She looks very different without her lab coat. "Hey Luci, I like your dress," I tell her.

"Is it okay?" She glances down and smoothes her skirt.

"Yeah. You look great."

She hands me a small white box tied with a red ribbon. "House warming."

"Oh, thanks. Shall I open it now?"

"Yeah, go ahead."

I discard the ribbon and wrapping and push aside the tissue paper. Inside is an elegant, clear glass globe with an explosion of vibrant colors frozen within its center.

"It's a paperweight," Luci says. "Reminded me of a supernova … which in turn reminded me of you. So, I just had to get it."

"That's so sweet." She's caught off guard when I hug her. "I love it. It'll be perfect on my coffee table."

A server stops by to take Luci's drink order, as additional people appear in my doorway. I still haven't memorized everyone's name, but I've had fewer and fewer embarrassing moments lately.

"Hi, everyone. Please come in. What would you like to drink?"

Urick and Nila arrive in full uniform. It's unclear to me whether they just got off duty or whether this party is their assignment for the evening. It doesn't matter. I'm just glad they're here. Nila hugs me, and Urick grunts *hello*. He surveys the room with hooded eyes.

"Thanks for coming, guys," I say "There's food and drink inside."

Urick sidles just past the door and parks himself against a wall. "You go ahead," he says to Nila.

She rolls her eyes. "Can't take him anywhere." She laughs her rich laugh, and I wonder vaguely if they are dating. Urick's a cool customer, but Nila's smoldering beauty would be hard for anyone to resist—for *pleasure or procreation.*

Cute Jeffrey shows up with Monica, the churlish goth chick, on his arm. It reminds me of a *Ronald Weasley-Girl With the Dragon Tattoo* love match, but to each his own, right? At least she doesn't appear to be concerned about me and Ash anymore.

Asher works the crowd for me. He makes certain no one's glass is empty and keeps the guests circulating inside. Before long, my small living room and dining area are full of happy party-goers.

I keep an eye out for Narowyn and Hugh, but the party's been in full swing for more than an hour before Narowyn arrives alone. She stops near the door and exchanges a few words with Urick. He moves out into the hall, and I get a prickly sensation that something's not right.

"Jaden, everything is so lovely," she says, taking my hands in hers. "I'm so dreadfully sorry to have to interrupt your party, dear, but may I speak with you outside?"

I follow her into the hallway where Captain Watterson and Urick are in hushed conversation.

"What's wrong?" I ask.

"We have a bit of an unpleasant situation," Narowyn says. "Lieutenant Michaels and Officer Ross are downstairs. They have a warrant for your arrest and a court order requiring me to deliver

Ralston into their custody.

Dread slams every drop of party juice out of me. "They're arresting me on Saturday night? I'm going to jail?" I ask in disbelief.

"Ted King filed your answer to IUGA's counterclaim yesterday, which must have precipitated IUGA's filing a criminal complaint," Narowyn says. "Lieutenant Michaels says IUGA provided a partial facial identification on you from their security cameras. They insisted that you be arrested immediately, claiming that, as a Transcender, you might attempt to flee the jurisdiction."

"The whole thing stinks to high heaven," Watterson says. "If they're pulling strings at police headquarters, I'm concerned about your safety there."

"What do we do?" I ask, clouds of fear gathering inside my chest.

"I've called Ted King," Narowyn says. "He's attempting to arrange an emergency hearing before Chief Judge Laurence of the criminal division to have you released immediately. He's told the clerk it's a matter of life and death."

"What about Ralston? You're not going to turn him over are you? They'll destroy his stored memory the second they get their hands on him." The promise I made to him echoes inside my head.

"I have no choice," she says. "We plan to ask the judge to release him on a bond with my personal guarantee that he'll not be removed from the jurisdiction."

"But that could take some time to arrange. What do we do until then?"

"Judge Laurence is at dinner with his wife. His clerk is attempting to reach him. If he's unsuccessful, Ted will try a different judge. We hope to get a hearing very soon, but in the meantime, I'm afraid you'll need to go with Lieutenant Michaels."

"No! Narowyn, no. I don't trust him."

"I understand, but we have no choice at the moment. It's best to go voluntarily. We'll send Urick with you. If they won't allow him to accompany you in the normal way, he'll shift inside police headquarters to wherever they are holding you."

Urick speaks up, "I will not let any harm come to you." His eyes tell me he'll die protecting me. Let's hope it doesn't come to that.

Lieutenant Michaels and Officer Ross wait inside Narowyn's office. "Here is Miss Beckett," Narowyn says. "She will accompany you of her own accord, but I'd like my Lieutenant to go along also."

"For what purpose?" Michaels says.

"For additional protection."

"Officer Ross and I can handle anything that's likely to come up while Miss Beckett's in custody."

"Look Michaels," Watterson says gruffly, "two attempts have been made on Miss Beckett's life in the last several weeks. We have reason to believe she's still in danger, and we believe IUGA filed this bogus criminal complaint to manipulate her into a vulnerable situation."

"We're in the process of arranging an emergency hearing before Chief Judge Laurence," Narowyn tells him. "Should something happen to Miss Beckett in the meantime, I assume you do not wish to have to explain to the Judge why you refused additional law enforcement assistance when it was offered."

Michaels scowls. "All right. Your Lieutenant can accompany us as long as he keeps his mouth shut and doesn't impede our processing of Miss Beckett. Where's the robot?"

"He'll be here momentarily," Narowyn says.

Officer Ross extracts something shiny from his pocket. "We won't restrain her hands since she's coming voluntarily, but she'll have to surrender her Trans-Dimensional Positioning Device and she'll need to wear this." He holds up a silver collar similar to the one IUGA's robot clamped on me. My brain goes numb and my hand goes protectively to my throat.

Narowyn glowers at him. "Put that thing away," she says through clenched teeth.

Ross looks to Michaels for direction. "Put it away," Michaels says.

"Jaden, I'll take your bracelet for safekeeping." Narowyn holds out her hand.

I slip it off and give it to her. Ralston steps into the room and I mouth "I'm sorry," to him, but he just shakes his head.

"I know you're vouching for both of them," Michaels says to Narowyn, but we've got to put restraints on the robot. We're told his program's been tampered with."

"That's absurd."

"It's all right." Ralston says.

Officer Ross positions Ralston's wrists behind his back and locks a heavy metal clamp across both of them.

"Let's go," Michaels says.

* * *

Once we're inside police headquarters, Lieutenant Michaels instructs Officer Ross to handle my processing. Another uniform steps up to take Ralston away to be cataloged as evidence. I silently pray that the emergency hearing happens before someone from IUGA gets to Ralston. I feel heartsick for letting him down.

Ross leads Urick and me to an area designated for processing accused criminals. The walls are starkly white. Long strands of strange, blue tube-lighting snake along the ceiling. The floors are white tile and unexpectedly shiny and clean. The room contains three rows of small metal tables with black flat-screens on top. A bald man with thick red tattoos decorating his scalp sits in handcuffs at one of these tables. He turns and scowls at me as we walk through the door. He opens his mouth as if to say something, but Urick casts a warning look his way, and the man clamps his mouth shut and turns back to the officer processing him.

Ross tells me to have a seat at one of the tables. He explains that the next steps will be to take a photo of me, run an iris scan of my right eye, and record my imprint.

The photo and iris scan take only a few seconds. But when Ross attempts to record my imprint with an illumometer, he says he can't get the instrument to work properly. Stomping to a closet on one side of the room, he chucks the device inside and removes another from the shelf.

"This can't be right," he says, whacking it on the table top. "I've never seen one register this high."

"It's correct. Just record it," Urick growls, giving him the wolf-eye treatment.

Ross shrugs and enters the data into his computer.

"We're done here," he says, getting to his feet. "This way to the holding cell."

He leads us to a thick metal door guarded by a giant, robotic guard. Ross peers into a retinal scanning device on the wall, and the door opens onto a long, cell-lined hallway.

Our shoes clatter loudly on the concrete floor, drawing the attention of the collection of characters populating the nearby cells. I ignore the muttered comments as we pass. Glancing into a cell on our right, I see two tall, thin beings inside. They appear to be dressed normally for Arumel, but they are clearly non-human. I avert my eyes, but my knees quake to think I might be housed with interesting cellmates.

We approach an empty cell near the end of the row, and I nearly swoon with relief. Ross unlocks the door and holds it open for me. I wobble unsteadily inside.

"You can't go in with her," he says to Urick. "You have to wait out here." He locks the cell door behind me.

Urick lazily props himself against the bars. Ross eyes him warily before clacking back down the hall.

The cell is pungent with the odor of disinfectant. I choose to believe that means it's clean. The bare slab floor is a Rorschach of unidentifiable stains. A dilapidated metal toilet occupies one corner—I'll die before I use it. A shiny metal bench runs the length of the three unbarred block walls, and I balance carefully on its edge.

"Shall I ask them to bring you a chair or something?" I say to Urick.

"No need." In a blink, he's standing in my cell. "I'll sit with you."

He eases himself onto the bench next to me and leans back against the wall. His solid presence is comforting in this jarring environment. We sit silently for several minutes, listening to the indistinct prattling of the other inmates, as my stress level inches steadily higher.

"Urick, can I talk to you about something? Actually, I need to ask a favor."

"What is that?" He sits up and studies me with interest.

"A few days ago, Ralston came to see me." I lower my voice to a whisper. "He was all worked up over the possibility that he might be sent back to IUGA. Anyway, I promised him if that happens, I'll get him, or at least his stored memory components, out of Arumel."

Urick's lips twitch slightly, which I take as his version of a smile. "You are going to smuggle him out of the country?"

"*Shh.* The thing is, I might need your help. I'm not sure I can do it by myself."

"You know I am a law *enforcement* officer, don't you?" he says with mirthful eyes.

"Don't give me that crap, will you help me or not?"

"I do not believe it will come to that." He relaxes against the wall again. "But I will help you."

"Thanks." I feel some of the tension fall from my shoulders.

After another few minutes of silence, I ask him, "So, is Urick your first name or last?"

He rests a hand on the hilt of his Throkken, which amazingly they allowed him to keep. "In Demonstadt we do not have last names taken from our fathers, as they do here. We are given designations at the age of fifteen, based upon the jobs we are assigned."

"Really? So what was yours?"

"My designation was *hunter*. I'm known as Urick Hunter."

"Okay. That's cool. What did you hunt?"

He stares at a distant point on the other side of the cell. "Men," he says quietly.

"You hunted men at age fifteen?" I gasp.

He props his elbows on his knees and rests his chin on his folded hands. "I had a period of training first, but then I hunted the enemy alongside others in my cohort. It was my duty." He turns his liquid amber eyes on me. "Do you think less of me because it was my job to kill men?"

I inhale deeply, struggling for words. Though I'm sickened by the thought of it, I understand he lived in a different world. "No. I would never judge you. But that must have been a hell of a way to grow up."

He shrugs. "It was all I ever knew until I came here. My life was no better or worse than anyone else's."

"Did you ever wish you could have another job? One that wasn't so violent."

"No. I was good at it."

My throat feels thick and dry. "Do you ever miss it ... that life?"

He looks away for a moment. "I have no enemies here. In Demonstadt I killed only men who wished to kill me or my people. I never killed for pleasure or sport. It was a service for my country." His voice is thick with emotion.

The realization of the kind of life Urick endured on his home earth crashes down on me. How does a boy, or anyone for that matter, ever recover from that kind of fear and brutality? My eyes swim with tears, and I'm embarrassed and ashamed. Getting to my feet, I turn and brush away the tears with my fingertips.

"Why are you crying?"

I shake my head. "I'm just so sorry. Sorry for what you had to go through, and sorry for being such a jerk."

"Do not pity me."

"I don't. It's just ... I shouldn't have questioned you that way." I hate that I'm crying right now, but this night has not gone at all the way I planned.

"Save your tears for something important." He stands and surprises me by gently drying my cheeks with his thumbs. "Do not let these people see you cry. Show them your true strength. They will respect you for it."

His words prop me up, and just in time, too. The click-clack of footsteps echoes in the hall, and Lieutenant Michaels and Officer Ross appear at my cell door.

"What's this?" Michaels says when he sees Urick. "You're not supposed to be in there." He glares at Ross.

Urick obliges by shifting out of the cell to a spot directly beside Michaels.

"Jesus! Don't do that in here," Michaels says flinching. He unlocks my cell door. "Your hearing is set up in Courtroom One. Come with me, both of you."

THIRTY-NINE

Courtroom One looks pretty much like the rest of police headquarters. The walls are hospital white, and the glare of the lighting is painful on the eyes. Instead of bare concrete, though, the floors are covered with thin, gray industrial carpet. Plastic chairs line the spectator area. The judge's wooden bench is perched on a raised platform at the back of the room, flanked by four large flags. We pass through a short metal gate to an area with two long wooden counsel tables and an assortment of chairs.

Ted King and Narowyn occupy one of the counsel tables. Michaels ushers me over to them. Urick joins Watterson in the row of seats directly behind us.

Narowyn stands and embraces me. "Are you all right?"

"Yes, just nervous."

I take the chair between Ted and Narowyn. Ted pats my arm reassuringly. "We should be underway soon."

The metal gate behind us creaks open and a tall woman with a porcelain complexion and a dark, angular bob steps through, followed by a small entourage. The woman and her male counterparts wear robes similar to Ted's except in a maroon shade. They sit at the counsel table opposite ours. Two men dressed in navy blue suits take seats behind them.

"Who are they?" I whisper to Narowyn.

She leans in. "The prosecutors are seated at the table. The man with the dark hair is Director Canto. I assume the other man is one of his assistants."

I glance at the two men. It's obvious which one is Canto. His suit is finely tailored, his black hair impeccably coifed, and he's staring at me intently with lethal brown eyes. He exudes a kind of dangerous power. Remembering Urick's words, I give him an *eff-off* jut of the chin, and look away.

A door opens behind the bench and a woman in red robes steps out onto the dais. "All rise," she says. "This honorable court is now in session. Chief Judge Robert Laurence presiding."

Everyone stands and Judge Laurence steps out of the same door and places a pile of papers and an electronic tablet on the bench. His robes are a dark, royal blue. "Please be seated," he says.

He scans the faces of those present in the courtroom. Tipping his head to Narowyn he says, "Mrs. Du Lac, welcome."

"Thank you, your honor," she says.

He squints toward the back. "Is that Director Canto, I see?"

"Yes, your honor," the director says. "Good evening."

"Well, well, quite a notable gathering this evening. Shall we begin? The court will come to order." He strikes his gavel with a crack, and then taps his computer screen to life and dons a pair of black reading glasses. "This is an emergency hearing for a Writ of Habeas Corpus, brought on behalf of Jaden Beckett to address the matter of her arrest earlier this evening."

The judge looks over at me. "Is that you, young lady?"

"Yes, sir," I say.

"Your honor," Ted whispers to me.

"Your honor," I add.

330

"Are you by any chance related to Eleanor Beckett, the chairman of the Arumel Societal Commission?"

My heart wrenches at the mention of my mother's name. So, she has a *mirror* here. I could happily have gone the rest of my life without knowing that.

"No, your honor. I'm new to Arumel."

"I see." He turns again to his computer screen. "Well then, Ms. Beckett has been charged with grand theft in the form of one automaton belonging to the Inter-Universal Guidance Agency. Is that correct Ms. Prosecutor?"

The judge removes his glasses and looks to the woman sitting in the first chair at the prosecution table. She stands. "Yes, your honor. Elaine Crawford on behalf of the people. To be more accurate the accused is charged with extracting the mass storage data and stealing the memory module of an automaton belonging to IUGA and transferring it into another automaton."

Judge Laurence nods. "And Mr. King you have filed papers indicating that the arrest of Miss Beckett and the confiscation of the automaton in question is a gross miscarriage of justice that needs to be rectified at," he checks his watch, "ten fifteen on Saturday night."

Ted stands. "Yes, your honor. The unlawful arrest and detainment of Miss Beckett constitutes sheer harassment. IUGA has filed a false complaint against her in retaliation for her civil lawsuit against it and the fact that she has successfully obtained a restraining order barring its employees and representatives from any contact with her. In addition, we are gravely concerned that agents acting on behalf of IUGA may attempt to harm her while she is in police custody."

Judge Laurence leans forward and squints at Ted. "Is that so? Well, Mr. King, you filed this motion, so I will hear from you first."

Ted goes over the general allegations of our civil suit against IUGA for the judge. He recounts the facts of the automaton attack against me in Connecticut and refers to the IGC Court restraining order against IUGA. He then addresses the issue of the stolen property charges.

"The automaton in question with its mass storage unit and memory module intact had been discarded by IUGA," Ted says, "and was recovered in a lawful operation carried out by the Transcender Police Force, with Miss Beckett's assistance, to prevent the data's imminent destruction. The automaton's memory data is of vital importance to the pending civil action. Further, we believe if IUGA is granted custody of the automaton in question, it will proceed with its plans to destroy the material evidence he possesses."

"Thank you Mr. King. All right, Ms. Crawford, go ahead with your response."

"Your honor, this is a case of theft for personal gain, plain and simple. We have evidence in the form of a partial facial identification placing the accused at the crime scene with a group of co-conspirators, who took pains to conceal their identities." She holds up two black and white photographs. "You should have these in your file," she says. "We didn't have time to make copies for Mr. King."

The judge takes a few minutes to examine each photograph carefully. He raises his eyes to the prosecution table. "Ms. Crawford, where were these taken? It appears to be a refuse dump."

"It's an IUGA parts facility, your honor," Crawford says.

Ted gets to his feet. "Your honor, may we see the photographs?"

"Most certainly." The judge hands the photos to his clerk who walks them to our table. One photo is of me barfing on the ground next to Ralston's beat-up head and torso. My chin and mouth are partially visible. The other is of Ralston being strapped to Urick's back.

Judge Laurence continues. "Ms. Crawford perhaps you will explain to me what use IUGA planned to make of an armless, legless, dented automaton torso that appears to have been thrown onto a refuse pile. You've stated in your complaint that the property is worth in excess of one hundred thousand Confederation Dollars. This looks like nothing more than scrap to me."

"Your honor," Crawford says, "the memory components of this automaton are beyond value. They are chock full of confidential propriety information belonging to IUGA. The agency believes the Transcender Society intends to use this information to damage IUGA's operations. Director Canto has given a sworn affidavit that the automaton remains had been placed on the scrap pile in error and, therefore, technically had not been abandoned. Hence it still belongs to IUGA."

"May I respond, your honor?" Ted asks, returning the photos to the clerk.

"Certainly," Judge Laurence says.

"As clearly shown in these photos, the garbage heap on which the automaton was discovered was located outside the fence surrounding the IUGA facility. Various companies in the area routinely place scrap on this pile to be picked up by a county truck and taken to the public incinerator. It's our position that IUGA intended the automaton and its memory data to be hauled away and destroyed. The law is well established that once property is abandoned by the owner, it can be claimed by anyone."

"What about IUGA's assertion that the automaton remains were placed on the scrap pile in error?" Judge Laurence asks.

"Even if the property was abandoned in error, which we dispute," Ted says, "it certainly was no crime for the Transcender Police and Miss Beckett to recover it in order to preserve material evidence in a pending lawsuit. This is not an instance of corporate espionage, as the prosecution would have you believe."

"All right people," Judge Laurence says, stacking his papers in a neat pile and placing the photographs on top. "I have your positions. Give me a few moments here."

He taps some keys on his computer screen and jots some notes on his electronic tablet. Removing his reading glasses, he looks up and announces, "I'm ready to rule."

Resting his hands on the bench, he says, "My findings are these: The question of whether the robot was thrown on a refuse heap in error or because IUGA expected it to be removed and incinerated is not one that needs to be addressed in this forum. Nor is this court obliged to reach the issue of whether the memory data was taken as part of a lawful Transcender operation."

He leans across the bench, addressing the prosecutor. "In fact, Ms. Crawford, I'm a bit mystified as to why this criminal complaint was ever issued. Where is the criminal intent here? As far as I can see from your own photographs, any reasonable person coming upon this garbage pile would have presumed the property had been abandoned by its owner and was, therefore, free to be claimed. Mr. King is quite correct on the law in that regard. If the property was thrown away in error, the agency is free to bring that up in a civil lawsuit. It is not a matter for the criminal courts."

"But these people were wearing gear to thwart the security cameras," Crawford says. "Clearly this was a covert operation to gain corporate secrets."

"I don't care what they were wearing, Ms. Crawford. Taking abandoned property is not a crime, and I trust I will not see any further complaints from your office based upon similarly flimsy facts, no matter who has provided a sworn affidavit."

"No, your honor," Crawford says. Her posture is defiant, despite just having had her nose tweaked.

Judge Laurence focuses on me. "Miss Beckett I apologize for the inexcusable inconvenience this has caused you. I'm ordering that all charges against you be dismissed, and any reference to your arrest be expunged from the record. You are free to go."

"Your honor," Crawford says. "One item still remains to be resolved. The automaton is here in police custody. IUGA has requested that it, or its memory data at least, be immediately returned to the agency until the civil court can resolve this issue."

"If I may, your honor?" Ted says.

"Yes, Mr. King."

"Mrs. Du Lac has gone to considerable expense to have the memory data transplanted into a new automaton shell. As the data's ownership is still in dispute, it would be highly inequitable to require Mrs. Du Lac to turn over a two hundred and fifty thousand CD automaton, or to render it useless by removing its memory data. The Transcenders are willing to post a bond to insure the return of all memory data to IUGA should a civil court find in its favor."

"That sounds reasonable to me," Judge Laurence says. "Accordingly, I order the automaton be returned to Mrs. Du Lac upon the posting of a five thousand CD bond."

Judge Laurence stands and gathers his papers. Everyone in the courtroom stands also. "Good night people," he says. "Try to enjoy the remainder of your weekend."

Narowyn hugs me and shakes Ted's hand. "Thank you so much, Teddy. We appreciate your coming out so late."

"My pleasure, Nary. I suggest you transfer the funds for Ralston's bond immediately, if possible. Watterson can wait and return him to the Chateau this evening. I don't recommend leaving him here overnight."

"I'll do so at once." She picks up her tablet. "Jaden, give me a few minutes to arrange this, and Urick and I will accompany you home."

When we reach the Chateau, Asher's waiting for me in my darkened apartment. Callie's sitting next to him on the couch. My apartment has been tidied-up, and all traces of the party, except the fresh flowers, have disappeared.

"You didn't have to wait up for me, Ash. And I can't believe you cleaned up."

"I had lots of help. We were all concerned about you—especially this one." Callie nudges my hand, and I tickle her ears. "Kind of puts

335

a damper on the party when the host is arrested and carted off to jail, but at least your friends had someplace pleasant to hang out and wait for word."

"Did Narowyn call you?"

"As soon as the judge ruled. Your guests went to bed relieved. Can I fix you something?"

"No. I'm a little tired. I think I'll just turn in."

"Can't blame you for that. You have tons of leftovers in the fridge, if you're hungry."

We walk together to my door. "By the way, you need to help me think of something nice to do for Urick," I say. "He really propped me up tonight. I'd like to get him a gift, but all I can think of is a tattoo."

He laughs. "Urick's kind of an enigma. I have it on good authority, though, that he loves flowers."

"You're such a liar!"

"No, I'm serious. I've heard he's always bringing lilies or daisies or whatever into the police barracks."

"Okay, flowers it is. I'll take some of these arrangements over to the barracks tomorrow. Thanks. And Ash, I mean thanks for everything—for taking care of things here and waiting up and all."

He uses his fingertips to gently tuck a strand of hair behind my ear. "Just try to stay on the right side of the law, please. I don't like worrying about you like that."

He grazes a kiss across my eyebrow and slips out the door. His scent lingers in the air, and I wonder for the hundredth time why I can't just fall in love with Asher. I've always found him attractive, and he's one of the most decent men I've ever known. But my mom always used to say, "The heart wants what the heart wants." Or, in this case, doesn't want. It's pointless trying to make sense of it.

FORTY

Autumn unfolds gradually in Arumel. The air takes on a fresh, clean flavor, and the days grow slowly shorter and cooler. The grounds of the Chateau reflect the change of seasons as the gorgeous red and purple flowers of summer give way to the bright oranges and russets of the autumn leaves.

In the days and weeks following my unpleasant brush with the Arumel City Police, I slip into a quiet routine: Firearms Training and classes in the morning, workout sessions and fencing in the afternoon, dinner with my fellow Transcenders in the evening, and occasional tutoring with Ralston afterwards. I'm becoming stronger and better educated all the while, but each day hooks onto the next like the uniform cars of a railroad train—chugging down a track to an as yet unknown destination.

My adoption of Callie is quickly approved. She spends most of her time with me these days, but visits the center when the notion strikes her. I have a tracking monitor in my apartment now, so I always know where she is. I've stocked up on her favorite healthy treats to make sure she keeps coming back. Thanks to Asher's excellent taste and decorator touch, my little apartment makes a warm and comfortable home for Callie and me.

My battered heart begins to heal a little more with each passing week. Thoughts of Ryder and his painful death haunt me less now.

One morning as I'm making my bed, I remove the fading sketch from beneath my pillow and press it between the pages of my favorite poetry book. Someday I'll find someone to restore it or at least preserve it for me, but there's no rush.

I worry less about Domerica these days. In a strange way, studying other earths and the quirky events that shape their destinies, has helped me adopt a philosophy of *what will be, will be*. I hope one day to see my Domerican father and possibly Gabriel again, if only from a distance, but I've made peace with the fact that my future is now in Arumel.

My nineteenth birthday rolls around quietly. It's the first time I've been away from home on my big day, and that makes me a little sad. I'm not sure if anyone at the Chateau knows my actual birth date, but I'm kind of hoping dinner passes without anyone mentioning it. Since my infamous arrest, I've been working hard to keep a low profile. I'd rather not have a big fuss made over me.

I plump up the cushion on my desk chair and settle in to read my email. I'm emailing in real time now, so I may have some birthday messages waiting. Before I switch the computer on, though, my front door swings open, and a small flash mob appears in my hallway.

"What's all this?" I ask as Asher, Eve, Nila, and Urick bustle inside.

"Put on something sexy," Eve says. "We're taking you away to celebrate your new trip around the sun."

"My what?"

"Your birthday, earth girl."

A goofy smile spreads across my face. "How did you find out?"

"Oh, please," Eve says. "We've been planning this for weeks."

"Girl, we're taking you to Venice," Nila says. "So wear some comfortable shoes, and bring a jacket, 'cause we're going for a gondola ride after dinner."

"Whoa. Did you say Venice? You're taking me to Italy for my birthday?"

"We're Transcenders, remember?" Asher says. "Hurry up. We have dinner reservations."

Nila and Eve help me pick out a dress to wear, and I snag my purse from the hall table. Asher gives us the coordinates for our destination, and we click our latches simultaneously. *Zzzt.*

We land in the Piazza San Marco, outside an enormous gothic style building facing the waterfront. Asher tells me it's the Doge's Palace, and we're on the Grand Canal. I pirouette in awe, taking in the mind-boggling sights around me. The air is rich with the tang of the ocean, the weight of history, and the crackle of ancient magic.

"The restaurant's this way," Ash says, taking the lead.

We stroll along the canal as vendors hawk their wares from small, colorfully painted carts. Poets, puppeteers, actors, and musicians vie for the attention of passersby from slapdash stages. We veer onto a narrow side street, cross two small footbridges, and turn left onto Calle Bempo.

"There it is!" Asher says. "Le Bistrot de Venise." The aromas coming from the open front doors are heavenly. "Does the birthday girl want to eat inside or out?" he asks.

"It's gorgeous out tonight, and I don't want to miss a thing. Let's sit out here."

The evening overflows with enchantment—strolling minstrels serenade us at our table, the food is divine, and the lights glitter like stars on the canal. The combination of droll Nila and kooky Eve makes for spirited and sometimes hilarious conversation. I even catch a smile on Urick's face once or twice.

It's late when we finish our Italian coffee and servings of house-made gelato, but Nila insists we must have a gondola ride before we leave. We wander back through the Piazza San Marco. The crowds have thinned as we make our way to the gondola stand.

Our gondolier is dressed in the traditional horizontal striped shirt and straw hat with a red ribbon band. He introduces himself as Paulo, and graciously helps us into the long low boat. We take seats on the velvet covered banquettes on either side.

Once we're all settled, Paulo uses his long pole-like oar to expertly back the boat out of its slip, and we begin our floating tour of the city. Paulo steers our boat from the Grand Canal onto a smaller canal near the Doge's Palace. Glowing lights mounted on the building facades glint and ripple across the inky water. He narrates along the way in heavily accented English.

"We are coming now to the most famous bridge in all of Venezia," he says. "The Bridge of Sighs connects the Palace with the Prigioni … the prison. This was the last image of freedom for many of the condemned. One final glimpse of their beloved Venezia."

The white covered bridge is breathtaking with the stars twinkling above and the water glimmering below. I'm awestruck by the fact that I'm actually riding in a gondola beneath the Bridge of Sighs in Venice to celebrate my nineteenth birthday. It's a night I'll never forget, and though nothing will ever erase the pain of losing Ryder, I'm happy to be making new memories—good memories—to tuck away and think about when I'm feeling blue.

It's around one a.m. when I arrive back in my apartment, exhausted, sleepy, and clutching a sequined and plumed carnival mask I picked-up as a souvenir. I kick off my shoes, drop the mask and my purse onto the floor, and fall across my bed. Callie hops up and snuggles up beside me. "Vasa, lights off. Wake me at eight, please."

"Of course, Jaden. Pleasant dreams."

Instinctively, I know it's not yet eight o'clock when my ringing phone wakes me.

"Narowyn Du Lac calling," Vasa says.

"What? What time is it?" I ask.

"It's seven a.m. Would you like to speak with her?"

"Yeah. Of course."

"I'm sorry to disturb you so early," Narowyn says, "Do you have a few minutes to visit with me before your firearms class? It's not an emergency, but I have something important to discuss with you."

"No problem," I say groggily. "I'll be right down."

"Actually, if it's convenient, dear, I thought I'd come to you."

"All right, sure. Give me ten minutes to dress." I bolt out of bed and stumble over my discarded purse and shoes. My knee hits the floor, crunching my new Venetian mask. Guess that means I'll have to go back someday.

Hurrying to the bathroom, I wash the leftover traces of makeup from my face, run the toothwand over my teeth, and pull the brush through my hair.

"Vasa, coffee on," I say, slipping into slacks and a sweater.

As I show Narowyn through the door, she surveys my rooms curiously. "With all the excitement the night of your open house, I never had an opportunity to really see what you and Asher had done with your place. It's charming."

She hands me a flat silver box tied with a wide matching ribbon.

"What's this?"

"A combination birthday present and apartment warming gift. Sorry to be late on both counts."

We take seats in the living room, and I place the box on the coffee table between us. "Would you like coffee?" I ask.

"None for me. Thank you. How was your celebration last night? I understand your friends took you to Venice."

"Yes. It was amazing. Do you mind if I fix myself a cup?"

"No. Please go ahead."

I jog to the kitchen and fix a giant mug of milky, sweet coffee.

When I rejoin Narowyn in the living room, she says, "It seems you're settling nicely into your new life. I do so want you to be happy here. I'm certain you're still heartsick over your loss, but I hope you're beginning to feel more at peace as time passes."

"Honestly, I am. I never would have believed it a few months ago, but I'm starting to feel kind of normal again, and don't worry, I am happy here." I gulp some coffee and set my mug on the table.

"That's wonderful, dear." She lowers her eyes for a moment and chews her lower lip. "Actually, I didn't come here only to bring you this gift. There is a matter I need to discuss with you, and I ask that you keep an open mind and hear me out before responding."

"Okay, what is it?"

"Eleanor Beckett would like to meet with you."

"What? No!"

"Jaden, please." She rubs her fingertips across her brow. "You said you would listen to me before making up your mind."

"I'm sorry. I can't imagine what you could say to change my mind, but go ahead." This whole topic makes me squeamish. I snag the paperweight Luci gave me off the table and nervously shift it back and forth between my hands.

"Judge Laurence told Mrs. Beckett of your presence here in Arumel. He also advised her that, in his opinion, you were being harassed by IUGA because of your pending civil suit against it. She looked up the case and has taken a strong interest in it. She wishes to file an amicus curiae brief on your behalf."

"What's an amicus whatever brief?"

"Literally, it's a 'friend of the court' document. They're filed by persons, not parties to the lawsuit, who wish to set forth arguments in support of one side or another. She feels strongly that IUGA's interference in Domerica's affairs and its assistance in the assassination plot against you was outrageous and should not go unpunished."

"It's nice she feels that way, but does her opinion make any difference?"

"As chairman of the Arumel Societal Commission, she's quite influential on such matters. She is willing to state that if the allegations against IUGA prove to be true, she would support expulsion of the agency from this country."

Narowyn leans in toward me and clasps her hands tightly. "I can't stress enough how important this could be to insuring your safety here."

"And you think if I don't meet with her she won't file the brief?"

"No. I'm quite certain she will file it either way. But I'd like you to seriously consider this invitation."

"Geeze, Narowyn." The paperweight slips from my hand and thuds loudly against the table, sloshing my coffee and rolling onto the floor. "Aren't you the one who warned me about getting involved with people's *mirrors*? I see nothing but more heartache coming out of this. I don't want to know her. I don't want to be her friend."

"I understand why you would feel that way." She retrieves the paperweight and replaces it next to my mug. "In this particular instance, however, I wish you would reconsider. She could be a powerful ally."

"Isn't it enough that I've had two mothers die on me already? Did you tell her about that? Did you tell her she'll probably die shortly after she meets me?"

"No I did not. She knows your mother is deceased. If you wish to convey your fears to her, that is your choice. I don't believe it will scare her off, though. Jaden, she's an educated, level-headed woman. She knows you're not her daughter. She has an interest in your case, and she wishes to meet with you."

She studies me for a moment, her fingers twining through her long strands of jet beads. "You've not asked for my opinion, but I shall offer it anyway. You learned much through your experiences in Domerica. You may choose to have a social relationship with Mrs. Beckett or not. That is entirely your prerogative. But having a preplanned meeting with her is surely preferable to bumping into her on the street."

My temples throb. "So, you think I'm just postponing the inevitable?"

"I do. Actually, she lives quite close to us."

"This really isn't fair of you to ask." I sound like a whiny child even to myself.

"I'm sorry you feel that way, dear, but it's Mrs. Beckett doing the asking, and I do need to give her your answer."

I slouch back in my chair and cross my arms. "If I agree to meet with her, there would have to be some conditions."

"Such as?"

"I want the meeting to be just me and Eleanor—no one else. If my father and Drew have *mirrors* here, she and I can discuss it at that time. But I'm not ready to meet the whole damn family, if you know what I mean."

"That's reasonable. I will convey that to her very clearly. She suggested tea at her house tomorrow afternoon. Is that acceptable to you?"

"So soon? That barely gives me time to get used to the idea."

She tilts her head. "Less time to fret over it."

I sigh. "All right. Tomorrow at three."

"Lovely. I think you'll find her delightful." She slides the gift box toward me. "Aren't you going to open it?"

I unfasten the ribbon and open the lid. Inside is a bronze on bronze patterned silk throw. The subtle sheen of the delicate fabric is exquisite. "It's gorgeous, Narowyn. Thank you very much."

"It's Fortuny. I heard you were fond of the Italians. It seems to go well with the rest of your things."

"It does, doesn't it?" I toss it across the back of my salmon colored arm chair. "I love it."

"Well I'd best be going. Thank you for being so gracious about this." We stand, and her hand reaches for mine. "I'll send you directions to Eleanor's home. Have a wonderful day, dear."

I'm tempted to climb back in bed and pull the covers over my head, but I hit the shower instead, hoping the remainder of my Friday won't be quite so stressful.

* * *

I wake on Saturday morning with an uneasy hangover from fragments of a vaguely disturbing dream about Ryder. Once my feet hit the bedroom floor, though, all my thoughts turn to my meeting with Eleanor Beckett this afternoon. I don't have classes on Saturday, but if I stay inside my apartment, I'll most likely sit around and stress about it all day. I need a distraction.

It's been a week since my Spontaneous Shifting sessions came to a close, and I've missed working with Luci, so I decide to pay her a visit. Also, I've been postponing telling her about the strange phenomenon that occurred during the automaton attacks in both Domerica and Madison. I know I should discuss it with someone knowledgeable, and she's the most likely person to help me figure it out. I'm certain she'll be in her lab, even on Saturday morning.

"Hey, Luci, you got a few minutes?" I say, poking my head inside her door.

"I always got time for you SG." She holds up a glass beaker filled with brownish liquid. "Tea?"

"Nah, just finished breakfast. Mind if I close your door?"

"Sounds serious. What's up?" She sets the tea on her desk and regards me curiously.

I scoot up on top of one of the lab tables. "Not sure how to say this, but I think something might be wrong with me."

She reaches over and lays a cool hand across my forehead. "You coming down with something?"

"I feel fine. It's just that I've had a couple of well, *incidents*. Twice it seems like I sent someone flying through the air by aiming my palm and shouting at them." I hold out my hand for her inspection.

She examines it cursorily, flipping it over and back. "Looks like a normal hand to me. Tell me what happened."

After I describe the two situations to her, I say, "The similarities seem to be that both times automatons were involved, and I was scared out of my wits. Plus, I screamed *get off*, or something like that. Do you think any of that's relevant?"

She rubs her chin with the back of her hand. "Don't know. Can you do it for me here?"

"What? Like you want me to send you flying across the room?"

"Not me, but pick an object. How about my tea?"

I laugh nervously. "It's not like that. I can't do it on command. I'm not angry or scared or anything."

"Well, just close your eyes and concentrate on what you were feeling when that robot attacked you in the road. Then give it a whirl." She shrugs. "Can't hurt."

I close my eyes and inhale deeply, conjuring up that night in my mind. It all comes flooding back again—pinned to the blacktop, my heart pounds frantically, I'm scared as hell and roaring mad. A jolt of remembered fury flashes through me. My eyes burst open and I swing my palm up toward the tea, wanting to smash it against the wall. The beaker soars off the desk and crashes into the cabinets behind. Tea and shards of glass splatter everything in sight.

"Holy shit! Sorry," I say, flabbergasted by what just happened.

Luci bounces on her feet and claps. "Woohoo! That was mega cool, SG. You gotta do that again. But wait. Wait 'til I get my goggles." She runs to the cabinet and pulls out her illuminosity goggles.

"Okay, pick something else." She scans the room. "The microscope. That thing weighs a ton. See if you can do it to the microscope." She adjusts the goggles on her head.

I close my eyes again, but this time I don't envision what happened that night. Somehow I understand that it's only necessary to summon up the intensity of emotion. Opening my eyes, I fix on the microscope, and then *wham*. My hand sends it airborne. It smashes into the wall, leaving a dent and a huge black mark before crashing to the floor and shattering to pieces.

"I knew it! I knew it!" Luci says, wrenching off the goggles. "A big bolt of energy just shot out of your hand." She looks at the destroyed microscope, and her triumphant expression falls away. "Uh oh, that was a really expensive piece of equipment. Probably should have practiced on something else. Narowyn's not going to be happy, but maybe she won't mind when we tell her how it happened."

"No! We can't tell Narowyn yet. We can't tell anyone until we find out what this thing is."

"It's just your energy, SG. You've stumbled on a way to harness your illuminosity and use it."

"Yeah … as a weapon. Some people might not think that's so great. It's just one more thing that makes me weird. IUGA will probably try to have me arrested if they find out—*unlawful use of hands*, or something."

She hops up and sits next to me on the lab table. "That's hogwash. Look SG, this *is* great. The power comes from here." She uses two fingers to tap my forehead. "Your palm's only the conduit. Once we figure out how to get it under control, you can move objects around any way you want by just using your mind. That's a good thing. After we understand how it works, I bet any of us can learn to do it."

"But that's what I'm saying. We need to figure it out first. You and me. I don't want to be studied or experimented on like some guinea pig. Narowyn wouldn't do that on purpose, but if she finds out about this, you know she won't rest until she gets to the bottom of it. You have to promise me—not a word to anyone until we understand it better."

She puffs out her cheeks. "Okay. It's a promise. But I need to research this, and we need to work together to try and tame this power. You gotta devote some time to it."

"Yeah, fine. Believe me, I want to understand it as much as you do."

"All right, I'll clean up this mess and hide that broken microscope. You run along, but stop by here in the mornings or at lunchtime or whenever you can, and we'll work on tweaking this thing 'til it's under control."

"Deal." We shake hands, and she makes a sizzling noise like my hand just burned hers. I roll my eyes and leave, thinking I may get in a workout before lunch.

Eve intercepts me before I get to the stairs, though. "Hey I've been looking for you. You wanna go to Virtual World with me today? They have a new werewolf adventure."

"What's Virtual World?" I ask.

"You never heard of it before? Oh man, It's so great. You choose the fantasy you want to experience. You know, they have things like outer space and medieval times. Then you go in this chamber and put on this cool eye gear, and you have this whole realistic experience in a virtual world where you're the hero in some epic story. It's a real adrenaline milkshake."

"I don't know Eve, I need to be somewhere this afternoon."

"It only takes a couple of hours. I'll have you back right after lunchtime. I promise."

"Can we do it together?"

"Yeah, that's the fun part. We'll be partners. I thought we'd be werewolf hunters. They'll give us fake pistols and silver bullets and everything. I've been dying to try it. We'll finally get a chance to use all that firearms training we've had. C'mon," she coaxes.

It does sound kind of cool, and it would be as good as a workout for getting rid of my nervous energy. "Okay, but I have to be back here by two so I can change for this tea I have to go to."

"No problem. We'll take an air taxi home."

FORTY-ONE

Eve and I have a blast playing werewolf hunters in an amazingly lifelike virtual environment. The werewolves are scary as hell—life-sized, mangy, monsters with fangs and claws. I swear they even smell like wolves. We have to dodge and run and even climb a tree to escape them. Eve bags a lot more of the bloodthirsty beasts than I do, but we both win trophies for being the high scorers of the week. As we're leaving, a small group of teenagers approaches us and asks for autographs. We modestly consent. Then they ask for a little spontaneous shifting demonstration, which we artfully decline. This is a first for me, but Eve says it happens to most Transcenders at one time or another.

The air taxi ride home is almost as much fun as the werewolf game. Soaring above the gleaming skyscrapers with their rooftop gardens, I gain an even greater appreciation for how beautiful the Emerald City is.

Back home, I take a long shower and change. By the time I set foot out the front door of the Chateau, I'm having fresh misgivings about the wisdom of this meeting with Eleanor. There was a time, back in Domerica, when I felt meeting my mother's *mirror* was nothing short of miraculous. But now, I worry that my heart's just going to get broken one more time.

The afternoon air is crisp and refreshing and helps to clear my mind. The short five-block walk to Eleanor's neighborhood persuades me that it's probably best for us to meet like this instead of leaving it to accident. Though my heart flutters as I round the corner onto her street.

An unexpected but familiar wet nudge against my palm sends a wave of relief through me, and I turn to find sweet Callie behind me, eyes bright, tail wagging. "Hey, what are you doing here?" I sit on my heels and hug her. "Thanks for coming, girl. I need the moral support."

When we reach Eleanor's home, I have to double-check the street number. The house looks like an old English cottage rather than the grand estate I expected. The exterior features an authentic thatched roof and giant leaded glass windows. Vining red and white flowers completely swallow up the low picket fence surrounding the property. A small wooden gate opens onto an uneven stone walkway. Callie and I climb the steps onto a wide, gray porch. The red front door is merrily welcoming.

I knock tentatively, and after a moment, the door opens with a whoosh, and she's there. I don't have the urge to run into her arms, but I can't hold back the smile of pure pleasure at the sight of her lovely smile. She wears a long, flowing dress of peach-colored linen. Wisps of hair frame her flushed and beaming face.

"Jaden, it's so good to meet you." She holds out her hand and I shake it.

"I see you've brought a friend," she says, bending to pat Callie's head. "Come in both of you."

"She'll be happy to wait outside if you prefer."

"Nonsense. She's welcome inside."

Callie and I step into the foyer. The interior of the house is as warm and inviting as the outside. Fresh flowers in mismatched vases sit atop nearly every flat surface, including the haphazard stacks of books propped against chairs and tucked into corners.

"I've been working in the garden this morning," she says. "I think flowers make everything so much more festive don't you?"

"I do."

"I have tea laid out for us in the solarium. We are completely alone, as you requested. I normally have some housekeeping help, but I've given her the afternoon off." She escorts us down a short hallway to the back of the house.

The glassed-in room is bathed in afternoon sunlight. A cluttered desk sits near the back. Stacks of files cover the desktop and spill over onto nearby chairs and even the floor. The remainder of the room is taken up by a charming sitting area worthy of the faerie folk. Colorful chintz-covered chairs and a matching couch are surrounded by potted plants of many sizes and shapes. A glass-topped coffee table with metal legs carved to look like tree branches sits atop a thick, flowered rug.

"This is beautiful," I say.

"Thank you. It's my favorite room. John grumbles about the cost of cooling and heating it, but we live rather modestly, so I allow myself this one extravagance."

Her reference to my father's *mirror* answers one of my unspoken questions. She motions for me to have a seat in an overstuffed chair with a whimsical footstool in the shape of an elephant. It reminds me of a silly Fargen footstool Ryder and I received as a wedding present. Callie makes herself comfortable on the floor next to my chair.

"Now, how do you like your tea?" she asks, perching on the edge of the couch.

"Two sugars and a little milk, please." I notice a glass door leading out into an extraordinarily lush garden. "Your roses are amazing. My mother used to grow roses too."

She passes a delicate teacup and saucer to me. "Isn't that remarkable? I do love them. Please forgive me for not being completely educated on how this *mirror* thing works. You certainly do bear a remarkable resemblance to my late daughter, but in many ways you're quite different."

That intrigues me. "How different?"

"Oh, her life was very quiet, and she loved it that way. It revolved around her horses, riding students, and family. She rarely ventured outside her sphere of familiarity. You've lived a much larger and varied existence." She pours tea for herself and drizzles some honey into her cup. "What about me? Do I resemble your late mother?"

I bite my lip and study her. "Yes and no. I think the differences between you are more cultural than anything else. My mom had short hair, and she normally wore business suits. She was a very engaged mom, but she was usually kind of harried. Typically, *mirrors* are very much alike except for the way their unique life experiences have influenced them."

"I see. I find the whole thing rather fascinating, don't you?" She settles back in her seat with her tea.

"It can sometimes get confusing." I sip my tea and gaze out at the garden, to avoid having to explain what I mean.

She artfully changes the subject. "Well, I'm delighted that the IGC Court hearing is coming up soon. I'm very much looking forward to it."

"You're coming?"

"Yes, I thought I'd sit in the upper gallery. I don't want my presence to be a distraction to any of the parties, including you. So, if you'd rather I didn't …"

"No, that's fine. It won't bother me." I'm relatively certain that I'll have bigger things to worry about at that point.

She tilts toward me, her eyes twinkling with girlish excitement. "Please tell me all about yourself, Jaden. I understand you've had some remarkable experiences. What was it like being a queen?" She passes me a plate of assorted cookies.

"Frightening but fun." I say, taking two small lemon cookies and placing them on my saucer.

"Did you have lots of wonderful things? Gowns, and servants, and private jets?"

"The Domerican people are not as advanced technologically as we are. In fact, horseback is still the main mode of transportation there, so no fancy cars or jets, but I did have some extraordinary things. The clothes were beautiful beyond belief, and the palace was super-luxurious."

"How exciting. I have to say, I'm a bit envious. It must have been an incomparable experience. But I was terribly sorry to hear of your tragic loss. You're so very young to be a widow."

"People in Domerica marry quite young. I suppose that's part of being a less advanced society."

"Not necessarily," she says. "Several years ago, the marriage rate in Arumel was at an all time low, as was the population growth. Our lawmakers thought it wise to provide some significant incentives for young people to marry and have children. It worked better than anyone anticipated. Not only did the rate of marriage increase appreciably, but the average age of newlyweds dropped dramatically. My son Drew is married and already has a small child at age twenty-one. My daughter was also married briefly before she died. She never got to meet her nephew, Jeremy."

I'm intrigued by the information that my *mirror* was married, but I don't want to delve any further. The thought of Drew with a toddler makes me smile. "My brother Drew in Connecticut won't be ready to be a daddy for years," I tell her. "But his *mirror* in Domerica is married and will soon be a father also."

"Tell me about your family and your life in Connecticut. Is it terribly different there?"

"Yes. The United States, on my earth at least, is fairly technologically advanced, but not like Arumel. And it will be some time before the people are ready to embrace the existence of beings from other planets or even relate to the fact that other dimensions exist. Religion and superstition keep many people from being open minded about such things."

She nibbles on a macaroon. "So living there is not an option for you?"

"Not if I want to use my gift. These cookies are delicious, by the way."

"Thank you. Please have some more." She slides the plate toward me. "And your father, what does he do?"

"He's a nurse in the cardiac unit of a local hospital. You already know my mom died a few years back. She was a judge. Dad's been dating a real nice woman lately. I won't be surprised if they decide to marry in the next year or two. My brother's in college in North Carolina, and I imagine my dad's kind of lonely without us."

Eleanor is easy to talk to, unpretentious and kind. She seems fascinated with the Transcenders, and I share some of my more remarkable stories with her. After a while, though, I steer the conversation away from me.

"How long have you been on the Societal Commission?" I ask.

"Oh goodness, it's been twelve years now."

She explains that the commission deals with the major issues confronting Arumelans—healthcare, public safety, and quality of life. I have the impression that her calm wisdom and keen sense of justice make her well suited for the position.

"I love my work," she says. "But I've been increasingly troubled by the pervasive presence of IUGA in this country. Its actions are frequently detrimental to the public welfare, in my opinion. And it strikes me as unethical that its executive officers have grown extraordinarily rich using confidential information generated by the Agency. It makes no profit, per se, but I'm convinced that, in some cases, events have been manipulated to the advantage of its operators. Without more transparency, however, we have no way to prove it."

"I appreciate so much your willingness to file a brief on my behalf," I say. "That's so kind of you."

"It's my pleasure. No one should be allowed to control the destiny of another. That is the antithesis of freedom. Your case is a perfect example of that." She glances at my empty tea cup. "Would you care for more tea?"

"No, two's my limit." I glance at my watch. "Callie and I had better be going. I still have a few things to do before dinner." I stand and Callie jumps to her feet, tail wagging furiously.

"Thank you so much for coming, Jaden. This was just delightful."

"Thank you for—"

I'm interrupted when a small child darts into the room from the hallway. "Nana, Nana," he cries.

Eleanor scoops him up into her arms. Then she glances at me with worried eyes. "Jeremy, what a surprise. Did your father bring you?"

"No, Unca Ry."

His meaning rockets to my brain, and my head whips around to the door at the same instant that Ryder's form fills up the frame. His eyes meet mine, and within the space of two seconds his expression morphs from abject joy, to disbelief, to comprehension, to anguished pain—and finally, pure hatred. He turns abruptly and flees.

The air is sucked from the room, and I crumple into the chair, my heart deadened by shock.

Eleanor sets her grandson on the floor, and he wobbles to Callie, giggling as she licks his face.

"Oh god, Jaden, I'm so sorry. I had no idea Ryder was watching Jeremy today, or that they would come by unannounced. I thought it best not to even mention that he was my late daughter's husband, since I'm aware of your reluctance to know about your family's *mirrors* in Arumel. Are you all right?" She kneels next to my chair and takes my hand.

"I'm fine," I say, feeling as if someone just kicked me in the stomach. "Is there another way out of here? I don't want to run into him."

"Yes. Use this door." She takes me to the glass garden door. "The back gate leads to an alleyway. Turn right and it will let you out one street over. Please forgive me, Jaden. I'm so terribly sorry."

"It's okay, Eleanor. It's not your fault. I'll be in touch."

Callie and I trot through the back gate and into the deserted alley. We make a right turn onto the street parallel to Eleanor's. I spot a small park situated on the corner, and plow ahead to the entrance. Cutting across an expanse of grass, we manage to avoid other people. Tears stream down my face and trail inside my collar.

We don't stop jogging until we're deep inside the park. A small bench rests in the center of a deserted copse. I collapse onto the hard concrete seat and howl my heartbreak to the trees. I didn't believe I could hurt like this again.

Callie sits quietly at my feet staring at me with anxious eyes. She nudges my knee in concern. It's okay, girl." I run my hand along her silky fur. "Everything's going to be all right," I say to myself more than to her.

I rest my cheek against the cold concrete of the bench for a few minutes. Then, after a flurry of hiccupy breaths, I manage to reel my emotions back in.

"Come on, girl. Let's go home."

We walk back to the Chateau and duck up the stairs to my apartment. I flop down on top of my bed and shed a few more tears, remembering the look of utter devastation on Ryder's face. He was so heartbreakingly beautiful in his pain. The sorrow in his eyes was all too familiar. I see it in the mirror every morning. I also understand the final flash of loathing in his eyes. I hate him too—because he's alive and my Ryder is gone.

A knock at my door startles me out of my thoughts.

"Jade, are you here?" Eve calls from the doorway. "You left your trophy at my place." Callie runs to meet her, while I use my sleeve to dry my eyes.

"What's wrong, girlfriend?" she says coming through the door.

I raise a shaky hand to my forehead. "Unfortunately, I just saw a ghost."

"Huh?"

"Come in. I'll tell you all about it."

I grab two juices from the fridge, and we sit on my bed while I describe my encounter with Ryder.

"Sweet Giza! What a douche. How could he just run away like that?"

"I guess he was … I don't know, traumatized by seeing me."

"Still he didn't have to be such a jerkwad." She pats my leg reassuringly. "The good news is you don't ever have to see him again."

"That's not necessarily true. Eleanor's house is only blocks from here. For all I know he lives on the next street over. I could bump into him at any time." I sink down into my pillows.

"Well, if you do, you just act like he doesn't exist. He's lower than snot." A mischievous smile plays at her lips. "But I think you should look him up online and see where he lives, just in case. Maybe he's got a social page."

"What? No. I'm not going to do that. I've been down that road before. It's too much like stalking."

"No it isn't. It's for your own protection."

"Forget it Eve. I just want to put it behind me."

"Okay. I was just headed down to dinner, wanna come with?"

"Yeah. Give me a minute to wash my face."

FORTY-TWO

On Sunday morning heavy gray clouds perch low in the sky. The air is a good ten degrees colder than it was the day before, and my mood has taken a plunge also. I call Rals to invite him over for brunch.

"I could use a shoulder to cry on," I say. "I accidentally bumped into the local version of Ryder Blackthorn yesterday."

"Oh my, where was this?"

"At Narowyn's urging, I had tea with Eleanor Beckett at her home. I guess I should have been prepared for something like this, but she assured me we'd be completely alone. Anyway, come over, and I'll tell you about it over Eggs Benedict."

"Goodness, you've learned to make hollandaise sauce?"

"Nah, it's from a carton. All I have to do is heat it up, but it tastes pretty good."

Ralston's a sympathetic listener. I describe my visit with Eleanor and Ryder's surprise appearance. He's caring and supportive as usual, and wisely advises me to try to put the incident out of my thoughts.

"Look at it this way, now that you've experienced the shock of that initial first meeting, you never have to go through it again."

"I know, but it kind of ripped the scab off of all the painful memories that were beginning to heal. And that wasn't even the worst part."

"What do you mean?"

"For a split second, before he ran out of the room, he looked as if he hated me. I think I understand why, but I don't want him to hate me." I blow out a sigh. "I don't even know why I care."

He gazes at me with tender eyes. "I'm certain it was only his astonishment you witnessed, my dear, and you care because of the *perpetual contract*. Remember what I told you in Domerica? Now that you two have met and the connection has been made, it's not unusual that you would feel something for him, perhaps even be drawn to him. The important thing to understand is that the way you handle those emotions is entirely up to you."

After we clear up the brunch dishes, Ralston and I set up the board for a game of chess. A grueling two hours later, I finally manage to put him in checkmate. For some reason, though, I have the sneaking suspicion that he let me win.

"Well done, old girl!" he says.

"That better not have been a pity-win," I say as we walk to the door.

"You know my pride would never allow that. I would like a rematch soon, however."

"Anytime you think you're up to it, old man." I smile and kiss his cheek. "Thanks for the talk, Rals. I needed it. Would you mind letting Narowyn know I won't be at dinner tonight. I'll finish the leftovers from brunch, and I have a lot of studying to do."

"Of course, my dear. I shall see you tomorrow."

The week starts out sunny but cold. I concentrate on my classes and try to put the incident at Eleanor's out of my mind. Eve and I go shopping Tuesday afternoon for warm scarves and gloves, but I keep my outside excursions to a minimum for the rest of the week for fear of running into Ryder Blackthorn again.

Friday morning, Eloise waits for me inside the firing range for our final Firearms Training class. A few of my paper targets are good enough to have been put on display on the *wall of fame* behind the counter. I can't help but feel a little proud when I see them.

"Have you been practicing outside of class?" she asks after our session. "You were extra sharp today."

I laugh. "I did go virtual werewolf hunting last weekend. Maybe that's why."

"Well whatever it is, you've come a long way in the past weeks, Jaden. You're one of my sharpest pupils. I'll be filing my report with Narowyn today, and I expect she'll have you out in the field in no time."

"I owe it all to you, Eloise. You really are the best. Thanks for everything. Hope to see you again soon."

"You will, once you get another newbie in here. Seems about time y'all added a new Transcender."

"We really don't control that, but you never know. Maybe soon." I hug her goodbye and head back to straighten up my apartment before Alternate Earths.

After classes and a quick lunch, I decide to see if Ralston can fit in a fencing session.

When I arrive in the large gym-like room where the fencing piste is located, Ralston is working with a student. He has taken on a few other pupils, and I wait in the stands for him to finish his lesson.

"Do you have time for me this afternoon, old man, or are you too tired?" I ask, once his pupil leaves.

"I never tire of dispensing a good thrashing to arrogant and deserving students, of which you are my favorite," he says with a taunting grin.

I change into my silver mesh fencing suit with the protective head gear and select an epée from the rack.

Ralston and I face each other on the strip, our epées up. "En garde," he says, the signal that we are about to begin. "Allez, allez," he shouts, meaning *come and get me*.

I lunge at him, and he deftly parries my blade, then quickly scores a touch. "Touché," he cries. The lamé on our suits is electronically equipped to buzz when the epée touches the mesh in the target area. In epée, basically the entire body is fair game.

We separate and take our stances again. Ralston's speed is literally superhuman this afternoon, and he quickly scores several more points on me. I squint at him suspiciously through my mask. It occurs to me that his handsome new shell must have some special, super-fast reflexes the old one didn't.

Laughing heartily, he yanks off his head gear. "Had enough yet, Supernova Girl?"

Oh, he did not just say that. His condescension kind of pissed me off, but calling me Supernova Girl means war. He's not the only one who's got skills.

I pull off my mask and sneer at him. "Not a chance, grandpa. I'm all warmed up now."

We replace our masks and take our stances once again. "En garde," he says. "Allez, allez."

I lunge at him. He parries the move with lightning quickness and attacks. I vanish into the air for a heartbeat, then reappear in front of him and score a touch on his chest. His suit beeps.

"Touché!" I shout.

"I trust you know that is cheating, Jaden." He circles me warily.

"Sorry, Rals."

"We'll do that point over," he says. "En garde. Allez, allez."

I lunge, he parries. I disappear and reappear to his rear touching

363

his back with my epée. *Beep.* He whirls around, and I vanish again reappearing at his side. I touch his thigh. *Beep.* I do the same routine twice more. His suit buzzes with each touch.

"Enough!" he shouts, smashing his epée into the floor.

I'm laughing so hard I can barely stand.

He throws off his head gear, his face flaming. "I've never been treated so disrespectfully in my entire life."

"Calm down, Rals." I take off my own mask. "I had the impression you were using an unfair advantage against me when we began. If I was wrong, I apologize. I only meant to remind you that it's not sport unless we're on equal footing, old chum."

His chin juts sharply, but then he bows graciously. "Touché, my dear. And so, the student becomes the master. It is I who must humbly apologize to you, dear friend. I'm afraid my new and improved body has caused me to act rather arrogantly. I meant no disrespect whatsoever, and I hope you will forgive me."

"Don't worry about it, Rals. Apology accepted."

He smiles, eyes twinkling. "And may I add that your spontaneous shifting skills are much improved. I'm quite impressed."

"Why, thank you." I make a little bow and stride toward the locker room.

* * *

After dinner, I put the finishing touches on my Science of Transcending homework, and I'm about to change into my pajamas when Narowyn calls and asks to see me in her office.

She's seated in an armchair reading when I arrive, and I take the seat next to hers.

"Thank you for coming, Jaden." She sets her book aside. "I suppose I owe you something of an apology. I heard from Eleanor Beckett that Ryder Blackthorn unexpectedly made an appearance at her home on Saturday. She was quite concerned and sorry about it, but she wasn't certain you would wish to speak with her."

"It was a pretty large jolt," I say. "But I know it wasn't your fault or Eleanor's. So please tell her not to worry."

"Still, it must have been painful for you. Would you care to talk about it?"

"No. Actually, I'm trying to forget it. Obviously I knew there was a possibility that he existed. Hiding my head in the sand was probably not the right approach to take. But Ralston and I had a nice talk afterward, and as he points out, now that the initial surprise is behind me, I can go on with my life as if he's irrelevant—because he is."

She watches me with guarded eyes. "Then you're feeling well emotionally?"

"Yes. I feel good. I finished up Firearms Training this morning, and I whipped Ralston soundly at fencing this afternoon, so things are looking up."

She smiles. "Yes, I got your firearms report today. You've progressed brilliantly in all your training, Jaden. Eloise couldn't say enough good things about you, and of course Dr. McDonald is one of your most ardent fans."

"They're both good teachers. I enjoyed working with them." I don't feel the need to tell her Luci and I are continuing to work together on my other little project.

"Wonderful. I wanted to let you know that Ted King got in touch with me today. The IGC court granted our request for a postponement of the hearing. Unfortunately, it seems they have a rather full docket, and the earliest date they can have a panel in Arumel City is January fifth."

"Hmm, so a few months from now?"

"Yes. Does that concern you?"

"I guess not. I'd like to get it over with before the holidays, but I feel safe with the temporary restraining order in place."

"Good. Then since we have some additional time, and since your mornings are now mostly free, I thought perhaps you would enjoy taking on an exploration or two. We've just had something new come in."

"Really? An exploration?" My stomach snaps to attention. "Are you sure I'm ready?"

"Oh yes. It would only be for a few days. And I'm afraid it's not a terribly exciting assignment. We received word that Earth P17L, an Outlier Earth, nicknamed Twin Moons, suffered a catastrophic tsunami two days ago after a major earthquake in Alaska. Many of the coastal areas of California have been destroyed. Tragically, tens of thousands have been killed and many thousands more are missing. We've been offered a large grant by the government to go to Twin Moons and conduct a bit of research, in the hope of preventing a similar catastrophe from occurring here or on another Confederation earth."

"Oh my god. That's horrible. Is it safe to go right now?"

"Yes, with precautions. The area's contaminated with all the detritus from the flood. But we already have established contacts there, and you'll be provided with everything you need. I'd like to have a team on the ground quickly to put together the pertinent geological data and disaster statistics, as soon as possible."

"Who else would be on the team?"

"Asher has been to Twin Moons before, so I imagined you two would be partners on this assignment. This is not a place where we can go in as ourselves. The concept of Transcenders is beyond the understanding and acceptance of the society. You will pose as relief workers. A husband and wife."

That gives me pause. Asher and I posing as husband and wife might get a little sticky. "It sounds interesting, Narowyn, but are you sure I'm the right person for this? I mean, I don't know anything about geology or disaster statistics. I'm not even sure what relief workers do."

"You would only be collecting data from other sources, not analyzing it. And I felt this might be a good initiation for you. Judging from your experience in Connecticut, you and Asher seem to work well as a team."

It's true we did work well together in Connecticut. But Narowyn doesn't know about my concerns that Asher may have feelings for me that aren't strictly professional, and I'm not prepared to share that with her just yet.

"I really appreciate this opportunity, and the confidence you've placed in me, but I'd like some time to think it over. I'm not sure I'm ready."

"Naturally, dear, I do not wish to send you in if you feel uncomfortable. I'll need your answer in the morning, though. Time is of the essence here."

"Understood. I'll let you know in the morning." My stomach does a slow churn.

"That will be fine." She stands to see me to the door. "And, Jaden, should you run into Mr. Blackthorn again or should he try to contact you, please know that I am available any time to discuss it."

I really wish she hadn't said that. Her words just upped the blender speed in my belly. I hadn't considered that he might try to contact me. I head back to my apartment and splash cold water on my face.

"This was supposed to be a quiet evening," I say to my reflection in the mirror. One thing I know for certain, I can't avoid it any longer—I need to have a talk with Asher tonight.

I pat my face dry and dab on some lip gloss. Then I quickly wipe it off. Lip gloss is not appropriate for this discussion. I trudge down the hall to Asher's apartment and knock softly on his door.

"Ash?" I say, leaning in close.

After a moment, I hear footsteps. The door opens a crack.

"Jade? What are you doing here?" His hair is tousled and his eyelids are heavy like he fell asleep in front of the TV.

"I need to talk to you about something."

"This isn't the best time for me. Can it wait until morning?"

"Nope, sorry buddy, it can't." I push past him into the apartment, picking up the faintest whiff of perfume on the way. I freeze at the entrance to the living room when I see Nila sitting on Asher's couch in a short yellow sundress. Her long legs and bare feet are tucked beneath her, and her loose hair billows around her shoulders like volcanic smoke.

I raise my hands to my face. "Oh shit. I am so sorry, Ash. I didn't know you had company."

"Hey Jaden," Nila says, bending down to retrieve her sandals. "Sounds like you two have some things to discuss."

"Nila, this is so embarrassing. Stay. Please. I can talk to Ash later."

"Don't worry about it, girl. I was just leaving anyway." Her long sensuous fingers trail across Asher's shoulder as she passes. He follows her to the door, and they exchange whispered goodnights.

"So," he says to me, closing the door. "That wasn't awkward or anything."

"Oh man, Ash. I don't know what to say. *I'm sorry* doesn't quite seem to cover it."

He picks up a tray with a half empty bottle of wine and two glasses and glumly carries it to the kitchen. "You want some wine while we talk about this urgent matter that just can't wait?"

"No. You go ahead, though."

He pours a little wine into a glass, and we sit at his kitchen table. "What's up? Are you all right?"

"Yeah. I'm fine. It's just that Narowyn spoke with me tonight about sending us on an exploration together."

"Yep, she mentioned it to me earlier. You got a problem with it?"

"You know what? Right now I feel like such a dumbass, I don't even know how to say it."

"Just say it. It's me remember? You've said plenty of dumbass things to me."

That makes me smile. "Okay, but promise you won't laugh."

"Scouts honor." He holds up three-fingers.

"Well, we'd be going away together for a few days, posing as husband and wife, and I didn't really know what your current feelings were toward me, so ..."

He grins, but doesn't laugh. "So you were worried that I might still be carrying a torch for you and that would be ... umm, maybe even more awkward than tonight?"

"Well, nothing could top that, but yeah."

He nods still smiling. "Okay, I get it. So, you want me to tell you that I have absolutely no designs on you and you're safe pretending to be my wife."

"Uh, I don't think you need to tell me that after tonight. I saw that love-sick puppy look on your face."

He throws back his head and plunges both hands into his hair. "Ah, Nila, Nila, Nila."

"Boy's got it bad, huh?"

"God, Jade. I've never felt this way before. The woman's about to drive me mad. She's all I think about. I can't sleep at night. I have to stop myself from calling her twenty times a day. She's like love heroin or something. I can't get enough of her."

His mournful green eyes delve into mine. "Do you have the vaguest idea what I'm talking about?"

"Oh, yeah." I nod slowly. "Nothing else like it on this earth … or any other, for that matter."

"This is how you felt about Ryder?"

"Yep."

"Shit. No wonder you wouldn't give me the time of day. I guess that explains a lot of things."

"Like why I married him?"

"Like why you married him."

"So how long has this been going on between you two?"

He takes a slug of wine. "We've known each other for a few years, but I guess I never really saw her until that night at the pub in Oxford. We stayed up and talked all night after we got back to the flat. I guess she must have cast a spell on me or something. God, I never thought I'd be dating a cop." He slaps a palm to his forehead.

"Uh, she's really not your average cop, Ash. She's more like an intergalactic law enforcement ninja."

He barks a laugh. "She's a ninja all right, in every way. But sometimes I feel like a complete Neanderthal around her."

"Ha! You're not a Neanderthal. You're Mr. Suave. Anyway, are you sure you want to go away on exploration right now?"

"Yeah. I think we should go. It'll be invaluable experience for you, and it'll do me good to get away for a few days to try to recoup some of my old machismo. Besides, I think she's a little jealous of you."

"I hate to break it to you, Ash, but you don't need any more machismo. Nila likes you the way you are, and while I highly doubt that she's jealous of me, a little distance might do you some good. You know, give her some time to miss you."

He grins. "Does that mean we're going to Twin Moons?"

"We're going to Twin Moons," I say, getting to my feet. "I'll let Narowyn know in the morning. Why don't you call Nila and see if she wants to *pop* back over here?" I waggle my eyebrows.

"You don't think I should play hard to get? Let her wonder about what we're doing?"

"Life is short, my friend." I head for the door. "Don't ever forget that."

FORTY-THREE

"Jaden, good morning," Narowyn says when she finds me sitting in her office. "You're here very early." She lays some files on her desk and comes around to join me in the armchairs.

"I didn't get much sleep last night," I say. "I don't like to leave things hanging, so I wanted to get this out of the way early."

"I assume that means you've reached a decision?"

"Yes, I have. I'd like to go to Twin Moons with Asher. I spoke with him about it, and he agrees it would be a good first experience for me."

"Excellent. We'll get you two set up immediately. Can you leave tomorrow?"

"I don't see why not." So much for my quiet little routine. "What do I need to do to prepare?"

"I'll have Gil put together some information for you on Twin Moons. It's not terribly different from your home earth, with a few notable exceptions. Also, you'll need to be fitted for a uniform. That is done over in the police barracks. If you go this morning, it should be ready for you by tomorrow."

"I thought we were supposed to be aid workers. Won't the

uniforms kind of stick out?"

"You'll be given appropriate local clothing when you reach Twin Moons. Transcenders always travel in their uniforms when on official business. It's in the back of the handbook."

"Oh, sorry."

"It's quite all right. It takes time to learn the rules and regulations. In any event, that's all you need to do today. We'll have everything else ready for you and Asher in the morning. You'll be briefed at that time. Do try to get a good night's sleep, though."

"I'm sure I'll sleep better tonight."

I go directly from Narowyn's office to the Transcender police barracks to get fitted for my uniform. Turns out, sunny Jeffrey from the armory is also responsible for the uniforms. He has me try on a couple of different sizes and makes some notes on alterations. He promises the uniform will be waiting for me in the morning, as will a utility belt equipped with a holster for my sidearm and a pouch for a penlight and emergency meds.

Gil finds me when I land back at the Chateau. "I have a packet of information for you on Twin Moons," he says, passing me a slim file. "Narowyn tells me you're going tomorrow."

"Yeah. My first exploration." I flip through the file, not much here.

"Such a pity what happened," he says. "Please do bring back photos. I can use them in class."

"We plan to bring back lots of useful information, Gil. I have one question for you, though. How can this earth have two moons when the rest have only one?"

"Well I assume you're familiar with the Giant Impact Hypothesis?"

I twist up my mouth. "No, can't say that I am."

"Briefly, it states that the moon was formed out of the debris left over from a collision billions of years ago between the earth and a body approximately the size of Mars."

"No kidding? I'd never heard that."

"The majority of scientists who subscribe to the hypothesis believe that every earth had more than one moon at some point, but the sun's gravity caused these multiple moons to move in unstable orbits. Eventually they all collided with each other forming themselves into one big moon."

"So what happened on Twin Moons?"

"The theory is that the debris from the giant collision formed two moons of a similar large size—twins, if you will—which had concordant orbits. Consequently, they never had occasion to collide. You'll see from the information I gave you that this anomaly causes some tidal differences, and of course the nights are certainly brighter, but other than that, Earth 17L2 is not that different."

"Good to know. Thanks for the tutorial and the file."

"My pleasure." He smiles cordially, but he's still not quite as humanlike as Ralston.

I spend the afternoon reading over the materials in Gil's file and reviewing the Transcender Handbook. Even though I just cleaned my pistol, I do it again for good measure. After that, I call Luci to let her know our secret work sessions are on hold until my return. She says she has plenty of research to do in the meantime.

Finally, I make all the arrangements to have Ralston and Gil take care of Callie while I'm gone. As I'm gathering up dog food and treats to take down to their apartment, a soft but adamant tapping at my front door causes me to stop what I'm doing and see what's going on. I open the door to a flushed-looking Eve.

"Jade," she whispers. "There's someone downstairs to see you."

"Okay, but why are you whispering?"

"I don't know if you're going to want to see him. It's that Ryder

Blackthorn guy."

I grip Eve's arm and yank her inside. "What does he want?"

"He didn't say. I put him in the front drawing room and told him I'd see if you were at home. What shall I tell him?"

I shake out my hands and bounce on the balls of my feet. "I don't know. Just say I'm not here, and you don't know when I'll be back."

She scrunches her pert little nose. "Umm. Maybe you should just talk to him for a minute, Jade. He looks really hot. I mean, not just normal hot, but like melt your nail polish kind of hot."

"I know what he looks like," I say irritably. "Okay, tell him I'll be right down."

She claps her hands and grins. "Oh, goody. Can I listen at the door?"

"Go!"

I sprint to the bathroom and check myself in the mirror—hair still looks good. I could use a little mascara and some blush, but I don't want him to think I got all dolled up for him. I still haven't forgiven him for being such a massive jerk at Eleanor's. I pinch my cheeks, apply a coat of nude lipstick, and head downstairs.

As I enter the drawing room, he unfolds his lanky frame from the chair. *Holy sweet mother.* A hot chill jags through my body at the sight of him. Eve was right about the nail polish thing.

"Hello Mr. Blackthorn," I say, working to keep my voice even. "What can I do for you?"

He tucks his hands in his pockets. "I just stopped by to apologize for my terrible behavior the other day." He looks away for a moment and then returns his eyes to mine. "It's no excuse, but I was in shock seeing you at Eleanor's. It didn't take long for me to realize that you must have been as blown away as I was. Anyway, I'm sorry for being such an ass, and I hope you'll forgive me."

Nice speech. "Don't worry about it," I say "It wasn't pleasant for either of us, but I'm over it now. So let's just forget it ever happened. Thank you for coming by."

He doesn't make a move to leave. "I wonder if you'll let me buy you a cup of coffee to make up in some small way for my rudeness."

My chest throbs at the thought of having coffee with him. "Sorry, but I'm in the middle of packing for an exploration. I really don't have time."

"Then can we sit here for a minute? I have something I'd like to say to you. I promise to make it quick."

"All right. Have a seat." I gesture toward the chair, and I take the one opposite his.

He reseats himself and leans toward me, elbows resting on his knees. "I ... by way of explanation, I did know about you before that day. My mother-in-law told me you lived in Arumel City, and I'd heard some of the news accounts about your lawsuit against IUGA. But nothing could have prepared me for the impact of seeing you again."

"Again?" I squint at him.

"No. Not again ...I mean of seeing you."

"Listen, Blackthorn, you don't have to explain. I know exactly how you felt. And just for the record, I *didn't* know you existed. I specifically didn't want to know. So I'm guessing I was probably the more shocked of the two of us." My words come out kind of snarky, but I'm not sure of the proper etiquette for speaking to your dead husband's body double.

He combs a long fingered hand through his hair. "I'm sorry Miss Beckett, I'm handling this all wrong. I know you're not her."

"And you're not him," I snap. The huge chasm in my heart aches, and I wish he hadn't come.

"No, I'm not." He lowers his eyes and stares at his hands a

moment. When he looks up again his face is cloudy, and my heart involuntarily squeezes.

"No one can ever replace the loved ones we lost," he says. "I just thought ... well, I hoped that one day we might be friends."

Friends? Could I ever be in the same room with this man without attraction and repulsion dancing a tango inside me?

I shake my head. "Nope. Not a good idea. This whole thing is way too confusing for me, and to tell the truth, it hurts just looking at you."

He closes his eyes, and softly as a prayer he says, "Please. I ask you not to make up your mind so quickly. I get why you think it sounds a little sadistic. That's what I thought at first. To me, your moving to Arumel was a total disaster. I dreaded running into you. I even considered leaving town—moving away to make sure it wouldn't happen. But incredibly, now that it has, I feel different."

"Different, how?"

He dips his head and looks up at me through his coal black lashes. "Honestly, I can't stop thinking about you. I find myself wanting to see you again."

Gulp. My insides quiver at his words.

"What about you?" he asks. "Have you thought of me at all?"

Oh lord, how am I supposed to answer that? *Only every day since I saw you.* I remind myself that it's probably only the *perpetual contract* at work here.

"Of course, I have. It's not easy putting something like that out of your mind. I was devastated seeing you that way."

"I know, but that's what I wanted to tell you. The more I think about it, the more I'm convinced we're looking at this all wrong."

"I don't understand. Wrong in what way?"

"What if this isn't some kind of cruel cosmic joke? What if this is

377

just how it's supposed to be?" He tilts his head, and his eyes sparkle maddeningly. "What if there's a way to transform something that seems intolerable into something good?"

A mini-explosion goes off in my stomach. I'm not sure if it's a burst of springtime butterflies or an eruption of slimy black worms.

"What does that even mean?" I drag my eyes away from his.

"All I mean is, wouldn't we be happier and more at peace if we were friends instead of two people anxiously trying to avoid each other?"

I study the rug for a second. "Look, Blackthorn, I'm not sure what you want from me. I hope this isn't some kind of sick psycho-attachment thing like you think I might be your lost wife, and you just want to pick up where you left off."

He shakes his head. "No. It's not like that at all. The thing is, we live in the same city and we're liable to run into each other from time to time. We have a lot in common just from the fact that we've both lost spouses recently. In the end, we may not find each other interesting at all. But, honestly, I'm just asking for a chance to get to know you."

He seems so earnest, but at the moment I can't even make eye contact with the guy without my heart being razored to shreds. I don't really picture us hanging out together sharing a pizza.

"I appreciate that it took a lot of guts on your part to come here today," I say. "And you're right—I don't want us to tiptoe around trying to avoid each other. But I've got a lot going on in my life at this point, and it hasn't even been six months since my husband's death. Emotionally, I'm not in a place right now where I can be friends with you."

"Fair enough," he says softly. "I can wait ..."

Something in his voice pierces all the way to my soul. Like his words carry some unspoken promise I understand subliminally. I shoot him a sideways look. His gaze remains steady on me. "May I ask one thing, though?" he says.

"Depends."

"After a while, if you're feeling more comfortable with, well, the idea of us being friends, will you consider having coffee with me?"

"Sure, I'll consider it." I get to my feet, hoping he'll take his cue to leave.

"Thank you." He pushes up from the chair. The simple joy in his smile does a number on my heart.

We walk together to the front door, his heat and scent pulling at something deep inside me, which I choose to ignore.

"Please tell Eleanor *hi*," I say as he walks outside.

"I will. Be safe on your exploration."

I close the door behind him, and slump against it, sighing loudly.

"So?" Eve stands in the foyer, hands on her hips. "How did it go?" Did he apologize? Are you going out with him?"

"He apologized. Says he wants us to be friends." I use my fingers to make quotation marks around 'friends.'

She groans. "Oh that's so transparent. He's hot for you, and you know it. He practically devoured you with his eyes."

My lips curve up involuntarily. "Maybe, but I'm not ready to go out with anyone yet, and when I am, I'm not sure I'll want to go out with him."

"Are you nuts?" she says clutching her heart. "I mean he came all the way over here to apologize in person. And he looks like a smoldering volcano of ..."

I flash her a scowl.

"Okay, you already know what he looks like. Give the guy a chance. You loved him once, you could love him again."

"That's the problem. He's not the one I was in love with. Yeah, he's great eye-candy and all, but I don't even know what kind of guy he is."

"Well don't wait too long to find out. A hot sex sundae like that doesn't stay on the market long," she says, fanning herself.

"What did you call him?"

"You heard me. Add a little whipped cream and a cherry, and *mmm, mmm.*" She licks her lips suggestively.

Laughing, I grab her hand. "Come on, earth girl. I think my manicure needs a little touching up."

FORTY-FOUR

In the morning, Jeffrey has my gear ready and waiting for me. I take it all back to my apartment, and Callie watches curiously as I change into my uniform. It fits perfectly. A patch with the official Transcender seal has been sewn onto each shoulder. I strap on my utility belt and secure my pistol in its holster. After I fasten my hair into a single braid, I check myself out in the full-length mirror.

The sight makes me giggle. If only Liv could see me now. She'd think this was the best Halloween costume ever. With a pang of guilt, I wonder what my father would think of his gun-toting daughter heading out on a potentially dangerous exploration. *Better that he doesn't know.*

I dash off a text to him and one to Drew, since communicating with them will probably be difficult while I'm away. I let them know all is well with me, and express the hope that we'll all be together at Christmastime. I sign off by saying how much I love and miss them both.

After dropping off Callie at Ralston's door, I meet Asher in Narowyn's office. She has our coordinates, ID cards identifying us as relief workers, and a few last minute instructions.

We enter the coordinates into our TPDs, and on the count of three, *Zzzt*, we're streaming stars across the dimensions.

We touch down in the courtyard of a beautiful Mexican-style hacienda in East San Francisco. I scan the sun filled sky for signs of the two moons, but neither is visible. Asher leads me through an arched portico to the back door. He knocks three times.

The door is opened by an attractive, dark-haired man who appears to be in his late forties. "Asher, welcome," he says.

"Jack, this is my partner, Jaden. Thank you for agreeing to host us."

He shakes my hand. "Please come in. I'm happy to help. We've suffered such an enormous tragedy. I hope your work will help prevent this in the future, or at least ameliorate the effects."

Jack's home is beautifully decorated in traditional Mexican furnishings—lots of dark wood and painted tiles. He leads us down a Saltillo-tiled hallway to some bedrooms.

"Asher, I've put your clothing and toiletries in this first room." A folded stack of clothing and a backpack lie on top of the bed. "Jaden, your things are in there." He points to a room at the end of the hall. "After you've changed, I'll drive you down to the site. I'm afraid your accommodations will be pretty rough, but I know you want to be at ground zero."

"That's right," Ash says. "We appreciate your making the arrangements. We'll be ready shortly."

Asher follows me to the room where Jack has left my stuff. "You should have everything you need, but if anything is missing, we can pick it up later. Just leave your uniform and gear in the closet."

"Should I bring my gun?"

"Better not. We don't have the appropriate local permits. Bring your cash, though."

"Uh oh." *Damn!* I knew I'd screw up somehow.

"You didn't bring cash?"

"I didn't know I was supposed to." I wring my hands contritely.

"It's okay, Beckett, I have plenty for both of us, but for future reference, *always* bring local currency. The saying *Cash is King* usually holds true." He smiles making me feel slightly less stupid.

I sort through the clothing on the bed. People must dress like farmhands on this earth. A plaid flannel shirt, a pair of oversized bib overalls, and some Mariachi sandals are to be my outfit for the next few days. After slipping everything on, I look in the mirror and change my mind—*this* would definitely be the best Halloween costume ever.

My back pack is well stocked with toiletries. I even find a pair of John Lennon sunglasses and a blue bandana which I pray I'm not expected to wear on my head.

I hang my uniform in the closet, and stash my utility belt and gun on the top shelf. Another glance at myself in the mirror leaves me mystified—who wears this stuff? There's no accounting for taste, I suppose. We're required to dress like the locals, so *when in Rome ...*

I shoulder the backpack and meet Asher in the hallway. He's wearing faded jeans, a black t-shirt, a corduroy jacket, and running shoes.

"Whoa, look at you," he says with laughing eyes.

"Wait a minute. How come you're dressed like Justin Timberlake and I'm dressed like Greta the Goat Girl?"

Jack walks up behind me. "That's my fault. I guess I didn't do a very good job with the clothes. I lent Asher some of my things, but my wife took her elderly mother out of town when the tsunami warnings went into effect, so I picked out your clothes myself. It's what I thought a relief worker would wear."

In Kansas maybe.

"It's all right," I say, embarrassed to be caught complaining. "It really doesn't matter what I look like. We're here to do a job."

"Amen," Asher says. "Let's go."

"The car's this way." Jack motions us to follow.

We traipse after him to the garage and climb into his white Range Rover. "It'll take us about twenty minutes to get down there. I've told the folks at the World Aid Organization that you're a married couple here to gather data for the International Disaster Relief Fund. That's the cover Narowyn gave me."

"That's what our IDs say." Asher tells him.

Jack's neighborhood is lovely, with palm trees, bright bougainvillea, and large houses on enormous lots. "Our area got away unscathed," he says. "But prepare yourselves for some disturbing sights."

As we draw nearer to the water, we catch the first glimpses of damage to buildings and piles of collected debris. After a few more miles, it looks more like a war zone than the San Francisco waterfront. The golden gate bridge still stands majestically over the bay, but beneath it are acres of ravaged neighborhoods. Derelict boats and cars lie scattered miles inland from the coastline. Carcasses of trees, destroyed bits of furniture, and mangled household appliances litter the roadways.

"How high were the waves?" Asher asks.

"They estimate twenty to twenty-five feet in this locale."

"Was the area evacuated in time?" Asher says.

"Most got out. But we only had a few hours warning, and nobody predicted the wave would travel this far inland. Alameda was totally deluged with water. Alcatraz and some of the smaller islands were swallowed up completely. No sign left of them."

"What are the casualty estimates?" I ask.

Jack shrugs. "Hard to say. Around thirty thousand confirmed dead so far, but a hundred thousand or more still unaccounted for. By far the largest non-war disaster in the country's history. Probably take months before we get the final numbers."

We drive into an area where rescue workers and earth moving equipment are sifting through mountains of wreckage. "They're still pulling survivors out of there," Jack says. "You hear a lot of miraculous rescue stories along with all the bad stuff."

Jack parks in a make-shift parking lot next to a line of pickups and vans. "We'll have to walk from here. The roads are washed out. We're headed down there." He points to an area about a hundred yards away where a small tent city has been erected. "That's where you'll be stationed."

The air is a complicated muddle of unpleasant odors as we climb out of the SUV. "I've set up a couple of meetings for you today," Jack says, "and I've arranged for a helicopter tour tomorrow. The information's all here." He hands Asher a sheet of paper.

"Can you give me a hand with this water?" He opens the back of the Range Rover.

Asher and I slip our packs over our shoulders and each grab two cases of bottled water. Following Jack across the mucky lot, we pick our way around random debris. I don't even want to think about what's in the toxic stew oozing between the straps of my sandals.

When we reach the tents, Jack approaches a short man wearing a surgical mask and latex gloves. "Asher, Jaden, this is Parker Moses, of the World Aid Organization. Parker's heading up the WAO effort in the bay area."

We shake hands with the harried, bespectacled Mr. Moses. "We appreciate your letting us operate out of your camp," Asher says.

Moses pulls his mask down and tucks it under his chin. "Not a problem, as long as you're here to help and not impede our efforts."

"I assure you we won't be in your way," Asher says.

"Good. We've got a table and two cots set up for you in one of the tents. I'll show you the way. Just stack that water over there." He points to an area where workers are unloading food, water, and other supplies from trucks.

After we drop off the water, Jack bids us farewell. "Call and let me know when you want to be picked up," he tells us. "And good luck."

Moses shows us to our tent. It's tiny, and the walls seem paper thin. Large squares of cardboard have been laid down to form a makeshift floor. A folding table and chair sit on one side of the tent, and two cots are pushed together on the other. A lantern and a small space heater are tucked into the corner.

"It's pretty rustic," Moses says, "But I imagine you're used to that. You got surgical masks and gloves on the table." He points to a row of white boxes. "You already saw where the food and water is stored. Port-o-lets are located on the south edge of the tent line. Our main operations are in the big tent to the north. If you have any extra time, we could use your help checking-in people, passing out food, and well, you know the drill."

"Thanks," Asher says. "We're happy to help when we can."

"Be seeing you," Moses says. He replaces his mask and hurries off.

"Holy crap. Is this what you expected, Ash?" I say, still struggling to process the enormity of the devastation.

"You never know what to expect, but I try to mentally prepare for the worst." He spreads out the sheet of paper Jack gave him on the table. "Our first appointment is with Dr. Cara Meyers of the U.S. Geological Society. That's at two. What do you want to do until then?"

"I guess we could help out at the main tent."

"That should give us a good feel for what's going on with the survivors," he says. "We need to take photos of everything, but tomorrow can be our filming and photo day. Ever flown in a helicopter before?"

"Nope."

"It's an experience you won't forget."

We pluck surgical masks and latex gloves out of the boxes on the table and make our way to the main tent. Lines of dazed looking people snake outside the tent entrance. Workers inside are writing down names, passing out blankets, tending to injuries, and comforting frightened survivors.

"Can I help you?" A woman with curly red hair and freckles approaches Asher and me. Her WAO badge says her name is Linda.

"Hi Linda," Asher says. "We're with International Disaster Relief. We'll be on site for a few days. We had some extra time and wondered if we could help out in any way."

"Yeah, we can use all the hands we can get. You look pretty strong," she says to Asher. "You can assist the guys unloading the donation trucks. We're getting in supplies faster than we can unpack them."

"Okay, sure," Ash says.

She sizes up my unusual outfit. "You can't work in those shoes," she tells me. "You're going to need some boots or something. Do you know what we're walking on here? It's a mish-mash of raw sewage, boat fuel, and rotting animal carcasses. You don't want that on your skin."

"This is all I brought." I glance cautiously at Asher.

"There's an army surplus store open in Union Square. Only reason they're open is because of the high demand for guns, what with all the looting. I'm sure he'll have something for you. I got a truck heading up there now to pick up more blankets and lanterns. If you hurry, you can hitch a ride."

"That'd be great. Thanks." I turn to Ash. "So, honey, can I have some cash for new boots?"

He rolls his eyes and reaches for his wallet. "I guess so. How much do you need?"

"I'll just take that," I say, relieving him of the wallet.

"Woman thinks I'm made of money," he says to Linda.

The army surplus store turns out to be a nice little find. I ditch the overalls and plaid shirt and buy a pair of jeans, a t-shirt, and a cotton military jacket. The owner of the store recommends knee-high, lace-up motorcycle boots for mucking around in the flood zone. I use Asher's cash to pay for everything, but he brought a ton of it, so I think we'll be fine.

I help the others load up the blankets and lanterns on the truck, and we head back to camp.

When I stop by the supply tent to return Asher's wallet, he does a double-take. "Whoa, that's an improvement. You look kind of hot in those boots."

"Thanks, honey," I say. "See you back at the tent at two."

Linda seems to approve of my new boots and puts me to work at the intake table. My job is to record the names, addresses, injuries, if any, and missing family members of the people in line. Then I'm to direct them to the first aid station, the missing family member board, or the chow line, depending on the situation.

The first person to approach me is a young woman around my age. Her hair is a matted mess, and her clothes are filthy. Silent tears leave dirty streaks on her cheeks. She manages to say her name is Sarah Jameson, but she's too distraught to give me her address.

I walk around the table and offer her a wet wipe from the dispenser. "Tell me what happened to you."

"I was camping with friends," she sobs. "We scattered when we saw the wave coming. I've been searching for three days, but I can't find anyone. I'm afraid they're all dead, except I don't know how to find out."

"Do you live around here?"

"No ... I live in Colorado. I'm on break from school."

"Have you called your parents to let them know you're okay?"

"Nooo," she wails. "I lost my phone. No one will help me."

"I'll help you." I wrap my arm around her. "Come over here. We have some phones available."

"You can't abandon the intake table," Linda barks at me as she rushes across the tent.

"This girl needs help. She's been wandering around for days searching for her friends. She hasn't let her family know she's alive, and she probably hasn't eaten anything."

Linda's scowl softens. "I'll take her. You get back to the table."

The next people in line are a mother, father, and son. Their house trailer was washed away. They've been living in their car, but they need food and a place to stay.

"Lunch is being served at the back of the tent," I tell them after taking their information. "You can stay here for the time being. Check in at the housing table. They'll assign you to a tent temporarily. Representatives of FEMA and the Red Cross check with us daily for people who need supplies and more permanent housing."

They thank me, and I move on to the next sad story, and the next, and the next. The line of misery seems endless.

When it's time for our meeting with the seismologist, I don't feel like I can leave the intake table, the line is still a mile long. I decide to let Ash handle it himself. When I finally make it back to our tent, Dr. Meyers has already come and gone.

"Sorry I missed the meeting, Ash," I say, sinking into a folding chair.

"No worries. Dr. Meyers brought us a ton of useful information on the quake in Alaska as well as the formation of the tsunami. She even brought art." He holds up a colorful red, orange and yellow picture that looks like an abstract painting.

"What is that?" I ask.

"It's an infrared picture of the wave amplitudes."

"Oh. That's good, I guess." Even though I only worked a few hours, I'm emotionally and physically drained.

"You all right?" he asks.

I rest my head in my hands. "Oh god, Ash, it's completely overwhelming. So many people are suffering. Their needs are so great. What we're doing seems totally inadequate. Can't we do more?"

He runs a comforting hand over my hair. "This is the hardest part of any exploration, Jade. But you have to remember that's not why we're here. We're only observers. In the first place, we don't have the resources to run to the rescue whenever a disaster occurs in the galaxy. And, in the second place, we'd be doing exactly what we're accusing IUGA of doing— interfering with the natural order of things."

"I know, but it's just so hard not to care."

He sits across from me and pats my knee. "You don't have to be uncaring, but you do have to find a way to detach. This city and this nation will find a way to deal with the disaster, and maybe bounce back even more resilient. We take away what we can learn from it, in the hope that our knowledge will prevent something similar from happening on our earth or somewhere else."

"I know, I know. I'm just so tired. When's our next meeting?"

"In thirty minutes, why?"

"I need to rest for a bit."

I stretch out on a cot and face the wall of the tent. Closing my eyes, I attempt to disengage my emotions from the chaos around me. Asher sits at the card table and quietly sifts through the files of information Dr. Meyers left.

Just before four o'clock, he wakes me for our meeting with the American Red Cross representative. Glen Burke is a wiry, studious looking young man. Dusty brown hair falls across his forehead as he reads from his notes, carefully reciting disaster statistics collected by his organization to date. He cautions us that the information changes on an hourly basis.

"The numbers of casualties and the amount of property damage is staggering," Burke says. "It'll take San Francisco at least a decade to recover from the devastation."

"We appreciate everything you brought us today," Asher tells him. "We'll be in touch."

"You have all my contact information," he says. "If you call me in a week or so, I'll have more accurate numbers for you."

Once Burke leaves, our schedule is free for the rest of the evening. "What do we do now?" I ask.

"How about a break?" Ash says. "I'm starving. Let's get away from ground zero for a bit and have something good to eat. Have you ever tasted authentic San Francisco sourdough bread?"

"I hear it's pretty amazing. But are you sure it's okay for us to leave?" I ask.

"It's more than okay. We've accomplished a lot today. I know a nice Italian place near the Civic Center. Far enough inland that I'm sure it'll be open."

We begin walking in the direction of the Civic Center, hoping to find a cab or some type of public transportation, but it appears nothing's operational yet. At Ash's suggestion, we step into a deserted alley and shift to a spot near our destination.

FORTY-FIVE

Dinner is a nice respite from the sullen spectacle of the tent city. The dimly-lit restaurant is charming with its checkered table cloths and candles in Chianti bottles. We sit on opposite sides of a comfortable booth, and Asher puts me at ease by chattering about normal things while we eat. He updates me on his mother and sister, both of whom I met a while back in Asher's hometown.

"I'm hoping to go home for Christmas," I say. "Do you think that'll be okay with Narowyn?"

"Sure. Lots of people travel over the holidays. We usually don't schedule explorations during that time."

"You'd be welcome to come home with me."

He smiles enigmatically. "Thanks, but I think I'll see what Nila's doing before making any plans. Don't know if she's ready to spend the holidays with me yet, but I'm going to ask her."

I haven't had a chance to tell Ash about my encounters with Ryder Blackthorn yet, and this seems as good a time as any to bring it up.

"Guess who came to see me yesterday," I say.

"Who?"

"Ryder Blackthorn."

He stops buttering his bread and gapes at me. "What? You're not serious. He just showed up out of the blue?"

"Not exactly. Narowyn convinced me to have tea with Eleanor Beckett last week, and I first ran into him there."

"That's nuts. Why would she do that?"

I fill him in on Eleanor's intention to file a brief on my behalf with the IGC court, and I explain how Ryder just popped in unexpectedly and then rushed out without a word.

"Anyway, he stopped by the Chateau yesterday to apologize. He invited me out for coffee and said he wants us to be friends."

"I hope you told him to go to hell," Ash says.

"I didn't put it like that. But I told him I'm not ready for any kind of friendship with him."

Asher leans across the table, his lucent, green eyes intense. "Jade, you need to nip this thing before it gets started. You shouldn't have coffee with that dude—ever. You're just asking for trouble if you try to start some kind of relationship with him."

His arrogance irritates me, and I slant away from him in the booth. "Listen, Ash. First, there's nothing to *nip*. Second, I have no intention of starting a relationship with him. And third, I don't tell you who you should or should not be involved with. I expect the same courtesy from you."

His body relaxes. "Sorry. I just don't want to see you hurt again, that's all."

Our server brings us complimentary chocolate soufflés for dessert, as a thank you for our business during this turbulent time.

The wonderful smell of fresh-baked chocolate takes the edge off my momentary anger. "I know you mean well, Ash. But we all have to make our own mistakes. I'm happy you found Nila. She may turn out to be the best thing that ever happened to you or the worst—or possibly both. You need to trust your own heart, and I need to trust mine."

I scoop up a spoonful of the hot gooey soufflé and let the warm chocolate melt on my tongue. It takes me less than five minutes to gobble up my entire dessert, and, since Asher doesn't like chocolate, I help myself to his as well.

"So how much longer do we need to be here?" I ask, changing the subject.

"We've already made some serious headway," he says. "If we hit it hard all day tomorrow, we should be able to finish up and go home tomorrow evening."

A surge of relief buoys my spirits. "Really? That'd be great. I know it's weird to say, but I feel like such an outsider here—sort of like an alien."

"That's completely normal. If these people knew what we were, they'd treat us like aliens." He signals our server for the check.

"What about Jack? Obviously he knows we're Transcenders."

"Jack's the younger brother of Narowyn's first husband. She's kept in touch with him for many years. He's the only one on this earth she's ever confided in about her real reason for leaving. He agreed with her that his brother wouldn't be capable of accepting the truth."

"Oh man, that's so sad."

"Something we all have to deal with."

Stepping outside into the cool night air, I'm floored by the surreal sight of two dazzling moons lighting up the evening sky. I laugh out loud. "Are you freakin' kidding me? This is awesome."

"Keep your voice down," Asher whispers. "It's nothing out of the ordinary for these people."

"Sorry," I say grinning like an idiot. The brilliance of the radiant orbs causes the stars to pale to near invisibility, but the moons' silvery luminescence more than makes up for the loss. Internally, I add to my gratitude list: *the sight of twin full moons suspended over San Francisco bay.*

On our return to camp, we stop in at the main tent to help pass out food and water. But even with the light of two moons, it soon becomes difficult to function using only lanterns, and the main tent is forced to close for the night.

Back in our tent, I climb into one of the cots and draw the covers up to my chin. Asher turns on the space heater and puts out the lantern before he stretches out on the other cot.

"Goodnight, honey," he says.

I laugh. "Sleep tight, dear."

* * *

We get an early start in the morning, quietly vacating our tent while most of the others are still asleep.

"The helicopter's due at noon," Asher says. "Let's get as many photos as we can before then."

"Works for me. You want to split up?"

"No need for that, really. I want to visit what used to be the Fisherman's Wharf area first."

"Okay, lead the way." We munch on protein bars for breakfast while we walk.

It's impossible to make it all the way to the wharf. Much of it is still covered in murky water. Many businesses have been gutted or completely torn from their foundations. The area is littered with destroyed boats, jagged pieces of concrete and wood, and decaying sea life, including the sad remains of numerous seals. I'm glad we remembered to bring our surgical masks.

Asher takes out his polycom and snaps shots of the area. I find the proper icons on my polycom and follow his lead. "What are we looking for?" I ask.

"Whatever you think might be of interest to the scientists back home."

We wander northwest from the wharf to what used to be the marina. Then we cut back through a residential area where we photograph recovery crews using heavy equipment to sift through the rubble.

"Time to get back to the tent city," Asher says. "We should eat before we go up in the chopper. We may not have time afterward."

We stop at the main tent where volunteers are serving ham sandwiches and warm tomato soup. Parker Moses finds us as we're finishing lunch and informs us our helicopter is waiting in the lot where Jack parked the Range Rover yesterday.

"We'll say our goodbyes now," Asher tells him. "We're heading back this evening. Jack's picking us up at six."

Moses raises his eyebrows. "So soon?"

"I think we have everything we need," Asher says. "We appreciate your help."

"I hope you'll tell the people at the relief fund their money would be put to good use here."

"I'm quite sure you'll receive a check from the fund soon," Asher says. We shake hands with Moses, shoulder our backpacks, and start for the parking area.

"Will they really get some money or were you just shining him on?" I ask.

"Narowyn will make a donation to the WAO through the relief fund. We wouldn't take advantage of anyone."

Our rented helicopter is a shiny black and red four-seater. The gum-chewing pilot introduces himself as Jim. He wears the stereotypical baseball cap and aviator sunglasses, and his bomber jacket looks to be authentic World War II issue.

Asher sits in front in the co-pilot's seat, and I strap myself into the seat behind him. Jim gives us a tutorial on operating our headphones, after which I slide on my Sgt. Pepper sunglasses and brace for my first chopper ride.

"I understand you want to see the areas with the heaviest damage," Jim says to Asher.

"That's right."

"I'd say the hardest hit area is Long Beach, but that's a little over two hours to the south. That okay?"

"It's fine. We just need to be back here by six."

Jim presses some buttons and the rotors begin to whir loudly. He double-checks to make sure we're securely buckled in, then he taxis a short distance before we lift off and away. My stomach flutters up into my chest and stays there.

Our route takes us over the Golden Gate Bridge and south along the shoreline. From this altitude, the sheer magnitude of the devastation below is indescribable.

Asher fishes a small video camera from his backpack. "I'll take care of the video, Jade," he says into the headset microphone. "Maybe you can make a few notes."

"Sure," I say, taking a paper notebook out of my pack. "So Jim, why was Long Beach the hardest hit?"

"It's the lowest lying part of the California coast," he says. "The waves weren't as high, but they came further inland 'cause there was nothin' to stop 'em. See these cliffs over here?" He points to some tall cliffs on our left. "They protect a lot of the northern shore. Don't have those in the south."

Asher intently records everything with the camera while I scribble a few notes.

As we fly along, Jim provides bits of information to help put everything in context. "This area we're flying over now used to be multimillion dollar mansions with miles of sandy beach. Turned to wasteland now. Luckily, most of those people can afford to rebuild. Don't know if I'd chance it again, though, no matter how much dough I had."

"Isn't this supposed to be a once in a millennium occurrence?" I ask.

"That's what some say, but why tempt fate?"

By the time we reach Long Beach, I think I've seen enough rack and ruin to last me for more than one millennium. Ash stows the video camera in his pack.

"This was just what we wanted to see. We got a lot of great footage," Ash says. "Let's take the quickest route back, Jim. Jade and I don't want to keep our six o'clock ride waiting."

"Sure thing," he says.

Jim twists his head to look over his shoulder as he begins an arching turn. That's when I see it—behind Jim's right earlobe—a tiny gray tattoo like a bar code. I yank off my sunglasses to get a better look. It's identical to Ralston's. No question, he's IUGA.

My heart gongs inside my chest. I don't know what to do, but I'm pretty sure if I don't do something fast, Asher and I will never make it back to San Francisco alive.

Jim's head is still turned, exposing the back of his neck to me. I angle myself on the seat and grip the sides tightly before ramming my boot into the base of his skull. He immediately shuts down and falls forward. The chopper wobbles from side to side, and the nose dips precariously.

"What the—! What did you do?" Asher yelps.

"He's IUGA. Grab the stick."

"What? I don't know how to fly this thing. We're going to crash!"

Ash latches onto the co-pilot control between his legs, and pulls it toward him. I'm thrown backward and the tail of the chopper drops.

"Not that hard!" I shout. "We're going to flip." He moves the stick forward slightly, and the helicopter begins to level off, but the wobbling gets worse.

"Should I do something with the pedals?" he asks.

"I don't know. Just try to keep us horizontal."

He holds the control steady with both hands, and we seem to level out a bit. "Get on the poly to Narowyn. Tell her we need a chopper pilot. Stat!"

Asher focuses on keeping us parallel to the ground while I call Narowyn. "We need someone who can fly a helicopter. Now! Our pilot's down," I say.

"On it." She disconnects.

In less than fifteen seconds, Officer Kai from Urick's team lands in the seat next to mine and quickly assesses the situation. "Holy shit! Hold her steady, Ash." He turns to me. "Help me switch places with the pilot, but watch the throttle." He points to a control between the seats.

Together we hoist Jim's body through the gap and onto the floor. Kai hops into the pilot's seat, grabs the stick, and puts on Jim's headphones. "Okay, I got it, Ash. You can relax." He confidently takes over the controls, and I feel I can breathe again.

"Anybody want to tell me what happened?" Kai says, once we're flying smoothly.

"I identified the pilot as an IUGA automaton by the tattoo behind his earlobe," I explain. "So I took him out."

Kai glances back at me. "Did he threaten you?"

"No. I wasn't going to wait for that."

"How do you know he wasn't just on assignment working the disaster for IUGA?"

Truthfully, the thought hadn't crossed my mind. I get kind of a sinking feeling inside. "Is that a possibility? I just assumed he was here for me."

"IUGA's licensed on this earth. They usually have agents in place before a huge disaster occurs. He may have been part of that force."

"Well hell, what was I supposed to do? Ask him if he had any current plans to murder me?"

Ash calls Narowyn back to let her know we're okay. Afterward, we fly in silence for a time before Kai puts the chopper down in a deserted field about five miles from the tent city. Once we're on the ground, we search Jim's body and the interior of the chopper.

"No sign of a weapon," Kai says. "Not even a dog collar. Call your host and tell him where to find you. After he picks you up, I'll reboot this dude and see if I can wipe a few hours of his memory. He'll never know what happened."

"Thanks for coming to the rescue, Kai," I say.

He smiles. "No problem. It was kind of a boring afternoon, anyway."

Within ten minutes of Ash's call to Jack, we catch sight of the Range Rover crossing the field. I remain quiet on the drive back to the hacienda, wondering how badly I screwed up. If that chopper was really going to crash, Ash and I could have shifted out of harm's way, but it might have slammed into a residential area, injuring people on the ground. I feel like crap.

Back at Jack's house, we quickly change into our uniforms and stash our relief worker clothes in plastic bags. Jack promises to dispose of them for us.

"We can't thank you enough for hosting us," Asher tells him.

"My pleasure. Please give my love to Narowyn. Let her know we're all fine here."

"Will do," he says.

When we're alone, I say, "Sorry, Ash. Hope I didn't ruin the whole mission."

"Don't worry about it, Beckett. I probably would've done the same thing in your place. Narowyn wants to see us right away."

"Yeah, I figured she would."

"Guess I was right about one thing," Ash says with a smile. "It was a ride you'll never forget."

When we arrive in Narowyn's office, she stands to meet us. "Are you two all right?"

We both nod.

"Sit down and take me through what happened." We take seats at the conference table, and I recount all the details for her.

"I just went with my gut instinct," I say. "In hindsight, I realize that he didn't have a weapon and may not have known we're Transcenders, since Jack booked the trip. But I believed he was going to try to kill us. I'm sorry."

She drums her fingers on the table, her expression grim. "You did the right thing, Jaden. Your judgment was sound. That agent may have been innocently on the scene, but it seems too much of a coincidence to me. We'll have to be a bit more careful on future explorations, if we're aware that IUGA maintains a presence in the location."

I quietly blow out a relieved breath.

"I'm sure you're both tired," Narowyn says. "We'll have Captain Watterson do a little more digging into this matter. I'll let you know if he finds anything new, but for now, we'll put it behind us—no harm, no foul. I'll see you both in the morning for your exploration report."

FORTY-SIX

Morning comes too soon, after a restless night's sleep. I feel a little lightheaded as Asher and I sit in Narowyn's office to debrief her on our exploration. Thankfully, Ash takes the lead in summarizing the information contained in each file we collected. He also provides her with copies of the photos and video recordings we made.

"It was very bad, as you can see," he says, "but probably worse because of the two moons. The waves were far higher than predicted. Sadly, the tsunami hit when the moons were nearly full."

"That is unfortunate." She lays the photos to the side. What are your impressions, Jaden?"

"The possibility of a similar quake in Alaska and a resulting tsunami on other Confederation earths can't be ruled out," I say, struggling to sound sharp. "When we share this data with the government, one of our recommendations should be to beef up the early warning system and evacuation methods. Fewer casualties would have resulted in Twin Moons with a little extra time."

"Yes, excellent. This is very helpful," Narowyn says. "Good work you two. It's likely that lives will be saved because of your efforts. I shall read through these materials with interest."

"Jack sends his love and wanted us to tell you everyone there is all right," Asher says.

She tips her head and smiles. "Thank you for passing that along." She turns to me. "Congratulations on your successful first mission, Jaden.

"I hope you'll see fit to send me on another one, in spite of what happened."

"Of course. This was only the beginning of many exciting projects to come. By the way, do you still have those glasses Ralston gave you in Domerica?"

"Yes. Why?"

"Take them to Dr. McDonald and ask if she can make some duplicates for you—sunglasses too. You should carry them with you on exploration so you'll have a way of identifying IUGA agents before you enter confined spaces with them."

"I will. Thanks."

* * *

Life settles down fairly quickly after returning from Twin Moons. No new information surfaces up about the automaton pilot. It appears most likely that he was there doing legitimate IUGA business, but an attempt on my life can't be entirely ruled out.

My studies in Alternate Earths and the Science of Transcending continue, and I add a class on Quantum Electrodynamics, taught by Luci. Our extracurricular work continues also.

Luci patiently coaches me on moving objects around the room gently instead of smashing them to smithereens. I still suck at it, but we have a mini-breakthrough when I'm able to slowly raise a book from her shelf. It hovers in the air for a moment before crashing to the floor. She says we're finally getting somewhere.

As the holiday season approaches, the household staff becomes busy as elves. They festoon the common areas with pine boughs, holly, colorful streamers, and ornaments. Hanukkah menorahs and decorated Christmas trees appear on tabletops and tucked into every nook and corner. The trees outside the Chateau are strung with twinkling lights. All explorations are suspended until after the New Year, and the atmosphere at the Chateau is joyful and festive.

Eve and I do a little holiday shopping together. She knows her way around the malls, or gallerias, as they are called here, and she's amusing company. But I'm always a little on edge about possibly bumping into Ryder when I'm out and about in Arumel.

It's a confusing kind of hope/fear. If I'm honest with myself, part of me would like to see him again. I'm curious about what he's like on this earth. But his suggestion that we form a friendship messes with my mind. Is that what he really wants? Would I be disappointed if it was? Is it only the *perpetual contract* that causes me to think about him more often than I'd like to? All I know for sure is that a flash of raven black hair or a familiar laugh in a crowd, sets my heart racing with a sort of eager dread that I might run into him.

Narowyn tells me to take as much time as I want to be with my family over the holidays, as long as I promise to be home at least a day before the hearing. She doesn't mention sending a protection detail with me, although I wonder if she's secretly assigned Urick or one of the others to watch my back while I'm away. I plan to take a pair of the special glasses Luci made for me, just to be on the safe side.

On the day before my trip home, Narowyn and I meet with Ted and Corinne to prepare for the January fifth hearing.

"Shall I order coffee and tea while we're working?" Narowyn asks.

"Certainly, if you like," Ted says. "This will probably take us a couple of hours. I'll take coffee, black."

Narowyn orders our drinks while the rest of us gather at her conference table.

"As we expected," Ted says, "when IUGA learned about the presence of Ralston's memory data in Arumel, they amended their counterclaim to allege that you have their stolen property in your possession and they want it back." He extracts some papers from a brown file and slides them across the table to me.

"That first document is the amendment to the counterclaim, the second is our response, and the sheet on the bottom is a list of the Justices we've drawn and their earth of origin."

I skip over the amended counterclaim and the answer and go straight to the list of justices. None of the names look familiar.

"We've done a bit of research, and we're fairly happy with the panel," Ted says.

"We drew three women and two men," Corinne adds. "We view that as favorable. Women tend to be a little more sympathetic to individuals rather than large organizations. And, though most justices on the court tend not to flaunt their political leanings, we do know that Justice Akbar has come out quite strongly in favor of volitionist issues in her past opinions."

"That's good, right?" I say.

"It's excellent," Ted says. "She frowns on the use of guided destiny, which is IUGA's whole reason for being."

"The senior presiding justice, Rosemary Goodspeed, also seems to have more liberal leanings," Corinne says.

"Oh, I've met her a few times," Narowyn says. "She spoke at one of the commission meetings last year. I rather like her."

"Good," Ted says. "We know relatively little about the other three panel members. Justice Cheung has a bit of a hard-liner reputation, Justice O'Brien's opinions rely heavily on the unique facts of each case, and Justice Juma is a relative newcomer to the bench, so he hasn't written much to date."

The drinks arrive, and Ted relaxes in his chair and enjoys a few sips of coffee before continuing. "Jaden, the IGC Court is a court of chancery, which essentially means they're not bound by the laws of any specific nation or earth in the Confederation. Their sole job is to find a fair and equitable solution for disputes between entities and individuals who operate inter-galactically."

"So they just listen to both sides, and try to make a fair decision?" I ask.

"That's basically it. We brief all the issues and provide the research, but they can do whatever they deem just, and there is no appeal. Their decision is final."

"Okay. What do I need to do?"

"We'll call you as our first witness," Ted says. "You'll be given an instruction regarding telling the truth. This court is equipped with sophisticated iris scanning equipment. Any deviation from the truth is picked up by the cameras and automatically noted on the transcript of your testimony. The justices are provided a report at the conclusion of the hearing highlighting any instances of detected deception."

"You're kidding?" The whole concept makes me uncomfortable. "I mean, can these cameras really do that? What if I blink funny or get something in my eye. Could the cameras mistake that for lying?"

Ted chuckles softly. "No. They've been in use for years in the IGC Court. They have a proven track record. This is state of the art equipment, Jade. You have nothing to worry about."

"I'll have to take your word for it," I say. "So, what happens then?"

"Well, after you've taken the stand, I'll ask you a series of questions. Address all your answers to the Justices, not to me or opposing counsel. Make eye contact with them, Jade. It's very important. After my examination, the other side will be allowed to pose questions. They'll try to trip you up, but just take your time before answering. Wait a beat or two before giving your response. After IUGA's counsel is finished cross-examining you, the justices may ask a few questions. Again, just take your time before answering."

"Okay, wait a beat before answering. Got it. But can you give me some examples of the kinds of things they might ask?"

"Yes. We'll go over all of it. The court has ruled that no direct evidence links the automaton attack on you in Connecticut to IUGA, so they've excluded any testimony about that. Be careful not to refer to it at all."

"It's a lot to remember." I guzzle my tea nervously.

"The most important part of your testimony will be when you relate the events that took place on the day of the attack at Warrington Palace," Ted says. "We'll run through your testimony several times until you feel comfortable with all your answers."

I stare at the bottom of my empty cup. "I think I'm going to need more tea."

Our meeting goes on into the evening, and even though we cover everything more than once, I'm anxious about the upcoming proceedings. More than ever I appreciate what's at stake here—my future safety and possibly Ralston's freedom. What really makes the acid swirl in my belly, though, is the thought that IUGA might come out of this without so much as a slap on the hand. Never having to answer for the devastation it caused in Domerica or for Ryder's death.

The next morning, I drop off Callie at Ralston's, distribute a few gifts to friends, and close up my apartment, before shifting to Oxford for the day to pick up souvenirs for everyone at home.

My insides quiver pleasantly as I board the flight from Heathrow Airport in London to JFK. When the jet touches down in New York, a warm feeling of home floods through me.

Dad and Lisa announce their engagement on Christmas Eve. I couldn't be happier for them. They make a good couple, and for the first time since mom died, Dad reminds me of the happy-go-lucky guy who raised me.

I spend some time with Liv, but our interactions are brief and somewhat awkward. Our lives have taken such different directions, and I don't feel good about making up Oxford stories to tell her. On my last night in Madison, I agree to meet her and a few friends from high school at Marou, a local dance club. I wear a pretty red dress I bought in Arumel, and I'm excited to see some of the old gang.

The music is loud and the place is packed, as I step inside the front door. I scan the crowd searching for Liv, but my eyes are drawn to a group in the corner and one very tall, handsome man with hair the color of a raven's feather. My heart skitters in my chest.

"Jade!" Someone on the other side of the room calls my name, but I turn and bolt out the door. Sprinting to my car, I can barely find my breath. I start the engine and pull away quickly. It was him. I know it was him. I'd forgotten he was due home from Zambia by Christmastime. *Damn!* Why did I have to go out tonight? Why did I have to see him?

My phone rings, and I turn it to silent mode. I pull onto the freeway and drive. I need to think. Part of me wants to go back and speak with him. I searched for him for so long. But I know that would just be inviting heartache. This isn't my world anymore. The sight of him stirred up all kinds of crazy emotions and I don't know what to make of them.

It's late and I'm nearly out of gas by the time I reach home. Dad's asleep and Drew's out with friends. I text Liv that something came up. She's pissed, but she'll get over it. I'm still shaken and confused, but I'll be home back in Arumel tomorrow, and I won't have to think about it anymore.

In the morning, Dad drives Drew and me to the airport. We both promise to return in June for the wedding. We wave goodbye to Dad, and Drew walks me to the international security checkpoint. As soon as we part, I sneak into the ladies room, lock myself in a stall, and immediately shift back to the Chateau.

Even though I mostly enjoyed my trip home, I'm thrilled to be back in my comfy little apartment with Callie curled up next to me. There's a peaceful kind of contentment in having my own space, being my own person, and charting my own path.

Before turning in for the night, I gather my electronic notebook and my files for the hearing in the morning and place them on the table in the hall. Then I skim through the small stack of mail that accumulated while I was away. An envelope addressed in a familiar hand catches my eye. I slide open the flap and draw out a red foil holiday card with a white dove embossed on the front. Inside is a simple inscription: *May your holidays be filled with peace and joy. Warmly, Ryder Blackthorn.*

I shake my head and smile. It's only a card and it doesn't say much, but the knowledge that he thought about me over the holidays kindles a small fire in my belly.

FORTY-SEVEN

The IGC Courtroom is located downtown in the same building as the Arumel Supreme Court. The awe inspiring structure is a tribute to ancient Greek architecture. The gleaming marble edifice features enormous columns and about a million steps leading up to three sets of ornately carved brass doors. My breath catches as Narowyn and I begin the somber ascent.

Ted and Corinne wait for us at the top of the stairs. They've brought a box-toting assistant along with them. Asher, Captain Watterson, Urick, and Ralston are also waiting to accompany us inside for the day's proceedings.

The courtroom itself is majestic and intimidating. Dark-green marble walls, soaring coffered ceilings, and massive gilded chandeliers create an atmosphere of pomp and gravity. The air is electric with pent-up tension. An acute sense of significance presses down on my shoulders. Much of my future depends on the outcome of this hearing.

Our footfalls are muted by the plush carpeting as we march down the center aisle. Dark pews of polished wood line both sides of the spectator area. Observers have already begun to filter in and take seats. They gawk at us and whisper to each other as we make our way to the front. Large galleries run along the upper walls. The section reserved for the media bustles with cameramen and reporters.

Spectators file steadily into the other sections.

Ted opens a short wooden gate leading to the gleaming counsel tables and motions us inside. The Justices' massive mahogany bench looms large on a raised dais before us. Tall columns, mirroring those outside the building, stand sentry behind the bench. Floor-length, golden velvet curtains cover the spaces in between. Computer monitors, name plaques, and water glasses are positioned on the bench in front of each of the five high-backed judges' chairs.

Opposing counsel table on the right is already alive with activity. An army of robed lawyers is engaged in filling water glasses, organizing files, reviewing notes, and conferring among themselves. Director Canto sits placidly at the table, his hands folded in front of him. A cadre of corporate types takes up a full row of chairs behind the lawyers. Canto's lackeys, no doubt.

Our small entourage follows behind Ted to the long counsel table on the left. Narowyn and I seat ourselves in thickly upholstered chairs between Ted and Corinne. The others take seats arranged along the rail behind our table. Ted's assistant removes two stacks of files from his box. He positions a stack in front of Ted and one in front of Corinne, then he nods at Ted and departs without a word.

"Seems like we're a little outnumbered," I whisper to Corinne.

"IUGA must be hoping a show of strength will make up for a loser case," she says.

I hope her robust confidence is justified. I place my electronic notebook on the table in front of me and take out the paper Ted gave me identifying each justice and their home earth. Behind me the hum of nervous anticipation grows louder.

A wooden door opens to the left of the Justices' bench, and a dignified looking white-haired gentleman in black robes enters the courtroom. He places a file on a desk below the bench and clips a tiny microphone to his robe.

He walks to the front of the courtroom, and the crowd falls silent. In a booming baritone, he declares, "Oyez, oyez. The Inter-

Galactic Confederation Chancery Court is now in session, the honorable Justices Akbar, Juma, Cheung, Obrien, and Chief Justice Goodspeed presiding."

The golden draperies behind the bench open automatically. Every soul in the courtroom rises, and the five justices step forward to claim their respective seats.

They each take a moment to get situated—activating computer screens, clipping on microphones, arranging papers and tablets. None of them appears younger than fifty. All of them look distinguished in their somber black robes.

Justice Goodspeed, positioned in the center of the bench, flips a switch to activate the microphones and taps her gavel once. "Please be seated," she says crisply.

According to Ted, she's the presiding justice for this matter. A senior judge from Sillouhy on an OE ominously nicknamed Darkland. She wears her steel gray hair in an attractive French twist. A jeweled dragonfly brooch is pinned at the neck of her robes.

"This morning we have before us the case of Jaden Beckett and the Transcender Society versus the Inter-Universal Guidance Agency, and the accompanying counterclaim. Are all parties present?"

Ted, Corinne, and the bevy of IUGA lawyers get to their feet.

"Yes, Madame Justice," Ted says. "Theodore King and Corinne Barker for Miss Beckett and the Transcender Society."

"May it please the court," IUGA's lead attorney says. He's a portly man with thinning brown hair and a striped ascot tucked into the neck of his gray robes. "C. Bertram Cathcart and Associates on behalf of Director Canto and the Inter-Universal Guidance Agency."

"Excuse me, Mr. Cathcart, but is Director Canto a party to this lawsuit?" Justice Goodspeed says.

"No Madame Justice, he is with us today as a representative of the IUGA." He sweeps his hand toward the director who nods and smiles modestly.

"Thank you for clarifying that," she says. "We have only two days to conduct this hearing, let us be precise in representing the facts, shall we?"

"Yes, Madame Justice," Cathcart says.

"That applies to both parties." She looks directly at Ted.

"Yes, Madame Justice," he says.

"This matter has been fully briefed by both sides," Justice Goodspeed says. "We have been provided with a list of stipulated facts on which the parties agree, as well as a list of exhibits for both parties."

She consults the notes on her screen. "Essentially this suit centers around a thirty-day time period in which Miss Beckett was returned by IUGA to the country of Domerica on Earth H87D. Her return was precipitated by a previous order of this court finding that IUGA had overstepped its authority by forcing Miss Beckett to abandon that country against her will. You will confine your arguments and testimony to that thirty-day time period, understood?"

"Yes, Madame Justice," Ted and Cathcart say in unison.

"Each side shall have one day within which to present its case. You shall both be allowed five minutes for opening statements, and ten minutes for summation. Time limits will be strictly enforced. Mr. King, as the claimant's attorney, you will proceed first."

Ted stands and walks to a podium in front of the Justices' bench. He straightens his robes and squares his shoulders. "Honorable Justices, the claimant's case is simple. Miss Beckett, a first time Transcender and unsuspecting teenager, was duped by the powerful IUGA into returning to a situation where her death was all but a certainty.

"IUGA took these actions knowingly and with malice aforethought after it gained the knowledge that if Miss Beckett were ever allowed to join the Transcender Society, she would put into motion a sequence of occurrences which would inevitably lead to the complete downfall of the agency.

413

"The evidence and testimony will show that not only did IUGA mislead Miss Beckett into returning to Domerica, it also infiltrated a criminal enterprise which was plotting her assassination. The agency provided advice and assistance to this enterprise in formulating a precise plan, based upon IUGA's advanced prediction technology, which had the highest probability of resulting in Miss Beckett's death. In addition, IUGA unlawfully supplied automatons to participate in the attack on Miss Beckett and the Domerican royal family. At least one of these automatons caused human death in the process of attempting to murder Miss Beckett.

"All of this was done out of greed and self-interest in order to ensure that Miss Beckett's true destiny with the Transcenders would never be fulfilled. Thank you." He makes a small bow to the justices and returns to his seat at the counsel table.

C. Bertram Cathcart rises majestically in his robes and ascot and takes his place at the podium.

"May it please the court," he says. "The claimant's case is pure fantasy." He spreads his arms grandly, and affects an indulgent smile. "When given the opportunity, Miss Beckett jumped at the chance to return to Domerica. No trickery was involved. She had left a young man there with whom she had a *perpetual contract*, and she could not wait to see him again. More importantly, Ms. Beckett was a princess in Domerica and first in line to become its queen. Every young girl's dream.

"While it is true that once Miss Beckett made her decision to return to Earth H87D, the probability of her assassination increased, IUGA had nothing whatsoever to do with that. The independent plot to eliminate her was based solely upon political and economic factors of Dome Noir, an enemy nation. It had nothing to do with IUGA's desires. Once the agency became aware of Miss Beckett's revised destiny, it did what it does in every case of such significance—a case involving the head of a country—it oversaw and facilitated the fulfillment of that destiny. IUGA's sworn duty.

"If there is a culprit in all of this, if there is a greedy party or an obstructer of destiny, it is Miss Beckett, herself." He turns and points to me. "She altered the program of a very valuable IUGA automaton, causing him to disobey IUGA orders and turning him into a spy. The information she received—"

"One minute remaining, Mr. Cathcart," Justice Goodspeed says.

Cathcart nods and continues, "… the information was then used to hamper what had already been preordained for her. In so doing, she altered not only her own destiny, but she also unlawfully altered the destiny of the entire Earth H87D." He walks to the front of the podium and smoothes his robes. "In closing, I will add that Miss Beckett freely signed a binding contract to remain in Domerica When the tampered-with automaton improperly reported the assassination plot to her, she fled that earth, thereby breaching her contract with IUGA and cheating destiny in the process. We beg the court—"

"Thank you Mr. Cathcart, time is up," Justice Goodspeed says.

Cathcart's face flushes. He obviously didn't get to deliver his scintillating closing line.

"Mr. King, please call your first witness."

Ted gets to his feet. "I call Jaden Beckett to the stand."

My stomach clenches and my mouth suddenly blooms with cotton as I roll my chair away from the table. Ted directs me to the witness box at the right of the Justices' bench. I take a seat inside the box and clasp my hands together in my lap to control the tremors running through them.

Justice Goodspeed addresses me. "Ms. Beckett, it is my duty to inform you that special iris scanning cameras are present in the courtroom today to monitor the truth of your answers. Any deviation from the truth detected by this equipment will be noted in the transcript of your testimony and highlighted for the Justices. Do you understand?"

"Yes, Madame Justice."

"Thank you. You may proceed, Mr. King."

Ted smiles at me reassuringly. "Please state your full name for the record."

"Jaden Victoria Hanover Beckett," I say, my tongue sticking to the roof of my mouth.

"Bailiff, bring Ms. Beckett some water, please," Justice Goodspeed says.

A uniformed woman promptly delivers a glass of water to the witness box, and I take a sip. "Thank you Madame Justice," I say.

Ted continues with a few softball questions designed to put me at ease—what is your address, how old are you—that type of thing. I find myself more relaxed by the time he moves on to the meatier issues.

"Miss Beckett, did Agent Ralston of the Inter-Universal Guidance Agency visit you at your home in Madison, Connecticut in May of last year?"

"Yes."

"Were you expecting a visit from him?"

"No, it was a complete surprise."

"What did Agent Ralston say to you at the time?"

"He said that the powers that be had decided I could return to Domerica for thirty days with no impact on my life in Connecticut." I make eye contact with the Justices, as Ted instructed. "After the thirty days, I would have the opportunity to choose where I wanted to live out my destiny—in Domerica, back in Connecticut, or with the Transcenders in Arumel."

"Did you accept this deal?"

"Yes."

"Did he pressure you in any way to accept?"

"No. He did say my mother's *mirror* in Domerica was ill, but that wasn't why I accepted. I wanted to go back to Domerica for reasons of my own."

"Did Agent Ralston inform you that if you accepted this deal, the probability existed that you would be assassinated?"

Mr. Cathcart bounds to his feet. "Objection, Madame Justice." He rests his hand on his generous midsection. "That question assumes the probability of her assassination existed at that time. A fact which is not correct and not in evidence. In addition, this entire line of questioning relies completely on hearsay. This is merely Miss Beckett's version of the conversation."

"May I respond to that?" Ted asks.

"Make it brief, Mr. King," Justice Goodspeed says.

"Mr. Cathcart is entitled to cross examine Miss Beckett and present any witness he chooses to refute her testimony. In fact, former Agent Ralston is here in the courtroom and available to testify as to the conversation."

Cathcart coughs loudly. "That's absurd, he's an automaton."

"He was IUGA's representative and a first-hand witness to all of IUGA's shenanigans," Ted says hotly.

"Enough, gentlemen," Justice Goodspeed says. "I will not have petty bickering in my courtroom. Mr. Cathcart, your objection is overruled. May I remind both of you that this court is not bound by the laws or rules of evidence of any specific nation. We are a court of equity. As such we have wide latitude to explore the facts as thoroughly as we deem necessary and base our decision upon what is fair and just in our sole discretion."

"Yes, Madame Justice," the men say.

"Let's keep our objections to a minimum, gentlemen," Goodspeed says. "Mr. King you may proceed."

Ted turns to me once again. "I'll rephrase the question. Miss Beckett, when, if ever, did Agent Ralston inform you that a high probability existed that you would be assassinated if you remained in

Domerica?"

"About a week before my scheduled wedding," I say.

This seems to interest the Justices. Akbar and Juma exchange a glance, and Justice O'Brien leans forward in her seat, reaching for her stylus.

"Please explain to the court how this conversation between you and Agent Ralston came about," Ted says.

"Ralston had just returned from a visit to IUGA headquarters to finalize my contract details. Even though I still had several days to decide, I told Ralston I'd already made up my mind and wanted to sign the contract as soon as possible."

"And what option had you elected to take?"

"At that time, I had intended to stay in Domerica."

Ted steps around the podium and rests an elbow on top. "Miss Beckett, please tell the court what happened when you and Agent Ralston met to sign the contract?"

"I was about to sign my name on the final page, when Agent Ralston snatched it away from me."

"I see. And what did he say to you after pulling the contract away?"

Out of the corner of my eye I see Cathcart squirming in his seat as if he wants to object, but he remains silent.

"He said that if I signed the contract I would die on my wedding day." A flurry of gasps and surprised exclamations rumble through the spectator sections.

"Order!" Justice Goodspeed cracks her gavel. "Anyone unable to maintain appropriate courtroom decorum will be removed by the bailiff."

Ted continues, "What occurred after Agent Ralston made this revelation?"

I describe for the Justices how Ralston informed me of the plot by the Noirs to kill me and the royal family members. I also go over what he said about IUGA's involvement in the scheme.

"And did he say why IUGA wished to facilitate your assassination?"

Cathcart hoists himself up. "Madame Justice, again I must object. This calls for the disclosure of confidential proprietary information of IUGA, information that this woman had no right to know, and would not have known had it not been for her unlawful corruption of the automaton's program. Disclosure of this information would be extremely detrimental to IUGA's business interests."

"Madame Justice," Ted says. "This is the very basis of our case. IUGA cannot keep this information from being disclosed simply by declaring it confidential. I'm not asking for business secrets. IUGA holds itself out as a public service agency. The manner in which it conducts itself with the public should be transparent. The case law supports this view."

"Give us a moment," Justice Goodspeed says. She turns off the microphones and the Justices turn away from the bench and move their chairs together for a quiet conference. After a minute or two, they turn back to the bench and Justice Goodspeed reactivates the microphones.

"Mr. Cathcart," she says. "My fellow justices and I agree that the information you wish to keep out of the record cannot be deemed confidential and proprietary in this instance. Mr. King is not seeking confidential information on how the business is run, he is laying out the claimant's theory for why IUGA took the actions that it did. A long line of cases exist which hold that the information gleaned from IUGA's prediction models is discoverable in court if it pertains to allegations of IUGA misconduct. Objection overruled. The witness may answer."

A deflated looking Cathcart reseats himself. Ted repeats the question more forcefully. "Miss Beckett, did Agent Ralston say why IUGA wanted you dead?"

419

"Yes. He said that IUGA's prediction models showed a ninety-six percent probability that if I chose any option other than to remain in Domerica, I would be responsible for setting off a chain of events that would lead to the eventual demise of IUGA."

Quiet murmurs ripple throughout the spectator section.

"Thank you," he says.

"I believe this is a good time for a ten minute break," Justice Goodspeed says with a crack of her gavel. Everyone in the courtroom scrambles to their feet as the justices remove their microphones and exit through the golden curtains.

"You're doing great," Ted whispers helping me from the box.

FORTY-EIGHT

After the break, Ted asks me to detail for the justices the elements of the plan Ralston and I put together to thwart the Noirs' attack. I go over each component of our strategy, making sure not to leave out any important facts. Two justices take furious notes during my testimony, while the others sit in rapt attention.

Once I've finished, Ted checks his notebook. Thank you Miss Beckett. Now, I understand that because the attack was intended to take place on your scheduled wedding day, you and Chief Blackthorn were married in a secret ceremony prior to that day. Is that correct?"

"Yes, that's true."

"But you also continued with the original wedding plans as if the ceremony would take place as scheduled?"

"Yes, Ralston told me that it was crucial for IUGA to believe everything was going according to plan so that they wouldn't act before we had all our ducks in a row."

"I see. Then will you describe for the Justices what took place when your scheduled wedding day arrived?"

I take a sip of water and a deep breath. Facing the justices head-on, I begin my recounting of the events of that fateful day. When I get to the details surrounding Patrick's death, I have difficulty keeping my voice even. And, as I describe the horrible sights I witnessed during the battle, silent tears begin to roll down my cheeks. My voice begins to quaver when I relate the events that took place in the tower room after the Noirs broke inside.

"Urick, uh, Lieutenant Hunter, was there," I say. "He pointed a gun at me, as we planned, and he signaled me with his eyes that it was time to go out onto the walkway and shift to Arumel."

"Did you do that?" Ted asks.

"I … I put one foot out onto the walkway, but then I saw my husband and some of his warriors burst into the room. I turned to come back inside, but the walkway fell apart under my feet."

"I know this is painful Miss Beckett, but please tell the court what happened next."

Words mix with tears in my throat and my voice comes out strangled. "I shifted to Arumel like we planned, but not before I saw my husband reach out to save me and fall from the tower behind me."

Ted pauses for a moment. "What did you do when you arrived in Arumel?"

"I shifted right back to Domerica, but it was too late. My composure cracks completely at the memory. "He was dead." I sob into my hands, aware that the world is watching as I fall apart.

"Does the witness wish a moment?" Justice Goodspeed asks gently.

Ted passes me a tissue box and raises his eyebrows.

"No, I'm okay," I say, plucking a few tissues. The courtroom is hushed except for the sounds of quiet snuffling from the spectators.

"Did you go back to Arumel at that point?" Ted asks.

"Yes, Narowyn Du Lac came and took me back." I dab at my eyes with the tissue.

"And did Agent Ralston join you there as planned?"

"No. IUGA had gotten to him first. We found what was left of him several days later lying on a garbage heap outside an IUGA parts facility on another earth."

Cathcart clutches the arms of his chair and makes to rise, but Goodspeed stops him with her raised hand. "Keep your seat, Mr. Cathcart. You'll have your opportunity."

"What happened to the now former agent Ralston once you rescued him?"

"He was too damaged to be repaired, so the Transcenders purchased a new automaton shell for him. The information from his mass storage, his memory module, his eyes, and his voice box were transplanted into the newer model."

"Please tell the Justices, to your knowledge, other than the transplanting of the items you just mentioned, did you or anyone else under the Transcenders' direction ever tamper with or alter the software or hardware of Mr. Ralston in any way?"

"No, never."

"Only a few more questions, Miss Beckett. Did you ever sign the contract provided to Mr. Ralston by IUGA?"

"Yes. I signed it three days before the attack."

"And in that signed contract, which option did you elect?"

"I elected to join the Transcenders in Arumel."

Several Justices make a note of this.

"And have you been back to Domerica since your return to Arumel?"

"No."

"Why not?"

"Because that would've been a breach of the contract with IUGA."

"Thank you very much, Miss Beckett. No further questions," Ted says.

"Cross examination, Mr. Cathcart?" Justice Goodspeed says.

Cathcart clears his throat and holds himself erect. He carries a thick book with him to the podium. "A few questions if it please the court. Now, Miss Beckett, you freely admit that you returned to Domerica of your own volition, is that correct?"

"Yes."

"Good. And after your return, you eventually ascended to the throne and became Queen of Domerica. Is that true?" He clasps his hands behind his back and leans toward me.

"Yes."

"And you began to plan your wedding to Chief Blackthorn?"

"Actually it was being planned prior to Queen Eleanor's death," I say.

"I see. Thank you for correcting me. So is it fair to say you were very happy being back in Domerica and soon to be wed?"

"Yes, until I found out I was going to be killed on my wedding day."

"Precisely." He pokes the air with his index finger. "And you gained this knowledge by rewriting certain areas in the software programs of Agent Ralston so that he would report such things to you. Correct?"

"No, that is not correct."

Cathcart holds up the book he brought to the podium. "Madame Justice, this is IUGA's Exhibit 1. I would note for the court that I have marked the pages relevant to my next question."

"Very well," Goodspeed says. The Justices each locate their copy of Exhibit 1. Cathcart carries the book to the witness stand and places it in front of me. "Have you ever seen this manual before, Miss Beckett?"

I examine the cover. "No."

"Please read the title for the court," Cathcart says.

"Inter-Universal Guidance Agency Automaton Specification Manual," I read it aloud.

"Now please turn to page ten of that manual and read for the court the highlighted paragraph."

I turn to page ten and locate a paragraph highlighted in yellow. "It says, *All automatons employed by IUGA are specially programmed to protect confidential information of the agency. A custom designed, multi-level system of safeguards is utilized to prevent IUGA automatons from disclosing: (1) the identity of any subject or subjects under observation by the agency; (2) any and all prediction methods utilized by the agency; and (3) any probability distributions or other information gleaned from the agency's destiny prediction models, to any parties other than their IUGA supervisors.*"

"Thank you," Cathcart says. "Tell me then, Miss Beckett, how do you explain the fact that an automaton, which is precision programmed to follow only the orders of its owners, and never to disclose confidential prediction model information to anyone outside the agency, confided such information to you?"

"He told me he altered his program himself to allow him to make such decisions on his own."

Cathcart's mouth twitches unpleasantly. "Really? This automaton altered his own program? And exactly, how did he go about doing that?"

"I really don't know. You'll have to ask him. But he said it's a widely held secret in the IUGA automaton community that they can rewrite their programs to allow them to exercise free will. It's really not surprising considering they're smarter than the average supercomputer." I pat the thick book in front of me. "It probably says that in here."

Cathcart bristles at my answer. "Madame Justice, I move that the witness's answer be stricken from the record as unresponsive."

A small laugh issues from Goodspeed's pink bow-shaped mouth. "Mr. Cathcart, you asked the question. There is no jury present. We all heard this witness's answer. If you wish to call the automaton to refute this, we will consider such a request."

"Thank you Madame Justice," he says, although his brow remains creased.

"Now, Miss Beckett, once you learned of your predicted destiny, you and the automaton Ralston took drastic steps in order to make certain that your fate did not unfold the way it was described to you. Correct?"

"Well yeah. I wasn't going to just let a bunch of lowlife mercenaries storm in on my wedding day and kill me and my family without doing something about it."

Titters go up from the spectator area.

"Madame Justice." Cathcart blusters. "Please instruct Miss Beckett to confine her answers to the question asked."

"Miss Beckett," Goodspeed says, "I know it is tempting to elaborate, but please listen to the question asked and answer only that question."

"Yes, Madame Justice," I say.

Cathcart grips both sides of the podium. "Miss Beckett. What gives you and the Transcenders the right to complain to this court about IUGA's actions, which were only intended to facilitate the unfolding of destiny as it was predicted, when you have taken even more radical action to prevent destiny from taking its appropriate course?"

I look at Justice Goodspeed. "Madame Justice that's a complex question, am I allowed to answer it fully?"

"Of course, Miss Beckett. It does seem to go to the heart of your case."

"Mr. Cathcart," I say, "I took what you describe as 'radical action' because I don't believe IUGA has the authority to choose my *true destiny*. Those QPs, or whatever you call them, are nothing more than sophisticated fortune telling machines. I believe my true destiny was to form a friendship with Agent Ralston so that he would make a choice to do what was right rather than what he was ordered to do."

"Thank you, Miss Beckett," Cathcart says cutting me off.

"Wait, I'm not finished. You asked what gives us the right to complain about IUGA's actions." I look to Goodspeed and she nods for me to continue.

"IUGA's job is supposed to be 'guidance.' In this case, IUGA used its vast resources to try to force a particular destiny on me and the country of Domerica for its own purposes. Assisting in murder should never be within a public service entity's jurisdiction, in my opinion. That's just playing God, Mr. Cathcart."

Applause breaks out from the spectators' section and the gallery.

Justice Goodspeed takes her time in banging her gavel. "Quiet people," she says. "Well then, Mr. Cathcart, any further questions for this witness?"

He clears his throat. "Only a few regarding the contract, Madame Justice."

"Proceed," she says. "We'll break for lunch afterward."

Cathcart steps to the counsel table and removes a document from a file. "This is IUGA's Exhibit 2," he says to the court. "May I approach the witness?"

"You may." Goodspeed says.

"Now Miss Beckett, do you recognize this document?"

"It looks like the contract IUGA prepared for me."

He flips to the last page. "And do you recognize the signature on the final page?"

I squint at the page. "No."

"No? Please look at it again. Is that not your signature electing to stay on in Domerica?"

"No it is not," I say, holding the document in my hand.

"Well, whose signature is it?"

"I really don't know, Mr. Cathcart."

"Is this not the document you gave to Agent Ralston to file with IUGA's legal department?"

"I've never seen that signature before in my life." I make certain to phase my answer so that it's one hundred percent true.

"Mr. Cathcart, we had a question about that also," Justice Goodspeed says. "The document you filed as Exhibit 2 does not match the document provided to us by the Arumel City Office of Records."

"That's impossible," Cathcart splutters.

"I have it right here," Goodspeed says. "Mr. Clerk, please give this to Mr. Cathcart."

The gray-haired clerk hands the document to Cathcart, who takes it and turns to the last page as he walks to counsel table. He lays the document on the table for the others to see. The attorneys and Director Canto have a hushed conversation before Cathcart returns to the podium.

"Madame Justice, I'm not certain why we have a discrepancy here. We will research it further and provide our answer in a supplemental brief."

"That will be fine," Goodspeed says. "Are we ready for lunch?"

"Yes, I have no more questions for this witness."

* * *

We walk to a fancy looking restaurant across from the courthouse for lunch. Ted has reserved a private room for us so we can discuss the case without being overheard. The hostess shows us to our table and passes out menus as we take our seats. I find an empty chair between Ralston and Urick. The conversation remains light until our entrees have been served and the door is closed.

"Teddy, how do you think it's going?" Narowyn asks.

"It's going well, but we'll see what the afternoon brings," he says. "We've scored a few points, and Cathcart has made a couple of missteps. That contract thing was just sloppiness. His team should have caught that before they came to court. It's like any good laserball game, though, they'll likely regroup this evening and come out strong for the second half."

"What happens when we go back in this afternoon?" I ask, pushing food around my plate with my fork. "Am I finished testifying?"

"The Justices may have a question or two for you, but then you're finished. I'm going to try to put Ralston on next. Cathcart will raise a big fuss about automatons not being allowed to testify in legal proceedings. But it's not unheard of, and these Justices may allow it."

Ralston nods solemnly. He hasn't eaten a bite of his cheese soufflé, causing me to wonder if automatons can get a nervous stomach even if they don't have stomachs.

We return to the courtroom and get ourselves situated at counsel table once again. The spectator crowd has swollen since this morning. People overflow into the aisles, propping up against the walls or sitting on the stairs.

The clerk steps to the front of the room. "All rise," he says. The draperies part, and the Justices appear once again and take their seats.

Justice Goodspeed clips on her microphone. "Miss Beckett," she says, "would you please return to the witness stand? The Justices have a few questions for you."

I move to the witness box and resume my seat.

Justice Goodspeed nods to Justice Juma on her left. He's a large man, with graying, curly, black hair. If I remember Ted's cheat sheet correctly, he's from Kenya on an earth I'd never heard of.

"Miss Beckett," Justice Juma says in a deep baritone, "the automaton that attacked you at the palace, was he positively identified as an IUGA automaton?"

"Yes, Mr. Justice." I glance at Ted and he nods. "I identified him using special glasses Ralston lent to me. I was able to get a photo and an ID number. It should be in our filings."

"And did you personally see this automaton kill someone?" Juma asks.

"As I previously testified, my guard, Patrick, ran onto the balcony to disarm the automaton. What I actually saw was Patrick being blown backward by the force of a rifle shot. Then I heard another shot, and I assumed the automaton had killed the guard with him on the balcony. After that, I saw him emerge from the balcony aiming a rifle. He threatened the guards in my room. Later I saw him shoot at me, but he missed."

"How did you finally escape from him?" the Justice asks.

"Several of my guards and I attacked him. He was thrown against the wall by something or someone and landed face-down on the floor. I grabbed his rifle and used the butt to disable the nerve center at the base of his neck."

"I see. Thank you," Juma says.

Justice O'Brien, a thin woman with a dishwater blonde bun speaks up. "Miss Beckett, were there any other behaviors of Mr. Ralston that indicated he was operating outside the authority of IUGA?"

"Yes, a few. He disclosed other information to me that, according to that manual, he shouldn't have. Oh, and he secretly took a necklace from IUGA's vault. The necklace belonged to me, and he

430

knew it had sentimental value. He did it as a favor."

"Did you ask him to?" she asks.

"No, Madame Justice. He did it on his own."

She nods, and Justice Cheung from Hong Kong asks the next question. "Miss Beckett, I am troubled by what you call your rescue of the automaton Ralston. This appears to me to be a theft of property and information. On what basis do the Transcenders claim that ownership of the automaton, or his memory data, has passed to them?"

The question throws me a little, and I gulp loudly. Can they really be considering returning Ralston to IUGA? I compose my answer carefully.

"Mr. Justice Cheung, I'm not a lawyer, but I will tell you what I know. Ralston feared that IUGA would dismantle him and use him for parts once they discovered his disloyalty. Since he had just saved my life and those of several others, I promised him I wouldn't let that happen." I take a sip of water, recalling what Ted had argued in the criminal court.

"When he went missing, we had some ideas about where to look for him. IUGA had removed his arms and legs. They threw the rest of him onto a pile of garbage outside their fence that was scheduled to be picked up by the city and incinerated. The lawyers tell me this is called *abandonment*, and that anyone who claims abandoned property is the new owner."

"But IUGA says in a sworn affidavit that the abandonment was accidental, and they did not intend to relinquish ownership of the automaton," Cheung says.

"It didn't appear accidental to me, Mr. Justice. It looked like they intended to have him burned to ash."

He cocks a dark eyebrow and nods grimly.

Justice Goodspeed glances to her right and then to her left. The other justices shake their heads. "Miss Beckett," she says. "Before we excuse you, I have a few questions. Do you have any special knowledge or training in computers or robotics which would render you capable of altering Mr. Ralston's programs?"

"No Madame Justice. I'm okay with my home computer, but anything more complicated than that, and I'm lost."

"Are you familiar with the term *source code*?"

"Not really. I think it's something software programmers use."

"And you've never had any experience writing source code?"

"None at all."

"Thank you Miss Beckett. You may step down. And Mr. King, you may call your next witness.

"Madame Justice, I wish to call Constantine Albrecht Ralston to the stand."

FORTY-NINE

Cathcart is up and out of his seat with lightning speed, impressive for a man his size. "Madame Justice, as was indicated earlier, this Ralston character is an automaton. It is well established in the law that automatons may not testify in legal proceedings. The iris scanning equipment is not effective on robots, and we've already heard testimony that this particular robot has the ability if not the propensity to lie whenever it wants to."

"Mr. King, the weight of the law is in Mr. Cathcart's favor on this point," Goodspeed says. "Do you have anything that might persuade us to rule otherwise?"

"Honorable Justices," Ted says to the panel. "I could give you the emotional argument that Mr. Ralston's actions in saving numerous human lives have shown him to be an individual of principle and morals. But I prefer to give you the logical argument. Why not?" He holds up his palms and shrugs.

"Mr. Ralston is a key figure in this lawsuit," Ted continues. "Why not hear what he has to say? Mr. Cathcart implies that since the iris scanners do not work on automatons, you will not know if he's lying. Therefore, you may be duped. I disagree. You are five distinguished Justices with decades of experience among you. Who better to judge whether or not Mr. Ralston's words ring true? What harm is there in hearing him out?"

"Give us a moment," Justice Goodspeed says. She turns off the microphone system, and the justices huddle behind the bench once again. This discussion takes longer and appears to be more contentious than the previous one. After a nerve-racking five minutes, they return to their positions at the bench.

"Ladies and gentlemen," Justice Goodspeed says. "We have decided to allow the testimony of the automaton, Mr. Ralston, with the stipulation that should this court determine at the close of Mr. Ralston's testimony that it has muddied rather than clarified this case, we reserve the right to have the testimony stricken from the record."

"Thank you Madame Justice," Ted says. He motions for Ralston to come forward to the witness stand.

Justice Goodspeed doesn't give Ralston the instruction on the iris scanning equipment. Instead she says, "Mr. Ralston, you are expected to speak the truth to this court. I caution you that if we believe your testimony is untruthful in any way, we will strike it in its entirety from the record and not consider it in making our decision. Do you understand?"

"Yes, Madame Justice," Ralston says. He looks handsome in his tweed suit, hands folded neatly in his lap.

On Ted's request Ralston states his full name for the record. "And what is your registration number?" Ted asks.

"My current Arumel Registration Number is XM261702."

"Thank you Mr. Ralston. And what was your IUGA ID Number when you worked for that agency?"

"D7829," he says.

"Thank you. Now, please tell the court how you first learned about Miss Beckett."

"I was assigned to Earth H87D at the time. The then IUGA Director, Zarbain, called me into his office and told me Miss Beckett was predicted to accidentally shift into my sector, thereby disrupting a significant event about to take place there. He pulled me from my current assignment and ordered me to assist her in assuming a temporary identity, and to watch over her until IUGA could work out a way to send her home."

"Was Miss Beckett aware at the time that she was a Transcender?"

"No. She was a first-timer. Normally these first shifts come as a complete shock to the unsuspecting person."

"Were you instructed to conceal the fact that she is a Transcender from Miss Beckett?"

"Yes. I was told to keep the Transcenders away from her at all costs."

"Do you know why you were given that instruction?" Ted asks.

"At the time, I assumed it was because my director had a prejudice against Transcenders. But I've since been told that it was because he knew she posed a threat to IUGA, and he wanted to send her back to Earth 7Y12 permanently."

Cathcart stands. "Objection, Madame Justice. This is hearsay, twice removed."

Goodspeed addresses Ralston. "Who told you that the former director knew she was a threat to IUGA?"

"Director Canto," he says.

"Mr. Cathcart I assume you intend to call Director Canto," Goodspeed says, "since he is listed as your only witness. Hence, you may ask him what he did or did not tell Mr. Ralston. Objection overruled."

"Yes, Madame Justice." Cathcart reseats himself.

Ted continues. "Now Mr. Ralston, the court is most interested in the events that took place beginning with the day you visited Miss Beckett in Connecticut up until the present. On the day you offered Miss Beckett the opportunity to return to Domerica, were you aware that anyone at IUGA perceived her as a threat to the continued existence of the agency?"

"No I was not."

"Did Director Canto ask you to persuade Miss Beckett to accept IUGA's offer?"

"No. I was promised my old position back as a Senior Agent if Miss Beckett agreed to return to Domerica. But Director Canto told me he was quite certain she would readily accept since she had been forced to leave Domerica against her will."

"And who forced her to return to Connecticut against her will?"

Cathcart is on his feet again. "Objection. This is in the stipulated facts. We're covering old ground here."

"That is true," Goodspeed says. "Mr. King, please move on."

"Apologies Madame Justice," Ted says. "Mr. Cathcart is correct. The parties have stipulated that IUGA forced Miss Beckett to leave Domerica."

"Madame Justice," Cathcart blusters, "is counsel now testifying?"

"Mr. Cathcart, sit down," Goodspeed says. "Mr. King, move on to new ground or this witness will be excused."

"Sorry," Ted says. "Mr. Ralston when did you first become aware of Director Canto's concern that Miss Beckett posed a threat to the agency?"

"On the day I returned to headquarters to have the legal department prepare the final contracts for Miss Beckett's signature."

"What did Director Canto tell you at that time?"

"He said it was imperative that Miss Beckett sign the contract electing to remain in Domerica as soon as possible. He showed me the information gleaned from the prediction models regarding the agency's likely demise should Miss Beckett elect to join the Transcender Society. He also showed me the data predicting her death, should she stay in Domerica. Director Canto said it would be in everyone's best interest, including my own, if the latter destiny was fulfilled."

"So he told you that Miss Beckett had at least two possible destinies, but that she should be guided into the destiny which kept her in Domerica and led to her death?"

"That's correct," Ralston says. "He went on to explain that IUGA agents were assisting a group of soldiers from Dome Noir in a plot to assassinate Miss Beckett. He shared all the pertinent details regarding the location of the soldiers' hideout and plans for executing the attack."

"Now, Mr. Ralston, please tell the court what you did after receiving this information."

"In all good conscience, I could not allow Miss Beckett to sign the contract until she was told the entire truth about what would happen to her and other members of the royal family should she elect to remain in Domerica. Consequently, I informed her of what I had learned."

"After you gave her this information, what happened?"

"I shared with Miss Beckett a plan I had formulated on my journey back to Domerica to save her life as well as the lives of her loved ones, and we agreed to put the plan into action."

Ted consults his notebook a moment. "Mr. Ralston, what steps did you and Miss Beckett take to put this plan into motion?"

"We enlisted the cooperation of the Transcenders, the Enclave army and the Unicoi Warriors to entrap and fight the foreign attackers on the palace grounds. Most of the royal family was sent to a safe haven in Old Unicoi prior to the attack."

"Please describe for the court what transpired on the day scheduled as Miss Beckett's wedding day."

Covering much of the same ground I did, Ralston faithfully recounts the events as they unfolded on the day of the attack. He goes over the arrest of the princes, the Noirs' invasion of the palace grounds, and the ensuing battle. He details how he positioned the princess's body at the base of the tower as if she had just fallen. Then he describes sneaking into the stable to wait for the Transcenders to come for him.

"And what happened when you entered the main stable at Warrington Palace?" Ted asks.

"I was attacked from behind by two automatons. They immediately began to dismember me and throw my limbs into a cart. Eventually, I short-circuited. I don't remember anything until the moment that Jaden, excuse me, Miss Beckett, and the others revived me and rescued me from the refuse pile."

"Now, Mr. Ralston," Ted says. "One of the allegations of IUGA's counterclaim is that Miss Beckett altered your program turning you into her spy and causing you to disobey IUGA's orders. Did that in fact happen?"

Ralston chuckles softly. "Absolutely not. Miss Beckett possesses neither the knowledge nor the skills to alter my programs, and she certainly could not have accomplished it against my will."

"Did anyone alter your program, Mr. Ralston?"

"Yes. I did."

"Will you please explain to the court how you did it?"

Ralston looks pained. I know he's worried that if he explains how it's done, IUGA will be able to prevent it from happening in the future.

"The explanation is rather technical Mr. King. But, to put it in layman's terms, I possess the ability to make repairs on myself and to update my own programs. By using this know-how as a back door, if you will, I was able to rewrite segments of my own source code to allow for the behaviors I desired."

Ted doesn't press him for a more thorough explanation. "Very well," he says. "I understand you are currently working for the

438

Transcender Society at the Chateau du Soleil. Please describe your duties for the court."

Ralston presents a nice portrait of the work he does at the Chateau from teaching classes on fencing and world governments to helping out with the cooking and gardening.

"Thank you, Mr. Ralston. I have no more questions, Madame Justice."

"Mr. Cathcart," Justice Goodspeed says, "do you wish to cross?"

"I have a few questions, Madame Justice." Cathcart carries his notebook to the podium.

"*Ahem. Mr.* Ralston," he says with obvious distain, "you've testified that, 'in all good conscience' you could not allow Miss Beckett to sign the contract with IUGA until you disclosed confidential information to her about her future. Is that correct?"

"Yes."

"You are aware that you are an automaton and not a human, are you not?"

"Of course."

"Yet, you expect us to believe that you possess a conscience?"

"To be accurate, Mr. Cathcart, the phrase 'in all good conscience' simply means, 'while being fair and reasonable.' I believed that it was only fair and reasonable for Miss Beckett to have all the pertinent information. But, in answer to your question, yes, I do possess a conscience."

Cathcart's mouth twists into a mocking smile. "Well, then Mr. Ralston, will you be so kind as to explain to this court how a machine, such as yourself, came to be endowed with a conscience?"

"It would be my pleasure," Ralston says, assuming a professorial tone. "The term 'conscience' refers to a sense of right and wrong. As is set forth in the Automaton Specification Manual, which you brought with you to court today, I was expertly programmed by my manufacturer with a keen ability to distinguish between what is generally accepted to be morally and socially right and wrong. I further enhanced that program by endowing myself with the ability to choose between the two."

"I see." Cathcart rubs his double chin. "And yet, despite your so-called 'conscience,' you contend that you secretly altered your program a number of years ago to allow yourself the ability to disobey your owner's direct orders—to be disloyal, in other words?"

"Yes."

Cathcart nods smugly, as if he's scored a point. "Did this alteration to your program also provide you with the ability to lie?"

"Oh, heavens, no. I had been lying on behalf of IUGA for the previous forty years," Ralston says.

Laughter breaks out in the courtroom. A few IUGA lawyers cover their mouths to conceal their amusement.

Cathcart's jaw clenches. "Then this alteration provided you with the enhanced ability to lie to representatives of your owner, IUGA?"

"Yes."

"So, not only are you disloyal, you are an admitted liar, Mr. Ralston."

"I have admitted lying on occasion, yes."

"Now then, during your visit to IUGA headquarters to pick up Miss Beckett's contracts did you take a Mini Quantum Predictor without authorization?"

I was hoping Cathcart wouldn't bring that up.

"Yes," Ralston says.

"So, that would make you an admitted thief as well as liar?"

"Actually, I only borrowed the QP. I returned it later."

"But you did steal a necklace from IUGA and give it to Miss Beckett?"

"Yes. That I did. But it was her necklace."

"Let's get back to the QP, why did you steal, er, borrow it to begin with?"

"In order to save lives."

"Exactly what do you mean by that?"

"I borrowed it so that Miss Beckett and I would have the ability to devise the most optimal plan possible to save her life and those of the royal family."

"*Ah ha!*" Cathcart pulls himself up to his full height. "Then you and Miss Beckett used equipment belonging to IUGA and taken without its knowledge, to obstruct her preordained destiny. Isn't that correct?"

"It is correct to say we used it to achieve the outcome we most desired, which is the same purpose for which IUGA employs QPs every day."

Cathcart picks up his stylus and rolls it between his fingers. "Do you at least admit to using this surreptitiously procured equipment to directly defy orders given to you by IUGA?"

"Yes, I proudly admit it."

"Then I ask you this, Mr. Ralston, why should this court accept the word of an admitted liar, thief, and traitor as to anything?"

"Whether it should or shouldn't is not for me to say, Mr. Cathcart. If this court does not believe my testimony, the Justices will disregard it. But if, as Mr. King has suggested, my testimony has the *ring of truth*, then justice will be served. Isn't that what we all seek here? Justice?"

Cathcart's eyes turn to slits. "You aren't nearly as clever as you believe you are, robot," he says, pointing his stylus at Ralston. "You are the property of IUGA and will be returned to them for appropriate disposition."

Ted springs from his chair. "Madame Justice, is Mr. Cathcart really threatening this witness in open court?"

Mr. Cathcart, I caution you. You are skating dangerously close to being sanctioned by this court. Please remember where you are and conduct yourself accordingly."

"My deepest apologies, Madame Justice." Cathcart bows contritely. "I meant no disrespect to this court. I have no further questions for this *robot*."

Cathcart turns his back on Ralston and saunters to his counsel table.

"Mr. Ralston, I have a question for you," Justice Goodspeed says. "I understand IUGA automatons are generally programmed for self preservation."

"Yes, Madame Justice."

"Why, then, did you make the decision to assist Miss Beckett when you knew the consequences for you could be dire?"

Ralston's eyes mist up as he turns his head toward me. "Because she is the closest thing I have to family. She can be a bratty, unreasonable teenager at times." He smiles and turns back to the panel. "But she is one of the most courageous, compassionate individuals I've ever encountered, and I care for her a great deal. She and the others did not deserve to die. They were innocents."

Justice Cheung speaks up. "And you would have us believe that your conscience told you this?" he asks skeptically.

"I would not attempt to persuade you one way or the other on that point, Mr. Justice Cheung. I ask only to be judged by my actions."

"Thank you Mr. Ralston. You are excused," Goodspeed says. "Mr. King the afternoon is rapidly slipping away from us. Please be brief with your next witnesses. Remember you have only until six o'clock."

"Yes, thank you, Madame Justice. I call Narowyn Du Lac to the stand."

Narowyn rises and glides to the witness box. Her auburn hair falls in a shiny sheet to her shoulders and her understated black dress is finely tailored to flatter her trim figure. Sitting perfectly erect with her hands in her lap, she brings an aura of grace and sophistication to the courtroom.

Goodspeed delivers the standard speech about the iris scanning cameras to Narowyn.

"Please state your name for the record," Ted says."

"Narowyn Helene Du Lac."

"And Mrs. Du Lac, what is your current position with the Transcender Society?"

"I am Chief Executive, for the Society and Chief of the Transcender Police Force."

"You run the place?" Ted says.

She smiles demurely. "Yes."

Ted leads Narowyn through a series of questions essentially designed to corroborate the facts Ralston and I have already testified to. Her answers are articulate and concise. Then he moves on to new ground.

"Mrs. Du Lac," Ted says. "When you were informed by Miss Beckett that IUGA's prediction models showed an almost certain probability that she would succeed you as Chief Executive of the Transcender Society and that during her tenure IUGA would fall out of public favor and eventually fail altogether, were you surprised?"

"No, I was not," she says.

"Why not?"

"The Transcender Society has a cooperative information sharing arrangement with an organization known as the Auguaries. A few years ago they informed us that a new Transcender was foreordained to join our ranks and that this person would spark a resurgence in the volition movement. During her tenure as Chief of the Transcenders, advocates of destiny control would falter and IUGA would cease to exist."

"So, IUGA's prediction models only confirmed what the Auguaries had already told you?"

"Yes. That's correct."

"Would you say, Mrs. Du Lac that if the Auguaries foresaw this coming to pass, and the IUGA prediction models confirmed it, it might be referred to as Miss Beckett's preordained destiny?"

Narowyn turns to the justices. "As Transcenders we don't normally use those terms, but I would unquestionably say that it is most likely Miss Beckett's purpose in being here."

"Well put, Mrs. Du Lac," Ted says. "Thank you. No further questions."

"Do you wish to cross examine?" Goodspeed asks Cathcart.

IUGA's attorneys huddle together with Director Canto in animated conversation. After a moment, Cathcart lumbers to his feet. "We have no questions for this witness, Madame Justice."

"All right," Goodspeed says. "Mrs. Du Lac, thank you for being here today. You are excused. Anyone else, Mr. King?" She lifts the sleeve of her robe and checks her watch.

"One last witness, Madame Justice. I call Lieutenant Urick Hunter to the stand."

Urick strides to the stand in his dress uniform looking gloriously golden and a bit dangerous. After he states his name and current employment, Ted centers most of his questions around the time Urick spent with the Noirs holed up in the caves waiting to attack the palace.

"How pervasive was IUGA's influence with this Dome Noir faction living in the hideout?" Ted asks.

"A group of three men made all the decisions regarding the upcoming attack," Urick says. "The leader was Luc Canard, a former lawyer from Dome Noir. The two others were IUGA automatons."

"So, would you say IUGA had great influence among the men?" Ted asks.

"Yes."

"Were many other IUGA agents present among the ranks of these men?"

Urick rubs his chin pensively. "I would say one in ten men were IUGA agents."

"And did the Dome Noir soldiers know they were automatons working for IUGA?"

Urick snorts. "No. They have no concept of *automaton* in that country. They believed them to be human. They believed them to be mercenaries."

Through his questioning, Ted takes Urick forward to the day of the attack and asks him to describe the events that took place in the tower room. As Urick relates the events leading up to Ryder's death, I feel a vise grip around my insides. Narowyn rests her arm gently across my shoulder, and I lean into her for comfort and support.

Ted winds-up his questioning of Urick by focusing on the Transcenders' efforts to locate Ralston and the events on the night of his rescue.

"Lieutenant, is it your testimony that Mr. Ralston's torso and head were discovered by your team outside IUGA's property on a refuse pile that was scheduled to be picked up by the city and incinerated?"

"Yes."

"Thank you Lieutenant Hunter. I have no further questions for this witness."

"Your witness, Mr. Cathcart," Goodspeed says.

"Mr. Hunter," Cathcart says, rising and straightening his robes.

Urick fixes him with amber eyes. "That's Lieutenant."

Cathcart coughs into his hand. "Excuse me. *Lieutenant* Hunter, no one pushed Chief Blackthorn from that tower, correct?"

"He was attempting to save his wife," Urick says.

"Just so. And no representative of IUGA precipitated his fall in any way, correct?"

"His wife would not have been in peril, if it had not been for IUGA."

"But … Strike that." Cathcart seems reluctant to press him on this issue. He scrolls through his notes and surprises me by saying, "I have nothing further for this witness."

When Cathcart takes his seat, Justice Akbar, a petite woman from Mumbai speaks for the first time.

"Lieutenant Hunter, did you personally witness an IUGA automaton kill a human at any time?" Her voice is soft and slightly accented.

"Yes. I did, Madame Justice," Urick says somberly.

"How many humans?"

"I did not keep a casualty count, but more than a few were slaughtered by automatons."

"With firearms or swords or other weapons?"

"Mostly with guns and swords, but some explosives were also utilized by the IUGA agents."

Justice Akbar shakes her head, scribbling quick notes on her tablet. "Thank you, sir."

"I believe that is all we have, Lieutenant Hunter," Goodspeed says. "You are excused, and this court is adjourned until nine tomorrow morning."

"All rise," the clerk says.

The justices disappear through the curtained doorways, and the courtroom quickly and noisily empties out into the streets.

Overnight, the media outlets run the story of the day's court proceedings focusing on the startling allegations made by the Transcenders that IUGA used automatons in a failed coup and plot to assassinate me on my wedding day. Sound bites of Ralston's testimony are played over and over again.

"In a surprising development, the IGC Court allowed the testimony of an automaton to bolster the Transcenders' case," a polished, businesslike commentator says.

The camera then cuts to a shot of me crying in the witness box. "The claimant, Jaden Beckett testified—"

"Off. Vasa TV off," I say, determined to get a good night's sleep before round two begins tomorrow.

FIFTY

In the morning, Narowyn and I join the rest of our group at the foot of the courthouse steps. As we approach the front door, a horde of reporters rushes forward to meet us, firing questions and snapping photos. The spectator sections are already filled to capacity when we step inside the courtroom. Court deputies have begun turning away disappointed members of the public who hoped to hear first hand Director Canto's response to the allegations. An air of excited anticipation hangs in the room.

We assemble at our counsel table once again. Despite the fact that the atmosphere is more circus-like today, my insides are much calmer as I take my seat. My part is over, and I'm looking forward to the end of the day and putting the hearing behind me.

My eyes scan the upstairs spectator gallery for Eleanor Beckett. I didn't see her yesterday, but Narowyn said she was there. My heart contracts when I find her in the front row seated next to a gentleman who looks very much like my father. My eyes rest on him a brief moment and then move down the row where they meet the smoldering gaze of Ryder Blackthorn. He tips his head to me. I nod back and quickly turn away, my pulse galloping.

The same distinguished looking clerk calls the court to order, and the justices enter through their gold-draperied doorways and retake their seats at the bench.

Justice Goodspeed wears a pearl brooch today with earrings to match. She bids the courtroom a pleasant "Good morning," and then gets straight down to business. "I plan to break for lunch at one o'clock today," she says, "and reconvene at two for closing arguments. Mr. Cathcart, you may call your witness."

Cathcart rises, a whale in gray robes. Today he sports a lavender paisley ascot. "Thank you Madame Justice," he says. "May it please the court, I call Director Marcus Anthony Canto to the stand."

Director Canto rises elegantly and strides to the witness box. His suit is expensive and finely cut. Even though his slick charm's a bit douchy for my taste, he definitely adds a splashy star-quality to the proceedings. He takes his seat and swivels in the witness chair so that he faces the Justices.

Justice Goodspeed delivers the same iris scanning camera admonishment to him. "Any deviation from the truth detected by these cameras will be noted in the transcript of your testimony and highlighted for the Justices," she reminds him. "Do you understand?"

"Yes, Madame Justice," he says, his voice a vanilla smoothie.

Cathcart has Director Canto state his full name and his position at IUGA.

"Director, how long has the Inter-Universal Guidance Agency been in existence?"

Canto clasps his hands across his trim midsection and beams, the epitome of a poised public figure. "Over eight hundred years."

"And on how many earths is IUGA chartered?"

"Over a thousand at last count," Canto says with a satisfied smile.

Cathcart asks Canto to briefly review for the court some of IUGA's major accomplishments over the years. Obviously prepared for the question, Canto is all charm and polish as he breezes through IUGA's role as the anointed guardian of destiny. Most of his claims are astounding, such as IUGA's role in orchestrating the events that ended World War II.

The spectators seem mesmerized by his every word, and thoroughly impressed with IUGA's momentous achievements. But I can't help but wonder if any of his grand assertions can actually be substantiated.

Ted seems to be having the same reaction. He fidgets in his seat as if he fervently desires to object. But he keeps his peace. He'll have his shot at the Director on cross.

After Canto finishes his litany of IUGA's divine acts, Cathcart says, "Thank you, Director, and how long have you been employed at IUGA?"

"It will be thirty years this December."

"How long have you held the title of Director?"

"I was promoted two years ago."

"Please tell the court why your predecessor, Director Zarbain, was removed from that position."

Canto assumes a concerned expression. "Zarbain was removed by the agency's directors for his actions in returning Miss Beckett to her home earth against her will and for concealing the fact that she is a Transcender from her."

Cathcart paces behind the podium. "Then the board of directors of IUGA did not condone Zarbain's actions toward Miss Beckett, but rather punished him for them. Is that correct?"

"Yes. That's correct. He was let go from the agency," Canto says.

"Now Director, was it your province to fulfill the order of this court and offer Miss Beckett the opportunity to return to Domerica?"

"Yes."

"And what were the terms of the offer made to Miss Beckett?"

"They were quite straightforward, actually. She would remain in Domerica for thirty days after which she would freely choose her own destiny."

"Did you make this offer to Miss Beckett personally?"

"No. Because Agent Ralston had a previous relationship with Miss Beckett, I thought it best that he deliver the offer to her. He had previously been demoted, and I gave him the opportunity to regain his old position."

"And according to Agent Ralston's testimony, Miss Beckett readily accepted the offer?"

"Yes, she did."

"Director, why was Miss Beckett not informed at the time the offer was made that a possibility existed that she would be assassinated if she returned to Domerica?"

"Because no such possibility existed at that time," Canto says with a relaxed smirk. "Her loved ones and the rest of Domerica had presumed her dead for twelve months. Also, and perhaps more importantly, we never disclose to a subject predictions regarding their future. It would be a direct violation of our charter."

"I see," Cathcart says. "Now sir, I ask you, did you or anyone acting under your orders deliberately instigate a plot or conspiracy to assassinate Miss Beckett?"

All good humor vanishes from Canto's demeanor. "Certainly not." He gathers himself up with dignity. "That is not the function of IUGA. Our function is to guide and direct matters once a clear destiny path emerges."

"At some point, did you send agents to Domerica to assist a group of soldiers from Dome Noir with their already developed plan to assassinate Miss Beckett?"

"Yes."

"And when were these agents first dispatched?"

"Immediately upon learning of Miss Beckett's clear destiny path."

"What was the purpose of sending agents to join the Dome Noir forces?"

"To advise and guide them in order to ensure that Miss Beckett's destiny was properly fulfilled."

"In accordance with IUGA's public charter?"

"Exactly."

"Exactly," Cathcart repeats. "Now, were you aware of this supposed alternate destiny of Miss Beckett to one day become the leader of the Transcenders and facilitate the downfall of IUGA?"

Canto flutters a dismissive hand. "We had been aware of it, but it was not a likely scenario since Miss Beckett planned to remain in Domerica."

"Very good. And were the agents IUGA sent to Domerica ever intended to be actual combatants in the attack on Warrington Palace?"

"No. Never. They were present only in an advisory capacity."

"What about the automaton who attacked Miss Beckett at the palace? I believe the Transcenders have furnished a photo and an IUGA ID number on this agent."

"That agent's shell was recovered and analyzed after the battle," Canto says. "It appeared to our technicians that its programs had been corrupted or tampered with in some way. In any case, it was deemed to be a malfunction."

Cathcart leans an arm on the podium, "What about the testimony of Lieutenant Hunter that he witnessed IUGA agents kill humans during the battle?"

"Not a shred of evidence exists to support that. I can only surmise that Lieutenant Hunter was mistaken. Perhaps he was suffering from combat stress reaction or something similar. His violent background in his home nation of Demonstadt is fully set forth in our filings. I urge the justices to review his testimony in light of those facts."

Ted jumps to his feet. "Madame Justice, this is outlandish, No evidence regarding combat stress reaction or anything remotely similar exists in the record pertaining to Lieutenant Hunter, and Director Canto is certainly not qualified to render an opinion regarding anybody's mental state but his own."

Goodspeed leans forward across the bench. "Director Canto, please confine your answers to the question asked."

"Yes, Madame Justice," Canto says.

Cathcart makes an apologetic nod to the court and faces his client again. "Now Director, we've heard testimony that IUGA agents captured Agent Ralston during the battle at Warrington Palace. Is that correct?"

"Yes. It became obvious to us that this agent's program had been corrupted. It was guilty of numerous violations of direct orders. Agent Ralston was dismantled and taken to the parts facility on Earth Z772 for further examination."

"That is where its remains were found and removed by Transcender Police. Correct?" Cathcart asks.

"Yes," Canto says. "But the automaton's remains were never intended to be disposed of in the way they were—that is, placed on a refuse pile. I gave orders that the robot's memory module, software, and main processor were to be analyzed to determine in what ways they had been tampered with."

"Then the placement of Agent Ralston's remains on a garbage heap outside the facility was a mistake?" Cathcart says.

"Most certainly."

"Thank you, sir." Cathcart pauses and looks pointedly at the Justices as if the issue is now resolved.

"Director Canto," he continues, "how important is it to IUGA to retrieve the memory data from this automaton?"

"Goodness, it is of the upmost importance. Contained within that memory data is highly confidential information of IUGA regarding prediction model statistics. It must be protected at all costs. If this information fell into the wrong hands, it could be disastrous. Also, the data in that memory module is crucial to our investigation into what happened to this automaton that caused it to go rogue. It is vital to the public that this never happen again."

"Director, is it possible that Agent Ralston could have rewritten his own code to provide himself with the ability to ignore IUGA orders and disclose confidential information to others?"

Ted leaps out of his chair. "Objection, Madame Justice. The Director is not a technician or expert in the area of computers or robotics. He is not qualified to answer that question."

Cathcart quickly responds. "He has worked with automatons for thirty years, Madame Justice. He can certainly offer an opinion on the matter."

Justice Goodspeed rubs her fingertips along her temple. "Mr. King's point, that the witness has not been qualified as an expert, is well taken. I will, however, allow the witness to respond with a personal opinion, which we will consider in light of his experience."

"Director?" Cathcart says.

"Absolutely not," Canto replies. "Agent Ralston could not have altered his own program."

"Why not, in your opinion?" Cathcart says.

"The whole idea is preposterous. It would take an ultraintelligent, self-aware machine to reprogram itself in such a manner. If this were possible, not only would complete and utter chaos result within the ranks of IUGA, but our entire human society would be threatened. Under such a scenario, machines could reprogram themselves to take over civilization."

Canto leans across the rail of the witness box and speaks directly to the justices. "That is one more compelling reason why this memory data must be recovered and analyzed by our experts."

"Thank you," Cathcart says. "One last question, Director. Miss Beckett has asked this court to make the temporary restraining order against IUGA permanent because she feels her personal safety is threatened by the agency. Is Miss Beckett's life or safety in danger from any agent or employee of IUGA?"

Canto raises his chin. "Of course not. That's absurd. IUGA is not in the business of harming people. We are in the business of helping them. We bear no ill will toward Miss Beckett. We simply wished her true destiny to be fulfilled."

"Thank you Director Canto. I have no more questions, Madame Justice."

Justice Goodspeed looks to Ted. "Questions Mr. King?"

"Yes, Madame Justice." He walks to the podium with his notebook.

"Director Canto," Ted says, "during its long history, how many complaints have been lodged against IUGA agents?"

"I'm sorry," Canto smoothes his silk tie. "I oversee the entire IUGA operation—millions of employees, volumes of information. I don't keep track of those exact statistics."

"Would it surprise you to know it's close to ten million?" Ted asks

"No. Not over the course of eight hundred years."

"And on how many earths has IUGA's charter been suspended or permanently revoked?"

Canto shifts in his chair. "Again I don't have those exact numbers."

"Does six hundred and thirty-five sound about right?

"Well, over the course of our history that isn't such a bad number."

"What if I were to tell you that three hundred and twenty-two of those suspensions and revocations, that's over half of them, came within the last ten years?"

Canto's eyes skate to his lawyers for help. He's obviously unhappy with this line of questioning. "I'll have to take your word for that, Mr. King. I'm not currently in possession of that information."

"Hmm," Ted scratches his chin. "And yet, you're the Director."

"Objection!" Cathcart is on his feet. "Mr. King is badgering the witness."

"Mr. King, please refrain from commenting on the testimony," Goodspeed says wearily.

"Yes, Madame Justice. All right, Director Canto, although I suspect you may not know the answer to this question either, is it not true that IUGA's stated response to the majority of the complaints lodged against it has been that the agent in question had malfunctioned?"

"It would not surprise me to hear that. We employ over a million of these mechanical men. Failures in programming are inevitable."

"Very well, Director. Then, since IUGA's standard response to the vast majority of complaints is: *The agent malfunctioned,* would you concede that it's possible a portion of these malfunctions or failures in programming were due to automatons altering their own programs?"

"No!" Canto is adamant. "As I've already testified, I do not believe that is a possibility, and the human race better hope that it is not."

Ted shrugs. "Very well, Director Canto, let's move on. Why was Agent Ralston originally assigned to Earth H87D?"

"He was sheparding, er guiding, a high value subject—a subject whose destiny was to eventually save that earth from destruction."

"And who was that person?"

Canto ducks his head slightly and wets his lips "Chief Ryder Blackthorn."

"That would be Miss Beckett's late husband?"

"Yes."

"And did it show up in your prediction models that Chief Blackthorn would be a casualty during the battle of Warrington Palace?"

Canto swallows audibly. "It was a possibility."

"And was it IUGA's intention to allow this to happen, knowing of his importance to the fate of that entire earth?" Ted asks.

"No. We had a rescue team in place to ensure that Chief Blackthorn would survive the attack on the palace."

The breath abandons my lungs when I hear this. I had no idea they planned to save Ryder. I turn to Narowyn, clutching her arm. She shakes her head in bewilderment.

"So what happened, Director? If these prediction models are so finely tuned and accurate, why was Chief Blackthorn not rescued as planned? Why was he allowed to fall to his death while attempting to save his wife?"

"I can only surmise that it was due to the interference of Miss Beckett and the rogue agent, Ralston, as well as that of Lieutenant Hunter, who insinuated himself into the situation. They are to blame. Their actions would have thrown off all of our models. In such a case, there was nothing we could do."

"I see. Well then, please tell the court, what is the current fate of that earth, now that IUGA's rescue plan failed and Chief Blackthorn is dead? What's going to happen to it?"

Lowering his chin, Canto mumbles something inaudible.

"I'm sorry," Ted says, cupping a hand to his ear. "I didn't hear you."

"It is uncertain," he says stiffly.

"Meaning IUGA does not know whether that earth will even survive in Chief Blackthorn's absence?"

The Director studies his manicure. "That's correct."

"Thank you," Ted takes a moment to check his notes, letting the point sink in.

"Director Canto, you stated that you sent agents into Domerica to join the Dome Noir fighters as soon as Miss Beckett's destiny path became clear. At that time—at the point the agents were dispatched—what was the exact probability percentage of that destiny coming to pass for Miss Beckett? The probability that she would be assassinated?"

Canto rubs the back of his neck. "I don't recall exactly."

"Well then, approximately? Surely, since you dispatched the agents, you must know."

"I believe it was somewhere around a thirty-five percent likelihood."

Murmurs ruffle through the courtroom.

"A thirty-five percent probability? And you consider that a clear destiny path?"

"In some cases, it is. Yes."

"Well, at that same time, what was the probability percentage that her other destiny path would come to fruition? The destiny where she joins the Transcenders?"

"I believe it was around sixty percent," Canto says, looking at Ted and not the Justices.

Ted scratches his head. "Let me see if I understand this, Director. Your testimony is that there was a higher probability of Miss Beckett joining the Transcenders and taking down IUGA than of being assassinated by the Dome Noir thugs, but you sent agents in to facilitate the less likely scenario, thus raising the likelihood of its success?"

"Mr. King," Canto says with an edge of distain. "Agent Ralston had already informed us that he was certain Miss Beckett would elect to remain in Domerica. After all, she had just ascended to the throne and was planning her wedding. That was an observable fact which had not yet been programmed into the models. We independently took that into account before agents were dispatched. Sometimes one must apply reason and greater knowledge to these prediction models and make adjustments accordingly."

"I see," Ted says. "Who decides what adjustments are made?"

"On a matter of this importance, I do."

"Well then, Director, do you sometimes make adjustments in order to benefit IUGA and its interests?"

"Absolutely not. We have a duty to the public which we take very seriously."

Ted opens his mouth, as if to challenge this, but he appears to think better of it and scrolls down his notes instead.

"Director, you are a very, very rich man are you not?"

"Objection!" Cathcart roars. "The Director's finances have no relevance in this proceeding."

"Oh but they do," Ted says. "My intention is to show that Director Canto has become extraordinarily wealthy working for IUGA, and that it would mean a great deal to him if his livelihood were threatened."

"I'll allow it," Goodspeed says.

"What is your annual salary at IUGA," Ted asks, "including

459

bonuses and incentives?"

Canto brushes a hand across his shoulder as if to remove some lint. "Just over twenty-two million CD," he says.

"Twenty-two million a year," Ted says. "Then if the existence of IUGA were threatened, you would stand to lose a rather large fortune. Isn't that correct?"

Canto's lips form a tight line. "Oh, I imagine I could find another job Mr. King. I'm still relatively young."

"Good luck with that," Ted says under his breath.

Before Cathcart can object, Ted says, "Strike that. As a final matter, Director, please tell us, what is Miss Beckett's current destiny path? What is the current probability that she will put events in motion which will lead to the demise of IUGA?"

Canto bristles. "That is confidential."

Cathcart rises from his chair. "Objection, Madame Justice. IUGA is strictly prohibited under its charter from divulging such information about the future, especially in the presence of the subject." He tilts his head toward me.

"Madame Justice," Ted says. "This question bears directly upon whether or not the temporary restraining order should be made permanent. I'm trying to establish just how much of a threat IUGA and Director Canto perceive Miss Beckett to be."

Justice Goodspeed toys with her pearl earring. "Director Canto, I believe the cause of justice would require a small exception in this case. Without going into other specifics regarding Miss Beckett's destiny path, please tell the court the current probability percentage of Miss Beckett's taking over the helm of the Transcenders and instigating the collapse of IUGA."

He clears his throat. "As of today, I believe it is just above ninety percent."

A chorus of gasps and startled cries ripples through the

spectators.

"Thank you, Director," Ted says. "I have nothing further." He scoops up his note pad and returns to counsel table.

Goodspeed looks to her colleagues on the bench. "Questions?" she asks.

Justice Akbar raises her stylus. "Director Canto," she says in her soft voice, "besides the battle in Domerica, has IUGA employed automatons in the past to assist in combat situations?"

He crosses his legs resting his hands on his knee. "Madame Justice, in the past we have dispatched automatons to assist in similar coup situations, and as I noted in my previous testimony, we have had a presence during the crucial battles of all major wars."

"But my question is, did these automatons engage in actual combat in the past?"

"Only if threatened, Madame Justice."

"Tell me, Director, if you place these agents in the midst of a battle how can they not be threatened?"

"The vast majority of the time our agents are employed in an advisory capacity only and never see any combat."

"But that was not the case in Domerica." Justice Akbar wags her stylus at Canto. "The testimony is that one in every ten soldiers was an IUGA agent. I didn't hear you dispute it. That seems an excessive number of advisors. It sounds to me as if you supplied these people with an automaton army designed to kill humans. That is a clear violation of confederation articles."

Canto leans toward the bench resting his arms on the witness box. "Madame Justice, respectfully, that simply is not so. Our agents were present to advise and guide the Dome Noir soldiers. There is no direct evidence that any of our agents killed a single human being."

"Hmm." Akbar's face is tense. "Did IUGA remove its automatons from the battlefield prior to the locals going in?"

"We certainly did. Once we saw the likely outcome of the battle, we removed all of our agents—whether damaged or intact. We could not risk having this relatively unsophisticated population discover a disabled robot. That would have been disastrous."

"Then that would explain the lack of any direct evidence, wouldn't it." She lowers her head and makes a note on her pad.

Before Canto can respond, Justice Cheung chimes in. "Uh, Mr. Director, on a different subject, your prediction models show a rather high likelihood that your agency will not be in existence much longer if you do not take decisive action. Exactly what do you intend to do to save IUGA?"

Canto's posture stiffens. "Mr. Justice Cheung, we plan to conduct our business in the most professional and ethical manner possible, living up to the letter of our public charter. Internal investigations are currently underway to determine whether mistakes were made by us or our agents in Domerica. If they were, we will rectify them immediately. I believe as long as we consistently act in the highest and best interest of the public, IUGA will be around for another eight hundred years."

Justice Cheung nods. Goodspeed looks to the rest of her colleagues, and finding no further questions, cracks her gavel. "We'll take a one hour recess for lunch. Gentlemen, be prepared with your summations at two o'clock."

* * *

After the lunch break we traipse back into the courtroom. The media corps and the spectators' sections seem to have thinned out now that the main attraction is over. Once the justices have seated themselves at the bench, Justice Goodspeed calls on Ted for his closing argument.

He rises and walks to the podium. "Honorable Justices," he says, "in the beginning, IUGA's purpose may have been a noble one—to preserve order and prevent chaos—but over time, the agency has been transformed into a machine used to control events, not for the public good, but for the enrichment of a handful of men. This corruption of purpose is perhaps nowhere better illustrated than by IUGA's conduct regarding Miss Beckett, a young woman perceived as a future threat to its current operating environment."

The remainder of Ted's ten minute speech is eloquent and persuasive. He drives home the most important point: IUGA abused its power and violated its charter when it sent an excessive number of agents to assist in the Noirs' assassination plot in an attempt to save its own skin. When he returns to counsel table, Narowyn beams at him and pats his arm.

"Mr. Cathcart, we'll hear from you now." Goodspeed says.

He rises gracefully, smoothes a hand down his robes, and walks to the podium.

"May it please the court," he says. "What have Miss Beckett and the Transcender Society really proven here? They have shown only that IUGA, in furtherance of its sworn public duty, assisted in the fulfillment of a destiny which was already a near certainty—*a ninety-six percent probability*. On the other hand, Miss Beckett has admitted that she was in league with a rogue IUGA agent, and that she and the Transcenders did everything in their power to prevent that destiny from occurring. If certain unfortunate events took place as a result of Miss Beckett's unwarranted meddling in the natural unfolding of fate, IUGA cannot be held responsible. Miss Beckett brought it upon herself."

Cathcart blusters on for the remainder of his ten minutes, but his words sound hollow to me when compared with the weight of the evidence. I hope the justices feel the same way.

After court is adjourned, Narowyn and I gather our things and thank Ted and Corinne once again. I glance up at the spectator gallery, but see no sign of the Becketts or Ryder. It's not that I want to speak with him, that would seem awkward right now, but after two days of testimony re-living the events that took place in Domerica, it might be a comfort of sorts to glimpse his beautiful face and know that a spark of my Ryder lives on in some way.

FIFTY-ONE

Teetering on the brink of mental exhaustion, I sleep for most of the day following the hearing. I receive a kind message from Eleanor Beckett, praising my testimony at the hearing and expressing her good wishes for a speedy and favorable decision from the court. I return a short note thanking her again for her support and for attending the hearing.

My schedule quickly returns to normal. Although I've never been much of a winter girl, Arumel City is kind of a snowy wonderland in January. Callie loves the cold fluffy stuff, so we go for long walks when I need a break.

When I have extra time, Luci and I continue to work on my secret little skill. I've improved to the point where I can make my stylus float across the room and into my waiting hand. Luci thinks that's huge, but I think I still have a long way to go.

In February, when I'm beginning to tire of the icy chill, Nila and Asher persuade me to join them for a little ski outing to Switzerland. It turns out to be even colder but infinitely more fun than I imagined it would be. We eat fried Snickers bars in the 3 Tells Pub and do some scary-awesome cliff jumping in Interlaken.

Asher and I put two more explorations behind us, one to an Outlier Earth with three continents, only one of which is habitable, and another to an Archetypal Earth on the verge of discovering a new form of magnetic energy. I'm amazed and delighted by the new and exotic landscapes we visit, and I feel more skilled and confident with each successful exploration.

The glasses Luci made for me give me a greater sense of security when I'm away from Arumel, and I haven't had any brushes with IUGA agents since Twin Moons. Narowyn promises that soon I'll have the opportunity to head up an exploration team of my own. It sounds thrilling and daunting at the same time.

Despite all the frigid excitement of winter, I breathe a sigh of relief as the first whispers of spring descend on Arumel. There's still no word on our case from the IGC court, but it doesn't cross my mind very often. I'm happy living at the Chateau. The sunshine and warm weather feel like new beginnings and fresh starts to me.

One gorgeous Sunday I ask Eve to join me on a little shopping excursion to the Urban Bazaar in town.

"What are we looking for?" she asks as we wander among the artists' booths.

"I don't know, maybe some fun prints for the kitchen—just something bright and springy." I stop at a booth to thumb through a stack of matted photographs.

"Hey, Jade, look," Eve says. "Isn't that Hunky Dunky over there?"

"Who?"

"That Ryder guy."

I duck my head and pivot behind a rack of frames. "Where?" I whisper.

"Over there talking to that bleach-blonde set of boobs."

I peer around the side. In the next aisle of booths, Ryder stands with his hands tucked into the pockets of his jeans talking to ... "Oh my god, I know that girl—or her *mirror* at least," I say.

"Who is she?" Eve asks.

"Back home, she's my best friend, Liv Wallace. I don't know who she is here."

"Well whoever she is, she's about to steal your man. I told you, you should have made a move on him a long time ago."

"Shush. Can you hear what they're saying?"

"No, but she's totally macking on him. Look at her. She's practically shoving her cleavage in his face."

Just then, Liv places a long-fingered hand on Ryder's shoulder, and standing on tiptoes, she kisses him on the mouth before turning and walking away. My heart and stomach powerfully collide. Ryder stands and watches her for a moment, then he swipes the back of his hand across his mouth and turns in the opposite direction.

"Ha," Eve says. "Doesn't look like he's that into her. He just wiped off her lip gloss."

"C'mon. Let's go." I clutch the lapel of her jacket and pull her along. "I don't want him to see us."

"But I thought we were going to shop."

After watching Ryder and Liv together I feel kind of queasy and irritable. Something that tastes remarkably like jealousy coats my tongue and makes my mouth go dry. Liv's *mirror* back in Unicoi had a thing for my Ryder, and I didn't like it then either. "I need something to drink," I say.

"Okay. I know a great place for chocolate chai lattes." Eve takes the lead, and I follow her in kind of a dazed funk.

* * *

As the week begins, I try to keep myself focused on class work and my sessions with Luci, but thoughts of the scene between Ryder and Liv at the Urban Bazaar keep intruding. I can't seem to get it off my mind. I look up Olivia Wallace online and discover that she's had some success as a local actress. If she's anything like the Liv back

466

home, it's the perfect career for her. Her online publicity shots are gorgeous—sexy and self-assured. Nothing in her bio mentions a current love interest, though.

One sun-drenched morning, I decide to call Eleanor Beckett and invite her out for lunch. I tell myself it's because I haven't seen her since the hearing, and I never thanked her in person for filing the amicus brief in my case. But in my heart I know that I'm also motivated by my desire to learn more about Ryder. I promise myself I won't be the one to bring him up, but maybe I can find out whether he and Liv are an item.

At Eleanor's suggestion, we meet at a small café near her office. The hostess seats us at a pretty little window table with white linens and a vase of pink baby roses.

"Thanks for having lunch with me on short notice," I say. "I wanted to express my gratitude in person for the brief you filed. My lawyers say it was very persuasive and should bolster our case considerably."

"I'm so glad you called. I've been meaning to invite you to lunch," she says. "Let's hope we don't grow old waiting for the court's decision." Her smile is so like my mother's it makes my heart ache.

Throughout lunch, Eleanor is vivacious and inquisitive. She's eager to hear about my latest explorations, and she shares some sweet stories about her grandson. She's particularly animated when filling me in on her plans for a new garden this spring.

"You really must come and see it once it's all planted," she says. "John would love to meet you, if you feel up to it. We'll have dinner alfresco."

"That sounds lovely."

When the check is delivered to our table, I'm disappointed that Eleanor still hasn't mentioned Ryder. I reach into my purse for my cash card, but she intercedes.

"No. This is my treat, Jaden." She hands her card to our server.

"I hope in some small way it makes up for the dreadful experience you had at my home when Ryder stopped by unexpectedly."

Finally. I'm relieved she opened up the subject. "I got over that a long time ago," I say. "He came to the Chateau a few days afterward to apologize for his abrupt departure."

"Yes, he told me. He felt awful about his rude behavior."

"How is he, by the way?" I ask, careful not to appear overly interested.

"Doing well. The boy works too hard, I'm afraid, but he seems happy. He's moved on with his life, you know, since my daughter's death, and I'm glad. He's so young and has so much living still to do."

I toy with my dessert fork, averting my eyes. "Is he seeing anyone special?"

"Oh, I don't think so. He dated an attractive, young actress a few times—Olivia something or other—but they weren't really suited for each other, and he's not the type to go out with someone just for their looks."

I raise my eyes and smile. "He doesn't seem like that type."

She gazes at me for a moment, and I'm pretty sure she can read me like a book—my mom always could. "So … what about you?" she asks. "Anyone special in your life?"

"No." I shake my head vigorously. "I haven't dated anyone since my husband's death."

"Maybe it's time to think about getting back out there." Her eyes sparkle fondly. "I'll tell Ryder you asked about him."

"Oh, I didn't mean…" I begin to protest, but stop myself. "All right. Thank you so much for lunch, Eleanor. It was great to see you again."

She reaches across the table and squeezes my hand. "I hope to see much more of you in the future. I'll call you for dinner."

"That'd be great."

Walking home, I feel more peaceful knowing that Ryder and Liv aren't together, but I still don't know how to interpret my feelings for him.

$$* * *$$

The following day, Narowyn announces that we received a grant from the International Institute of Science to study Earth J999, a primitive OE discovered only last year. It sounds a bit like *Planet of the Apes*. The human population is tiny, but the simian population is enormous. The goal is to attempt to understand why.

Ash is the mission leader, and I'm second in command. We'll be accompanied by a small team including Luci, our resident scientist, and Joe, our animal expert. Asher warns me to be prepared. "If you think Twin Moons was roughing it, this will be ten times worse, and remember to pack bear spray. Some of those gorillas can get pretty territorial."

The day before we're scheduled to depart, I stop at a sporting goods store to pick up a supply of jungle-strength insect repellant, mosquito netting, and some final odds and ends. As I leave the store, I see a sign for *Handsome Harry's Hat Shoppe*. On a whim, I decide to pop in and buy Ralston a special thank you gift for taking care of Callie once again while I'm on exploration.

A light colored panama sits atop a mannequin head in the window, a jaunty little feather tucked into its shiny silk band. It's perfect. A bell chimes as I enter the shop, and a slim young man smiles at me from behind the counter. He wears a black fedora, a lavender shirt with rolled-up sleeves, and a vintage-looking vest.

"Welcome," he says, stepping around the counter. His soft hazel eyes connect with mine, and a look of recognition flashes across his face. Removing his hat, he places it over his heart and bows slightly. "Ah, the famous Miss Beckett. It's an honor to have you in my shop."

His easy charm and engaging smile are uncommonly attractive.

"You must be Handsome Harry," I say.

"Thank you for noticing. Harry Chambers, at your service."
Replacing his hat, he holds out a hand, and I shake it.

"Nice to meet you," I say, returning his smile.

"If you don't mind a suggestion." He reaches up and pulls a dark
pink, woman's hat from the shelf. "This fuchsia cloche would look
amazing on you. The color would be stunning with your magnificent
eyes."

My cheeks grow warm at the compliment. "Thank you, but I'm
shopping for a friend. That panama in the window is more what I
had in mind."

"Ah, an excellent choice. Let me get it for you." Returning the
cloche to the shelf, he walks to the window display and plucks the
panama from the mannequin head. "I can model it if you like." He
sounds only half-teasing.

I laugh. "That's not necessary, but I'd appreciate it if you'd wrap
it for me."

"It would be my pleasure."

I set down my bags and dig my cash card out of my purse. Harry
produces a beautiful chocolate brown hat box from behind the
counter and draws out several sheets of matching tissue paper.

He arranges the hat carefully inside the tissue, and then peers up
into my eyes. "Is this for a special occasion? Your boyfriend's
birthday, maybe?"

"It's a little *thank you* gift, and he's not my boyfriend—more like
a mentor." I don't know why I added that last bit, but it's probably
because his flirting is kind of fun, and I don't want him to stop.

The chime above the shop door sounds, and Harry momentarily
drags his lovely green-brown eyes away from mine. "I'll be right with
you, sir," he says over my shoulder.

He expertly ties a paisley ribbon around the box. "I can put this in a bag if you like, but it seems you've already got your hands full. I'd be happy to deliver it to you at the Chateau later this evening when I close up shop." His eyes dance with a hopeful light.

I don't have time to consider his offer, though, because the man behind me says, "I can help you with your packages, Miss Beckett."

My heart dives all the way into my shoes at the sound of the familiar voice, and I turn around slowly. The sight of him nearly brings me to my knees. The clear azure eyes, the sensuous lips, and the long graceful limbs send hot blood coursing through my veins. *Damn him!*

"What are you doing here, Blackthorn?" I say, doing my best to project *cool confidence* and not *blathering puddle of goo*.

His gaze sweeps me in like a hungry lion, and he runs his tongue along his lower lip. "I stopped by the Chateau, and they told me you were shopping in town. I saw you from across the street. I wonder if you're up to having that cup of coffee with me?"

He steps nearer, and I almost hold out a hand to ward him away. If I breathe in his scent, it will completely undo me.

"I'm in kind of a hurry," I say, irrationally unnerved by the thought of having coffee with him. "I'm preparing to leave on an exploration."

"Just a quick cup? Please?" He tilts his head and half-smiles.

My insides get all melty, and my good sense evaporates through my ears. "Okay, one cup," I mutter.

As soon as the words leave my lips, I'm sure it's a casmigorically stupid idea. I wish I could reel the words back into my mouth. I turn to Harry who also appears deeply disappointed with my response, but Ryder is already lifting the bags from my hands.

"We'll take this with us," he says to Harry as he slides the hat box from the counter. Turning to me, he says, "There's a place just down the block. I think you'll like it."

471

FIFTY-TWO

I follow him out of the shop, and we easily fall into step together. It's so freaking weird to be next to him—so familiar and yet completely surreal. *He's not my Ryder, he's not my Ryder,* I chant in my head.

The coffee shop is bright and homey and smells of cinnamon and vanilla. It's decorated to look like somebody's grandma's parlor with charmingly overstuffed sofas and arm chairs sporting tatted doilies on their backs.

"Is this all right?" He motions to a small bistro table near a sunny window.

"Sure."

"I'll get our drinks. What would you like?"

"Just a latte, please, small. I can't stay long."

We pile my packages on an empty chair, and I shrug off my sweater. *What are you doing Jaden? This is insane. Run while you still have the chance.*

But I don't run. I sit and wait until he returns with two steaming lattes. He sets one cup in front of me and takes the seat across from mine.

"Thank you for this," he says. "It's been a while since I last saw you, but I wanted to give you some time. Having been through something similar, I knew you needed it. I hope you're feeling a little more settled now."

"Actually, I am. Things are going well for me these days."

"The IGC hearing certainly went well for you, even though it must have been difficult to relive all of those terrible events. Your friend Ralston was a real scene stealer. The courtroom was mesmerized by his testimony."

"Thanks," I say, liking the fact that he called Ralston by name and acknowledged him as my friend. "It's nice to have that over with. It'll be even better when a decision is handed down."

"Yeah. Unfortunately, they take their sweet time in some cases."

Sunlight glints from his onyx hair, and he engages me with those impossibly blue eyes. He's so outrageously handsome, I experience that long ago feeling of *what's this guy doing with me*? Then I remember . . .

"So, this place is nice," I say. "Did you used to come here with your wife?"

His face falls and he rubs his chest as if I hurt his heart. "It hasn't been here very long."

"God, I'm sorry. I didn't mean to offend you," I say, feeling like a jackass. "I'm still trying to figure out how to act around you."

"Please, Miss Beckett, don't feel like you need to *act* a certain way around me. I have no expectations other than to get acquainted. Eleanor's told me a little about your amazing adventures. She's a big fan of yours."

I shrug. "Well I look a lot like her daughter."

"That's *not* why she likes you." His gaze is piercing, and his tone makes me feel as if I've wedged my foot in my mouth once again.

"I'm a fan of hers too," I say. "She went out of her way to help

473

me, and I appreciate it."

"She believes in you and your cause." He's annoyingly comfortable with himself, but he's also being very gentle with me even though I'm acting like kind of a jerk.

"Anyway," he continues, "it has to be strange to leave your family and move to an entirely new world. You've done it twice. Not many people alive can say that."

I'm not sure if it's the words he says, his obvious kindness, or the attractive way his hair flops over his forehead, but something goes off in my head—like a light switch being thrown inside me, and I see clearly for the first time. Other than my appearance, I'm nothing like his deceased wife. Eleanor said as much to me, and he knows it too. I'd never before considered that he might be interested in me because of my differences. I assumed he was only trying to get back what he'd lost.

With this new insight comes the disturbing realization that I've been doing exactly what I projected onto him. *I've been wanting to get a piece of my Ryder back.* The fundamental unfairness of it embarrasses me.

He takes a moment to shoulder off his jacket and drape it across the back of his chair. I use the time to study him. Up to now I'd done my best not to look at him too closely. His hair's shorter than my Ryder's, his complexion a little more copper hued, his eyes are the same endless ocean, but there's an unmistakable difference about him. Maybe it's his openness or the easy way he carries himself. I'm not sure. But if I didn't have all this other baggage screwing with my head, I'd probably think he was someone worth knowing better.

"Okay," I say. "I'll tell you all about myself, but I feel at a disadvantage. You already know a lot about me from Eleanor and from the hearing, and I know almost nothing about you. How about I ask you some questions first?"

"If you like." He smiles modestly.

"Do you have a job, or are you still in school?"

"I graduated college two years ago. For my senior project, I set up a small film production company. We do mostly indie films, documentaries, that sort of thing. We're still viewed as the upstart in the industry, but we won a couple of awards last year. So people are beginning to pay attention."

"Okay, that's a cool job. Film production." A flicker of memory niggles at my brain. "Hey wait a sec, you're Blackthorn Productions?"

"Yep. That's me." He grins over the rim of his coffee cup.

"I saw one of your films on TV. A sort of quirky thing about a community dog and the boy he adopted. I watched it with my adopted dog. We both loved it."

"Oh yeah. *Buddy's Best Friend.* We had a lot of fun making that. It got picked up by a major distributor, so it's gotten a wide audience."

"That's so great, and a little surprising. For some reason, I didn't see you as the creative type. I figured you'd be in politics or something like that."

He laughs richly. "*Noo.* Not my style at all. I leave all that to my father. He's a civil rights lawyer. I think he would've been happy for me to follow in his footsteps, but I can't see myself going to court. And those robes? Forget it. Civil disobedience is better suited to my wardrobe."

I'm glad to know his father is alive. In Domerica, both Ryder's parents were deceased. But that was due to environmental factors that don't exist in Arumel.

I try not to ask uncomfortably specific questions, but I probe a little more about his family. I'm curious as to whether his mother is also alive in this world and if his sister Catherine, my nemesis in Domerica, lives in Arumel. He tells me his mom is a prominent social worker in town. And the best news of all—he's an only child.

After a gulp of coffee, he sets his cup on the table. "My turn," he says. "Tell me about your family and where you grew up. I hear it was an Archetypal Earth?"

I describe Madison, Connecticut for him and give him a brief rundown on my dad and Drew. I describe my mother and a little bit about what it was like when she was killed suddenly in a car wreck. He already knows some things about my life in Domerica, but he seems curious to know more.

"So, you were queen for a while?" he says.

"Yeah, for about five minutes. It wasn't an easy job, but I think I handled it okay. It's weird to think about all that now." I toy with the handle of my cup. "Sometimes when I look back on it, the whole thing seems like a dream."

For the sake of maintaining the pleasant mood, I focus on the beauty of Domerica and challenges of life inside a dome, while avoiding the parts about Ryder and the events leading up to my relocation. He listens attentively and doesn't try to press for more information.

"My life's been kind of a crazy kaleidoscope ever since my first accidental shift," I tell him. "I'm still trying to get my arms around this whole Transcender business. Maybe after a few more years it'll become routine, but I have so much to learn."

"Do you like living in Arumel now? Do you think you might stay here permanently?"

"I can't realistically live anywhere else," I say. "Arumel has the only known Transcender community. I suppose I could always hide out somewhere and pretend to be normal, but that would be too much work. And I promised myself never to live a lie again. I'd rather put my gift to good use."

He smiles his approval. "That's admirable. But you didn't say whether or not you like it here."

"Yes, I like it. I've made some good friends. The thing is, when I was in Domerica, I was pretending to be someone I wasn't. It's not that my time there was wasted because I learned so much, and … well, I loved the people immensely. But I'm not sure what the future would have held for me if I had tried to stay there long-term. All I know for sure is that this is where I'm supposed to be now."

"Then you see this as your destiny?" He raises a questioning eyebrow.

I roll my eyes. "Don't try to lure me into that debate. I don't look at it in those terms. We all have something unique to contribute in this life, and as long as we're being true to that, destiny will sort itself out."

The antique clock on the fireplace mantle behind me chimes, reminding me that I need to get my packing done or I won't be ready to leave in the morning.

"I'm sorry but I'm going to have to cut this short," I say. "I really need to get home. I'm leaving on exploration tomorrow, and I still have a lot to accomplish tonight."

"Can we continue this another time?" he asks.

Long sigh. "Look, Blackthorn, you seem like a nice guy and this has been fun. I mean that. But I still have strong reservations about a friendship with you."

"I don't understand. Why?"

I tilt my head back and gaze at the ceiling a moment. I can't believe we're really talking about this, but since we are, we might as well get it all out on the table.

"Do you know what a *perpetual contract* is?" I ask.

"I've heard of it."

"And you know that supposedly such a contract exists between you and me?"

He shifts uncomfortably and stares at his coffee. "So I've been told."

"Well doesn't that bother you? I mean, don't you wonder if that's what this is all about? That because of some *woo woo* cosmic pact made a hundred lifetimes ago we can't stay away from each other? What if we end up ..." I fumble for words. "Well, what if it ends *badly*, like it has in the past?"

Our eyes meet and hold. "What if it doesn't? What if this," he waves his hand to me and back to him, "is how it's supposed to be? How it was always supposed to be? I mean, I loved my wife tremendously, but I don't believe I was meant to spend the rest of my life alone. Do you? Wouldn't you rather know?"

"Truthfully? I'm not sure. The pain ..." My throat swells, and I turn toward the window.

"I understand," he says gently. "Well, it's completely your call. If you tell me to go away and never contact you again, I'll honor that. I swear."

So, here it is—the moment of truth. Do I want him to go away? Now that I'm convinced he's not trying to recapture something he had with his wife, am I capable of letting go of the past and getting to know this man on his own terms?

I drink some cold latte to unknot my vocal chords. "It's just so complicated, and I'm into simple these days. I need more time to think about it."

The corners of his mouth fall, and he nods slowly. "Look, I know you have to leave, but can I ask a favor? Could I have a quick look at your TPD bracelet? I've heard about them, but never seen one up close."

The request seems odd but harmless, and I feel kind of bad for disappointing him. "Sure," I say, unfastening the bracelet and handing it across the table.

"May I?" he asks, his thumb poised over the latch to the medallion.

"Yeah, go ahead."

He lifts the top and a holographic map of Arumel City rises up. "Wow, cool." He turns it from side to side, examining it closely. "The detail is extraordinary."

"We have some talented cartographers at the Chateau."

The map disappears as he refastens the medallion. He opens the bracelet to the inside and reads the inscription out loud: "*Timeas non plures semitas vitae.* Fear not the many paths of life."

"Whoa, you read Latin?" I'm impressed.

"Who doesn't?"

"I don't."

He grins. "Neither do I. I'm just messing with you. I already knew the Transcender motto. I thought maybe you needed reminding."

I slump back in my chair and shake my head. "Well played, Blackthorn. I walked right into that one."

A slow smile creeps across his lips. "I'm not above a little trickery, if it will get you to change your mind."

I can't resist returning his smile. This guy's hard not to like. His eyes rest on me waiting for a reply. The want I see in them causes a strange stirring deep inside.

If I'm honest with myself I want him too, but I'm so profoundly scared. He's right. It's only fear that's holding me back, and I refuse to let the events of my life turn me into a spineless coward when it comes to love.

"Okay, Blackthorn, you win. I guess we can try. To be friends, I mean."

The joy in his grin sends a little thrill through me.

"Then will you have dinner with me?"

"Umm, no. Not dinner. Dinner's too much. We need to start slower. I haven't gone out since…"

He sits back and holds up both hands. "No problem. We'll do this any way that makes you comfortable. You tell me the next step."

I drum my fingers against my coffee cup. "I'll be on exploration for five days. How about I call you when I get back, and we'll set something up? Maybe you can show me your studio, or we can go werewolf hunting at Virtual World or something."

He laughs. "Sounds good. I'll expect to hear from you on the weekend, then?"

"Right." I stand and slip on my sweater.

"May I walk you home?" He helps me with my bags.

"No. I need some time to wrap my head around this. Thanks for the coffee, though."

He extends his hand to me. The gesture strikes me as ironic, but I set down my bags and slide my hand into his. The connection is immediate and electric. He startles at the energetic charge, but I expected it.

"Talk to you soon." I tuck the hat box under my arm and hurry through the door, feeling his eyes on me as I go.

Outside my feet barely touch the sidewalk. My previously agreeable mood soars to astronomical heights, and it hits me like a bolt of lightning—within the span of thirty minutes, my entire world has changed. Things that mattered so much this morning—my upcoming exploration, the pending IGC Court decision, working to control the strange power in my hands—have shrunk to near insignificance in comparison with the fact that I have a date with Ryder Blackthorn.

FIFTY-THREE

After dinner, I take Callie and her things to Ralston's apartment. I make a big deal of presenting him with his new hat as a token of my gratitude. He tries it on and preens in front of the mirror above his mantle.

"It looks good on you," I say. "The hat shop was very nice, and I ran into Ryder Blackthorn there. We had coffee together this afternoon."

His expression in the mirror registers astonishment. He turns away from his reflection and back to me. "Oh my, that must have been quite an experience. You seem in good spirits, though. It must have gone well?"

"Yes. I enjoyed myself. He's intelligent and interesting, and surprisingly laid-back. Very different from the Ryder I knew in Domerica."

"I imagine he must be. The environments they grew up in are strikingly dissimilar. Not having experienced the stresses and strains of losing both parents and assuming the role as tribal chief, I suspect our local Ryder is probably a more carefree soul."

"Yes, and creative, and kind, and funny too. He owns a small film production company. Hey, wait. How did you know his parents are alive here?"

"I looked him up online after you bumped into him at Mrs. Beckett's. Didn't you?"

"Uh, no. I think I was still in denial back then."

"Well, he sounds like a rather intriguing chap. Do you two plan to see each other again?"

"Yes." I conceal a sheepish smile with the back of my hand. "I promised I'd call him when I'm back from exploration. We plan to get together then."

His eyebrows shoot up. "I see. So does this mean you no longer have reservations about the whole *mirror* situation or the *perpetual contract?* Did he expect you to be more like his late wife?"

"I really don't think so. In fact I had a little epiphany at the coffee shop. I realized I was the one who was hung up on him being my Ryder's doppelganger. He seems cool with the fact that I'm so different. He pointed out to me that we could spend the rest of our lives trying to avoid each other or we could make an effort to be friends."

"Wise words, my dear. But I would be cautious until you know him better. I do not want to see you hurt again."

"I know Rals. I'm not going into this with any illusions. But he did force me to consider another possible perspective on the whole *mirror* thing."

Ralston takes off the hat and tucks it back into its box. "What perspective is that?"

"What if he's not my Ryder's *mirror?* What if he and I were supposed to be together all along and Ryder was his *mirror?*"

He smiles. "How cheeky. I like him already."

"Could he be right about that, Rals? I mean, that he's the one I was always supposed to be with?"

He lifts one eyebrow. "If you recall, I'm out of that business now, old girl. I'm afraid you're on your own with this one."

"Okay, that's fair, but can I ask you a personal question, Rals?"

"Of course, you may ask."

"Are you dating anyone?"

He blinks like the question didn't compute. "How do you mean that?"

"Well I heard that some humans here date automatons. I know you have a great capacity for love, but we've never talked about *your* love life."

Clearly uncomfortable with the question, he makes a production of refolding the tissue paper neatly around his new hat. "Actually, Gil and I have something of an understanding in that area, and that is all I'm willing to say on the subject."

"That's okay." *Because that's all I'm willing to hear on the subject.* "I just want you to have someone to love."

"I wish the same for you, my dear. Now come here and allow me to bestow a proper thank you hug upon you. I'm thrilled with my new hat. We must go to the yacht races next month. It'll be the perfect venue for showing it off."

"It's a date," I say. "Take good care of my girl. Love you guys." I kiss Callie on the nose and head back to my apartment to finish packing.

* * *

Five days on Earth J999, which we not so affectionately nicknamed *The Monkey House,* was about four and a half days too long. I land back at the Chateau, weary, filthy, and covered with flea bites. Even after spending a good thirty minutes under the shower lathering up with scented gel and washing my hair twice, I don't feel entirely clean. When Ralston brings Callie home, after her initial excitement to see me, she sniffs me up and down, as if the monkey smell still clings to my skin.

"How was the exploration, old girl?" Ralston asks.

483

"Hot, bug infested, and hostile. The apes we worked with were mean, but the humans were downright malicious. Our camp was attacked twice by the natives. We used flares to scare them off. But I would have been in fear for our lives if we hadn't brought firearms with us."

"Goodness. Were you able to collect any useful information at all?"

"Oh, yeah. We collected a number of blood samples and brain scans by bribing our human subjects with chocolate and other food and by using tranquilizers on the animals. We also got a ton of photos and video. I think the Institute of Science will be happy."

"Well, Callie was a perfect angel," Ralston says. "Gil and I will miss her company."

"Tell Gil thanks. You know I appreciate all you do, Rals."

Back in my apartment, Callie and I crawl up on my bed, while I check my email and think about getting organized for the upcoming week. I consider calling Ryder Blackthorn to set up our date, but decide to wait until tomorrow so as not to appear overly anxious. Though, I admit, the thought of coming home and seeing him again kept my spirits buoyed through some of the worst experiences in The Monkey House.

I never appreciated how comfortable my bed is until I spent several nights in a sleeping bag inside a crowded tent on a hostile earth. I awake on Saturday morning refreshed and thankful for my cushy surroundings.

After I've showered again and dressed, I allow myself to telephone Ryder. He seems happy to hear from me, and when I suggest we get together tomorrow, he asks if I am free to spend the day with him today. He proposes that we meet at the same coffee shop as before, and make plans from there.

When I arrive, Ryder's already sitting at the same sunlit table near the window. He stands when he sees me and holds out my chair. His grin is endearing, and he looks carelessly cute in jeans and a gray linen shirt.

"I got you an iced caramel latte," he says when I sit down in front of a tall frosty drink. "I hope that's okay."

For a fleeting second, I wonder if this was his wife's favorite flavor, but then I realize he's drinking the same thing, so I choose to believe it's his favorite instead. "Sounds perfect."

"I didn't know if you'd call me this weekend," he says. "I planned to stop by the Chateau if you didn't."

I smile at his seeming insecurity. "I told you I would. I usually do what I say I will."

"Now I know. How was your exploration?"

"Awful." I take a taste of my latte. "Mmm, that's delicious. Anyway, it was a primitive earth where the insects outnumber the mammals by ten million to one, the temperature hovers around ninety-five even at night, and it rains every day. We slept on the floor of a tent, and had no place to bathe—but those were just the good parts."

He laughs. "What were the bad parts?"

"The locals, both man and beast, were openly hostile to us. We were trying to understand why the simian population way outnumbers the human population on this particular earth."

"Amazing. Did you get your answer?"

"Our scientist, Dr. McDonald, says it appears to be a case of stunted human evolution. For some reason the people still look and behave like cavemen. They don't even have much language. We won't know why until all the data we collected is analyzed by the Institute of Science. But if they lack enough data to draw any conclusions, they may ask us to go back."

"I assume you won't be volunteering for that mission?"

Before I can answer, the polycom goes off in my pocket. "Sorry. I wasn't expecting a call," I say, pulling it out. "It's Narowyn. I'd better take it."

"No problem. Go ahead."

I punch the answer button. "Narowyn?"

"Jaden, I apologize for disturbing you." Her voice sounds strained. "Ted just telephoned. The IGC Court filed its decision moments ago. He and Corinne are on their way here. Can you come to my office right away?"

My stomach twists into knots. "I'm about ten minutes from the Chateau. Do you want me to shift?"

"That's not necessary. It will be a while before the lawyers arrive."

I sign off and quickly get to my feet. "I'm so sorry, but I need to go. We have a decision from the IGC Court."

Ryder reaches for my hand. "Are you worried?"

"Yes. Wouldn't you be?"

"I'd like to go with you, if that's all right."

The request throws me for a second, but then I realize I'd like him to be there—whether good news, or bad. "Yes you can come as long as you're prepared to see me cry, if they ruled against us."

When Ryder and I arrive at Narowyn's office door, surprise is apparent in her eyes.

"Narowyn, this is Ryder Blackthorn," I say. "We were spending the day together when you called. He sat through the hearing with Eleanor Beckett. I told him it would be all right if he came along to hear the court's decision."

She smiles graciously and shakes Ryder's hand. "Of course. Nice to meet you Mr. Blackthorn. Please come in."

I spot Ted and Corinne already seated at the conference table with copies of the court order in front of them.

"Is it good news or bad news?" I say to Ted.

He grins. "Good news."

"What about Ralston? Did they order him sent back to IUGA?"

"No, no. Ralston's safe. Please sit down. We'll go over everything with you."

Narowyn wraps an arm around my shoulder. "It's really quite wonderful news, dear. The court went beyond what we had asked for."

Ryder and I take seats at the table. I flip through the pages of the court order, while Ryder introduces himself to Ted and Corinne. It might as well be in Russian. My brain doesn't process the words, only that everyone seems happy, and I don't need to smuggle Ralston off of this earth.

"Let's go over our claims first," Ted says. "The court found in our favor on every point."

"That's great," I say. "But exactly what does it mean?"

"After reviewing all the testimony and briefs, the court found that IUGA had grossly violated its power and authority by helping the Noirs plan and carry out the attack on Warrington Palace. In addition, it found that IUGA took this action not to further the unfolding of destiny, as they claim, but to get rid of you because they see you as a threat."

"That's awesome, so did they make the Temporary Restraining Order permanent?" I ask.

"Yes," Corinne says, "and they extended it to include all members of the Transcender Society, not just you."

"But they went much further than that," Ted says. "They ordered IUGA to cease operating in the country of Arumel permanently. The justices gave it six months to wind up its business. They warned IUGA that another major violation such as this could result in the court permanently revoking the agency's charter to operate on this earth at all."

"Wow, that's pretty severe."

"It is, and IUGA also must leave Earth H87D where Domerica is located."

"What? Are you serious?"

"The court said that since this was IUGA's second major violation on that earth—the first one being the unauthorized erection of the domes—IUGA is no longer allowed to operate there. Period."

I clamp my hands over my mouth to muffle a laugh. Ryder smiles like he doesn't really get it, but he's happy that I'm happy.

"You haven't even heard the best part, yet," Corinne says.

"What could be better?" I ask.

Ted speaks up. "The court found that IUGA's actions in Domerica were so egregious, that it ordered them to pay punitive damages—fifteen million CD to you for the loss of your husband, and twenty million CD in reparations to Domerica to rebuild Warrington Palace and compensate for the loss of life there. The money will be distributed to the Domericans through various channels friendly to the Confederation."

I'm happy the victims will be compensated, but I'm stunned and a little embarrassed by the unfathomable sum of money IUGA's been ordered to pay me. "I didn't ask for that," I say. "Do I have to take it? What would I do with all that money?"

"Give it to charity. Use it for something good. The Court felt it was fair," Ted says.

Thoughts of the San Francisco tsunami victims float through my mind, and I wonder if Narowyn would object to me setting up a foundation to help fund work in some of the places where we conduct explorations.

"There's something else, Jaden," Ted says. "Let me read a paragraph to you. You'll find it halfway down on page three."

I turn to the appropriate page and follow along as he reads:

> *This Court is particularly troubled by the testimony indicating that IUGA may have employed automatons to fight and kill humans. If true, this flagrantly illegal use of automatons would constitute grounds for the revocation of IUGA's license to employ automatons anywhere in the galaxy. This court feels additional investigation is warranted, and hereby orders that a special investigatory commission be immediately convened by the Inter-Galactic Confederation for the specific purpose of determining if IUGA has employed automatons in such a way.*

"So they may not be allowed to use automatons at all? Ever?" I ask.

"That's a possibility," Ted says, "if the investigatory commission uncovers additional evidence."

I shake my head. "This is all so unbelievable. Where's the part about Ralston?"

"It's on the last page," Ted says. "Unsurprisingly, the court found in your favor on the contract issue. It also found that you did not alter Ralston's program or use information he gave you to thwart the orderly unfolding of destiny. Oh, and here it is right here." He points to the last paragraph.

> *In light of the facts and circumstances of this case and the heroic actions of the automaton, Constantine Albrecht Ralston, IUGA ID Number D7829, in defying IUGA's instructions, in order to save human lives, this Court cannot find any justification at law or in equity for returning the automaton, its mass storage data, or its memory module to IUGA.*

"That's so great," I say. "Can we call Ralston and tell him right now?"

"I'll send for him," Narowyn says smiling. "And, though it's not yet noon, I believe I'll send for a bottle of champagne also. This calls for a bit of a celebration."

Ralston and the champagne arrive at the same time. "What's all this?" he asks, stepping inside.

"We won, Rals," I say hugging him. "You don't have to go back, and IUGA is banned from operating in Arumel and in Domerica forever."

"What? The Court issued its order?" Ralston asks, clutching the back of a chair.

"Yes, this morning," Ted says.

I introduce Rals to Ryder. He nods politely, but still seems stunned by the news of the Court's decision. "Why would they release the decision on a Saturday?" he asks.

"Probably because it's likely to cause a big uproar in the media," Ted says. "Some will hail it as a landmark decision. Others will call the court biased and overreaching."

"IUGA's reaction will be sheer outrage," Narowyn says, pouring the champagne into flutes. "They have no legal recourse do they, Teddy?"

"They can't appeal the court's order," he says. "I suppose at some future date they may apply to have their charter in Arumel reinstated, but I don't see that happening for many years if ever."

"Rals, they also ordered an investigation of IUGA's use of automatons," I tell him. "If they find automatons killed humans at IUGA's direction, they'll revoke IUGA's license to use automatons anywhere in the galaxy."

His forehead wrinkles. "Oh dear, what will become of the million or so IUGA automatons if that were to happen? Will they be scrapped?"

I hadn't thought about that.

"Perhaps the price of automatons will decrease, and ordinary institutions and families will be able to afford to employ them in more intellectual and peaceful occupations," Narowyn says, passing out glasses of champagne.

"I hope you are correct," Ralston says.

Narowyn raises her glass. "I propose a toast to Ted and Corinne for their brilliant efforts on behalf of Jaden and the Transcender Society."

We all clink our glasses together.

Ryder leans in and kisses my cheek with champagne moistened lips. "Congratulations," he whispers.

"This is truly a momentous occasion," Narowyn says. "In fact, I believe I'll ask everyone to convene in the library to celebrate with us. This is a watershed day for the Transcenders. Ted, Corinne, Mr. Blackthorn, will you stay for a while?"

"Most certainly," Ted says taking another sip of champagne. Corinne nods.

"Actually, I should go and let you celebrate with your colleagues," Ryder says. "I'll stop by Eleanor's house and share the good news with her. May I take a copy of the order?" he asks Ted.

"Yes, and please tell Commissioner Beckett, how grateful we are for all her help. Her amicus brief added credibility and depth to our claims."

"Do you really have to go?" I say.

He smiles. "This is a major victory for the Transcender Society. I'm afraid I'd be a distraction. Can we make plans to get together this week?"

"Yeah, sure. I'll walk you to the door."

"You like picnics?" he asks when we reach the front door of the Chateau. "I live near Kistlethorn Park, and my neighborhood deli is on the way. I could pick up lunch for us."

"I don't know. I've been to Kistlethorn Park. It kind of creeped me out."

He throws back his head and laughs. "Those trees are seriously disturbing, aren't they? I'm shocked they allow school children inside. But there's this little pond, away from the trees, with swans and lily pads. Very serene. Trust me."

"All right, sounds fun. When?"

"Wednesday work for you?"

"Yeah, that's fine. I'll meet you at the main entrance to the park at noon."

"Fantastic. Savor your well-deserved victory today. Okay if I call you tomorrow?"

"I'd like that," I say with a shamefully happy grin.

FIFTY-FOUR

Sunday morning couldn't possibly be more glorious. The breeze is so mild it feels like I'm floating on a cloud as I sit and watch Callie romp around the Chateau courtyard while I mull over my day. I have kitchen duty tonight. For the first time, I'm in charge of planning the menu, which will necessitate several errands in town today. More importantly, I have a little clandestine excursion to make before I head out to do my marketing.

In light of the IGC Court's decision, I no longer consider myself bound by the contract with IUGA. That means a short visit to Domerica shouldn't ruffle anyone's feathers. To avoid any possible protests, though, I don't intend to let anyone know I'm going.

Back in my apartment, I slip into one of my uniforms to make it less likely that I'll be recognized should someone in Domerica happen to glimpse me. I also strap on my pistol and utility belt just to be safe. The coordinates for Warrington Palace are already in my TPD bracelet, but I lock-in on a musty little storage room on the third floor. It's almost certain to be empty, and it's near the queen's office—my intended destination.

Zzzt! After landing silently in the middle of the room, I tiptoe to the door and open it a crack. The hallway is darkened, which probably means no one is present on this floor yet. I hug the wall as I slink toward my former office, which I hope Lorelei has made her office now. After listening at the door for voices and hearing none, I turn the knob. *Damn, it's locked. Oh well.* I make the short shift to the other side.

The soft, silvery-pink morning light has just begun sifting through the window panes, and I gaze down into the once familiar courtyard. Stacks of lumber and slabs of marble tell me that reconstruction of the destroyed parts of the palace is still ongoing.

I take a seat at my former desk. A beautiful letter opener with an ornately carved handle sits to one side. Lorelei's remarkable silversmith work, no doubt. Taking the penlight from my utility belt, I parse through her files. When I come upon a file marked *Dome Noir*, I open it and skim through the contents.

Most of it is correspondence between Lorelei and a Prince Giscard. Recalling Ralston's history lessons on Dome Noir, I place Giscard as King Philippe's younger brother. With Prince Gilbert and Prince Jean Louis confined to Wall's Edge Prison and King Philippe in poor health, Giscard must be handling the fragile political situation—and probably governing Dome Noir as well.

After scanning several pages of correspondence, I gather that a negotiation is underway to restore peace between Domerica and Dome Noir. Giscard's tone is conciliatory and he renounces his nephews' actions as abhorrent. He begs Lorelei to reopen discussions on building a new dome in order to save his country from civil war and internal destruction. He sounds like a man on the edge of desperation.

I find information suggesting that Lorelei released the Grand Duke from prison due to his advanced age, but it appears the two princes are scheduled for reeducation soon. The reeducation procedure involves surgically altering the brain to wipe out a person's long-term memory, leaving them with no past or personal history. I view the practice as inhumane. As queen, I'd hoped to abolish it, but I never had the opportunity. Giscard formally requests that the young royals be exiled to Copula De Vita instead of reeducated. This would be a merciful but dangerous decision for Lorelei.

I search for her response on the opposite side of the file, but my hand freezes mid-air when I hear voices in the hallway. The voices stop at my door. At the sound of a key slipping into the lock, I slam the file closed and *Zzzt.*

I land back in the storage room and quickly reprogram my TPD with my next location. I didn't find out everything I wanted to know at the palace, but I saw enough to know that Domerica has the upper hand in dealing with Dome Noir, and Lorelei seems to have things under control. I double click my bracelet and alight in the middle of my old bedroom in Father's manor house at the Enclave.

Everything is exactly the same as it was when I left. It's as if Father expects me to return the way I did last time. It touches my heart to see a bowl piled with fresh pommeras sitting atop my desk. I slip two pieces of the bright pink fruit inside my uniform. Then I take a sheet of notepaper from the top drawer and, plucking the gold pen from its holder, I write: *All is well. ~ J.,* in the center of the page and tuck one corner under the fruit bowl. I hope Father is the one who changes the fruit, but if he isn't, I'm certain the housekeeper, Mrs. Hornsby, will show the note to him. She won't know what to make of it, but he will, and I hope it brings him a bit of joy.

My final stop is nearby. I want to see my horse Gabriel one last time, so I shift to the back door of Father's stables. Any number of stable boys are working this time of morning, but since the main doors are always propped open during the day, I'm comfortable landing here. After slipping inside, I take a moment to allow my eyes to adjust to the darkness. Two stable boys near the front banter back and forth loudly as they muck out adjoining stalls. They're occupied enough that I'm confident they won't notice me sneaking over to Gabriel's stall.

As I draw closer, I see the stall door is open. I worry that Father may already be out for a morning ride. But when I peer around the corner, I'm elated to see both Father and Gabriel inside. I quickly shift to the empty stall opposite them, where I can watch unseen. Their backs are turned to me as Father works to saddle Gabriel. They both look wonderful. Father is handsome and robust as ever and Gabriel's coat gleams. His tail is long and nicely groomed. Seeing Father is an unexpected pleasure, but it kind of blows my plan to feed Gabriel his favorite fruit, unless ...

I decide to give it a try. I set one of the pommeras on the straw floor of my stall, and using my palm, I gently guide it low to the floor and across to Gabriel's stall. I bring it to a stop just before it reaches Father's boot. It makes a small sound as it comes to rest in the straw.

Father turns his head as if he senses someone's presence, and then he notices the pommera at his foot. He picks it up and scans the stable area. "Jaden?" he says softly enough so that the stable boys don't hear. I'm tempted to show myself to him, but my heart and head agree that it's best to remain hidden. After a quiet moment, Father smiles widely. He tosses the pommera up in the air and catches it neatly in his right hand. "Thanks sweetheart," he says in the same soft voice. He turns to Gabriel. "Look boy, someone sent you a treat." Gabe takes the offered prize and munches it greedily. Father smiles again to himself and resumes his saddling.

Seeing him so well and communicating with him, indirectly at least, to let him know I'm fine, leaves me with a feeling of closure. I'm glad he and Gabriel have each other. I trust they will both live out happy lives in spite of the turmoil of the past.

My heart is light when I land back in my apartment. After changing into shopping clothes and grabbing my purse, I pull a slim red volume of poetry from my shelf and take out the faded sketch of Ryder. A few weeks back I came across a small art studio in town whose owner agreed to restore it and mount it in a small frame for me.

The weather remains gorgeous as I stroll down the city sidewalk. The combination of my satisfying visit to Domerica, the favorable court decision, and my upcoming picnic with Ryder has put me in the greatest spirits. I catch myself smiling at everyone I see. Half of them look at me like I've lost it, but the other half return my smile with good humor. One or two even give me a cross-arm salute—a sign of respect for Transcenders. Since the hearing and all the media coverage, I'm getting used to being recognized on the street.

I drop off the sketch at the art studio, and proceed to the farmers' market to gather supplies for tonight's dinner. I've decided to try my hand at making a baked pasta dish similar to the one I had in Venice on my birthday.

Narowyn asks me to sit with her at dinner. Thankfully, the meal turns out beautifully, and my fellow diners seem pleased—or at least not disgusted. I consider that a success.

"This dish is superb, Jaden," Narowyn says. "You're becoming quite a good cook."

"I had a lot of help," I say. "But, thanks."

"I wished to speak with you because we've had a new grant come in," she says, "and I'd like you to consider heading up the exploration team. I think you may enjoy this one a bit more than the last."

"Of course. What is the mission?"

"An intriguing earth where it's rumored that people indigenous to a particular rainforest have evolved with web-like arms, similar to batwings. It is said they can actually fly short distances."

"Sounds remarkable," I say, feeling thrilled and anxious at the same time.

"Come by my office in the morning, and we'll discuss the details."

FIFTY-FIVE

My exploration team and I are scheduled to leave Thursday. A host team will meet us in a small village near the rainforest. They will act as guides and liaisons with the Alarans, as the winged people are known.

I spend the beginning of the week making arrangements for being away and ensuring that my team has everything we need for the project. Asher won't be along for this exploration, and it'll seem strange not to have him to rely on. But Narowyn generously offers her assistance and guidance with all the planning and coordination of the mission. Things are coming together very well, and for the first time, I fully appreciate how much work goes into being a team leader.

Wednesday dawns golden, with cheery rays of sunlight dancing around the edges of my curtains. Thoughts of the upcoming exploration take a back seat to my excited anticipation of seeing Ryder and sharing a picnic with him. Though I've spoken with him briefly a few times this week, I'm anxious to be with him again.

I stand in my bedroom and stare at the contents of my closet. A half-dozen uniforms are lined up on the left side. On the right side are my everyday clothes, and in the middle I've arranged a few special outfits collected over the past year. In general, clothing in Arumel can be a tad boring. Eve introduced me to a couple of small boutiques downtown, though, that specialize in edgy but pretty women's clothes made of neoprene and other interesting fabrics. I pull out my three favorite dresses and lay them across the bed to be decided on later.

Slipping into my desk chair, I fire up my notebook to go over my lists of exploration supplies and instructions once more. The ringing telephone interrupts me halfway through the list.

"Asher Steele calling," Vasa says.

"Okay, I'll take it. Hey, Ash."

"Just calling to see if you're all set for tomorrow," he says.

"That's so nice of you. I think I'm good."

"You'll make a great team leader, Jade. Don't forget everything I taught you."

"I'll miss having you there, Ash. I hope you'll keep your poly handy in case I have an emergency."

"You'll be fine. Hey, you want to have lunch today? I could give you a few more pointers."

"I appreciate the invitation, but I'm having a picnic with Ryder Blackthorn today."

He's silent for a moment, and then he says, "Well … I hope you have a nice time. I mean that. Just be careful."

"Thanks, Dad. Bye."

I turn back to my notebook, but my phone immediately rings again.

"Dolce Art Studio calling," Vasa says.

"Put it through."

"Miss Beckett, this is Kelly at the art studio. I wanted to let you know that the restoration and framing of your sketch is completed and it's ready to be picked up."

"That's great. I'll stop by this afternoon. Thanks."

The art studio is one street over from Kistlethorn Park, so I can pick it up on the way home from my picnic. I finish reviewing the checklist for the umpteenth time and switch off my notebook.

After taking a warm relaxing shower, I blow out my hair with a round brush to form long loose curls. I try on each of my favorite dresses before choosing a multi-colored silk sundress with a flouncy skirt. The air is still a bit chilly outside, so I top it off with a light-weight jean jacket. My polycom and berry lip gloss fit neatly into one of the pockets, and I'm set to go.

Callie flashes me her saddest puppy eyes, as I open the door to a community car parked at the curb.

"Sorry girl. You can't come this time. I have a date."

She sits on the sidewalk and watches dolefully as I press my thumb onto the car's ID pad, and the engine hums to life. "Good morning, Jaden Beckett," the car says. "Where may I take you?"

"The main entrance of Kistlethorn park, please. Oh wait, drop me off a block from the main entrance." I figure the short walk will help calm the raging butterfly fest in my stomach.

"As you wish. Would you care for music?"

"Yeah. Love songs would be nice."

In ten minutes or so, the car efficiently pulls to the side of the road. "Kistlethorn Park is thirty meters ahead on your right. Have a nice day, Jaden Beckett."

I step out into the sidewalk and take a deep cleansing breath. By the time the Kistlethorn front gate comes into view, I feel fairly calm and collected. After all, it's just lunch, right?

My breath catches in my throat when I see him propped against the green wrought iron fence. A patterned blanket lays folded over one arm, and he clutches a brown shopping bag in his hand. His careless hair falls half-in, half-outside his collar. Not at all like the

Unicoi warrior I once knew, but remarkably appealing nonetheless.

He straightens up and smiles as I approach. "Thank you for coming," he says.

"Thanks for bringing lunch. Can I carry something?"

"No. I got it. The pond's this way." He gestures to a path on our right.

The gnarled limbs of the inky-black Kistlethorn trees are visible on the main road. Their leaves look sharp as volcanic glass. Today I notice giant buds of white and red scattered among the mass of shiny dark foliage.

"I've never seen the trees in bloom," I say.

"In another month or so the blossoms will be at their peak. It's an awesome sight, but still reminds me of a goblin's forest. The pastoral side of the park suits me better."

After several yards, we veer off the path. Ryder lifts up some low-lying weeping willow branches for me and I duck underneath. We emerge into a gorgeous green meadow complete with a tranquil, lily pad covered pond and a family of swans. It's like stepping from a Tim Burton nightmare into a Monet dream.

A woman and two small boys toss bits of bread to the swans. A few couples stroll along the path skirting the pond.

"Is this okay?" he asks.

"Perfect. It's beautiful here."

He spreads the blanket out in a grassy area near the pond. "I hoped you'd like it." We each find a spot on the blanket, and he pulls the shopping bag next to him.

"So, do you want to talk first, or eat first, or eat while we talk?" he asks.

"Why don't we eat while we talk? That way if it gets awkward we can just chew for a while."

He laughs. "It won't get awkward. I promise."

Dipping into the shopping bag, he takes out two wrapped sandwiches, followed by two bottles of water and a white bakery bag. "I got Portobello mushroom with goat cheese on multigrain and roasted red pepper with mozzarella on focaccia. Which do you prefer?"

"They both sound great. You choose."

"You want to share? Or shall we start with cookies?"

"Really? You brought cookies?"

His sky-blue eyes gleam. "Yeah. These are the best chocolate chip cookies on earth—well this earth, at least." He removes two enormous cookies from the white bag and hands one to me. "I got two more just in case."

I bite into the thick chewy disc. Warm chocolate chunks melt on my tongue. "*Oooh*, that's so good."

"I know, right?" He stretches out his long legs and props up on one elbow, gazing serenely at the pond as he chews.

He's so unbelievably attractive to me. I especially love the way his body is put together. For a second I'm struck by how weird it is that I've seen him without clothes. Though it wasn't really him, but my mind wanders … *Uh oh*. I feel my ears begin to burn hot. Not wishing to get caught having daydream fantasies about him, I take a stab at some polite conversation.

"So, what's going on at Blackthorn Productions these days?"

He shuffles a hand through his hair in a poignantly familiar way. "At the moment, we're working on two major projects, which is stretching our resources a bit thin. One is a short comedy feature written by two women laserball players about what it's like competing in a male-dominated sport. The other's a documentary I'm doing about the underground music scene here. Do you like music?"

"Yes, very much."

"I'll show you the rough cut when it's finished."

"I'd like that."

He fishes another cookie from the bag and breaks it in two offering half to me. I shake my head.

"Sandwich?" He asks.

"Not yet. I'll take a water, though."

He passes a bottle to me. "So what about you? I'd like to hear more about your explorations. Anything new on the horizon?"

"Yeah. In fact tomorrow, I'm heading up an exploration to a newly discovered earth where it's reported that some humans have developed wing-like appendages and can actually fly."

"Oh, so nothing out of the ordinary?" he deadpans, setting the sandwiches on top of their wrappers on the blanket between us.

I smile. "I've already told you it's not nearly as glamorous as it sounds. Last year we visited an earth with two moons where a tsunami had devastated a large portion of the California coast. It was heartbreaking. I wish we could've helped more, but we're kind of forbidden from doing that." I pick up half of the mushroom and goat cheese sandwich.

"No interfering with destiny?"

"It's more like allowing things to unfold naturally without introducing outside elements."

He takes the other half of my sandwich. "And you have your own team now?"

"Only for this one mission. I think Narowyn wants to see what I'm capable of—or incapable of, as the case may be. Fortunately the rest of the team members are all experienced Transcenders, in case I screw up."

"Somehow, I don't see that happening." He gazes into my eyes. "I hope you don't mind, but I just have to ask, do you believe what they say about you? That you're predestined to change the way the world views free will versus fate?"

"I wish that stuff hadn't come out at the hearing. I really don't feel like I'm here to do anything special. I'm just trying to be myself, and Arumel's the only place I can truly do that."

He chews slowly. "But you care about the whole *controlled destiny* versus *volition* debate, don't you?"

"Honestly? I care because what IUGA did to me was wrong. But I never intended to be the lynchpin in a major inter-universal controversy. I guess it's possible the debate will spur some big change in the world, but I didn't pick this fight."

He leans his head back and takes a deep drink of water. I like watching his throat as he swallows. My stare seems to amuse him but he continues to quiz me.

"Then you believe any attempts to control destiny should be outlawed?"

"Hey, what's with all the questions? I thought you weren't interested in politics."

"I'm not asking from a political perspective. I'm interested in your views on the subject."

"Okay. My view on destiny is pretty simple—no matter how hard we try, destiny will not be controlled. In fact, the more we try to control it, the more it laughs in our face and says *my, my, but you're just making this more interesting.*"

He grins and sets his sandwich on its wrapper. "Well, we agree on that, at least. Which leads me to my next question. Do you believe what I suggested before is possible—that you and I meeting the way we have was our fate all along? That maybe everything that's happened to us from the moment we were born was meant to lead us right here?"

I squint at him. "Have you been maneuvering me into some logical trap?"

He laughs lightly. "I'm not nearly that clever. I just want to know what you think."

"I don't know. It seems unlikely."

He tilts his head. "But still possible?" Something honest and raw shines through his eyes.

My heart gets tangled in my vocal chords, and I drink some water before answering. "Yes, I suppose it's possible."

He nods slowly, and I sense he already believes it's true. I don't know what to believe anymore. I swore off this whole *mirror* thing, but what if he's right? What if he's the one?

"Can I tell you something?" he says.

"I guess so. Go ahead."

"When I saw you walking down the sidewalk this morning, your hair streaming out behind you, the hem of your dress floating on the breeze, it felt like being kissed by the first brilliant rays of sunlight after a long winter's night."

I squint at him. "I thought you said this wasn't going to get awkward."

"Sorry. I didn't mean to embarrass you. I just wanted you to know." He keeps his eyes fastened to mine. "I waited six months to approach you, and I know I'm taking a risk by saying this, but I don't want to wait another six months. Scratch the friend stuff I said earlier. I'm too attracted to you to keep this on a friendship level. I knew it the second I saw that shopkeeper flirting with you. Will you consent to see me—on a more personal basis?"

My chest flutters, and I set my sandwich next to his.

"Ry. Hey, Ry!" a lanky young man in running clothes calls from the pathway.

Ryder looks up, smiles, and waves. "Hold that thought," he says, getting to his feet. "It's an old friend." I watch as he walks to the path, admiring the way his jeans fit him, and wondering how I'm going to answer his question—things seem to be moving so quickly. Maybe it's time to slow them down.

"Blake, how are you man?" Ryder says as they shake hands.

"I'm doing okay. What about you?"

"Can't complain. Fantasy laserball sucks this year, but business is good."

"So I hear. Someone told me the big dogs have been sniffing around looking to buy your outfit."

Ryder tosses his head back and laughs. "Vicious rumors. All the big dogs do is lift their legs and try to piss all over us. Besides why would I sell? I'm having the time of my life."

"You got a great thing going, man. The truth is, I've been meaning to call you. I'm sort of looking around for another job. Things are getting kind of weird where I'm at. Do you think you might have something for me?"

"Sure, come by the office tomorrow," Ryder says, slapping him on the shoulder. "We're always looking for good editors."

"Thanks, man," Blake says with a big grin. "Hey, how's the song writing going? Anything new on the horizon?"

"Nah. Haven't had much time to write lately."

"Well, we need to get together at my place and jam sometime. It's been too long. You can bring your lady." He glances at me for the first time, and his brows pull together. "Hey is that …?"

"No, it's not." Ryder cuts him off. I turn my face away, mortified to be mistaken for Ryder's dead wife.

"But she looks just like …"

"It's not, Blake."

"… that Transcender lady, Jaden Beckett," he finishes his sentence. I smile to myself for jumping to the wrong conclusion.

"Just come by tomorrow, man. I gotta go."

FIFTY-SIX

Ryder turns away from the path and saunters back to the blanket."How about a walk?" he says, holding out a hand for me.

"Sure. Can we leave our things here?"

"Yeah. No one will bother them."

We stroll side by side along the path circling the pond. "Sorry about that back there," he says. "You probably get recognized all the time."

"Don't worry about it. So your friends call you *Ry*?"

"Yep. Childhood nickname that stuck."

The swans glide over to us hoping for food. "Oh, I didn't bring anything for the swans." I glance back at our lunch on the blanket.

"It's all right. They get fed too much anyway. Before you know it, you got overweight swans, and then what do you do?"

"I don't know. Send them to Duck Zumba?"

He barks a short laugh. "Or maybe stock up on swan Spanx."

"Ha! Even better." I like his off-beat sense of humor. "So what instrument do you play?"

"Guitar ... and badly. It takes talent and time to practice, neither of which I possess. A couple of my songs have been picked up and recorded by other bands, though."

"A songwriter too, huh? Would I have heard any of them?"

"I don't know. Are you familiar with the Killers?"

My mouth drops open. "The Killers recorded one of your songs?"

He shoves his hands in his pockets. "Nah, I'm just trying to impress you. Someone who used to play backup for the Killers recorded one of my songs. It hasn't gotten much air time yet."

"That's amazing, but you really don't need to try to impress me."

"Seriously? You're like a rock star. A super-Transcender who took on big bad IUGA and kicked their ass. Obviously I'm going to try to sweep you off your feet."

"That's nice, but I hope you know that's not really me."

He glances at me sideways and reaches for my hand. My pulse quickens at his touch. "I'd like to know more," he says.

When the pavement ends, Ryder leads me to a grove of shady trees with a small bench beneath. He turns to me and gently takes my face in his hands. My knees feel unsure of themselves.

"You were about to tell me if you'll consent to see me on more than a casual basis," he says brushing the pad of one thumb along my lower lip. My heart pounds wildly, and a pleasurable tingle runs down my spine. I look up into his eyes, certain he's about to kiss me. Instead, he just grins.

"What?" I say.

"You have chocolate on your mouth."

"Oh, nice. That must be attractive." I run my tongue along my lip.

"It is to me. I love the taste of chocolate."

Either this guy's a huge tease or he's completely unaware of the effect he has on me. Doesn't matter, because I'm not shy about taking what I want, and I've made up my mind, I want him.

I wrap my hand around his neck and bring his mouth down to meet mine. His lips are warm and salty-sweet. He's tentative or maybe startled at first, but then he circles my waist with his arms and pulls me close, his tongue flickering across my lips. My mouth parts and he deepens the kiss, pressing his body into mine. I think my heart may explode inside my chest, and I'm sure my brain isn't receiving any oxygen. *So much for going slow.*

I move away slightly, allowing him an escape in case I'm being too forward, but his mouth follows mine, nipping my lower lip, coaxing, renewing the kiss. When we finally pull apart, he beams.

"Uh, wow. That was … pleasantly unexpected."

"Does it answer your question?"

"I'd say it does, unless I was just the recipient of the most amazing goodbye kiss in the history of mankind."

I smile and shake my head. "It wasn't goodbye."

"God, I hope not." He pushes a wayward lock of hair off his forehead. "Because I'd sure like to do that again sometime."

He pulls me over to the bench and we sit together, our knees touching. Taking both my hands in his, he looks deeply into my eyes. "There is one thing, though … I need to know if you consider me only a faint reflection of the husband you lost."

"I don't. Not at all." I study his face. "But what about you? Do you think of me as an echo of your late wife?"

He raises his eyes skyward for a moment and sighs. "She was an indescribably fine person, as I suspect you are," he says quietly. "But she was just a girl when she passed—a bit timid and almost achingly vulnerable. You are none of those things. It's your spirit that draws me to you."

"That's good to hear." I smile and raise my hand to his cheek. "I don't know what you and I were or will be to each other, but I'm ready to see where this will take us."

"You can't imagine how happy that makes me," he says, covering my hand with his own.

"Unfortunately, it's going to have to wait," I say. "I leave tomorrow on exploration, and I'm not sure when I'll be back."

He lowers his head, deflated. "Man, my timing really sucks. You're sure you have to leave tomorrow?"

"'Fraid so, but I'll call as soon as I'm back. I promise."

He laces his fingers through mine. "Will you call me while you're away?"

"If it's possible, but I'm not sure what to expect on the earth we're visiting."

"So what are you doing tonight?" he asks, a playful gleam in his eye.

"I'm sorry to say, I still have a million things to do before I leave. In fact, I'd probably better get back soon or I'll be up all night. Shall we finish our lunch?"

We walk hand-in-hand back to the picnic blanket. The atmosphere between us has palpably changed. We met for a picnic as friends and now we're dating, with all the wonderful and scary implications that go along with that.

Ryder stretches out and watches me while I finish my sandwich.

"You're not hungry?" I ask.

"I just want to soak up these last few minutes with you. They're going to have to last me for a while."

My cheeks flush under his gaze, and I begin wrapping up the

leftovers. We stuff everything back into the brown bag and fold up the blanket together. He takes my hand again as we follow the path back to the main entrance.

"So, I'm told you have a very high illuminosity," he says as we walk.

"Eleanor needs to quit talking about me."

"Well, it comes through strongly when you touch me. I feel it now holding your hand, and the kiss, well that was … nuclear fission."

"I've got news for you, it runs both ways."

"Really? You feel it too?"

"I do, but not with everybody. In fact, not with anybody …but you." *Now.*

"I like that." He squeezes my hand. We pass through the main gate and onto the sidewalk.

"I had a really nice time. I wish I wasn't leaving tomorrow," I say.

"At least let me walk you home."

I hesitate. My plan is to stop by the art studio on my way home and pick up my restored sketch. It's too much to try to explain to him. "Actually, I have a stop to make before I head home— something to pick up."

"I don't mind, if you'd like company."

I shake my head. "I need to do this by myself, but thanks."

"All right. Please call me if you can." His eyes reflect the sadness at parting that I feel inside. I lean in to kiss his cheek and he draws me close. "Stay safe." His warm breath tickles my ear.

FIFTY-SEVEN

It's all I can do not to skip down the sidewalk like a child. I'm completely Ryder-stoned and high on the mind-blowing afternoon.

In my distracted state, I almost miss the small side street where the art studio is located. I catch myself just in time and hurry toward the colorful storefront. As I cross a little alley and step onto the sidewalk in front of the store, something jerks me backward, and a cold, hard object snaps around my neck. *A dog collar.* Panic swells inside me, but my startled scream is muffled by a large gloved hand pressed roughly over my mouth. My attempt to spontaneously shift to the Chateau is futile, as I knew it would be.

I claw at the giant mitt over my mouth, kicking and twisting to get free. A massive arm vises around my shoulders, and I'm violently dragged backward through the alley and into a stand of dense bushes.

My attacker forces me to the ground and pins my arms under his knees. He leans his face close to mine. Instead of the automaton I expect to see, I'm confronted with something barely human. Its lips draw back baring yellow and brown teeth.

"Jaden Beckett?" The voice is deep and growly, the breath noxious. Sunken coal black eyes stare out at me from a mass of wiry black whiskers.

In response, I shriek my lungs out. His meaty gloved fist

smashes into my nose. Rockets of pain shoot through my head, and I choke on my own blood.

"Shut up," he croaks, tugging off one glove. He jams the foul tasting leathery thing into my mouth. Ryder's face floats across my mind. All I can think is: *I don't want to die. Not now.*

My knowledge of self defense screams for me to get out from under him fast, but my efforts to flip on my side and wrench myself free fail miserably. The gargantuan ape man succeeds in keeping me pinned. He's too large for me to try a headlock with my legs, so I continue to buck and squirm, hoping to free one of my hands and maybe use my illuminosity on him. All I succeed in doing is emptying my pockets of my polycom and lip gloss.

My poly! If I can push the red alarm button someone will come.

Although my arms are pinned, I open my palm and concentrate all my effort on willing the polycom to come to me. It sails into my left hand, but before I can press the button, Ape Man seizes my wrist and wrenches it until it snaps. The pain is agonizing. The phone tumbles to the ground once again.

He ignores the polycom and brutally yanks the TPD bracelet off my mangled limb. Clicking it open, he scans the inside. "Jaden Beckett," he reads aloud. The satisfaction in his voice curdles my blood. "I knew it was you." He tosses the bracelet aside.

All awareness of pain vanishes now as I numbly watch him draw a long blade from the sheath at his side. "Shall I carve up your pretty face or just do you the quick way?"

A strange calmness descends on me. *So, this is what it's like to die.*

Using both hands, he raises the weapon high. "No time for fun today."

A streaking flash of yellow fur pounces on Ape Man's back with a snarling growl. Fierce jaws snap and rip at his neck. The Ape Man grunts, and his blade falls away, clunking to the ground beside me.

My screams for Callie to run are dammed up against the gag in my mouth. The Ape Man clutches at her. He wrestles her from his back and violently hurls her against a tree trunk. She yelps pitifully before her lifeless body thuds to the ground. My heart bursts inward with a fury I've never known.

I whip my head to the side, and a roar from deep within me propels the glove from my mouth. Then I turn my wrath on Ape Man "GET OFF," I bellow.

Remarkably, he's blown a hundred feet backward. I don't know if the force came from my throat or my chest, or someplace else, but it worked.

With my limbs now free, I flip onto my stomach and scrabble across the ground groping for his fallen weapon. Ape Man is momentarily stunned, but rapidly recovers and quickly closes the distance between us. He grips my ankle and jerks me back toward him. Rolling onto my back, I raise my palm but realize I'll be carried along with him if I send him soaring now. Instead, I ram my foot into his face. The heel of my sandal pierces his eye, and blood spurts from the socket, splattering me and gushing down his hairy cheek. He yowls in pain, hands flying to his wound.

I jump to my feet, and scoop up the weapon, bracing for another attack. Ape Man extracts a small knife from the side of his boot and charges me in a half-blind, half-berserk frenzy. I hold my ground as he lunges toward me. Feinting to his blind side, I draw the razor sharp blade across the back of his leg, severing the tendons behind his knee.

He stumbles for one heartbeat, then two, and at last crumples to the ground.

Searching the grass, I spot my polycom. It flies into my good hand, and I manage to press the red emergency button. "Help me, please. Emergency. Emergency. Somebody, help me," I plead.

Not waiting for a response, I cram the poly back into my pocket and take up the weapon again, preparing for another onslaught. It's clear, though, that Ape Man isn't going anywhere. He awkwardly pulls himself up to a sitting position, blood puddling on the ground beneath his leg.

I point the blade menacingly at him. "If you killed my dog, you'll pay for it."

His lips draw back in a smarmy sneer. "Go ahead and do it. I'm dead anyway."

Urick lands at my side with barely a sound. "Jesus, Mary, and Joseph," he says. "What happened to you?"

My dress hangs in shreds and my nose and mouth are oozing blood. I gesture with the blade toward my assailant. Urick's lupine eyes flare. "Garugian," he mutters, as if the word tastes like excrement. He assesses my condition. "Are you all right?"

"I think my wrist is broken," I say, holding my left arm close to my side. "And probably my nose, but other than that, I'm okay."

"I will take care of this filth. Go to the Chateau. Find Narowyn."

"No. Callie's hurt, maybe dead. I'm staying with her." The weapon falls from my fingers, and I trudge to the tree where Callie lies, dreading what I may find.

Urick uses his polycom to summon his team members. "Roper, bring Nila and come at once."

I kneel at Callie's side and lay my hand on her chest, unsure if she's still breathing, "Callie," I croak, tears pouring down my cheeks. "Please be okay." I rest my ear near her heart and believe I pick up a faint beat.

Nila rushes to my side. "Jade, what happened?"

"A Garugian, I guess. Callie needs help."

She quickly places a call for assistance. "Help is on the way," she says. "They advised us not to move her. I'll stay until they come. But you need to have your injuries tended to."

"After Callie," I say, using the back of my hand to swipe the blood and tears from my face.

"At least let me take that collar off you." She reaches for the metal dog collar still locked around my neck. I lift my hair, and she unlatches it from the back and chucks it into the bushes. We sit on the ground on either side of Callie. I stroke her head gently and whisper desperate prayers into the ether. *Please let her be okay. Please let her be okay.*

Urick and Roper secure the hands of the Garugian, and we watch as they question him. He's belligerent at first, cursing and spitting, but after a few minutes he calms and seems to be answering questions. Roper takes out his polycom and snaps some photos of the scene. The Ape Man hangs his head, using his greasy long hair as a curtain to hide his face.

"What are they doing?" I ask Nila.

"I don't know. Maybe trying to get a recorded statement."

The Garugian vehemently shakes his head and refuses to look up while Roper attempts to record him. After a minute, Roper stows the device back in his jacket. The Garugian holds up his bound hands pleadingly to Urick. I'm shocked when Urick uses his Throkken to slice through the plastic wrist restraints, freeing the man's hands.

"They're not letting him go are they?" I ask in disbelief.

"No. You may not want to watch this." Nila lays her hand on my arm.

But I can't tear my eyes away as Urick passes his Throkken to the wounded Garugian. The man grips the hilt with both hands and plunges the blade into his own abdomen, making a slicing motion from left to right. His body topples forward onto the ground.

"Oh my god, he killed himself," I cry. "Why did they let him do it?"

Nila shrugs. "Garugians are wanted dead or alive by IGLE. His own people would have killed him anyway for failing at his mission. It's their code."

"What the hell is IGLE?"

"Inter-Galaxy Law Enforcement."

"Geeze. So they don't mess with any of the niceties like a trial or anything?"

"Not for their ilk." She gestures toward the body. "Garugians know the price when they claim the title."

Two men in white scrubs, carrying a small stretcher appear at the edge of the clearing. The sight of the Garugian stops them dead in their tracks. They glance warily at each other and then continue on toward Nila and me.

"Looks like you've had some trouble here," a man with thinning brown hair and worried eyes says. "Is that a Garugian?"

"Yes," Nila says. "Did you come about the injured dog?"

"She's right here." I get to my feet. "Hurry, please."

While the men work quickly to strap Callie onto the portable stretcher, I explain what happened to her.

The brown-haired man uses an instrument to scan Callie's chip for her vital signs. He gently runs his hands along her legs. "Her pulse is weak. She may have a broken bone or two and possibly some internal injuries," he says. "We'll take her to the veterinary hospital. Would you like us to call you?"

"Yes. She's … I'm … we adopted each other. Please save her."

"We'll do the best we can, ma'am. Where can we reach you?"

"At the Chateau du Soleil. I'm Jaden Beckett. How do I reach you?"

He pulls a card from his pocket and hands it to me. "Pardon me for saying so, but you look like you could use some medical attention yourself."

I examine his card. His name is Dr. Milo Lane of the Countryside Veterinary Hospital. "I know. I just wanted to make sure she was taken care of first. Thanks for coming so quickly, Dr. Lane."

The two men carry Callie from the clearing as Urick joins Nila and me. He replaces the bloody Throkken in its scabbard.

"This is for you." Urick dangles a metal chain with a disc attached.

"What is it?" I ask, taking it from him.

"ID tag for the pile of dung that tried to kill you. He told us who hired him, but he wouldn't say it on video."

"He told you? Who was it?" I ask.

"Director Canto, himself." Urick's eyes burn with disgust.

"Oh God, do you believe him?"

"He had no reason to lie. I promised I would let him use my blade if he gave us the name. We'll deposit the body with IGLE."

It's all too much to process. The director hires a Garugian to murder me. The man commits seppuku right in front of me. What next?

My knees wobble precariously. "I think I need some help now."

Nila grasps my uninjured arm. "Hold on to me," she says, and *Zzzt.*

FIFTY-EIGHT

We alight in the middle of Narowyn's office. She flies to my side. "Good God. What's happened?"

"Garugian attack," Nila says.

Narowyn eases me down into one of her chairs. "Are you certain? A Garugian in Arumel City? It's unheard of."

"The body's in an area on the edge of Kistlethorn Park if you want to see it," Nila says.

"Who's with it?" Narowyn asks.

"Urick and Roper. They're waiting for the rest of the team to transport it to IGLE."

"I'll see to Jaden's injuries. You may join your team if you wish. Ask Urick to return as soon as possible, though. I'll need a full report."

"Yes, ma'am." Nila vanishes.

"Can you stand, dear?" Narowyn supports me as I get to my feet. "I'm taking you to the infirmary." She clamps an arm around my waist and *Zzzt*.

The infirmary is bright and completely deserted. Narowyn helps me onto an examination table, and lowers the lights. I realize I'm still clinging to the Garugian ID tag Urick gave me.

"Will you put this somewhere safe for me?" I hold it out for her. "Oh, and Callie got in the middle of the fight. She's at the veterinary hospital. I need to know as soon as Dr. Lane calls."

Narowyn pales as she removes the tag from my hand. "I'm so terribly sorry about all this, Jaden. I assure you we'll ferret out who is responsible for hiring this assassin."

"He already told Urick it was Director Canto."

She clutches the colorful crystal beads hanging at her breast. "He actually disclosed that the director hired him?"

"Yes. But he refused to say it on video. So after they got all they could from him, Urick lent him his Throkken and the guy gutted himself. We just sat there and watched him do it. I don't get it. It's completely crazy." I close my eyes, trying to blot the image from my memory.

"I know it seems unconscionable, dear. I'm certain it was terribly disturbing, but that is their code. If they fail in a mission, they either take their own life or it is taken for them. His death was a foregone conclusion." She makes it sound so normal. Like the guy just turned in his resignation.

Narowyn slips on a pair of latex gloves and removes an instrument from a white cabinet in the corner. "This will show us the extent of your injuries." She grasps the handle and passes it up and down both sides of my injured arm while watching the screen.

"You have a clean fracture of the radius, just here." She shows me on the screen. The tiny break appears to be just above my wrist.

"Although, it's not a complex fracture, it is severe. To treat it, we'll inject the bone with an osteo-adhesive to stabilize it while it heals. You'll need to wear a cuff for a week or two. I suggest you wear your TPD on your other wrist. Where is your bracelet, by the way?"

"Oh god, it's back where I was attacked. Can you ask Urick to find it for me?"

"I'll get Dr. McDonald to send someone. She has all the devices on her tracking system."

She lifts my arm gently. "I'm placing your wrist in a brace. It's quite important that you keep it absolutely still during the procedure. The injections must be precise."

Narowyn sets the brace on the table and places my wrist inside, tightening it to hold everything in place. She rolls a piece of equipment to the side of the table and positions it over my wrist. It looks like a flat screen TV on wheels.

"This is a type of x-ray," she says. "It shows me if I'm positing the needle accurately. We wouldn't want the bone to fuse incorrectly." She pushes the needle into my wrist a few times injecting the glue into the bone. It burns for a few seconds, but then my wrist feels numb.

After rolling the screen out of the way, she brings over a hard plastic splint with Velcro straps. "This is your cuff. You may take it off to bathe, but it's important that you sleep in it at night, and no strenuous activity, please. Fencing is out of the question."

"All right, I'll baby it for a while. What about my nose?"

"Let's have a look." She gently probes my face with her gloved fingers. Then she runs the hand-held instrument above my nose and cheeks.

"You have a minor nasal fracture. I don't notice any disfigurement, so it won't need to be reset. Once the swelling recedes, though, if you believe something is not quite right, we'll take further steps."

"Should I put ice on it?"

"You can if you like, but I have a remarkable new medication here that's very effective at reducing the swelling, bruising, and soreness. It requires facial injections, though."

"Wait, what? You have to stick needles in my face?"

"I'm afraid so, dear. It's not very painful if we use numbing gel. The needle is quite thin."

"Okay," I reluctantly agree, "if you're sure it works."

She gently swabs the blood from my face with cotton pads and then rubs cool numbing gel across my nose and cheeks. We wait ten minutes before she begins injecting me with the miracle medicine. It's not so bad, really.

Once she's finished, Narowyn helps me to a sitting position on the table. "Give me a moment to put these things away, and I'll take you upstairs."

"All right, but I need to talk to you about something else."

"Certainly, dear. What is it?" She sits in one of the infirmary chairs, her eyes searching mine.

I clear my throat. "Something happened out there with the Garugian that I don't completely understand. It's happened before, and Luci, Dr. McDonald, has been helping me figure it out. It's time you knew about it."

"What is it? What happened?" Her brows knit together.

"It's weird, and you're going to think it sounds impossible because that guy probably weighed around three hundred pounds. But he sat right on top of me, and I couldn't move until he hurt Callie. Then something in me snapped—like all this collected fury exploded. Anyway, I shouted at him to get off, and he just flew backward, like from the force of an explosion."

She cocks her head. "And you feel you somehow caused that to happen?"

"I know I did. I've done it before."

"Goodness, when?"

"Remember when that automaton attacked me at the palace, and

523

I told you he was inexplicably thrown back against the wall? It was the same thing that time, and also when I was attacked in Madison. Except those times I pointed my palm at them and shouted. Luci's working with me to try to control it. I've gotten to where I can deliberately move objects around with my hand. I'm sorry I didn't tell you before, but I've been kind of freaked out about it."

She raises her eyebrows. "Yes, I can imagine. Does Dr. McDonald have a theory as to how it works?"

"Kind of. She says it has something to do with my illuminosity. She thinks I stumbled on a way to concentrate it and use it. Her theory is that everyone has the ability, it's a matter of learning to harness it."

Narowyn nods. "To be honest, I've heard of this before. Stories exist of past Transcenders who were reported to have possessed similar powers. It hasn't been attributed to anyone in hundreds of years, but it may have something to do with your elevated illuminosity. It seems to manifest itself during times of great stress."

"That's what Luci says, but she thinks I can use it in other ways when everything is calm. I've been making some progress."

Our heads turn toward the door as Asher bursts into the infirmary. "Jade, I just heard. Are you okay?" He rushes to my side "Was it really a Garugian?"

"That's what Urick says."

"What did he do to you? You look awful."

"Asher, that's not particularly helpful," Narowyn says.

"I'm sorry, but it looks like it hurts." He raises his fingertips to my swollen cheek.

"Narowyn fixed me all up. I'll be okay. Callie's badly hurt, though. I'm waiting to hear from the vet."

"Asher," Narowyn says, "Jaden and I were in the middle of a conversation that we need to finish. I plan to set up a meeting for later regarding our strategy for responding to this latest attack. I'd like you both to attend, but we need a few minutes alone right now."

"Ash kind of knows about this," I say. "I talked to him about it in Connecticut."

"Talked to me about what?" he asks.

"You know that thing I did with my hand to that automaton."

"It happened again?"

"Yeah and … well look." I stretch out my right arm and aim my palm toward a tray of medical instruments on the counter. I concentrate on the tray for a few seconds and then raise my arm. The tray lifts off the counter and becomes level with my arm. I hear Narowyn's sharp intake of breath.

I use my mind to draw the tray toward me. It glides smoothly into my hand. Then I release it and send it back across the room. I employ a little too much force on the return trip, though, and some instruments bounce and spill from the tray as it thuds onto the counter. "Oops."

"Holy shit!" Asher says. "When did you learn to do that?"

"I've been practicing, but I'm really better at bringing things to me. They always zoom away a little too hard."

Narowyn comes to my side. "Good Lord, Jaden, this is remarkable. We must certainly delve deeper into this—when you're feeling better, of course." She smoothes a motherly hand across my hair. "We'll have some time to work on it in the coming weeks. I'm afraid you're not in any condition to go on exploration tomorrow. You need to rest and recuperate."

"After today," Asher says, "it looks like you're not safe going on exploration—or anywhere else in the galaxy, for that matter."

Narowyn shoots him another *you're not being helpful* look. "Asher, would you please see Jaden to her apartment so she can shower and change before our meeting? I'll clean up in here."

"Sure." Ash holds my right arm and helps me down from the table.

I know he's just worried about me, but his ominous words fill my head with anxious thoughts. *Will I ever feel safe here or anywhere again?* If IUGA is willing to risk attacking me here in Arumel, they won't hesitate to track me down on another earth. Cold dread fills me up inside at the thought of living under constant guard again. I'll escape to a galaxy far far away if that's what I need to do to be free. I'll take Callie with me, and maybe Ralston will come too.

But my insistent heart pushes memories of the afternoon with Ryder into my mind, pleading with me to find another way.

Asher walks me to the elevator and punches the button for the third floor. "So, do you rent yourself out for parties and bar mitzvahs?" He gives me a sideways smile.

"Not funny, Ash. This just makes me a bigger freak than I was before. You know Narowyn won't rest until she figures out how this works."

"Hey, I'm just playing with you because I'm jealous. I wish I could do that. Do you really think I could learn how?"

"I don't know. That's what Luci says." I take hold of his arm and look him in the eye. "Do you really think I'm not safe anywhere in the galaxy?"

"Oh, hell, Jade, I'm sorry if I stepped on my tongue. I didn't mean to upset you." The elevator doors open and we step out. "We'll find a way to keep you safe. Your afternoon was bad enough. Please don't stress about that right now."

When we reach my apartment, he opens my door. "Was the picnic nice at least?"

"Actually, it was very nice." I step inside and shuck what's left of my jacket onto the floor.

"That's awesome. So, you're going to see him again?" Ash follows me inside.

"I think I might."

"Come on spill it. What's he like? Is he an okay guy?" His curiosity's kind of endearing, even if he is being annoyingly nosy.

"Yeah, he's kind of cool. He has a little film production company and he writes songs. He's not really much like my Ryder at all."

"Is that good or bad?"

"Don't know yet. I guess time will——." The ringing phone interrupts me.

"Countryside Veterinary Hospital calling," Vasa says.

"Put it through." I glance anxiously at Asher.

"Miss Beckett, it's Dr. Lane."

"Hi Doctor, how's Callie?"

"We just finished surgery. She had some internal contusions, and we needed to remove her spleen, but she'll be able to function without it just fine. She's resting comfortably now. We'd like to keep her for a few days. After that I believe she'll be ready to go home."

Whew. "That's great. When can I see her?"

"Give her tonight to recover. You can come by and check on her tomorrow morning."

"Thanks so much Dr. Lane."

"No problem. Have a good evening," he says and ends the call.

"Well, that's good news, at least," Asher says.

"I called on every angel and deity known to man to help her. Someone must have heard me. I'm just so relieved." I kick off my shoes. "There's food and drink in the fridge. I'm going to grab a shower."

"Need any help?" he asks.

"Ha ha. Don't let Nila hear you talking like that."

"She knows I'm a harmless flirt. Seriously though, Jade, you holding up okay? Don't you want to rest for a few minutes?"

"Honestly, I'm kind of numb right now. As long as Callie's going to be okay, I'll find a way to deal with the rest of this."

The hot shower feels like a baptism of sorts. I thought I was dead, but I somehow survived and received a new shot at life once again. I don't want to blow that. And I also don't want anyone else dictating my future. I mean how many second chances does a person get?

All the filth and scum of the bloody fight washes away from my body and my spirits lighten. Maybe I can find a way to stick around long enough to figure out if Ryder is part of a new beginning for me. I can't let Canto drive me away. I refuse to let IUGA win after all I've been through.

I slip on a pair of jeans and a t-shirt and blow out my hair. My face looks slightly better than it did before. Narowyn's magic meds must be kicking in. I dab concealer under my bruised eyes and apply a coat of lip gloss. The stiff splint for my wrist is a little tricky to put on with only one hand, but I eventually secure it in place.

Ash knocks on the bathroom door as I'm finishing up. "Jade, there's someone here to see you."

"I'll be right out."

"When I reach the kitchen, I'm shocked to see Eve and Asher in quiet conversation with Ryder Blackthorn.

"Ryder?"

"I had to come. I hope it's okay." He looks harassed.

An involuntary grin spreads across my face, at the same time unexpected tears spring to my eyes. I didn't know how much I needed to see him.

He reaches me in two strides and folds me in his arms. "Thank

528

god you're all right. How did this happen?"

"It was a hired killer. He was stalking me." I burrow deeper into his arms, and he rests his cheek on the top of my head. We stand in silence, shrouded in unutterable emotions—the fear, hope, and pain of loss—that only we two can understand.

"Uh, Jaden?" Asher says, like *remember us?*

Eve takes hold of his arm. "I think we should go now." She drags him toward the door. "Nice to see you, Ry."

"But, but …" Asher protests.

Eve squints at him, one eyebrow raised. "Get going." She motions to the open door. "Jade, I'll let Narowyn know you'll be along in a bit."

"Thanks," I say, still clinging to Ryder.

He cups a hand under my chin. "Let me see what he did to you."

"I look hideous."

"You look beautiful." He places a whisper of a kiss on my nose. "Asher says you have a meeting to go to, but can you spare a few minutes to tell me what happened? Eve called and told me you'd been attacked. That's all I really know."

Good old Eve. For once I don't mind her being all up in my business.

I take Ryder's hand, and we sit together on my couch while I explain what happened after we parted. I leave nothing out, but I gloss over the part where I sent the Garugian soaring through the air.

When I'm finished with the whole account, he shakes his head in amazement. "God, Jade, it's a miracle you're alive. But how did you get the guy off of you so you could grab his weapon? Did you use your martial arts or something?"

I'm tempted to say *yes*, but I'll have to tell him the truth eventually. "I know I never mentioned it before, but I recently found out I have this kind of strange power."

"Stranger than traveling to parallel worlds?"

I only half-laugh. "No, not really. It's a telekinetic kind of thing. Dr. McDonald thinks it has something to do with concentrating my illuminosity in order to move things. Anyway, when he hurt Callie I went crazy inside. I pushed up against him and screamed at him to get off me. He just went flying. I was as shocked as he was."

Ryder looks uncertain. "Can you show me what you mean? Can you safely do it here?"

"Sure." I scan the room for something unbreakable. Pulling a decorative pillow from the chair, I give it to him. "Hold this up."

He lifts it by the corner, dangling it in the air. I aim my palm and send the pillow rocketing out of his hand. It hits the wall and explodes. Stuffing flies everywhere.

"I really haven't perfected my technique yet." I rub my palms against my jeans.

"Damn. And you can do that to a three hundred pound man?"

"Apparently so." I hold my breath waiting for his judgment.

"You're one amazing lady, Jade. Any other powers I should be aware of?"

"Nope. Sorry. That's it."

He lifts my hand, his eyes a dark, turbulent sea. "Listen, I know you can take care of yourself. But this isn't something to be taken lightly. What're the Transcenders planning to do about this? We have to make sure it never happens again."

I like the way he includes himself in that. "It's not that easy. That's why we're meeting downstairs. We have no real proof that Canto hired the Garugian. It's his word against ours. The law's not very helpful in such cases, as we've discovered in the past."

Asher's words of warning echo in my ears. "It's only fair that I tell you, if we can't come up with a workable solution, I may need to leave Arumel to be safe."

"Whoa, whoa, wait a minute." His spine goes rigid. "There's got to be a better way. Maybe it's time you found a more creative solution."

"Like what?"

He rubs his thumb across the top of my hand. "I don't know, but running away will only encourage him. The director obviously has no problem ignoring the law for his own purposes. Handling this outside the available legal channels may be the best option."

My mouth falls open. "You're not suggesting we put a contract out on him?"

"God no. What he did was deplorable. I'm only suggesting that the Transcenders have certain powers that far exceed the director's. You just demonstrated that very effectively." He nods to the pile of pillow stuffing on my floor. "Canto feels threatened by you in more ways than one. Maybe you can use that to your advantage."

"I'm not sure I know what you mean."

"I'm not sure either, but bringing the police in on this is like asking the poodles to protect the pit bulls. If I had powers like yours I wouldn't take shit off of anybody. All I know is, the director's making reckless moves because he's scared. Fear is a powerful weapon, Jade. He who controls the fear, controls the game."

"I hadn't really looked at it like that before."

His fingertips gently skim across my bruised cheek sending goose bumps down my arms. "Just please don't go."

"Believe me, I don't want to." I wonder how he'd feel if he knew that it was his face I saw when I thought I was about to die. "Anyway, one good thing has come out of this. I'm not leaving on exploration after all."

He grins. "Does that mean I can see you tomorrow? Will you go to dinner with me?"

"I'd rather not go out looking like this, but we could fix something here."

"Sounds great. Let's not cook, though. I'll pick something up. Do you like Andalusian food?"

"I've never had it."

"Up for something new?"

"Sure."

"It's a date then." He gets to his feet and hoists me up by my good hand. "Is seven okay?"

"Yes, and bring your guitar."

He winces. "Okay, but don't expect too much."

We walk to my door, and I turn to him. "It was sweet of you to check on me, Ry. It means a lot." His nickname tastes strange on my tongue, but it suits him—easy and light.

"I feel responsible in a small way. You had been with me. I should have seen you safely to your door."

"The guy was a paid assassin. He would have found me sooner or later."

He tenderly takes my face in his hands. "Would it hurt badly if I kissed you?"

"It would hurt worse if you didn't."

His lips brush mine, soft as a feather—once, then twice. I tremble at their whisper touch. Then he circles my waist with one arm, gently bringing me in closer. His luscious mouth covers mine and he moves so sweetly, so carefully. My whole body groans for more. After the day I've had, restraint be damned. My good hand grips the back of his neck and I curve into him, kissing him for all I'm worth. He gets the message, and his mouth responds to mine with a fierce need. A low moan issues from his throat and vibrates all the way to my bones.

When we finally break for air, I feel dizzy, and thoroughly kissed. "Thanks," I say breathlessly. "That should last me until tomorrow."

FIFTY-NINE

The euphoria of Ryder's core-jolting kiss quickly fades as I approach Narowyn's office door. The room feels stuffy and over-crowded with Watterson, Urick, Nila, Asher, Luci, Ralston, and my two lawyers already waiting inside. A palpable tension permeates the air.

Luci stops me at the door and holds out my bracelet. "Hey, SG. Sorry about what happened to you this afternoon. You holdin' up okay?"

"Yeah. It looks worse than it is." She helps me fasten the bracelet around my right wrist.

"Narowyn asked me to return this to you also." She places the dead Garugian's ID tag in my palm.

"Uh, thanks." I shove it in my pocket.

Narowyn motions me inside. "Come in, Jaden. You're the last to arrive. Would you mind closing the door?"

I do as she asks and take the remaining empty seat.

Standing in front of her desk, Narowyn addresses the group. "Thank you all for coming. Our goal here tonight is to devise a united and forceful strategy for dealing with the Garugian attack on Jaden earlier today. To state our quandary succinctly, we know that

534

Director Canto was responsible for the attack, but we are hindered in filing a criminal complaint against him by the fact that we have no direct evidence of his involvement.

"Director Canto's motivation may have been revenge for the IGC Court's order or a desire to prevent Jaden from harming IUGA in the future. Regardless, his actions indicate a man on the edge, willing to go to extremes to achieve his ends."

Narowyn scans the faces in the room, her expression stony. "At this point I am open to any suggestions as to how we may put an end to this insanity once and for all."

"If I may, Chief," Watterson speaks up. "This guy's got to be put away for a long time. Jaden won't be safe until he is. You're right when you say we don't have enough for the locals to arrest him, but what if the Transcender Police arrest him?"

"On what grounds?" Narowyn asks. "We don't have jurisdiction unless the crime involves another dimension. That's not the case here."

"I believe we can make a strong argument that since Canto traveled to another dimension to hire the Garugian, that makes it a Transcender matter," Watterson says. "We've always had jurisdiction when the Garugians are involved."

"Yes, but we don't know if he did that," Ted says. "The Garugian may have been hired right here. The jurisdictional lines in Arumel are tightly drawn. We'd have a huge fight with local law enforcement if we tried to cross that line. In addition, with no direct evidence of Canto's involvement, the case will eventually get tossed out anyway."

"Maybe so," Watterson says. "But we can put him away until his lawyers get him out. We have all kinds of ways to delay his release for a good long while."

"It would have to be handled delicately," Ted says, grasping the arms of his chair. "We don't want the Transcenders to come off looking worse to the public than IUGA does."

"Is there any way the Garugians would provide us with the evidence we need?" Corinne asks.

A few muffled chuckles rise from the group.

"Not a chance," Narowyn says. "Transcenders are the Garugians' sworn enemies. Not to mention that it would kill their business—no pun intended. Who would hire them again if they helped us?"

"Well, at a minimum, Jade needs to have a guard around her whenever she leaves the Chateau," Asher says.

Narowyn's gaze settles on me. "Yes, I'm afraid that's true, and we can't chance sending you on exploration until this is resolved."

"No!" I say springing to my feet. "You can't make me a prisoner in the Chateau. I'll leave if I have to, rather than be guarded around the clock."

"Well, it's not safe back in Connecticut," Asher says. "They know where your dad lives."

"This is crazy." Frustration burns a hole in my chest. "Don't we have any recourse to the IGC Court?"

"We can try going to them, but I doubt we'll get anywhere," Ted says. "They've already ordered IUGA to wind up their business here and get out. We just don't have the required proof. It's only Urick and Roper recounting what a Garugian told them. The court won't lock up someone on that basis alone—especially the Director of IUGA.

"I don't accept that," I say. "You're telling me Canto can hire someone to kill me, and I can't do a thing about it? If that's true, I have no choice but to disappear. You told me I'd be safe in Arumel. You told me it was the only safe place for me."

Narowyn holds up her hands to quiet the discussion. "Jaden, I know this is upsetting for you. You've already had enough trauma for one day. Perhaps we should table this conversation for tonight and take it up again tomorrow."

She turns to Watterson. "Captain, please do some further research on the jurisdictional issues. Perhaps your suggestion that the Transcender Police step in will buy us some time until we can come up with a longer-term solution. In the meantime, I'll reach out to my contacts at IGLE, maybe they'll have some suggestions. It wouldn't hurt to get them involved since the Garugians are now part of the equation."

Luci pipes up for the first time. "I think I can rig up some kind of early warning system to let us know if any Garugian ever enters this dimension again. We have all of their imprints. I can program the system to send out an alarm if one of them gets within six thousand miles of Arumel City."

"That would be helpful Dr. McDonald. Thank you," Narowyn says. "Please all of you, put some thought into this, and let me know if you come up with any other ideas. It doesn't matter how outlandish they may be, any thoughts will be appreciated. Thank you for coming."

My spirits plummet as I trudge for the door. I can't believe this is happening. Just when I thought I'd found my permanent home, just when I thought I had another shot at happiness, my world comes crashing down again. I stand to lose everything once again. A dark despair worms its way into my heart, threatening to overwhelm me.

Ted and Corinne stop me to say how sorry they are about the attack. I thank them for their concern and slip out the door.

Ralston stops me in the hall before I reach the stairs. "Jaden, are you all right?" he asks, his forehead lined with concern.

"No, I'm not all right. I thought things were better here. But it seems I'll never be safe anywhere ever again."

"It's not as black as all that, old girl. Shall we have some tea and talk about it?"

"Not tonight, Rals. I need time to figure this out. I'm not good company right now."

"As you wish, my dear, but know this without a doubt—

whatever you decide to do, I will be with you through it all."

"Thanks, Rals," I say, hugging him. "That means so much to me."

My empty apartment reminds me that Callie and I both nearly died today. It's a small consolation to know that if I'm forced to relocate to some deserted outpost on a no-name earth, at least she and Rals will be with me.

I collapse onto my couch in the darkened living room. My broken wrist throbs, my head hurts, and I'm heartsick with the knowledge that my blossoming relationship with Ryder will likely die on the vine. My only option seems to be the life of a galactic nomad, in search of a place where nobody wants me dead. Where is the justice in that?

Unhappiness oozes from my every pore, and I'm on the verge of a serious crying jag when my apartment door swings open, and Urick strides inside. He spots me on the couch. "Jaden, may I have a word with you?"

"Oh man, Urick, I'm not in the mood for visitors tonight. I feel like hell."

"I believe I may be able to help." Something in his tone convinces me to hear him out.

"Vasa, lights on," I say. "Come in and sit down."

He sits in the armchair across from me. "Please turn off your Vasa."

He's acting strange, even for Urick. "Okay. Vasa off."

"Signing off," she replies.

"What's up Urick? What's on your mind?"

"Director Canto is a desperate man. He took a great risk in hiring a Garugian to kill you."

"I know. But that whole meeting downstairs was a complete

joke. This guy's obviously willing to stop at nothing. Arresting him and chucking him in jail for a few days will only make him more pissed off. If I stay here, he'll find a way to get me eventually."

"I believe you are right. Conventional methods will not work against this man. He is willing to operate outside of the law, and he is clever enough to cover his own tracks. I have come to offer you an alternative solution."

"What kind of alternative?"

His golden eyes glint in the lamplight. "I will take him out for you. You need never know the details, and I will never be found out. But he will not trouble you again."

I compose my facial muscles to conceal my utter shock, reminding myself of Urick's background and why he's making the offer.

"Urick, I'm very touched by your willingness to do that for me. I know the offer comes from your heart. But I have to refuse. I can't even consider it."

"He is a bad man, Jade." His voice is an angry rumble. "He is responsible for the deaths of many."

"I know that. And a time or two I've considered circumventing the law to do what I believed was right, but my own code won't allow the taking of his life. We can't resort to his tactics. That makes us no better than he is."

"Surely you see that your very existence threatens the thing he loves most in the world? He will stop at nothing to save it ... including murder. As long as he lives, he will be a threat to you, and even if you run, he may someday succeed."

I study Urick for a moment. "Maybe not. Something you said just gave me an idea. Maybe Canto loves something more than IUGA."

"What do you mean?"

"Hang on a second." I hurry to my desk and rummage through my drawers until I find what I'm looking for. It's an old magazine article about Canto I tucked away months ago.

I open up the magazine to the piece on Canto and give it to him. "I don't know why I saved this, but look at it. That's Canto's wife and two daughters. The article gushes about what a tremendous family man he is."

Urick's brow creases. "What are you saying? You want me to harm his family?"

"No. Of course not. But maybe the threat is enough. If you give me permission to use your name, maybe I can scare him into making a deal. Fear is a powerful weapon." I borrow Ryder's line from earlier today.

He stares at the glossy photo for a moment. "You believe if I threaten to harm his family, it will be enough?"

"Well, yeah, I mean look at those beautiful girls. But the threat shouldn't come directly from you. I'll drop in on Canto and have a little chat with him."

"I'm going with you."

"No. You can't be there. He'll panic if we both show up. He's not afraid of me … yet. Can I use your name, though? I think that'll be enough to put the fear of God into him."

"You may use it in any way you choose. But I wish you would allow me to do this for you, or at least go with you."

"I have to do this myself, Urick. It's time I took control of my own life. I need to be the one to deliver the message. I need to look him in the eye and know he's no longer a threat to me. Otherwise, I can't remain in Arumel."

He fingers the hilt of the Throkken at his side and nods slowly. "I understand, little sister. You should be the one, but take your firearm."

"Right. Just give me a minute to put on my uniform."

I slip into the bedroom to change. After getting into my uniform and boots, I strap my holster and pistol around my hips, and stuff my polycom and the Garugian's ID tags into my pockets. In the bathroom I pull my hair back into a high, tight pony tail, adopting Nila's badass ninja look. Then I cake on several layers of eyeliner and a slash of red lipstick, and I'm ready to go.

I find Urick pacing in my dining room. "Security cameras cover the Director's entire office," he says, "and a panic button is installed under his desk drawer. If he pushes it, you must shift back at once. I will wait here to make certain you return safely. Do you have your polycom?"

I pull it out of my pocket.

"Push the red button if you need me. No need to speak. I will come right away. Now, let me see your bracelet."

I hold up my wrist. Urick opens the TPD and zeros in on the Director's office. "You're all set. Give the bastard hell."

Zzzt.

SIXTY

I land on the Persian rug in front of Canto's Titanic-sized desk. He startles and glances up at me. Shock and disbelief distort his features.

He jumps to his feet. "What in the name of heaven are you doing here?"

My insides churn with nerves and loathing, but I maintain a cool façade. "What's wrong Director, you look as if you've seen a ghost."

"I must say, I've seen you looking better, Miss Beckett." He scrutinizes my battered face. "What happened to you?"

"I think you know exactly what happened, Director. You took an enormous gamble, and you lost."

His eyes travel to my gun, and I notice his hand slowly inching toward the panic button beneath his desk.

"I wouldn't call security just yet," I say. "I didn't come here to kill you, if that's what you think. I came here to deliver a very important message."

"Is that right?" He moves his hands to the top of the desk and leans toward me. "And what message is that?"

"It's two-fold, actually. First, your Garugian is dead." I remove the ID tag from my pocket and drop it on his desk.

"I don't know what you're talking about."

"Sure you do." I pick up the tag and read the name out loud. "Langor Burdige. Did you even know his name? The Garugian you hired to kill me?" I dangle the tag in front of the security camera, then turn back to Canto.

"He died right after he ratted you out, Director. Urick ran him through with a Throkken. "Do you know what that is? It's a long and deadly blade."

Canto visibly blanches. My lie has the desired effect.

"You remember Lieutenant Hunter don't you? The guy from Demonstadt? Used to hunt and kill men for a living? He took great satisfaction in dispatching your hired assassin."

"This is preposterous," Canto sputters. "I didn't hire that Garugian. If he said I did, he was lying. It's the word of a dead Garugian against the Director of IUGA. Who do you think will be believed? Now get out!" He points to the door.

"Sit down, Director! You haven't heard the second part of my message." I hold the palm of my hand toward his chest and concentrate on releasing a small jolt of energy. Instantly he's thrown backward into his chair, and it rolls across the floor colliding roughly with the credenza.

Fear flickers across his eyes. "What did you just do?"

"Nothing compared to what I can do." I lift my hand to the Chinese vase sitting on the credenza to his right, and I pulse a little shock wave across the room. The vase shatters sending chunks of porcelain flying through the air. He ducks as the shards bounce off his shoulders.

"What the hell are you doing? That was a priceless Ming dynasty vase." He brushes pieces of porcelain from his suit.

My eye is caught by a framed photo of Canto's wife and children on his desk top. "And this must be your family." I hold out my hand, and the photo moves smoothly across the room to me. "Very nice."

"Leave my family out of this, Beckett. If you're not here to kill me, just say your piece and get the hell out. I don't have time for your parlor tricks."

"The second part of my message is from Lieutenant Hunter." I say. "It seems he's grown quite fond of me since I joined the Transcender community. I'm like the sister he never had."

"How touching." He curls his lip at me. "And I care because …?"

"Urick wants me to tell you this: If anything unpleasant should happen to me or any of my loved ones, including my dog, anything at all—an unexplained accident, a tainted piece of food, even a bad case of the sniffles—he knows where to find you, and your wife, Irene and your daughters, Lydia and Rebecca. In fact, he wants you to know that he has all of your imprints, and he promises that there is no place on this earth or any other where you or your family can hide from him. Believe me, Director, he's good at hunting people, and he was especially taken with your daughters."

Canto's jaw clenches. "This is outrageous. Security cameras are recording everything you say. All I need do is give this recording to the international media and you'll be finished. You and your Lieutenant."

"I know all about your security, Director, but I don't believe you'll turn anything over to the media, because, if you do, we'll respond by releasing the recording of the Garugian confessing that he was paid by you to murder me," I bluff. "But mostly I don't think you'll do it because of Urick's message. His promise applies to this situation also."

His eyes turn to slits while he contemplates this. "Are you really that ruthless, Miss Beckett?"

"No, Director, I'm not. But Urick and his men are. Don't doubt that for a moment. I'm only warning you because I wouldn't want anything unpleasant to happen to these lovely girls." I hold up the photograph.

"You people are the lowest kind of filth." Spittle collects on his lips and he swipes at it with the back of his hand. "You'd stoop to threatening children?"

"I believe your oldest daughter is just about my age. You had no similar compunctions about threatening me. Misfortunes come in threes, Director. That's the third time you've tried to kill me. Three strikes and you're out."

"What is it you want from me?"

"I'll tell you precisely what I want. I want you to swear on the lives of your wife and daughters that you'll call off the Garugians and that you will never again attempt to harm me or any of my loved ones. Nor will you hire anyone to attempt to harm us. I want you to abide by the letter of the IGC Court's ruling and clear out of Arumel, but most of all I want you to promise that I'll never have to lay eyes on you again."

"And if I don't do as you wish, you will harm my family?" A vein throbs furiously at his temple.

"I prefer to keep things positive. If you do as I ask, you'll be able to sleep serenely at night. Otherwise … I can't be held responsible for what might happen. I'm afraid I have no control over Lieutenant Hunter and the others." I shove the photo across the desk to him. "I offer you what you stole from me, Canto, the chance to choose your own destiny. What's it going to be?"

He collapses into his chair looking old and defeated. "Miss Beckett," he says quietly. "This agency has operated for hundreds of years, ensuring that destiny unfolds for the highest possible good of the public. You can't imagine what harm you're doing by attempting to dismantle this venerated organization."

"I know exactly what I'm doing. IUGA has become a corrupt tool for making rich men grow richer. If the agency ever served a valuable purpose, it's been completely obliterated by the greed and self-interest of its operators. It has to go."

He gazes at me with watery eyes. "I will agree to your terms, Miss Beckett. I swear on the lives of my wife and children that neither I nor anyone under my direction, including the Garugians, will attempt to harm you and yours again. I further swear to abide by all of the terms of the IGC order. Please, just stay away from my family."

I study his eyes for a long moment. "You've got yourself a deal, Canto."

"Do I have your word?" he says.

"Yes."

He lumbers out of his chair. "I know you will find this difficult to believe, but I held no personal ill will toward you, Miss Beckett. My actions were prompted by my belief that IUGA's work is crucial to the orderly functioning of the galaxy. I felt I needed to save the agency at all costs for the good of the whole."

"Director, I hate to be the one to deliver the bad news, but IUGA never really was the overseer of destiny in this galaxy. Destiny has always and will always unfold exactly the way it's supposed to, with or without IUGA's interference.

His voice grows thick with emotion. "I'll never believe that all our good work was for naught."

"What you believe doesn't matter anymore. The history books will decide how IUGA is viewed by future generations. Don't expect to go down as a hero. In fact, I'd go home now and hug my wife and kids if I were you. Goodbye, Director." *Zzzt.*

Landing back in my living room, I'm surprised to find Narowyn on the sofa waiting with Urick. They both get to their feet.

"Jaden, are you all right?" Narowyn asks, rising from her seat. "Urick tells me you went to see Director Canto."

"I'm fine. Everything went as well as could be expected."

"Tell us what happened," she says. "Did he agree to speak with you?"

"I didn't give him much choice, but let's just say we arrived at an understanding. I don't believe he or anyone else from IUGA will bother me again. At least he gave me his word on it."

"That's quite remarkable," she says. "How did you get him to agree? Were you forced to bribe or threaten him?"

"I'm sorry, Narowyn, but the details of our agreement are confidential—between the Director and me. You'll just have to trust me on this."

Her eyes flare as she contemplates whether to pull rank on me. She glances at Urick. His face remains impassive.

"Very well," she says at last. "It was your life at stake this afternoon. Just tell me whether I should expect a visit from the local police this evening."

I smile. "No. Canto won't involve the police. In fact, I think he's gone home to be with his family for a while." I shoot a look Urick's way. "How about some tea? Would anybody like tea? It's been a hell of a day."

I sleep remarkably well in light of my unsettling day, and awake in the morning with two goals in mind—visiting Callie and spending the evening with Ryder Blackthorn. The swelling in my face has gone down considerably. I call the veterinary hospital, and they report that Callie is doing well. I arrange a time to see her this morning. Then I plan the rest of my day around figuring out what I'm going to wear, buying fresh flowers for my apartment, and selecting tonight's music.

Ryder arrives at my door at six forty-five carrying a bag of delicious smelling food in one hand and a black guitar case in the other.

"I know I'm early," he says, grinning, "but I've been looking forward to seeing you all day."

A wave of warmth floods through me at his words. "Come in." I take the food from his hand and set it on the kitchen counter. "Are you starving or do you want to sit first?"

"Let's sit. You look great, by the way. But tell me how you're feeling and what's going on with the whole IUGA thing."

I light scented candles on my mantle and coffee table, and we sit in my living room while I tell him about my surprise visit to Director Canto. He listens with rapt attention as I relate all the important details. When I tell him how I delivered Urick's message to the Director, his eyes widen, and he shakes his head. A small piece of me worries that he might think me callous for threatening Canto's family in that way, but when I finish with the story, his eyes shine.

"That was brilliant, Jade. You found his weak spot and played him perfectly. Bravo."

"You gave me the idea. I'm so used to doing things by the rules. You helped me realize that's not going to work if the other side is making up its own rules."

"Do you feel confident he'll keep his word to you? I mean, confident enough for you to stick around Arumel for a while?"

"From the look on Canto's face, I have no doubt he'll keep his word. Urick can be a pretty intimidating guy. Canto knows all about his background and what he's capable of. I'm just grateful he let me use his name. The director wasn't at all impressed with my mighty powers. He called them *parlor tricks.*"

He laughs. "It's not a bad thing that people don't fear you, Jade. I would like to meet this Urick character, though. I owe him a debt of gratitude. He must care for you a great deal."

"He was one of my first friends in Arumel. Anyway, those food aromas from the kitchen are making my stomach growl. Shall we eat?"

We fill our plates with seasoned rice and vegetables and some kind of fried cornbread. The food is spicy and filling. For dessert, we share a slice of chocolate cheesecake and some fresh berries Ralston brought over earlier. When we're finished we stack our plates in the sink, and I press Ryder to play his guitar for me.

I take a seat on my floor while he perches on my couch and strums a few bars. The melody is hauntingly beautiful. Then he closes his eyes and begins to sing. His voice is surprisingly strong and unexpectedly good.

> *If we could travel back in time, I'd recreate this perfect day.*
> *With sunlight streaming through your hair,*
> *you'd kiss me that same way.*

> *I know you're scared and so am I.*
> *But please don't let this be goodbye.*
> *Give our hearts a chance to fly.*
> *Stay with me awhile.*
> *Please, please stay with me awhile.*

> *I promise I can make you smile.*
> *Just stay with me awhile.*

He hums for bit, and then he stops playing and looks over at me tentatively. "Sorry, it's not finished yet."

It takes me a second to catch my breath. "Wow, what you've got so far is amazing. Did you write that for your wife?"

His eyes hold mine. "I wrote it last night."

I can't find the right words to express how happy I am that he has come into my life, so I lift the guitar from his hands and prop it against the couch before climbing into his lap. I nestle deeply against his chest hoping that somehow this overwhelming emotion will flow from my heart directly into his, letting him know how I feel.

He clings to me and whispers into my hair, "Please don't go."

"I'm not going anywhere." I say. "My life is here, now." As the words leave my lips my spirits, the universe, and the entire galaxy feel a little lighter, as if destiny is smiling on me tonight.

EPILOGUE

TEN YEARS LATER

Barefoot and shirtless, Ryder stands in the middle of our bedroom rocking an air guitar to a tune only he hears. I pause quietly at the door for a moment, admiring the way the muscles ripple across his back with each imaginary strum. And what he does for a pair of blue jeans is, well … thought provoking.

"Nice moves Clapton," I say, "but it's time for you to get ready. I don't want to be late for my own swearing in."

He flips the hair out of his eyes and grins, only half-embarrassed at being caught performing his rock and roll fantasy. "Sorry. Am I holding us up?"

"Nah, you're okay. Nobody's here yet—not even Ralston, and he's always twenty minutes early. I'm just a little nervous." More accurately, it feels like a hamster is running laps on an exercise wheel inside my stomach.

"Are Eleanor and John riding over with us?" he asks.

"No they're going with your parents. I've ordered an air taxi, though, since we'll have Ralston, Gil, Eve, and Asher."

"No Nila?"

"She's working security, so she won't be able to sit with the rest of you. We'll see her at the reception after the ceremony."

He comes to me and runs his hands along my arms. "I like your new dress."

"Thanks. Would you mind zipping me the rest of the way?"

I turn my back to him and sweep my hair aside. Instead of pulling the zipper up he glides it down, pressing velvety kisses along my spine and sending delicious chills down my back.

"Does this calm you?" His breath is warm and moist against my skin.

"It does exactly the opposite of calm me. And we really *will* be late if you keep doing that."

"It's just that you are so devastatingly sexy."

I swing around, alarmed. "It isn't the dress is it?"

"No, no. The dress is appropriately conservative. It's what's underneath that's so distracting." He circles my waist with his arms.

"Well, you're the only one in Arumel who knows what's underneath, so I guess we're safe. But how are you doing with all this, Ry? Are you nervous about it?"

"You mean about the fact that my wife is about to become one of the most powerful women on the planet?"

I cover my face with my hands. "Oh god, when you put it that way it sounds totally ridiculous."

"Ridiculously hot." He wraps his arms around me. "I think it's kind of a turn-on."

"Be serious for a minute. Do you wish we lived a … quieter existence?"

"Never. We'd be bored silly. And actually, I'm very happy that you won't be going out on exploration anymore. We'll have more time together."

I smile up at him. "Now we can start the family we've always talked about."

He arches an eyebrow. "You mean like right now?"

"Nice try, buddy." I duck out of his arms. "Have you even thought about what you're wearing today?"

"Why don't you pick out something for me? You're better at that than I am."

I scan the room for my earrings, and spotting them on the dressing table, I hold out my hand. They glide smoothly across the room and into my waiting palm.

"You know it still kind of weirds me out when you do that," he says.

"I think you'd be accustomed to it by now."

"Oh, I suppose it has its uses. How about getting my phone for me from downstairs?"

"No phone. Shower." I point sternly to the bathroom. "I'll dig out a suit for you."

He sits on the bed and pulls me down beside him. "In a minute. I wondered if you saw this morning's news?"

"About Director Canto, you mean?"

"Uh huh."

"They say he died quietly in his sleep. Too peaceful a death for someone who caused so much misery in life, if you ask me."

"He did keep his word to you these past ten years."

"Under no small threat," I point out. "Urick visited him every year on the anniversary of the Garugian attack to remind him of our deal."

"Yes, well Canto's had a few other things to occupy his time lately. I don't see how IUGA continues to function now with all the controversy swirling around it."

"Brought about in large part by Blackthorn Production's exposé on the agency's manipulating destiny for its own purposes." I brush the errant lock of hair from his forehead.

"I like to do my part, ma'am."

"After IUGA lost its license to employ automatons, I think Canto just kind of gave up. It's fitting, though, that he died on the day of Narowyn's retirement."

"And the day of your taking over the reins of the Transcender Society." He gets to his feet. "Stay here for a sec. This may be the only moment we have alone all day, and I have something to give you."

He opens the top drawer of the dresser and takes out a long navy blue box tied with a white ribbon. He plops down next to me again and places it in my hand. "A little congratulatory gift."

"Ry, that's so sweet." I fumble with the ribbon and open the hinged box. Inside I'm stunned to find a platinum necklace with a diamond pendant in the shape of an infinity symbol and a brilliant emerald set inside each sworl.

"This is gorgeous," I say, lifting it from the box. "Will you put it on for me?"

He fastens the chain around my neck. "It's very similar to a piece of jewelry I had years ago. Where did you find it?"

"Ralston took me to that antique jewelry store on Fifth. The emeralds remind me of your eyes. He thought you'd like it."

"He was right. I love it." My arms circle his neck, and he scoops me up into his lap.

Placing one hand behind my head he brings his mouth slowly down on mine. "*Mmm*, he murmurs from deep within his throat. He uses his lips to tease, excite, and arouse me.

"You're not playing fair," I say. "You know we're expecting visitors any minute."

"I know." He nuzzles my ear. "I just get carried away sometimes. Have I told you how proud I am of you?"

"Only about a million times. But I always love hearing it."

"Today marks the beginning of a new life for us, Jade, and a new world order, really. The Age of Illuminosity, the media are calling it. They say the energy of the entire planet will be raised because of the Transcenders' work. You'll now have your rightful place on the world stage. You've certainly earned it."

"I would never have gotten here without you, Ry. You've made me softer but stronger somehow. This is what I've been working so hard for, and it's what I've always wanted, but I'm not sure I'm completely prepared." My eyes search his for reassurance.

"Who can ever be completely prepared, love? We can't be certain what destiny holds for us in the next year, or the next hour, really. But you know what the Transcenders say ..."

"Fear not the many paths of life," we say together, laughing and falling back onto the bed.

THE END

ACKNOWLEDGEMENTS

I have so many remarkable people to thank for supporting and assisting me in completing this, the final book of my first trilogy. As usual, my extraordinary sister, Shelly, has been my chief advisor, proofreader, cheerleader, and psychotherapist through the writing of *Illuminosity*. Don't know how I'll ever repay her, but I see a trip to Italy in our future.

Dr. Christina Hickey deserves special recognition for her support and encouragement over the past few years as this trilogy took shape. We met over the internet when she reviewed *Transcender* on Goodreads. She has been a tireless promoter of my books ever since, and she did me the honor of acting as my editor on *Illuminosity*. She's a true renaissance woman and an amazing friend.

Of course, my sweet family, Mike, Colter, and Jessica, have all contributed in many ways to the successful completion of this trilogy. I could not have done it without their unwavering love, understanding, and indulgence. Jessica's comments and suggestions on the manuscript were particularly helpful.

As with *Transcender* and *Streaming Stars*, I have my beautiful and talented friend, Carrie Drazek, to thank not only for the *Illuminosity* cover, but also for being such an inspiration to me. She's an incredible lady and a kindred spirit.

Thanks once again to my friend Marsha Quinn for being one of my first readers. Her insights were invaluable. I also appreciate the editing contributions of Sylvia Anglin. Her comments were most helpful.

I'd also like to thank my friend, Donna Jordan, the most philanthropic woman I know, and the Doctors and staff of St. Joseph's Hospital, the Shimberg Breast Center, and the St. Joseph's

Cancer Center for their excellent care and kindness. Because of them, I am cancer-free and looking forward to many more writing projects in the future—a few of which I've already started!

Thanks to my beta readers. I appreciate your important contributions. Finally, heartfelt thanks to all the loyal readers who stuck with me to the end of this trilogy. I will miss Jaden, Ryder, Ralston, Asher, and the rest. I hope you loved them as much as I did.

ABOUT THE AUTHOR

Vicky Savage, her real name by the way, grew up gazing upon the beauty of the Wasatch Mountain Range right outside her family's kitchen window. She thought the Rocky Mountains would always own her heart, until she moved to sunny Florida for law school and instantly fell in love with the ocean. Her passion for new adventures and exotic locales led her on a circuitous path to writing science fiction/fantasy about strange new worlds and parallel universes.

Although she has lived in seven different states and London, England, the siren call of the ocean always brings her back to her beloved Florida, where she currently lives with her husband, son, and two dogs.

www.ingramcontent.com/pod-product-compliance
Lightning Source LLC
Chambersburg PA
CBHW070351030726
47504CB00001B/142